The Sanibel Arcanum

'Terrific blend of history and mystery—absolutely absorbing. He'll have to write another one now!"

Tom Kierein, WRC-TV (NBC), Washington, D.C.

"A promising debut . . . well-paced tension . . . A trained eye that misses little detail . . . wrestles with hefty ideas in entertaining fashion."

Steve Hall, *The Indianapolis Star*

"A compelling read . . . the imagery is vivid, the story tightly written and fast-paced . . . I found it difficult to put the book down."

Anne Ryder, WTHR Television, Indianapolis

"Everyone who loves Sanibel should read it . . . [the] plot is intriguing . . . timely and provocative."

Rob Strickland, *Sanibel Island Reporter*

"A . . . good mystery . . . one of the nicest things in the novel is the portrait of fatherhood."

Marion Garmel, *The Indianapolis News*

The Sanibel Arcanum

by

Thomas D. Cochrun

Thomas D. Cochrun

Cover Design and Art
by
C.W. Mundy

Guild Press of Indiana, Inc.
Indianapolis, Indiana

Guild Press of Indiana, Inc.
6000 Sunset Lane
Indianapolis, IN 46208

Printed in the United States of America

First Printing March 1994
Second Printing July 1994

Library of Congress
Catalog Card Number
94-075223

ISBN 1-878208-41-1

Computer graphics for cover design by
Matt Rollins
Amazing Announcements, Inc.

Dedication

To Mary Helen Decker Cochrun—-supporter, teacher, mother.
Thank you always.

Acknowledgments

Thanks to Ed and Judy Dunsmore for the first soundings; to Ben Strout, a producer's producer, for his eye for detail; and to my St. Martin French West Indies reading committee of the Mundys, Hoggatts, and Cochrun ladies. Those were great hours on the veranda. My deepest admiration to C.W. for the most beautiful book cover a writer could hope for.

A special thanks to Nancy Baxter and Sheila Samson for their craftsmanship, finesse, and creative sparkle.

Night Surf

It was the kind of stupor the island sun—and a lethargy caused by a presunrise dash to the airport, coupled with a two hour flight delay and short night—can produce. Tim Calvin was planted, as much as seated, in a patio chair, sipping a beer and slipping deeper into a vacation mindset. He had told his colleagues he wanted to spend the next fourteen days just becoming a grain of sand on the beach. Now, as he lounged on a friend's terrace while the cleaning crew finished with his own condo, Sanibel was starting its work on him. He stared almost mindlessly at the pink of the blooms on the flamboyants and oleanders around the terrace and sniffed their sweet fragrance. A small lizard perched on a nearby fern branch, slightly moving its head as if to tilt for better exposure to the afternoon sun and deep azure sky.

Even after all these years, the island held an exotic charm for him. From the moment he paid the toll and began the drive over the causeway, a feeling began in his stomach and inched its way up his spine. The sunsplashes off San Carlos Bay, the palms and Australian pines catching the breeze, day-trippers wading and fishing off the small islets—all of these beguiling pleasures strengthened the relaxing hold Sanibel had on him. The deep foliage, the vast wildlife refuge with its graceful birds, the surf and sun at the beach, and the island food were essential elements of his annual spring tonic, parts of the compound which doctored him each year.

For the first time he had booked two weeks—fourteen days—away from business and stress. Two whole weeks of the exotic island charm, time with friends and "quality" time with the kids. He wanted slow hours to sit and stare, as though intoxicated by a pace which allowed him to feel for the moment a kinship with the sunning lizard. Fourteen days of this, he thought, and he would be a new man. Unless he decided he couldn't give it up and go back.

"We can pick up the key, and by the time we get there it'll be ready," Laney said as she and Barb Hockett descended from the house to the patio. Barb and her husband Dave had been friends of the Calvins since college, and their home had always been the first stop before the family drove across the island to West Gulf, to the condo. Laney was radiant when on Sanibel, and Tim enjoyed seeing his wife released from her busy schedule as teacher, volunteer, and shuttle-driver to soccer, piano, and Brownies, as well as being house manager-in-chief. Now she and the girls were excited about getting into the condo and checking out the beach.

"I'm ready, if I can get out of this chair. I feel like that lizard over there," he said, finishing the last of the beer. Tim stood, stretched, and gazed up at the tropical sky. He watched after Laney and Barb as they followed his daughters who were dashing out to the rental van, eager to get on the move. He drifted lazily out to join them.

He hugged Barb as she stood next to the van. "Tell Dave we'll see him this evening," Tim said. Dave was more than Tim's good friend; he was his daughters' godfather. He was also one of those rare people who could take on any task and succeed. Dave had given up a claim to his family's lucrative retail business in the Midwest to become a potter and small shop merchant. He and Barb had sold their belongings and driven to Sanibel, where they bought a small, shed-like pottery business which became their home as well as their shop. Eighteen-hour days of hard work, sacrifice, and lots of imagination had created a successful business. Somewhere along the way they had also purchased and rebuilt an island bungalow and become the parents of Celia. What some had thought was a foolish move and a long shot at best had become a wonderful life.

Now these yearly vacation trips gave the old friends time for each other. Tonight, Tim mused, he would see his tall bearded giant of a buddy who, as always, could make him laugh and give him the inspiration of his inexhaustible can-do spirit. That was also part of the vacation "treatment." Mostly, though, what the treatment meant was no problems. Absolutely none—except perhaps choosing which restaurant to eat in each evening. As he backed out of the Hockett driveway he turned to his family with a grin of anticipation.

"Let's go hit the beach," he said, rallying a cheer from his youngest daughter Katie and a "definitely!" from teen-aged Elizabeth.

"Coo-ol! Awesome!" was Elizabeth's assessment as she dashed through the condo to the screened porch overlooking the gulf. She and Katie would be only steps from the beach.

"Yeah, this'll be fine," he said to Laney as he pulled the curtains open in their room, revealing an idyllic panorama of palms, beach, and surf. "This is definitely going to work. Definitely!" Laney joined him at the window, and smiling indulgently up at him, slipped her arm around his waist. Tim hugged her to his side, and as they lost themselves in the beauty of the view, contentment washed over him.

After a relaxed supper of chilled shrimp and salad, Tim spent the evening watching the surf. The gulf sunset had been brilliant. It wasn't until the last swatch of color had gone from red to pink and finally to a deep purple that he noticed the lights of a small craft that seemed to be passing repeatedly in the water along the stretch of beach in front of their condo.

Between laps of surf he could faintly detect the sound of a small inboard-outboard. It sounded like a smaller boat than those which carried fishing outings, or even those pleasure craft which rode further out on the horizon. It also sounded closer, and one of the lights seemed to be a spotlight scanning the beach. Odd—he'd never noticed a boat so near the shore, much less alone on a quickly darkening gulf.

* * *

He had forgotten about the boat and the searchlight on the beach by the time he and little Katie had rounded up flashlights and armed themselves against the possibility of "no-seeums." Island veteran Barb had told them that regular skin lotion dabbed on with a piece of paper towel was an almost certain guard against the invisible biters. As he swabbed the arms of his seven-year-old, they laughed again at his explanation of no-seeums—"you no see 'em." Well, he thought, with the breeze at the beach there was little worry about being chewed, but it was good to take the precaution anyway. He wanted nothing unpleasant to intrude on this year's island holiday.

Since the time she was barely old enough to navigate the shelly sand, Katie had delighted in their nocturnal hunts for sand crabs. Tonight she led the way with her light, running just a few steps ahead of him. The pounding of the tide and Katie's laughter and exclamations wrapped him in relaxed pleasure. Business cares and worries were blown far away by the warm island breezes.

Then, just for a moment he heard it. It sounded like a scream. Katie seemed to hear it too and stopped abruptly a few yards ahead and turned, looking up at him with the eyes of a child unsure, a bit startled. The noise seemed to have come from up the beach. They stood silently, cocking their heads and straining to catch the sound, but only the rush of the surf filled their ears. Nothing more.

"I thought I heard something too," he spoke above the surf in answer to Katie's unspoken question. "Probably some kids at another condo, or maybe a TV." Odd how a piece of sound can be lifted out of the context of another life somewhere and set loose to sail on the wind, he thought. Not unlike the tide washing in traces of other times and places, offering them up like coins in a collection plate. Things with a history of their own drifting into your life.

* * *

They moved on down the beach, stopping to look at the nautical lights on the horizon and the stars in the sky. "Sweetie, before sailors had anything to help them, they used the stars to navigate, to help them get where they needed to go." He felt this was one of those cosmic moments between father and daughter, a moment to be etched in their memory, a time hoped for as parents bring up children.

"But aren't the stars different each night?" she asked, remembering something she'd learned in school.

"The ancients had no TV, and not many people read or even had pictures, so they knew the star field like…"

"Daddy, what's that ?" Katie cried, looking down the beach. She moved around and grabbed his waist, hugging for a kind of protection.

Some fifty yards away was a general commotion: a darting light knifing back and forth in short zigzag strokes, and the sound of voices, low yells, not understandable. The light and voices moved toward the water, and the sounds came to him more clearly. Was it an accent? No—another tongue, a pattern in cadence, a clip he could not recognize. He strained to listen to the frantic-sounding conversation of shouts between two men who seemed to be splashing through the water. Holding Katie tightly, he shoved their flashlight heads into the sand.

"Don't move, honey," he whispered softly, trying to lessen her confusion and fear. The low whine of an inboard-outboard choked across the surf, and a searchlight ripped the darkness, scanning the beach in a frantic arc. It caught them, and for an instant they froze in the bright light. Feeling like a startled deer caught in headlights, Tim poised on his left knee, his arm tightening protectively around his frightened child. But the spotlight whizzed past them, cutting a path further east on the beach.

Tim's heart lurched, and he felt an almost overwhelming sense of relief. He didn't know who these people were, but apparently in their haste they had not seen him and Katie. No sooner had he finished the thought than he was again blinded by the searchlight. Katie instinctively turned her head and buried her face in his shoulder, trembling. Again his heart raced, his throat burned and his mouth went dry. He tried to block the light with his right hand. He heard a male voice yelling from the boat, shouting something, maybe to him. Who *are* these people, he thought, what *is* this?

"Hey, what's the deal?" he shouted back. The light went out, there was another shout and the small boat throttled up. The telltale whine of the engine receded through the surf and he could see a red navigational light moving into the gulf.

"Well, that was pretty wild," he said with cheerful fatherly control he didn't really feel. He wanted to assure Katie everything was fine—he could sense she was a bit undone by the incident. He thought about returning to the condo to tell Laney and Elizabeth about their adventure, but something drew him up the beach a bit farther. He was curious about the area from which the men with the foreign accents had run. He also wanted to show Katie there was no reason to be frightened.

The tide was coming in, so they moved up on the beach behind the uneven line of shipworms and pin shells that marked the high water line. He widened the two flashlight beams to the flood position and studied the path of light. He was about to turn around when he saw lines in the sand, two trough-like patterns, not unlike spade troughs made for planting seeds in a garden. With his flashlight beam he followed the lines to his right as they moved toward the vegetation that stood as a buffer between the homes and condominiums and the gulf beach. Tim was struck by an eerie feeling, a sense that he was being watched, even though he had seen no one else around. Again he scanned the beach, assuming that after the business with the voices and light, his imagination was now working overtime. He reasoned the men in the boat were too far out by now, and it was too dark for anyone in the condos to be watching. Still he could feel eyes on him, and apprehension gripped him.

"Katie, stay here and watch for crabs; this might be a good place. I'm going to look around up here," his voice trailed off as he walked toward the patch of sea grass and the large seagrape bushes which were almost the size of trees.

"What are you doing, Daddy?" There was an edge of uneasiness in her voice.

"I just want to check something…" and he almost stumbled in the sand.

The word "something" echoed like a shout in his head, reverberating with the force of a gunshot as he stopped short. His stomach dropped into a chasm and his heart seemed to leap out of his chest, beating like a jackhammer in his ears. It felt like the very life drained out of him as he stood looking down on a body and a severed hand, just inches away from his foot.

Buried on the Beach

Tim sat on the porch, sipping coffee, eating toast, and trying to clear his head. The late morning sun gave the beach a sparkle. The water was still turquoise, the sky still a deep blue and the sand a glistening white. The scene was perfect, complete with the line of walkers and shellers bent over in the famous "Sanibel stoop" set against a curved horizon which seemed endless. But it all seemed distant, as though he were looking at it through a haze. The last twelve hours had rewritten his longed-for ideal island vacation plans, throwing his life out of kilter and thrusting him into some madness he didn't understand.

It was after two in the morning before he finished giving statements to the police and they finally left. It seemed hours before he could drop off to sleep. Katie was fine, still not quite sure what all the commotion had been about. She had been told her daddy found a man who had been hurt on the beach. The medical people told Tim that another few minutes undetected and the man would have died from loss of blood.

"Hey Pop, you OK?" Elizabeth yelled up from the path between the condo and the beach. "Get your number fifteen sunscreen on and come on down! We're going to build a sandcastle." This was Elizabeth's last year to have spring break with the family. Next year she would be in college and on another academic calendar. She was an exceptionally bright eighteen-year-old who had perceived the true horror of the night before. Now she was trying to gloss over it and force some normalcy back into their family time. She had returned to the beach with Tim last night to apply first aid to the man while they waited for the ambulance. Even then she had displayed an amazing composure. "Don't forget to use fifteen!" she called with an emphasizing nag to her tone.

Tim chuckled as he watched his soon-to-be-premed student daughter head back to the beach lathered in a considerably less-protective sunscreen, and wearing a bikini he didn't mind seeing on any young woman other than his daughter. The sunscreen SPF rating had been a running family joke for years. He had always insisted the kids wear a high sun block, but as Elizabeth had grown older she had taken a great interest in the "perfect tan." To avoid his nagging this year she had, against his protests and advice, gone to one of the tanning parlors to, as she phrased it, "build the base for the perfect tan." Tim noticed with some chagrin two beach walkers who turned to stare as Elizabeth strolled back to her lounge chair. One of the guys spoke out of the side of his mouth, and both chuckled. "Move on, you slugs," he mumbled as he sipped his coffee.

The phone on the bar rang, breaking into his trance-like state. Phone calls were something vacations were supposed to protect him from, but things had changed.

"Hello."

"How's everybody doing this morning?" There was both concern and strength in Dave's voice. Dave, godfather of his children and like a brother to him, was one of the most caring and gentle people he knew. He was also probably one of the toughest: the ceramic artist was a former drill instructor and rugged sergeant. In fact, Dave was the first person he had called after finding the man on the beach. Tim knew Dave would get quick emergency and police response by placing calls to some of his island friends.

"Everybody's fine. Katie doesn't know much. I'm still rattled."

"The chief called. Hospital says the man's going to be OK. He was beaten to a pulp. They've tried to save the hand, but it doesn't look good.

"This has really blown everyone away," Dave continued. "The worst crime we usually have down here is someone breaking into a car. The police figure they'll be able talk to him this afternoon. No one seems to know the guy.

"How about you?" he asked. "Are you going to be OK?"

"I just want to put it out of mind, you know," Tim answered. "This is supposed to be our break from the world, and we've got only so many days. I hate to sound callous about the whole thing, but...."

"That first Kir Royale at Jean Paul's tonight will put you back into the mood. We've got a table at the early seating. You'll love his new chef. We'll bring Cee out as soon as he she gets home. She's anxious to play with Katie. Go get some beach—it'll be good for you. You're on vacation, man!"

"Great! See you this afternoon."

"Who was that?" Laney asked as she came through the door with the breeze rushing in behind her.

"Dave. They're bringing Celia out to see us this afternoon. Katie'll like that. How's she doing with what happened last night?"

"She seems unfazed. She wants to go to the pool. When are you coming down to build the great sandcastle?"

"As soon as I get greased up."

Tim watched as her long legs and high fanny moved down the hall and out the door. She'd been doing exercises with Elizabeth and was looking trim. After twenty-some years she still excited him. Vacations were always good for them. The sun and beach, the time of relaxation, and the dining out all combined to weave a cocoon of romance.

As Tim spread sunblock over his arm and hand he couldn't help picturing the severed hand and the beaten body. After his initial fright he had run to Katie to prevent her seeing it. The jog back to the condo, the call to Dave, the return to the beach with towels, and the wait for an ambulance and police had all blurred to a thin memory. Until last night he'd never seen any vehicles on the beach. Once the injured man had been taken away, a large pickup with a rack of lights mounted on top of the cab lit up the beach in an odd luminescence. He thought now how the scene had looked like something from a Ridley Scott film, either *Blade Runner* or *Paradise*, with a kind of diffused glow shining through the palms and seagrapes. Silhouettes and shadows flickered in a kind of dance on a beach, the bright moon overpowered by spotlights. More spotlights on the beach, he thought. First the lights of the men with foreign voices; then the search-spots of the police, catching men bent over and searching, not unlike shellers. But this Sanibel stoop in the glow of spot lights was no benign hunt for the almost-mythical junonia shell. This bend-and-stoop search of a serene, gentle-looking beach was for evidence of an act of violence. They had found nothing, nor were they likely to. A crime scene on a beach has to be nearly impossible, Tim thought. Wind, birds, surf, and shellers, all conspire to wipe away or conceal what might be a clue.

He was about to open the door and start down the three flights to the beach, when the phone rang again. "Forget it," he thought, then reconsidered. It might be Laney's sister who was staying over at Fort Myers Beach.

A woman's voice greeted him. "Mr. Calvin, my name is Natalie Simmonds. I'm a reporter and I would like to interview you about what happened last night. We won't take long and promise not to spoil your beach time." The voice was pleasant, but determined.

"I don't know…I'd just like to forget about it and get on with my vacation." He tried to sound terse.

"But this man you found may have been involved in the bombing in New York City last month. You may have seen or heard something that could impact national security."

"Where are you getting this?" He was stunned by what she had just said—and curious.

"I'll fill you in when we meet. You ought to be on the beach enjoying the sunshine. That's where my photographer and I'll meet you in, say, about an hour. Thanks. Good-bye," she said and hung up before he could even respond.

He walked to the window and stared out at the sea. Terrorism! He was beginning to feel like a piece of driftwood caught in a powerful surf, unable to control its destiny. The events of the last twelve hours had washed over him like a rip tide and now seemed to be carrying him on their own current, and he resented it. And besides that there was something else—the sense that last night he was being watched.

Tim ducked as he passed the beach cabana to avoid knocking his head on the overhang, something he was famous for. The sight and sound of the waves washing onto the beach and the warmth of the sun cheered him. What was it about the sun? He felt almost in control and safe, here in its heat and light, among the people passing. This was part of the beach scene he loved so much, the shellers and walkers on the move. Some looked straight ahead, but most cast their eyes down, scanning the shells—a parade of sorts, people in a variety of hats and shirts, shorts and swim suits, shoes or sandals or barefoot. Some were leather-skinned veterans, others were dark-bodied torsos parading with a kind of pride, and there were the lobster-red necks and legs and shoulders of those who later on would surely feel the sting of venturing unprotected into the sunshine. But he watched with more than amusement, looking to see if somewhere in the lines of people was someone watching him.

"Daddy, I've got the moat," Katie called, breaking into his thoughts. "Can you help me with the bucket? It's too heavy!" she asked with the fierce determination of a child busy constructing a fantasy of sand and shells. She had walked past a couple and a family who had taken up spots just north of the entrance path to the beach, almost in the spot where last night he had noticed the unusual troughs. The police chief and Dave had speculated they were caused by the toes of the man as he was being dragged into the seagrape bush, face down after having been apparently beaten elsewhere on the beach and then pulled into the thicket. The bush and vegetation surrounding the area were marked with the yellow tape used at emergencies and crime scenes. It seemed strange to him the tape didn't look at all out of place here. The strict environmental code of the island often dictated that replantings were flagged and roped off, so it was not uncommon to find such markings along a stroll of the beach. To most who passed by in the continual stream of foot traffic, the area didn't draw even a second look. It was clear that many of these vacationers were unaware of the news. That might change when the reporter shows up, he thought.

"Daddy, you get wet sand and build the tower. This is going be a backlake," Katie pleaded as she knelt over a hole she was digging, enlarging it with a pinshell and small plastic shovel.

"Tell you what, I'll use the bucket to pull sand out of the hole for your lake," he said as he began to help her dig.

Time has no value on vacation. It can either stall, standing still, or race ahead; it makes no difference. Tim was oblivious to its cadence, his entire thought and awareness directed toward building the great sandcastle with his energy and that of his daughter combining in joyous teamwork. The only sign that time even moved along was the rhythm of the waves washing in a calming lullaby behind them.

The castle began to take great architectural form with Katie excavating to a depth of two and half feet.

"Daddy, I think I found something hard. The shell keeps hitting it." But before he could look to see he was interrupted.

"Mr. Calvin, I'm Natalie Simmonds," the woman said, extending her hand to him. "And this is my photographer, Steve."

Tim was annoyed. "You know, Ms. Simmonds, I'd really rather not get involved here. I was just...."

"But you are involved, Mr. Calvin. This is the biggest story to hit Sanibel in quite a while."

She was young, probably mid- to late-twenties, but she possessed a self-confidence beyond her years. TV people, he thought, they were different, no doubt about that. There was always a patina of knowledge, the public's need to know, which led to a kind of smugness, a take-charge personality. Natalie Simmonds was attractive, like most television reporters, and had a pleasant appearance. She had that designer-rack classy style of dress that betrayed a lovely figure which he imagined would look even better in a two-piece swim suit.

"You can really help us shed some light on what happened." She stared intensely at him with her large, liquid-blue eyes.

He met her stare. "Have you talked with the police? They can tell you more."

"They can, but they won't," she smiled, her eyes showing a flicker of mischievousness, her tone almost breathy. "That's why I need you." Did she really say that or did I imagine it? he wondered. Wishful thinking? He pondered silently, their eyes still locked in a kind of psychological battle—a kind of smirking test, a sporty tête-à-tête. He liked her spunk.

"Daddy, Daddy! I found a pirate treasure!" Katie broke in, and he disengaged his stare. He could see she was holding a large piece of metal. It looked like brass or maybe bronze, covered in sand and shell debris.

"Yeah, it might be off a pirate ship," he said, just glancing at the item she had pulled from the hole.

"Mr. Calvin..." Simmonds began.

"Tim is all right if you prefer," he countered.

"I'd like to interview you up near the location where you found the man with the severed hand. Please."

* * *

Tim recounted the incident for her, the glaring sea as a background. She asked for details, thoughts, mood. Had he gotten a good look at the men or the boat? What else did he see or remember? After a while Steve the photographer began walking around them while he continued to videotape. Natalie said he was getting "set up shots and B-roll" to use to help her make edits in their conversation.

Her eyes fairly glittered. "This is the most exciting story I've covered since the evacuation caused by Hurricane Andrew," she said as they walked over to Katie's sandcastle. Steve took a few more pictures including one of Katie digging away with her new scoop, the long piece of metal she had found, which was about the size of an address plate.

"A source of mine said the man you found was probably either Iraqi or Libyan."

"Iraqi?"

"Yes. There was speculation the men responsible for the beating and the severing of the hand were also Libyan or Iraqi." She smiled and, snapping her notepad closed, tucked it and her pen into her purse.

As she prepared to leave Natalie shook his hand again, and her deep blue eyes once more had that smoldering quality. "You've been very helpful to me. Thank you, Tim," she said and winked, ever so subtly. One last smile and she turned and walked away. He stood there feeling as though he had been seduced, or at least flirted into an interview he had not wanted to do. And she had said nothing about the new-found terrorist connection; he had forgotten to ask.

As he watched her walk away, the sun behind her dress revealing the shape of very lovely legs, his innocent voyeurism was interrupted by a prickling on the back of his neck—that eerie sense again that someone was observing him. He quickly scanned the perimeter of the beach and the few people who were idly strolling in the heat of the day. Nothing.

* * *

Katie had finished the castle, embellishing it with shells and a kind of sea vegetation washed in on the tide. The stuff was a hot pink color, and she used it atop the towers and plaza area nicely, like pink landscaped trees. He also noticed the metal plate she had found, which she had by now washed in the surf.

"Wow," he mumbled.

"What did you say?" Katie returned.

He took the plate from her in order to examine it more closely.

"Honey, this is really neat. This could be from a pirate ship, or from a ship of some sort. It looks old." He marveled at the heavy metal plate, about six inches by six inches, rough around the edges and weighty. It looked to be a couple of inches thick.

"I told you so," Katie peppered back. She peered closely at the writing that covered the plate. "What's it say, Daddy?"

"I don't know, sweetie. It's engraved in an old script, maybe Latin or Greek. This is a real find."

"Yes, it is, a real find indeed," a man's voice startled him from behind. "Mr. Calvin, allow me to introduce myself. I've been watching you."

The Watcher

Later as he showered, Tim mentally replayed the conversation with the man who had startled him on the beach. So, yes, he had been watched, last night and again today. He was told it was for his "security and that of his family." The only identity the man had given was to say he was Valmer, "well-known to your friend Dave."

This Valmer was a mysterious, though not threatening man in his late sixties or early seventies, carrying the tan of an island resident who spent time outside. His face was lined and he was somewhat stooped, and carried a slight paunch, but he appeared strong and especially sinewy for a man in his decade of life. He had the hint of an accent, and a powerful and penetrating stare. Speaking in a deep, calm voice, he fixed Tim directly with his eyes, which, though bright, seemed to be reservoirs of melancholy.

The eyes twinkled briefly when Tim asked him how he could have watched in the darkness of the beach last night. "There is quite efficient technology," he had said with a hint of a smile. "It is very important that you give this metal plate to our mutual friend Dave for its safe keeping immediately. We'll chat again."

Tim stepped out of the shower and wrapped a towel around his waist. As he stood looking out the sliding door of the bedroom onto a late afternoon beach, with the palms dancing in the breeze, the mood the scene was supposed to evoke escaped him. Instead, he felt something more powerful pulling on him, an amalgam of the events of the last eighteen hours and others, undefined, and as yet merely anticipated. The serenity of vacation had been wiped away by a sense of mystery and growing sense of anxiety.

Katie and Dave's daughter Celia, affectionately called Cee, had spent the rest of the afternoon in the pool, under the somewhat watchful eye of Elizabeth who broke up her child-watching duties by reading the current issue of *Sassy* and listening to a Cure tape on her Walkman. The gals were now putting on their evening dresses, Laney mixing rum cocktails as prelude to dinner at the French Corner. This annual outing was one of her favorite evenings of the yearly Sanibel visit. Jean Paul's French Corner was high on Laney's list as one her favorite places to spend time. Laney had put the Planet Drums CD on to play while they got ready, and the captivating percussion rhythm, artistically mixed and presented by Grateful Dead drummer Mickey Hart, produced a mellow mood.

Cee was a precocious child with a precise but extremely articulate manner of speaking. She regaled Tim and Laney with how the French Corner's new chef was "marvelous. He's done very nicely with the salmon in dill—I'm sure that's what I'll order." Barb and Dave's only child, and Tim's goddaughter, Cee was smart beyond her ten years. She was deeply cherished by her parents, two artists who had reared her with an exceptional affection. Tim thought how lucky she was to be living on the island of his vacation dreams. It delighted him to see his Katie and Dave's Cee growing up as friends, the second generation of a friendship which was closer than many family ties.

Tim hummed to himself as he slipped on his sport coat. This night had become a ritual in the history of the Calvin-Hockett friendship: cocktails in anticipation of the charm of Jean Paul's French Corner, and then dinner in the authentic provincial setting. Tonight, though, there was another item on the menu, the intrigue that he could not put out his mind.

* * *

Tim and Dave avoided any discussion of the recent bizarre events until the preliminary rituals had been executed. Jean Paul extended his traditional greeting; kisses for the ladies, kisses on the hands of the little ladies, and gracious handshakes for Dave and Tim. The group was then ushered to the round table in the middle of the French-country styled room, next to a wooden beam. From there they could see through the windows to the ferns and Australian pines, a natural wall of green which wrapped round the small structure, an unassuming and house-like abode of culinary magic tucked into the island's famous vegetation. To the other side was the bar with its colorful display of bottles, espresso machine, ceramic wall display, French country kitsch, and beautiful dark wood. This middle table had been "theirs" for some fifteen years, and the special night always began the same, with Kir Royales and rounds of toasts.

The room was suffused with an elegant, low, candle-like glow. Each table was enveloped with its own sphere of light and fresh flowers to beautify the center. The light and arrangement of the tables offered a sense of privacy, a natural environment for Dave to fill in for Tim the details of the mysterious Valmer, the man who had watched him on the beach.

As Dave began his description, Tim felt as though he were hearing of a character from a Robert Ludlum or Graham Greene novel.

"He's the son of middle European émigrés. He was a natural as an OSS operative during World War II—so good he was there at the creation of the CIA."

"I got that vibe from him. He sure talks like an old spy," Tim responded.

"More than a spy. He had a brilliant career and rose to Deputy Director for Operations. He was the man in charge of all field operatives and operations." More drinks arrived, bringing another round of toasts.

Tim mulled over what Dave had just told him. He knew that "operations" meant the human side of cloak and dagger work. "How long was Valmer in?"

"He was on the fast track all during the buildup of the Cold War. But he suddenly quit. He resigned in a dispute with LBJ. He won't talk much about it, but it happened during the early days of the Vietnam conflict."

Tim gazed out the window. "A lot of people had trouble with Johnson over the war policy. Remember how bitter it was back then?"

"Yes, even inside the CIA. But this falling out was over a matter of principle. Late one night after a good deal of brandy he opened up and told me he and the President got into a real heavy shouting match over a matter of interpretation of CIA charter and mission. Valmer thought LBJ had been wrong in a 'task' he'd assigned to him, so he just walked away. According to him he 'left from the corridors of power for the pace and nature of Sanibel Island.' Pretty strong stuff, huh?" Dave continued his quiet narrative, while Laney, Barb and Elizabeth chatted away. Katie and Cee were busy decorating doilies with colored pencils.

"Yeah, pretty amazing," Tim mumbled.

Tim felt like his stomach was tied in a knot by the time their dinners arrived. It was absurd! He was inadvertently involved in something in which a man had been beaten and had his hand severed, and now he was being watched by a mysterious old spy. He couldn't understand why, though. It just wasn't clear at all.

The roast leg of lamb en croûte, the Pouilly Fuisse, and the comfortable conversation of Laney, Barb and the girls reinstated his sense of reality and relaxation. The fine meal and evening were the kind of thing vacation was supposed to be. As they enjoyed the work of the restaurant's master chef, Tim was able to put aside all the nagging questions. The only other hint of the unpleasant underside came as they finished the entrees. When the ladies excused themselves to go to the powder room Dave reminded him that Valmer had asked that the metal plate be turned over to him for safekeeping.

"We'll keep it safe. Valmer said he could tell you more about it later."

"Why? Tell me more about what? Why don't we just give the

plate to Valmer and let him deal with it?" Tim said with a note of exasperation as he drained his wine glass.

"It's not that easy. Valmer says this whole situation is real tricky. That plate may be extremely valuable. And it could be tied up in some touchy international relations stuff or diplomacy. You know I'm not into that as much as you are. I told Valmer about your interests and background."

"Dave, for Pete's sake, I'm just a tourist trying to enjoy a vacation. I mean, two weeks a year I get *away* from hassles. The last thing I want now is to get involved in an international dispute over some old artifact or whatever else is going on."

Dave heard the edge of testiness in Tim's voice. "Look, Tim, all I'm trying to do is let you know what's going on in Valmer's mind. He says he needs someone he can trust. He needs someone with your background and skills."

"My background and skills? I'm a communications consultant. I help design location shoots for ad agencies. I train CEOs in how to talk to the media. I work in building corporate images and start in-house publications. What's that got to do with any of this?"

"You know what I'm talking about—the doctoral thing. He asked me about you, and then checked you out himself. Remember he was a honcho in the CIA and he still has access to information."

"Well, that's just great—he checked me out," Tim grumbled. "That old geezer's sure got his share of nerve."

The doctoral thing. The words prompted an almost visceral change in Tim. It spun his mind back into the one area of his life filled with regret. The Ph.D. that never happened and never stopped casting a shadow over his innermost perception of himself, regardless of what success or happiness he had achieved since.

As a doctoral candidate in history twenty years ago, he had completed his class requirements and was beginning work on his dissertation. He had done the preliminary research and was preparing to spend several months in Europe working on a study of the spread of secret military religious organizations and lodges, such as the Knights Templar, during the Crusades. It was an arcane topic which he attacked with relish, partly because it allowed him to indulge in fantasies he'd had since childhood when he had immersed himself in Edgar Rice Borroughs novels and episodes of Johnny Quest on TV.

While in graduate school Tim had supported himself with a job as a reporter on a local newspaper. He enjoyed the journalistic chase of a story, and approached his doctoral research with the passion of a reporter going after a hot tip. But his true longing was to write something that would have historical impact, to share his knowledge and love of history.

Tim was never able to complete his doctoral work. Two weeks before he was to leave for Europe his father became gravely ill, and Tim had to stay home to help support his family. In the months of his father's illness and recuperation Tim's dream of graduate school became increasingly remote. Although he had managed to go on to develop a satisfying career in which he had earned respect and admiration, his unresolved pursuit continued to haunt him. His profession allowed him to use his analytic and investigative skills, but he tended to shy away from actual reporting or history because they invoked the painful memory of the doctorate left in limbo. Dave's reference to "the doctoral thing" evoked that lingering doubt, the "what if" question of his life, that somewhere out there was an article on Byzantium or a dig in Turkey that should have had his name on it.

Tim was snapped back to the present by the ladies' return to the table and the delivery of their desserts. "OK, I'll talk to him. But I don't want to get into something heavy," he said with morose resignation. "This is all I want right now," he said, indicating the sweet confections the waitress set before them.

The arrival of the desserts brought another of their rituals, the sharing of bites of the marvelous creations of sweet paradise. Laney's favorite was the crème caramel, and Elizabeth and Barb opted as usual for the chocolate mousse. Cee and Katie split a snowball, a scoop of ice cream covered in nuts and chocolate. Dave went for the strawberries in Grand Marnier, and Tim was delighted by his pear poached in port and covered in chocolate.

The group was in a cheerful and satiated mood as they bade adieu to Jean Paul. As the girls headed to the rental van, Dave took Tim's elbow and pulled him aside.

"We'll take the gals with us to Timbers and wait for you on the porch. Jayne and Andy are singing blues. Valmer wants to meet with you at the crab bridge in Ding Darling. He promises it'll be very quick."

"It'd better be."

Tim was always enchanted by Ding Darling's more than five thousand acres of wildlife refuge. Its primeval setting was a trip away from modern civilization, back to a time before man inhabited this subtropical barrier island. Set aside in 1935 by Jay Norwood "Ding" Darling when he was Chief of the U.S. Biological survey, the area gained status as a national wildlife refuge in 1945, the year before Tim's birth. Since childhood he had felt a kinship with this home of cormorants, anhingas, roseate spoonbills, great egrets, white ibis, brown pelicans, red shouldered hawks, osprey, and other birds—and the 'gators. Darling had been a visionary, establishing four hundred and twenty refuges during that year of 1934–35. Here was the native and original Florida barrier island as it had been, home to native Americans from at least 3000 B.C. on. Natural, pristine, and beyond the reach of human development, the refuge had avoided the change which started with the first European settlers in the mid-1500s. Thank God Darling had moved to save this wilderness, Tim thought. Tonight he was on the five-mile "wildlife drive," a road on a dike built in 1962 as a mosquito control, holding the brackish water at a level which prevented summertime exposure of the mudflats, the favored breeding ground of marsh mosquitoes. During the winter the flood gates were opened, allowing tidal waters to wash in nutrients, which then became feeding grounds for dunlins, yellowlegs, and sandpipers.

The sun was beyond the western line of Brazilian peppers and Australian pines. A few osprey descended against the pink glow to their nesting stations high above the tree line, while hawks soared on thermal currents, circling over this paradise. The lagoons and lakes reflected the pink of the sky, and the white ibis, reminding him of a Matsumoto painting, gracefully waded in the pink water, the brilliant white of their plumage moving in a kind of staccato ballet. The darker the sky became, the more loudly the frogs croaked their rhythm, providing a base beat that accompanied the occasional shrill of a bird rattling through the branches and leaves of the lush overgrowth.

The sunlight had completely faded by now, so the last vans of wildlife photographers were packing up and passing him by on their way out of the refuge, their expensive long lenses and tripods tucked carefully away. He felt very much alone as he pulled his van to the side near the crab observation bridge, a wooden, pier-like walkway built out over a brackish bayou; it lead to a wider deck which fronted on a small lagoon. Below him were thousands of blue crabs. These little creatures, greenish to blue in color and only six inches wide, were particularly nasty, snapping viciously when caught by weekend crabbers. They looked odd and other-worldly here in the twilight.

Tim became increasingly annoyed as mosquitoes fed hungrily on his neck and arms. He walked out along the bridge, looking for this mysterious Valmer; he had not seen another car, and there was no sign of the man on the pathway. After walking to the end of the bridge to the widened observation deck he finally saw a note pinned to the rail: *"Mosquitoes fierce. Come to Tower 2."*

Shadows were deepening and the sky darkening as he slowly motored to the tower and parked just south of it. A gray Mercedes was parked just north of the tower steps. As he got out of the van and locked the door he heard a splash in the water behind him. He spun quickly and saw something that looked like a log floating in the freshwater channel. He noticed worn spots on the bank to his left. "Great, just great," he mumbled, realizing he was alone at dark just feet from one of the preferred areas of the sanctuary's uncounted alligator population.

The creatures grew from six to eight feet long and could travel up to ten miles per hour. He had always told the girls to stay at least fifteen feet away from them. Now he suspected uneasily that he was standing much closer than was prudent to a predator which had superior twilight vision. He started up the steps to the tower's observation deck at a brisk pace.

"If you look out from this point—you see that feathery line? That is where the Australian pine and the damned Brazilian pepper encroach upon us," said a voice coming from a silhouetted figure in the corner of the tower. "Two interesting varieties, and like you and I, neither are indigenous. Good evening, Mr. Calvin." The man emerged from the shadows.

"The pines are beautiful," Tim responded, staring at Valmer with suspicion.

"Like a tall and exotic lover who leaves you in the morning. Tallest thing on the island, some a hundred feet. But they have a very shallow root system and are the first to topple in high winds; then they break your heart. Some fool brought the Brazilian pepper here as an ornamental plant. But it's like a greedy man. It crowds out native growth, choking other plants, starving off wildlife habitat. We are trying to eradicate both." Valmer turned his view from the horizon and faced Tim. Tim could see him now, observe him more closely than he had been able to on the beach. Valmer was a lean, strong-featured man with a direct and unwavering gaze; his intense stare made Tim a bit uneasy.

Tim swallowed in an attempt to ease the dryness in his mouth. "I'm not really interested in environmental philosophy right now," he said. "I'd like to know what's going on. I gave that metal plate to Dave."

"Wise indeed, Mr. Calvin. What your daughter found is an object of great desire. Some who covet it are like the Brazilian pepper, greedy, and like the alligator you heard below, capable of great violence. What I have to tell you is not pleasant, but it is most intriguing. I hope it is adequate to lure your considerable curiosity Mr. Calvin. I seek your assistance."

Valmer's tone, combined with the oddly evocative sounds and scene, sent a slight chill down Tim's spine, and he shivered. The darkening twilight, ushering in a primordial soundtrack of frogs beginning their sawing rhythm, the squawking of tropical birds, the splashing in channels and lakes, and the rushing of the wind through the trees, further heightened his sense of discomfiture. Night was upon them, and Tim was feeling isolated and defenseless.

"I noticed you shiver. Are you chilled? We could sit in one of the cars." There was a note of sincere concern in Valmer's voice.

"A little bit, but I'm fine," Tim replied. "In fact I'm fascinated by the sound of this place after dark. I've never been here after sunset."

"Then please, sit," Valmer indicated a bench near the edge of the deck. "This chorus of nature, rarely heard by many, is a quite appropriate background for the bizarre and mysterious tale I have to tell you. And while it will not be heard by many, either, it is none the less profound."

"You're talking about the metal plate?"

"And the story behind it. At least as best as we understand it now. The exact origin of the metal plate is unknown," Valmer continued. "There are some widely divergent theories which associates of mine are checking. What we know is the identity of the man on the beach. He is a former Libyan military officer now in the employ of Tojo Rome, the privately held corporation of Aoki 'Calamari' Pasotti."

"That TV reporter, Natalie Simmonds, said there was a Middle Eastern connection to this. I don't like being involved in something with people like that," Tim snapped.

"Patience, please, Mr. Calvin," Valmer soothed. "This is a detailed story; hear me out. Pasotti's father was a wealthy Italian businessman who traded in art and artifacts. He was a confidant of Mussolini and had a high military commission, which he had used to amass by fraud and force an even greater collection of art riches during the war. Through his military connections, the senior Pasotti met the daughter of a prominent Japanese family. Aoki Pasotti was the issue of that union, and inheritor of the great wealth of both families. It seems a great injustice, doesn't it, Mr. Calvin, that while millions suffered or died, the influential among the Axis powers preserved their wealth with the help of Swiss banks and clever lawyers?"

"So some of the war's losers were actually its big winners. I don't think this kind of information is commonly known," Tim offered somewhat feebly.

"We are not trading in a common commodity, nor are we dealing with common people. The nickname 'Calamari' is not entirely endearing. It speaks of his passion for the dish—squid—but it also describes his tentacle-like hold over his business dealings and associates."

Valmer concluded his briefing with speculation that Pasotti was the leading dealer in the underground market of sacred art and artifacts.

"A zealot in his almost fanatical pursuit. To use an old company term, he's off the reservation," Valmer said as a prelude to a warning. "He tried to kill a man who was in possession of the metal plate your daughter found. We believe the attackers of the man you found are also his associates, possibly after a wayward colleague. I cannot be sure they are not still here on Sanibel. Mr. Calvin, I cannot emphasize how tenacious Pasotti can be. He was not unknown to me in my former job. Indeed, his tentacles stretch to great lengths."

Tim was disturbed by Valmer's tale, but his pride compelled him to mask it. "It is a fascinating and, as you said, a bizarre story. Bizarre that somehow it ends up on Sanibel. Why not just turn it over to the authorities? That way my family and I can get on with our vacation." He tried to sound slightly irritated, perhaps bored.

"If only life was a simple as that, as clear-cut as those whom we used to refer to as 'civilians' think it is. No, Mr. Calvin we can't turn the plate over to the authorities. While we don't know with certainty what it is, our preliminary speculations have put it in the classification of something which could have a quite unsettling and far-reaching effect. You can appreciate how delicate and tenuous Middle Eastern policy and diplomacy is. Until we have a better understanding of the Libyans and their role, and know exactly what Pasotti is up to and how he is involved, this matter is best left a quiet little secret. Some of my former colleagues are using their considerable skill to learn more."

"So what do you want from me?" It was a question Tim hated to ask.

"I am familiar with your background, Mr. Calvin. History is something of considerable significance to you," Valmer paused, as if searching for the correct words. "I only wished to inform you of the complexity of this matter and the possible history of the plate and its potential significance and impact. I'll have more details and further ideas to consider and present to you later. Please, consider seriously the things I have told you." He turned to face Tim and stepped closer. Again Tim was struck by the eyes that were steely, but at the same time sincere.

Valmer's comment "history is something of significance to you" really worked Tim over. The old master spy had struck a nerve by touching something Tim thought was buried, no longer part of his life.

Tim was numb as he drove out of Ding Darling onto the San Cap road. His head spun, and he was becoming angry. The more he thought about this last encounter, the more his rage built. For so long he had planned these two weeks of complete "R & R," a break from work, a time to catch his breath. It was a time to forget about conferences in New Orleans, seminars in Philadelphia, meetings in Denver or Indianapolis or wherever, airplane schedules, hotel rooms, hours on the phone. This was to be a time for no hassles, no problems—beach time with the kids, fatherly conversation with college-bound Elizabeth, and tender time with Laney, a chance for them to rekindle their flame, a time for passion. Instead he felt a sinking dread, and that he was being manipulated, grasped in the jaws of something large and terrible; and worst of all, he had no power to resist it.

As he turned onto Tarpon Bay Road driving to rendezvous with Laney, Barb, Dave, and the girls, he could hear Jayne's voice. The amplifiers at the Timbers Restaurant and Bar were apparently set with the wind, and her gutsy blues were being carried on the evening's breeze. Andy Walling, a local musician, had recently become Jayne's voice coach and they performed together a couple of nights a week at The Porch. Tim and Laney had met Jayne and her husband Brian through the Hocketts, and over the years they had become friends.

A couple of years ago they had all taken a diving vacation together to Grand Cayman. Brian and Jayne, who also owned the exquisite Mad Hatter Restaurant, had been like private island chefs in residence during the Cayman trip. An evening at the Mad Hatter was usually the *coup de maître* of the Calvins' Sanibel stay. Jayne, a fiery redhead with the elegance of a *Vogue* model sang blues as if she had been a street urchin from the southside of Chicago. These nights on The Porch provided good relaxation for her and Brian, a break from the restaurant business.

As he started up the veranda steps, Brian caught his eye and hoisted a beer, questioning whether Tim wanted one. Tim nodded with emphasis and flashed two fingers. Brian smiled and headed into the bar.

"What's wrong?," Laney asked, reading his face and worried by his grave expression.

"It's deep," he whispered. "I'll tell you about it later."

"I'm counting on it," she smiled, a hint of sensuality in her voice. She scooted closer to him and took his hand.

As they sat in the crowded nightclub, alive with the night rhythm of partying vacationers, Tim found it difficult to relax. What could Valmer possibly want from him? Obviously he had checked his past if he knew about his failed doctoral track. Why was he playing that card with him? Ah, the hell with it, he thought, as Jayne stepped up the tempo and launched into an Etta James song.

The music and good times lifted his spirits. After enjoying a few sets, Tim and Laney collected their girls, said good night to everyone and headed to Bailey's Market to pick up a few groceries for breakfast. Traffic was light at this hour, and there were only a few cars in the Bailey's lot.

"We'll have to remember this. The best time to come to Bailey's is just before closing time," he said. He turned to Elizabeth and Katie sitting in the back seat. "You gals want to come in or stay in the car?" They opted to wait outside.

Bailey's was an institution. An emporium operated by one of the first families to settle the island, it had since grown to a whole corner of commerce. He and Laney went in through the door near the bakery. She grabbed a cart, and he stood gazing at the tempting displays of breads, cakes, and cookies, row after row. Usually there was quite a line of customers, but tonight just a handful of people stood waiting their turn.

His automatic grocery store behavior kicked in. He could drift and dawdle through supermarkets, browsing along the aisles for what he might need, and more often selecting things that he didn't need. Laney, on the other hand, was very brisk and efficient and whipped past items not on her list.

They had just rounded the corner by the chip display and were headed to the checkout when he heard them. The voices he had heard on the beach the night before. The accent and cadence were unmistakable. Cautiously avoiding drawing attention to himself, he followed the sound of the voices. They belonged to two men who were leaving a checkout line and heading to the exit. He caught just a glimpse before the men went through the door to the parking lot. Both were dark haired, and looked to be in their thirties. One was muscular, like a weight lifter and the other was slightly built with a pocked face.

While Tim and Laney went through the checkout line, he looked through the door to see if he could spot the duo. Then, as they carried the groceries to the van he scanned the parking lot.

Elizabeth looked uneasy when they opened the door of the van. "Lizzie, honey, what's wrong?" Laney asked.

"It was weird. These two dudes, with real dark complexions—one had a lot of zits—got into the car next to us. One of 'em looked at Katie and started yelling in some language—I don't know what. The other guy got out and looked at her and started yelling, too. I didn't know what to do, so I told Katie to lie down and I honked the horn. Didn't you hear it?" The girl was clearly shaken.

"We didn't hear the horn," Laney said, her voice tense.

"You did the right thing. Don't worry about it now," Tim said with an assuredness he absolutely did not feel. As they drove along Tarpon Bay road to West Gulf and then to the condo, he attempted to behave in a cavalier and casual manner, but his stomach rolled uneasily. He checked the rear view mirror repeatedly to see if they were being followed, and for good measure even pulled into another condo. That drew a chorus of "Where are you going?"

"Just checking the tennis court here," he joked while surveying the rear-view mirror.

Minutes later the van pulled off West Gulf drive into the entrance road to their condo. The soft lights bathed the giant ferns and bougainvilleas, and the pool glistened in marine blue from its underwater lights. Lights were on at a couple of the doors of the nine-unit, three-story condo. The dramatic lighting on the palms painted the small, quiet building with deep shadows. They drove through the serene, nighttime setting, up the drive past the tennis court to the nine-space car port. Tree frogs croaked, but all else was silent. Getting out of the van, they headed for the elevator carrying sacks of groceries.

Once inside, with the door locked, Tim began to feel more secure. The sound of the surf rolled in from the terrace, and it drew him into its spell like a magnet. He climbed the small spiral stairs up to the private sundeck on the roof. Each of the three top units had its own deck, fenced for privacy, affording one of the highest views on the island. The star field was brilliant, from the horizon line over the water to as far back as he could see inland before trees eclipsed the view. Katie and Elizabeth came up for a look and a hug and kiss before turning in. Elizabeth, her sixth sense picking up his concern, stood behind him rubbing away the tension in his shoulders. As he pointed out Venus and Mercury, Elizabeth pointed to the Big Dipper. He was starting to describe Orion's belt when he heard a faint hint of a foreign voice. Elizabeth heard it too. She stopped rubbing his shoulder, and froze. Katie didn't hear it. "Why did you stop, Daddy?" she asked.

"I think your Mom's calling you, kiddo. Time to get tucked in. Give me a kiss." He hugged the little girl close. "God bless you, sweetheart. Daddy loves you. I'll check on you in little while."

As Katie headed down the stairs Elizabeth asked, "What's going on, Pop? Are those guys here? What do they want? Should you call someone?"

Before he could answer, the voices got louder, closer, sounding like shouts. He and Elizabeth ducked their heads and homed in on the sounds. They were coming from the south, to the side, the end of their building. They edged over toward the sundeck's fence and peeked out. What Tim saw made his heart stand still. Two dark figures lurked in the shadow of a tall ficus shrub between his condo and the building further south. A natural boundary of trees and shrubs outside of the decorative lighting of the two buildings provided a refuge for the two men. They had flashlights, and their attention was focused on the south building, beyond the vegetation line and past the sea grass and sandy open space. Access to the building was limited by a fence and wall, and they had taken a stand at the only open space between. Beaming their lights toward the other building, beyond the beach, pool, patio and shuffleboard court, they seemed unaware he was watching them. Quietly Tim and Elizabeth ducked down the spiral stairs. He pulled and locked the hatch cover behind him and went to the phone to call Dave.

The Potter's Wheel

Waking up early was part of his vacation behavior. It was as though an internal clock sounded, reminding him that sunshine was waiting on the Gulf of Mexico just steps away, a scene he had paid for and didn't want to squander by sleeping in. He had slept surprisingly soundly, considering the menace of the two men outside the building last night. It was his theory, a worrisome one, that the men had been interested in finding him and the girls, but were off in their search by one structure along the beach. After Tim had called Dave he in turn had called the resident manager of the neighboring condo. Within minutes, flood lights had brightly illuminated the vegetation buffer, forcing the men to flee, running like scared animals.

Tim had then been able to go to bed with a sense of relief. Laney saw to it he fell into a relaxed sleep. As he slid under the covers she had turned to him and begun a slow massaging of his chest, circling gently with her fingertips. The coded message of body language ignited a blaze in him, and together they caressed, stroked, and came together on a sea of passion while the surf rolled away and blew in with the breeze which fluttered the curtain at the window. Later, he lay on his back with her body curled into his, her head on his shoulder, her fingertips tracing his forehead and temples and along the bridge of his nose. This was his sweet dessert, the final inducement to deep sleep, a refuge from anger, fear, and the strange forces which seemed to be conspiring to steal his vacation.

* * *

The next day passed in brilliant sunshine spent in bursts of beach-walking and shelling, swims in the pool, lapses into the deep naps induced by the intense sun, and reading. He found it amusing that he had to arrange his reading glasses and sunglasses in an overlay on his nose. It was time to get prescription sunglasses, he thought, another sign the baby boomers had reached maturity, at least by the body clock.

Emotionally, however, he felt very much akin to the kid he was when he had made his first trip to the beach. That first glimpse of the ocean was one of those transcendent moments forever enshrined in his memory. The color of the water rolling up on shore to him, the wave tips curling in a white foam, the sound which reached into his nerves and fired synapses of relaxation, causing him to shudder, had stamped themselves in his memory and life at that moment. The white-hot heat of the sun seemed to transport him aloft then. It was as though the exotic palms, graceful and elegant, their fronds waving against a royal blue sky, beckoned that boy he had been into a world more perfect, more right than anything he had ever imagined. At once he was in a land of paradise and pleasure and mystery on the edge of the great water that had carried ships of history and adventure. Robert Louis Stevenson seemed to call to him from beyond the current. And later, he found he could never read Hemingway's passages of water or sky and not think back to that boyhood moment when he was forever changed, standing on a beach watching the sunshine reflecting on the gulf.

Now his self-doubts and the memories of his academic "failure" had been exhumed by Valmer, and they worked through his mind as he stood in the sun with the water lapping over his toes. He stared deep into the horizon and waited for that special feeling to come over him, that sense of awe and splendor that always rose from the sea. He had always brought his worries and problems here for resolution. Tim had come to believe that, like the waves and the surf, time curved back on itself at the beach. He was there as a kid with his parents and brothers, as he was there now, and knew he would be even when he had passed on, when Elizabeth and Katie walked in the surf with their children and grandchildren. Once, in a meditative mood, he had shared his thoughts with his friends that "eternity touches humankind in the tide, in the building of the barrier island, in its perpetual and gentle sift of sand. In the powerful hands of Providence time and lifetimes are easily molded." Now the magic of the beach and the philosophic musings it inspired eased his mind and soothed his doubts. It always had. Today he was adrift and at ease, all unpleasantness far and remote. At least for this moment, Tim was convinced God was in heaven, and with that he was content.

This third day of vacation seemed to suit them all well. The girls beamed, proud of what they could see were the beginnings of tans, and their eyes sparkled with the joy of vacation-time peace of mind. All of them were also voraciously hungry, another effect of time on the beach and hours in the pool. They planned to drive across the island for an evening of carry-out barbecue on the Hockett's patio. For this drive, Tim decided to stay on Gulf Drive, through its curves and winding changes to Middle Gulf before cutting back across to Periwinkle Way and on to the Hocketts. The homeward rush on Periwinkle, the island's main thoroughfare had begun, and the day-trippers would be bumper-to-bumper all the way to the causeway exit. Not that it was a major traffic jam, like those back north, but Tim and his family enjoyed the signage and roadfront presentations of the quiet and elegant condominiums of the more scenic West Gulf. The traffic flow was gentle and the lush greenery beautiful. This route allowed them to stay near the water and avoid the crowd. The sun was beginning its arc in the west and it cast that wonderful evening glow on this side of the island. Indeed it was a perfect evening, the cap to a wonderful day.

* * *

A Touch of Sanibel Pottery sat diagonally from the McT's Shrimp House and Tavern, two authentic Sanibel mainstays. The Hocketts had expanded and transformed their corner into a bit of island enchantment. The stucco building, like the pottery made inside, was unique, landscaped with palms and shrubs and lush vegetation. A giant handmade fish pond on a pedestal sitting in front, and decorative trim of purple and turquoise, made this one of the most charming buildings on the island. Benches flanked the front door, placed invitingly at the end of a custom-made tile walkway inset with shell patterns of Sanibel. There was nothing common about this shop, nor its potter owners.

Barb Hockett and her assistant June were closing out the books and greeted the Calvins with warm smiles. Barb's smile radiated a kindness that Tim was sure could melt the stoniest heart. She had a natural ability to greet customers and to immediately put them at ease. As they exchanged greetings, Dave walked in from the back of the shop in customary T-shirt and shorts.

"How ya doin'? Whoa, look at the tans here. Good day at the beach, huh?"

Barb came around the counter. "I want you to see the raku firing—some of the colors are great."

An iridescent gold pot with ragged edges and streaks of purple and green blending throughout the shining gold glaze caught Tim's eye. As Barb turned and lifted pieces on a display shelf and discussed the items with Laney, Dave tapped his friend's shoulder and pulled him aside.

"I had breakfast this morning at the Quarterdeck."

That was a morning routine for Dave, a place where the "ol' boys and gals," the inner circle of the island, took their regular table in the corner, for conversation, gossip, jokes, and breakfast, which had been served for years by a smiling Karen. It was ritual for these residents, people who began their working day on this island paradise which was sought by others as a refuge from work and routine.

Things got done in this manner.

"Valmer was there and we had a chance to talk privately," Dave continued. "He said if you're worrying about those voices you heard outside your condo last night, he made a call and took care of it. That's all I know."

"Well, I've been trying to forget it completely, but that does give me a little peace of mind. It's good to know this guy still has connections to people with power and information," Tim said wondering how far what Valmer had called "this little secret" had spread. If an old CIA man was having to get in touch with his contacts, didn't that mean they might be drawing the attention of and involving forces well beyond the peace of Sanibel Island? He decided that it didn't matter, though; he was determined to just get on with his vacation.

The Hockett's island bungalow was rich with the scent of cookies baking in the oven. Barb and Laney were busy in the kitchen while Cee and Katie watched a video. Dave and Tim had dropped Elizabeth off at a T-shirt shop when they drove to the end of the island to pick up some Buttonwood Barbecue. The Buttonwood Barbecue Restaurant was one of those special "finds" the island was famous for. Buttonwood was a hardwood which offered a unique, wonderful smoky flavor, and chicken and grouper were excellent mediums for its delicious effect. The restaurant further enhanced the culinary treats with a secret sauce. Tonight he and Dave were taking back a potpourri of the menu: chicken, grouper, ribs, and smoked shrimp. Tim was relaxed and hungry.

As they headed back north on San Cap road, the tree line at both sides of the road became a dark green, geometric frame for the brilliant island sunset. The sun, a giant orange ball, inched behind the tree tops and the sky lit up in a brilliant neon pink. Miles Davis' mellow tones filled the van and a richly scented breeze blew through the windows.

"I'm really happy with my new wheel," Dave remarked about

his latest acquisition at the shop. "It's truly the wheel from heaven!"

"Really an improvement, huh? Is this one motorized?" Tim asked.

"Yeah, it's great. I use my foot to control the speed instead of just to keep it going."

Over the years Tim had spent hours watching Dave start with a hunk of clay, slap it onto the wheel, then by a magical combination of the wheel's turn and his hands, mold and shape it into an object of beauty. The clay would rise or fall, flatten or curl, seeming to have a life of its own. But with Dave's expertise, it took on another life, another mission, another form as it spun on the wheel. It was an ancient craft, and in an odd quirk of fate, Dave had discovered his ancestors had also been potters.

Now as they drove, Dave seemed to want to talk shop. "At first I wasn't crazy about the new wheel. Neither Barb nor I wanted it—we didn't need it. But we had gone to a trade show and ran into an old associate who had worked for us, then set up his own shop down in Naples. He was liquidating so he could move into the Caribbean. And he was trying to move it."

"So you got a deal?"

"Yeah, but it just sat there for months. I kinda resented it, power wheel and all. Well, the old foot power wheels were fine. Anyway, about a month and a half ago I started to play around with it. The more I horsed around, the more I got into it. It actually is an improvement. I think some of the pieces I've been throwing have gotten better, you know? For so long it just took up space and was in the way. Now I don't know why I waited so long to try it."

Tim was puzzled as they walked into the bar at the Buttonwood. He had the distinct feeling that the new wheel wasn't really what was on Dave's mind.

"Something's bugging you, Dave. What's up?" Tim asked his friend of twenty years.

"Just a second," Dave said, holding up his right hand pointing with his index finger. He then walked away to turn in the order. On the way back he dawdled to marvel at the assortment of dessert cakes and tortes sitting on an old Hoosier cabinet shelf, the display case for the confections.

While he ordered a couple of beers, Tim watched Dave from the bar. He waited for him to amble over to him.

"Dave, you're stalling. I know you too well not to know you're trying to get at something. What's with this business about the new wheel?"

"I told Barb I ought to just come out and tell you. I'm not good at this double talk. I was just trying to explain that sometimes things you don't like at first work out."

"Like what?"

"Like this thing with the metal plate. What Valmer has in mind."

"How so? Exactly what does Valmer have in mind?"

"I really don't know a lot either. But I do know it's going to work out OK," Dave replied. "Valmer is real solid. He knows a lot about you and the family and how close we are. He wants your help with something, something he says he's too old to do. He wants to meet you at his house tonight after we've had dinner. I'll drive you there. But he says this will be just between the two of you."

Tim hadn't wanted to think about all of this tonight, and he sighed and frowned resignedly at Dave.

The rest of the evening was pleasant, though Tim was decidedly distant. More than once Laney asked him what was wrong. He was thinking about the conversation he and Dave had just had. Potters wheels and working with clay—he couldn't avoid the feeling that this trip to Sanibel had slapped him onto a wheel, and now he was clay in Valmer's hands. Perhaps tonight he would get some sense of what kind of shape things were going to take. It didn't matter to him what Valmer wanted. He wasn't about to let him manipulate him into something. He'd go and listen to him, and then bow out. Still, he had a nagging curiosity about what Valmer wanted from him and about the metal plate itself. Tim knew that it was very old, and the cryptic inscription intrigued him. His old fascination with antiquities, the one that had impelled him into the doctoral program, beckoned him.

Storm on the Slough

Like its owner, Valmer's house possessed an air of mystery. Distant from neighbors, it stood at the end of a winding stone driveway, set between a thick buffer of trees and bush and a private lake also bounded by deep foliage. The lake fed into the Sanibel River, actually a water-control slough. A screened porch, designed in the style of old Florida, wrapped the entire building. The house was all clapboard and tin roof and shutters, built up on pylons and possessing a well-scrubbed, clean look. Under screen was a large pool bordered by the porch and stairs, and on the other side a small guest house and porch. Candles or lanterns illuminated the porch, giving the inner core of the house a glowing, Saturn-like ring.

The house had fairly recently been built, and as they walked from the car, Dave told Tim how demanding Valmer had been during the construction phase.

"None of the builders had ever seen a home like this," Dave remarked. "What really knocked 'em out was the porch and how he used the space inside. It's definitely unique."

"Yeah. It sure is."

The two men were greeted by the vicious growls of Langley and King Charles, Valmer's canine sentries.

"At ease!" came a command from the inner sanctum beyond the porch. "Indeed these are capable guards, but as Dave and his beloved Celia will tell you, they are cream puffs too, who love to swim in that pool and clog my filter. Don't worry, Mr. Calvin, please come through." Valmer opened the door and stepped onto the porch. He was dressed in a short-sleeved white tropics shirt and khaki slacks. His dark hair was combed straight back, and his manner seemed somewhat more relaxed than when Tim had seen him before.

"David, I took the liberty of building you a Cuba Libre. I trust you will handle it well." Valmer handed Dave the chilled beverage and motioned for him to make himself comfortable in an arrangement of porch furniture overlooking the lake.

"Mr. Calvin, what is your medicine tonight?" he asked, placing his hand at the small of Tim's back and ushering him into a large room with cathedral ceiling. The room was divided at about the midway point by a large bar. At one end was a collection of elegant furniture and accoutrements. A high tech kitchen island, flanked by a long dining table set against ceiling-to-floor windows overlooked the lake. To the other side of the bar was a small breakfast nook with smaller windows. A twin stair arrangement broke the wall at one end, the lower stairs leading to the bathroom, shower room, art studio, laundry and pool entrance. At the midpoint in the large greatroom was a door, which Dave had told him led to the master bedroom—the only bedroom—and bath.

"I'd like a Stoli and mineral water please," Tim said, breaking his wide-eyed sweeping gaze at the considerable art collection.

"Yes, Mr. Calvin, I can see from your transfixed stare that you join the chorus of those who find our humble abode 'unique,' 'exotic,' 'eccentric.' It fits Jane, my artist bride, and me very well." Valmer poured the liquor into a glass. "Please excuse me, but I cannot find it in my constitution to splash water of any sort into a good vodka. May I suggest you not offend your host, and please drink it as it was intended. I keep it chilled to twenty-eight degrees."

As they stepped onto the half of the small stairs that led upward, thunder rolled across the sky and danced back up off the lake. "Heaven is about to baptize this affair," Valmer offered with a tone of resignation. At the top of the stairs was an office that looked much like a chapel, with vaulted ceiling and leaded window in an end recess. A cross hung on one side of the alcove. What looked to Tim like an El Greco oil faced it from the other wall. He stopped to study the piece and look for the signature.

"Yes, it is an original," Valmer offered, gesturing him toward a chair. "The furniture is from a monastery in Czechoslovakia."

Shelves lined the walls, filled with well-worn books—antique, theological, and political or historical. In a section at about eye level all of the titles appeared to be about nothing but World War II or intelligence operations. There were stacks of magazines and papers. A computer with a monitor and keyboard sat on an old, dark wooden desk with gargoyle legs and ornate sculpting. To the side was a tilt-top light table for the display of transparencies and overlays, and next to that was a map. The chairs and couch were masculine, comfortable, and commanding, showing signs of proper care and important use. Tim knew intuitively the room was like the private chamber of a monastery prior: office, library, and operations center. He sensed that history had been touched and shaped by men who had occupied this furniture, used the desk, studied the volumes.

A flash of lightning through the pointed leaded window in the alcove animated the haunting face of the El Greco. The eyes in the painting seemed to deepen and the head to tilt. Tim drained his tumbler of Stoli, sinking into the deep leather of the chair, almost hypnotized by the painting hanging just feet away and to his right at about a one o'clock angle.

"The doubts of Thomas," Valmer said looking over his left shoulder and gesturing at the painting. "Or is it the redemption of his soul in those eyes?"

He leaned forward to a mahogany chest at the side of his chair. The carved figures on the sides and front of the chest were of knights on horseback, lances held high aloft. The top was an heraldic shield, emblazoned with a cross and crescent moon and a pennant of lions. The first jolt of Stoli combined with the low light of the room and the dark wood, transporting Tim to another time and place—medieval Europe. The airy, green world of Sanibel could have been oceans and centuries away. Valmer lifted the lid of the chest, revealing a stainless steel compartment, iced and lined with bottles of Stolichnaya, Absolut, and Aalborg Akavit from Denmark.

"Another taste? From this enigma, Mr. Calvin?" Valmer's eyes reflected the mischievous sparkle Tim had noticed when they'd met a couple of days earlier. The man seemed to delight in the unexpected.

"The chest is twelfth century, originally designed to be a place for a knight's silks as he ventured and patrolled to and from Acre and Jerusalem. The conversion was done years ago by an old design hand—a colleague. The vodka I purchased from the bottle shop when I ventured into civilization last week."

Tim held his glass as Valmer poured liberally. The clear liquid, thickened to near ice, sparkled in the light of the desk lamp under its blue shade. A clap of thunder rattled overhead, but Tim took little notice.

"Are you a religious scholar?" he queried as he sipped.

"Mr. Calvin, I have spent much of my life under attack. It is as Jeremiah said when a siege was threatened by the enemy from the north: 'Stand by the ways and ask for the ancient paths, where the good way is and walk in it and you shall find rest for your souls.' I must tell you I seek those paths."

Tim looked at him directly. "Did you seek those paths when you worked for the government?" Valmer returned the stare, saying nothing, until Tim began to feel awkward. "I know you used to work for a federal agency," he said, trying to smooth the wrinkle.

Valmer seemed to exude formality. The way he turned his head to train on Tim's face was a motion filled with dignity. Finally his deep voice broke the long silence.

"You know? Or you have been told? How can you be sure enough of anything to claim knowing? Does it not become an act of faith? You know because your dear friend, whom you trust and love, told you, and you believe what he says. You have faith. You therefore believe and thus you know." His response sounded to Tim almost like a rebuke from a professor or judge.

"I'm sorry sir, I didn't mean to be inappropriate."

"It can never be inappropriate to seek truth, though it can sometimes be dangerous to attain knowledge." He paused, gazed into his glass and then fixed his deep eyes on Tim. "It was 1968 and the terrible war had fractured our nation. The President, as you know, was in great torment, and his advisors were cutting each others' hearts out. There was no consensus—the country seemed suicidal; we were coming unraveled."

"I remember. I was in school and working as a reporter."

"As you recall, the human toll had bloodied our hands, and anarchy seemed upon us. Your generation had lost faith completely. Some were growing in ways of anti-democracy and disorder, and a subculture of terror was spreading through our children. I was asked, or more precisely 'tasked,' by my superiors to begin a systematic process to employ our considerable ability to do in America what our job had been abroad. It was not to my mind within the context of our charter." He paused and picked up a book from the table between their chairs. "Do you know the book of Hebrews, Mr. Calvin?"

"I've read it. I don't, ah, know it, exactly."

"It's a good mystery. There is no agreement on its author. The message is a bit like that of Paul, but neither language nor style is even close. It's believed to have been penned before Jerusalem was destroyed, during the time of Nero's persecution, probably sometime between 67 and 70 A.D. Since you have asked why I left the agency, which had been my life, allow me to answer this most important question of my life by reading chapter thirteen, verses seventeen and eighteen." He licked his thumb and leafed to the page. " 'Obey your leaders and submit to them for they keep watch over your souls, as those who will give an account. Let them do this with joy and not with profit, for this would be unprofitable for you. Pray for us, for we are sure that we have a good conscience, desiring to conduct ourselves honorably in all things.' " Valmer closed the book, held its spine with his right hand, and cradled his knuckles into the palm of his left hand, the Bible resting against his chest. For a moment he stared into space, as if his mind was miles away. Then, returning his gaze to Tim, Valmer took a deep breath and continued.

"I could not in good faith consider the job with clear conscience. The mysterious writer spoke to me. But my pretense at nobility did little to slake the evil. It merely excused me from participating in it." The last words trailed off. He returned the book to the table. He looked at it for a moment, then retrieved his glass and took a long pull from it.

"But now, my friend, and you cannot escape that term since you know the inner chapter of my life's book, we have come to the moment where destiny is about to seize you."

Lightning flashed and illuminated the room in a burst of brilliant white, casting Valmer's face and the face in the painting behind him in an eerie glow. The eyes of El Greco's Thomas and those of the old spy seemed from the same source, both staring, appraising, pinning Tim for what felt like an eternity.

Valmer broke the silence. "Our learning curve has gone up. You have seen for yourself that the plate you found is quite old, and have heard that it is very important. I can affirm both of these assessments. It is, indeed, a world treasure of some sort." He swallowed the last of his drink and set the empty glass on the table. "The man I told you about, Aoki Pasotti, had purchased the metal plate some time ago from a somewhat shadowy Middle Eastern source who was able to smuggle it across the ocean. This source is also a bad player, but not important to us in this context. Pasotti dispatched one of his security staff, the Libyan you found on the beach, to handle the cash transaction and to secure the plate. He believed that being a former Libyan officer, this man could work around customs and security details. The transaction went smoothly, but Pasotti's man, realizing the value of the plate, decided instead to be enterprising and look for a buyer himself."

Tim sat up and leaned forward. "Now let me get this straight," he said. "The plate is an antiquity which this Pasotti bought under the table in the Middle East?" Valmer nodded, and Tim continued.

"But his messenger decided to make money for himself by selling to somebody else instead of delivering it to Pasotti." Again Valmer nodded assent. Tim leaned back, attempting to absorb all of this information. His head was swimming, and his tongue was beginning to feel heavy from the effects of the Stoli. "Did the Libyan come to Sanibel to hide?"

"No. Originally Pasotti had bid against another possible buyer, a man with connections to Captiva. That's the link. The seller told Pasotti's man that Pasotti had outbid the Captiva man. The light went on in the Libyan's head, so he made contact with the spurned buyer. Apparently more than happy to know he might actually be able to gain the plate, buyer number two arranged for a meeting on Captiva, thus bringing the whole sordid affair to our pleasant little neighborhood."

Valmer's matter-of-fact way of detailing this intricate and dark scenario, combined with the Stoli, the chapel-like atmosphere of the office, and the rolling echo of thunder made Tim feel as though he were hovering outside his body, an observer listening to and watching someone else. There were also split seconds when he felt as though he were pinned to the leather chair. His heart was in his throat and he could feel the metallic taste of fear, drifting in and out on the deep tones of Valmer's voice as the tale of strange names, places, and events unfolded before him.

"It's so odd to think that Katie and I literally walked into this," he said, snapping out of his reverie.

"Odd, yes, but fortunate too, certainly for the Libyan. After all, you saved his life. My friends in Langley tell me that Pasotti discovered the treachery and dispatched two other men from his security staff, also Arabs, to find the Libyan thief. Your discovery on the beach was evidence they had succeeded in at least a portion of their assignment. The severed hand was an apparent dispatch of an Islamic sense of justice. Somehow the Libyan had been able to pitch or bury the metal plate before his vengeful colleagues got to him. Your and Katie's crabbing hunt interrupted the men during their violent and frantic search for the plate."

"They must have seen us on the beach that night—they picked us up in their spotlight twice. It was so quick I don't see how they could have gotten a good look. But there has to be some explanation for their recognizing Katie at Bailey's, and trying to find our condo. What would make them think we had the plate or even knew anything about it?"

"The downside of notoriety," Valmer said. "Remember, the television reporter Natalie Simmonds interviewed you, and her report included tape of Katie holding the metal plate. It didn't take long for these men, who after all are professionals, to change the focus of their hunt." In the course of all that had happened, Tim had forgotten about the encounter with Natalie Simmonds. He cursed under his breath, angry that he hadn't been more firm and declined the interview. As a result he had placed his family in jeopardy.

Valmer quickly moved to soothe him. "After the incident at your condo I called some 'friends.' The menace of the hunters has been expunged; they are no longer on the island. They were given, should I say, a free flight to Miami where they are enjoying an all-expenses paid 'vacation' in a secure area."

Tim relaxed visibly, and his thoughts returned to the object that had caused all the furor. "But what about the plate—what have you learned about it? What is it? What does it say? Where is it from?"

"That, my friend, is perhaps the most elegant mystery of this matter," Valmer replied. "I expect more definitive information soon, and I will share with you what I learn. For now we don't know what the plate is or what it means. From the preliminary data we've reviewed we believe that even though it appears to be an ancient artifact it could still impact current political and/or economic issues and situations. I strongly believe that we must take a delicate approach to the investigation in order to avoid an insidious clash of history with our present fragile political stability. This need for delicacy requires a somewhat unorthodox methodology, Tim—we need to act quickly and unofficially—which is why I think this will take your help."

"My help? I'm already in this more than I want to be!" Tim

got up and strode over to the window. The flashes of lightning seemed to add to the surrealism of the situation. Turning back to face Valmer, he tried to justify his feelings. "This is government stuff; I'm just an ordinary civilian. This is too big for me."

"You'd be surprised how many things that the public considers to be government functioning are conducted in this manner. Besides, you are not just any ordinary civilian. You have a decent base of knowledge in this general period of history. Even though people in Langley can't say for sure what the implications of the plate are, they seem worried about it...."

Valmer was interrupted by a beep sounding from the computer on his desk. He walked over and tapped a key. The inbound message was from a research associate at Langley. Tim walked over and peered over Valmer's shoulder at the message on the screen.

"It's from the code people," Valmer said. "The engraving on the metal piece has been translated. They say the significance and origin of the plate and its inscription remain unknown.

"One side is written in Greek. It translates: '*Warrior of Light who guards the South where Christ rules and Judges enthroned to the setting sun. A second house on early spirit ground. Two sisters now reach to heaven.* The other side is in Latin: *For the love of God and all earthly issue. King of Ages here resides true light on sin.*' We need to print this out."

Valmer tapped the keys for the print command for two copies. He pulled the paper from the printer. He and Tim stared at the words. Both men seemed transfixed by the words, locked in their enigmatic message. Valmer handed one of the papers to Tim, who responded with a quizzical gaze. As Valmer began to usher him out of the office and down the steps to the main house he attempted to explain.

"Mr. Calvin—Tim—as I said, this situation may require your help. Your knowledge of medieval lore and history exceeds that of many museum professionals. Please take this paper with you and study it. If you have any ideas regarding the meaning of the message, based on your knowledge, let me know immediately." The sparkle in Valmer's eyes had been replaced by a pensive darkness. "Why are people worried by it? What might its implications be? What is it from history, with a message such as this, that could haunt us now? There must be some meaning beyond the chase of collectors like Pasotti. Think about it, please. For now, I myself must also spend time pondering this translation," Valmer sighed. He placed his hand on Tim's shoulder, as if attempting to comfort him, and almost apologetically said, "Try to sleep well tonight. This storm may pass us by."

"I can't tell whether the front is going to skip us or if we are just under a hole in the system," Dave offered from the living room as he walked in from the porch, meeting Valmer and Tim as they reached the bottom of the stairs. "Our tourists have a canoe outing tomorrow morning," he smiled, indicating Tim with a nod of his head. Tim was too numb to respond. His mind was not yet fully back on Sanibel.

He slept fitfully, tossing and turning, with strange dreams. The night was thick with humidity, and the sheets felt like a clammy shroud. He awoke with a headache and slight dizziness. When he looked out the window he found no cheer in the scene that greeted him. The sky over the gulf was gray, the water choppy, and a strong wind bent the heads of the palms at a hard angle. The blue sky of the previous day seemed distant and alien now, the warm sunshine as remote as his comfortable life back home.

In this twilight moment of morning, when he was half awake and feeling vulnerable, the bizarre events of the previous evening replayed themselves in his mind, seeming even more unreal. Libyan hit men, CIA analysts, international diplomacy? Strange religious messages from the ancient past? A sluggish anger crawled across his mind as he wondered what was happening to his dream vacation, the relaxation he craved so? Surely he still had some power over his own actions. This vacation was becoming a trap of anxiety. Perhaps he should cut his losses, gather his family and leave this strange episode behind. They could simply fly home, back to the security of life away from Valmer, the mysterious metal plate, Libyan hit men, and international schemers.

But there was something else at work and nagging at his mind—his curiosity about what it all meant. Valmer's orchestrated this whole thing, Tim thought, he baited me—unearthing my doctoral work, dredging up all those old feelings, all the old passion of the hunt. Tim went into the bathroom to get a drink of water, and gazed at the reflection in the mirror. Even that person looked unfamiliar, and he tried to read what was in the eyes that looked back at him. What did he really want? Valmer had laid out a richly tantalizing mystery and asked him for help. Tim recognized the lure and couldn't deny the fascination it held.

"Hey, Pop, are you up for this canoe trip?" Elizabeth stood at the bathroom door, Katie at her side. "Mom just called Bird, and he said because of the wind we're not going over to Buck Key."

Tim walked back into the bedroom and sat on the edge of the bed, trying to shake the doubts and strange shadows from his head. The girls knew little if anything of his mental torment. Dave had reassured Elizabeth and Katie by creating a story that the men who had followed them were interested in the metal plate, having seen Katie with it on the TV newscast. He had told the girls that the men had been "taken care of" and wouldn't bother them again, especially since the plate had been removed for safe keeping. At most, the ordeal of the man on the beach and business with the metal plate barely rated a second thought. Vacation was still the essence of what was happening for them. Their spirits were high, and today's canoe outing with wildlife expert Bird Westin was all that constituted their sense of adventure. The girls' voices and laughter bubbled with excitement, and anticipation sparkled in their eyes.

"Sure, let's give it a go." He put on his best father-in-the-morning face. No sense in spoiling this trip for them, he thought. For now he would go on as if nothing was out of order. But he knew intuitively last night's meeting in Valmer's office had been an initiation into a world beyond what he knew, a world which seemed intent on pulling him out of the safe circle of his family and his own world.

Andrew "Bird" Westin stood next to the canoe trailer behind his pickup, holding a small map inside a waterproofed hard page. The choppiness on the gulf and the brewing storm had forced them to cancel the six-hour paddle to Buck Key and back. As he described the alternative trip he had in mind, he repeatedly looked at the sky and checked his watch, saying he was sure they could get in a small trip on the slough.

"Since everybody's up early and since you've paid a deposit, we can take a short paddle on the Sanibel River. It'd be just too dangerous to even think about going out onto the bay. It's up to you." He looked at Tim and Laney and indicated with a "J" motion a path on his map for the trip. They decided to go for it.

The wind subsided, softening its sound as it rushed through the trees, shortly after they put the canoe into the water and lazily drifted away from the dike-road boat launch. The slough, the result of an Army Corps of Engineers dredge, ran through the thickest of the island's famous vegetation, and they paddled along under a canopy of branches and greenery in the heart of the island. This private world of Sanibel was home to a variety of birds and was a primary nesting area for alligators. Bird Westin, an ecologist of national stature, was completely at home in this tangle of nature. As they paddled he would call to his passengers to "look left to that group of reeds," or "right, under that lily pad," or "up there on the bank, right behind those branches," to spot baby 'gators with a protective mother nearby or to see well-camouflaged birds. Elizabeth's fascination with science and devotion to the environment made her a perfect companion on this nature ride, and she peppered Bird with questions that he repeatedly said were "great inquiries." Katie marvelled at the proximity to alligators and absolute denseness of the jungle-like growth.

At times the outgrowth seemed to engulf the slough, pushing in overhead and from the banks so closely that they all had to lie flat on their backs with their heads below the top of the long canoe so it could navigate a tunnel of thicket. The sheer nature of the ride was so all-consuming that Tim was able to put all thoughts of the intrigue surrounding the metal plate out of his mind, along with its accompanying fearful, nagging questions. As they paddled through the cocoon of foliage, Bird Westin's narrative on the passing scenery lulled him.

As they returned, a crack of lightning and a rumble of thunder shook the walls and ceiling of their nest-like surroundings, causing the leaves to tremble. Bird stopped paddling long enough to glance at his watch. "We should beat the rain by a couple of minutes. We'll get you out in time to keep you dry, although you wouldn't feel it in here until it really pounded."

They had just loaded the canoe onto the trailer when the first drops of the thunderstorm began to pelt their faces. They exchanged hurried good-byes and dashed for the van. As they bounced along the small sand-and-gravel road the sky opened and the tropical rain poured down as though the gulf had been inverted.

"Let's go to the shop and get what we want set aside," Laney suggested, "and maybe the girls would like some breakfast." Tim was beginning to feel as if he was on vacation again, and he discovered his appetite returning as they dashed up the ramp at Café Sanibel. They grabbed a booth by the window, and the gals made plans to shop on what by now was evidently a non-beach day.

Several cars were parked in the spaces at Barb and Dave's shop. Merchants of this island paradise benefited when the weather was unparadise-like, and this was definitely a good morning for business. As they entered the shop Barb called from behind the counter.

"Good morning! Dave has a message for you, Tim. He's back in the workshop loading the kiln for a firing."

Tim knew it was a routine but critical part of the potter's craft: stacking the raw clay objects properly and precisely mixing intense levels of heat and measures of time. He had often marveled at the awesome power of nature harnessed and controlled in the ancient alchemy of kiln firing as he peeked through the viewing hole into the white-hot kiln. Dave usually did not sleep for most of the twenty-four-hour firing period, checking temperature levels and attending to the intricate details. It was a time when his usually mellow personality was a bit strained. Dave was busily absorbed in the project and didn't hear Tim approach.

" 'Morning, Mr. Hockett. Looks like you're ready."

"Hey, so you got rained out this morning." Dave turned, wiping clay dust from his hand and extending it for a friendly slap on Tim's shoulder. Then his eyes narrowed and his brow furrowed. "Valmer wants you to come back to his place later today. He's got some more information. And he's got a game plan. He says he hopes you'll agree to take a few days and help on this."

"Yeah, that's what I was afraid of. Some beautiful vacation, huh?" Tim said, an edge of chagrin in his voice. But, as much as he hated to admit it to himself, he felt excitement mounting. It was a feeling he remembered both from doing his historical research and from his days as a reporter. Chasing a story had always gotten his adrenaline pumping; so did his first glimpse of the Tower of London. The pursuit of the unknown, the thrill of discovery, produced a kind of excitement that couldn't be compared to anything else.

* * *

Valmer apparently had not slept since their meeting. He looked drawn and tired, but focused nevertheless. He met Tim on the front walk and began immediately.

"Tim, I have a great deal to share with you. And I have no other recourse than to ask for your help. Since the translation came in last night I have been busy building a database. Please, allow me to show you and tell you what I have."

Valmer took Tim's elbow and led him to a corner of the porch arranged much like a TV room. Tim noticed stacks of video tapes, folders, and maps laid on a circular glass coffee table. Indicating a chair for Tim to sit in, Valmer sat down on a couch surrounded by more folders.

"These are laser-printed backgrounders," he said, tapping a stack of folders. "They are for your use, and I will get to them in a moment. The videotapes will be most instructive and will fill in many gaps. But first, the bottom line.

"I need—actually, *we* need—you to do some field research, to ask some questions. Nothing more."

"I don't follow. You've got tons of data right here." Tim gestured to the folders and tapes. "What more can you need?"

"Here's the problem, Tim. Our experts know what the metal plate is, but they don't know what it really is."

"Come again?"

"Yes, it is confusing. It is as though this plate is at the heart of an arcanum. A secret mystery, a puzzle within itself. As you can see, my friends and old colleagues have supplied a blizzard of information since they identified the plate your Katie found buried on the beach. It is an object of intense interest and there is fierce dispute over its ownership, even between nations, which is the reason we need your help."

Tim simply shifted a little in his chair. Disputes among nations over archaeological treasures was nothing unusual. He remembered a recent legal battle between a Midwest art dealer and the government of Crete over some mosaics. What was there about this particular brass or bronze plate with its cryptic message that was so vitally important?

Valmer continued. "Nothing in the files is conclusive as to the plate's origins, but there is no shortage of theory. Here it becomes intricate and complicated. Over the years, sources in the world's three great religions have laid claim to the plate and proclaimed its authenticity. Until the second world war there had been only legends, unproven stories about the existence of an ancient piece of metal that fits the description of this piece, engraved with what has been described as a code. These legends of an ancient artifact, so important that it was deemed sacred, passed through tribal histories, among bedouins, and in monastic orders. Christians, Jews and Muslims in their variety of ways kept this tale of a code alive."

"You know, I remember something like that, from Joseph Campbell, a series of articles published at Princeton. Something about comparative religious myths, repetition of icons." Against his will, Tim felt himself becoming engaged.

"Yes. Well, as the story of the plate passed through generations it permuted, and took on additional lives and nuances. Over time, the legends attached to the plate became almost as important to the cultures and religions as the plate itself. Which again is where someone with a good knowledge base is important to us."

"It seems like you've already got it. People who know more than I do."

"That is not entirely so. Our knowledge base on this plate is composed only of theories, rumors of the ages. No one in modern times had seen a sacred plate artifact, nor could even prove its existence. All we have to go on are these legends. Theories, Tim, theories! Policy and diplomacy have to turn on fact—not some fantasy or theoretical musings of ancients. We need to sort out the fact from these theories."

"What you're saying is that you have research about a strange talisman, an old superstition, a myth. All of which has been detailed in academic research. But what the scholars have ended up studying is the myth, the story—not the real meaning of the plate? So all of these reports on the plate's significance are nothing more than speculation and guess-work?" Tim shook his head in bewilderment. He was getting thirsty. "Could I have a drink?"

"Certainly. How about a port? It's handy. I have Taylor-Fladgate twenty years tawny." Valmer moved to a bar cart that sat nearby on the porch, and continued to speak as he poured two snifters full. "It is indeed a good mystery. Why did three religions carry a myth for hundreds of years, all relating to a mysterious artifact not seen in centuries—until its discovery in the second world war, when portions of an old Norman castle in France were opened for the war effort? The castle had been a private home, much of it sealed and unused, a large part of it dating back to the tenth century. At one time in antiquity it had been the residence of a grand master of an order of knights, a leader of a lodge. Local history and legend tells of how this order of knights, warriors in the Crusades, had suffered great losses and retreated. Some of the order fled to Rhodes, but a remaining band returned to Normandy and brought artifacts with them. These relics remained in the chateau, property of the master and his heirs. Through the centuries the knights' order's importance along with their artifacts were lost and forgotten. As the generations passed, the ancient treasures, most quite unimpressive-looking, were considered mere tokens of the past with little value, shoved away, and put out of mind. Some of those elements of antiquity were discovered when the castle's catacombs were opened during the war."

Valmer took a sip of the port and held the snifter to the light, admiring its warm russet glow. He set the snifter down and picked up one of the folders. "Records were poorly kept by the Army quarter-master's staff, but it seems certain many of the items, some of them priceless, were stolen by people who knew what they were, or were taken as souvenirs by GIs. Since then they have been a part of an underground trade of antiquities. Your plate has been traced to this time as one of the items discovered buried in the castle's catacombs and traded."

"So during World War II the reality caught up with the myth of some special coded plate. Or at least gave it some plausibility?"

"And it began to complicate things. Remember, I said elements of all three major religions—Christianity, Judaism, and Islam—lay claim to this item. Now, transpose this on top of touchy international relations and ancient hatreds, and you can begin to appreciate how this old piece of metal might be able to play hell with world politics."

"Well, we've got the plate. Why don't we just give it to..." Tim halted, puzzled, finding himself finally and inextricably snared in the mystery's web. "To whom?"

"Precisely!" Valmer pounced, drilling him again with his intense gaze. "But before we get to the 'whom,' we must learn what it is and what it means. We must separate the superstitions and legends from the reality. Your love of history and your civilian status will serve us well. A United Nations commission has been assigned the role of determining ownership and heritage of such objects in dispute. It's a kind of world-wide legal wrestling match: Turkish urns taken from Hittite sites, Egyptian artifacts taken by Napoleon to France. Some of these cases had been dragging on for decades. But we don't want to expose the plate to that front, if we ever do, until we know exactly what it is we have and what its implications may be. In just a moment I'll share with you the assessment of a risk analysis team at Langley, but first I want you to look at these folders."

Tim glanced inside the folders, finding pages of print and a photograph in each.

"You have here background on two people I want you to meet, men I knew when I was with the agency. They are both with the UN commission and scholars who have some considerable knowledge of this matter. They also understand the extreme delicacy of the case. I want you to meet with them, get their views, hear their thoughts and theories. Run some of our research here by them— they may very well be able to sort this out. Dr. Abu Shakir Haji, an Islamic scholar you will meet in Chicago. You'll have to work through his assistant, a Juni Khadija. There is a little on her in the file, but not much. The other man is Dr. Benjamin Stroutsel, who is probably on holiday in France. In a while I'll put on the video tape which contains news clips about Haji and Stroutsel and the UN commission. It also has some pieces on religious artifacts and museums and there are interviews with a couple of historians and curators. You'll need to be up to speed.

"As you're briefing yourself and confirming things with Haji and Stroutsel, you'll need to be doing other things too. For one thing, I think you need to visit the abbey library at Mont Saint Michel, off the Normandy coast. Stroutsel may be able to help you there. One of our people claims the library of antiquities there is without peer. The more informed you are, the more effective you will be, and the more quickly you can return to your vacation."

"With all due respect, I don't remember signing on to this yet," Tim interjected. "I won't deny that it sounds interesting, appealing, even. But I'm not sure. I mean, I've already been chased and stalked. My little girl has been plastered on the five o'clock news with the plate, and if I left my wife and daughters would be here alone." Tim shuffled the folders, unsure what to do with them. He felt that putting them down would be an indication that he wouldn't accept the assignment, and he wasn't altogether sure he wanted to turn it down.

"I don't know, Valmer," he went on. "I think you're going too fast. Who would cover my liability? I'm not sure I should take this risk."

"Tim, forgive me, but I believe you are posturing now. I assure you that your family is in no danger. The men who accosted you, as I told you, are safely held in Miami. And remember, your best friend Dave is here to look after your family." Valmer leaned back in his chair, assessing Tim with cool eyes. "I don't mean to be presumptuous, but my living and often my very life have depended on my being a good judge of character. I believe you want to go on this mission. In fact, I think you would never forgive yourself if you didn't go." Valmer picked up a travel packet and held it toward Tim. "I have your tickets and agenda here." As Tim opened his mouth to speak, Valmer held up a hand to silence him. "Before you say any more, look over the report the risk assessment people at Langley have put together:

" '*We have amassed volumes of material and synthesized it to a* bare minimum. *The plate is priceless—which is to say whoever holds it can determine and fix its value, beginning in the seven-figure range. Adding to its value are the multiple theories that its engraved inscriptions contain a code. But a code to what? Certainly to something also beyond value. This coded message is described variously as religious secrets, or a key to the location of a treasure or artifact. Only a small group of religious and historical scholars have knowledge of the plate. Contemporary study is virtually nonexistent; most data derives from primarily eighteenth and nineteenth century research. Even among academia, there is precious little current study of the plate or its origin.*

" 'A survey *of published material indicates a sense that the secret the plate contains could have disruptive power with impact on accepted religious history. It has been postulated that the secret might even upend existing belief patterns—something on the level of the Dead Sea Scrolls research. According to a now-deceased Harvard professor, the message of the plate might, by itself, or by pointing to another source, contain information which could by it's nature shake or even shatter the major religions at their foundational premises.'* So, the plate and its secret could, at the very least, initiate an enormous legal warfare over rights of ownership." Tim's face reflected the tightening he felt in his stomach.

"You see, Tim, this is not a simple matter. I'll skip to the conclusion here. I quote—'...*the implications could jeopardize government relationships, treaty arrangements, and probably derail delicate secret negotiations now ongoing. If there is an appearance government agencies have become involved, alert bells would sound, warning flags would be raised, undue attention would beget more undue attention, and things could spiral, gaining a force of their own. That scenario must be avoided, even at great cost. We urge a prudent plan of low key inquiry. It is imperative that there be no appearance that any agency of the U.S. government is involved either in possession of the plate or determination of its origin. Premature discussion could have serious implication.'* Close quote."

Tim sat leaning against the arm of the chair, his elbow on the arm rest, his chin cradled between his thumb and forefinger. He stroked his chin and stared at Valmer, who stared gravely back.

"I know this kind of thing, how men are stretched beyond themselves to uphold and protect the greater interests of their countries. Such is mission and duty." The old patriot and cold warrior rose and strode to the edge of the porch. For a long moment he looked out over the tops of the trees that surrounded his home. Drawing a deep breath, he turned and faced Tim again. "Whether you care to admit it or not, you are the man for this job," he insisted. "It must be done discreetly. You can achieve that. If anyone in an official capacity were tied to this affair, then the genie would be out of the bottle. That cannot—must not—happen." Valmer was emphatic.

An expectant silence hung between the two men. Eye to eye, they held each other's gaze. Tim realized that he had been holding his breath. He released it shakily and spoke. "For now, it seems only this Pasotti and his people, the Captiva would-be buyer and just the few of us on Sanibel, outside of your friends in Langley, know about the plate."

"Or even have an inkling of what kind of trembling ground it could produce. That's why your participation in this mission is so vital. *You* would be able to smother the fire before it can go beyond the smoldering stage."

Tim sipped his glass of port and considered the status of the situation. Because of the terrible potential and risk the discovery of the artifact involved, he thought, someone needed to unlock the code or the meaning of the plate, to innocently probe its mysterious history in a quiet way so as not to draw attention. Someone needed to travel to Chicago to meet with the Islamic Scholar at the University of Chicago; and someone had to travel to France, to the library of ancient manuscripts at Mont Saint Michel, where the riddle might be solved. Ultimately, someone would need to deliver all of the sensitive information accrued to the appropriate authorities. Valmer insisted he was to be that someone.

Maybe he would listen; maybe he would agree to be that someone. The old spymaster who had given up a career of power and influence over a matter of principle was impossible to ignore. Valmer's sacrifice had been great, and all he was asking him to do was give up a few days of vacation. Tim couldn't deny the appeal the research mission held for him, a once-in-a-lifetime chance to take a journey to uncover an ancient mystery. The more he thought about it, he could find no good reason not to go.

Driving back to the pottery shop, Tim felt as though a metamorphosis had occurred. He no longer felt angry or out of control, like a pawn being manipulated by forces larger than himself. Instead, he felt infused with a sense of duty and purpose. How incredible that just three days ago he was a mere communication consultant, with nothing else on his mind but enjoying the longest vacation of his life—extended time with his wife and daughters. Now he was preparing to embark on a quest, a mission of international proportion.

Inwardly, though, he knew the purpose of the mission, as important as it was, simply provided him with an excuse. He was unabashedly thrilled at the idea of responding to the siren-song call of the mystery, to be held in the grip of a conundrum. His pulse quickened as he thought of the fascinating trip to the place where time telescoped, and new realities lay waiting for the historical researcher.

He had planned a similar trip through history once before. Fate had denied him then, but now it seemed to offer him a second chance, an opportunity to fulfill the unrealized dream of his life. But this time the mission was of greater importance than his quest for a doctorate. This time he sought information which could avert and prevent potentially dangerous fallout to the religious and political order of the world.

He considered for a moment that he was not altogether unlike the people he saw on the beach, walking along bent over in the famous Sanibel stoop. After all, they too were on a mission, a search for the junonia, the next perfect shell. We're all chasing our own junonia, he mused.

As he thought about the impending adventure, he felt infused with energy, a vitality he had not felt for years. Then he pictured little Katie, Elizabeth, and Laney, the disappointment in their eyes, and his elation collapsed like a punctured balloon.

"Dear Lord," he sighed, as rain continued to blanket the windshield, the staccato movement of the windshield wipers like a metronome marking his vacillation between anticipation and anxiety. "Help me to explain this to the girls; help them to understand."

He knew something was wrong as soon as he walked into the pottery shop. Elizabeth huddled on a bench, her eyes puffy and red, as though she had been crying. He had planned on calling the family together to tell them that he was going to have to catch a flight to Chicago that afternoon, and then on to a wider trip. But his fatherly instinct initially compelled him to comfort his first child and find out what had happened.

"My ring—I lost my ring." She tried to hold back a sob. "I think it came off when we were loading the canoe. I didn't notice it was gone until we got back here."

Her ring was the custom design she had ordered, a high school graduation gift from him and Laney, and the pride of her life. A beautiful example of a jeweler's craft, it had been given in lieu of a standard class ring which Elizabeth considered "tacky and a waste of money."

"We'll go look for it," he soothed as he hugged her and kissed the top of her head. "Let's give it a shot."

"Not in this rain," Laney said coming in from the back room of the shop. "It's terrible out there. We'd never find anything."

Katie, sensed her big sister's despair, and was sad-eyed in sympathy. The girls and Laney were all near tears and gathered in a family circle for support. Tim was struck by the sadness on their faces, from something other than what he had been imagining would soon cause it. The announcement of his departure had been upstaged by a more immediate distress.

"I don't care if I get wet! I want to go look for Lizzie's ring now!" Katie insisted. Elizabeth pulled her little sister onto her lap and nuzzled the top of her head. The girls seemed to find comfort in their closeness.

*   *   *

Old, brown palm fronds, knocked down by the heavy rain and blown by the strong wind, littered the small road. The downpour remained intense and visibility was diminished, but Tim and the girls found the spot along the dike road where they had parked, and where the canoe journey had begun and ended. Soaked within seconds of getting out of the van, they fanned out and began searching, bent at the waist, stooping in order to better examine the ground. For several minutes they scanned the grass, sand, and the muddy bank, desperately hoping to spot a glimmer of gold. Nothing. Resignation and despair began to set in. Tim could see that Elizabeth was crying again. A strong-willed young woman, she was nonetheless very sentimental, and Tim thought that this had to be one of her toughest moments. Her last family spring vacation, and she had lost her beloved ring. Distant thunder seemed to rumble in from the gulf, filling the thick air. Tim signaled for Laney to get Katie into the van, out of the rain and possible lightning.

He and Elizabeth retraced their steps, scanning the ground even more closely. The footing was slick, and he slipped and slid a few feet down the bank on his knees and palms. A shot of lightning cracked close to the road, and thunder vibrated in the air. He found himself in a thicket of mangrove trees: they had always seemed sinister to him, with their roots in the air, like bony fingers groping through the water. To him they represented swamp and bayou, things backwater and hidden. But right now the roots were his safety handle and he grabbed at one to stop his slide toward the slough, and whatever crab, 'gator, or snake life might be lurking below the water's surface.

Another lighting crack, even closer than the one before, made him decide it was time to abandon the search. The glare of the lightning created a shadow effect across the picket fence-like stretch of mangrove roots he clung to. He looked up and saw Elizabeth was at the top of the bank, peering through the roots, which for an instant in the lighting looked like jail bars. An accomplished hiker and climber, Elizabeth grabbed a root and leaned forward toward him, extending her right hand. He wedged a foot against the roots and scrambled up, reaching out to her. He scanned the muddy bank, looking for another foothold, and at that moment he saw the ring. It lay just on the edge of the bank, embedded in mud, its backside shining like a nugget.

In order to pull her father back up onto the bank, Elizabeth gave one last mighty tug. In his excitement at finding the ring, Tim slipped as he cleared the edge, and they both fell flat into the muck. He sat up and wiped the mud from his eyes, and he and Elizabeth stared at each other. They both looked like swamp creatures, and they began laughing hysterically. Then he felt the hard object under his hand, and still laughing, held the gleaming trophy out to his grateful daughter.

A "Mucky" Meet

"I can't believe you're going to do this! Tim, you have been dreaming about spending two weeks on Sanibel since we were married. Now we can finally do it and you're going to leave!" Laney wasn't so much angry as she was incredulous. "You also really need to slow down. This is supposed to be a vacation. A break."

"I don't mean to butt in, but I guess I have been for twenty years anyway," Dave said from his position behind the kitchen counter where he was fixing a snack of bread and cheese. "But Valmer says Tim will only be gone three, maybe four days."

"How are you going to get from Sanibel to Normandy—with a stop in Chicago besides—in three days? There's no way!" She was emphatic.

"OK, so four days. Valmer's slick at working out the arrangements. I'll go pretty hard, get it done and get back to lie on the beach. Maybe I'll get lucky in Chicago and get all I need." Tim took her hand. "I know this is our vacation. I am sorry about that—I really am. But there is something about this that excites me. I get revved thinking about where I'll be. Do you realize I had planned to visit the ancient manuscripts library at Avranches and Mont Saint Michel when I was doing my doctoral research? This stuff is not that far from what I was going to do then."

"Besides living a dream— which I'm sure he does every day with you and the girls anyway," Dave interjected and ducked the couch pillow Laney flung at him. "He's got to do this. There is a lot at stake." His tone conveyed an unspoken seriousness, adding credibility to the situation.

"I know that, Dave. I also know Tim, and I know this is something he has to do," she said, smiling ruefully. "If he didn't go he'd regret it and he would never get over it. One disappointment like that in life is enough."

"I'd probably never let you forget it either, huh?" Tim said as he rubbed his hand over her shoulders.

"I guess I can manage for a few days without you," she sighed. "I do it all the time when you travel for work. I just wish it didn't have to be now."

"And don't forget how much he loves to eat! The chefs in France aren't too shabby," Dave offered a piece of gouda from the slicer. "Here, have a little nibble. Get some now before the little gals get back with Barb."

"All we need to tell the girls is that some business has come up, that I'll be back this weekend."

"All you need to tell us is what?" Elizabeth said walking down the hallway, drying her hair with a towel. Even though the rain had washed most of the mud off them, she had decided to shower at the Hocketts after the successful ring hunt.

Tim explained that he needed to do some field research for a sort of client, face-to-face, "away from fax machines, telephone calls, even computer circuits."

"What kind of research?" she wondered. "Why you, Pop?"

"Kiddo, you're old enough to understand that sometimes governments have to do things that are best done without a lot of attention. I need to talk to some historians about that metal plate your sister found. It turns out it could be something important, and if it looked like governments were getting involved then a lot of things could happen. Right now it's important to keep this real quiet. To keep it…"

"Undercover!" Elizabeth finished. "Cool. So you're going to be like a spy?"

"No. Like a historian. A researcher. Like an interested tourist."

"Yeah? So who is going to pay for this?" she asked.

"We certainly are not!" Laney shot in warningly.

"No, of course not. Associates of Dave's friend Valmer," Tim
said.

"You mean the old spy? Cool. My dad, Tim Calvin—undercover tourist-historian spy."

"Yeah—real cool, huh?"

As Tim drove the Hocketts' old van across the causeway, his
exit to the mainland was quick. Traffic was light as the rain was
keeping the day-trippers away. Driving away from the beautiful island gave him a hollow feeling. He took solace from the thought
that within three or four days he would cross back over onto the little
piece of paradise he spent most of the year longing for. The rain
seemed to be letting up as he moved along Sumerlin toward the
airport. Traffic was still light even here. He found it odd to be parking at the airport rather than returning it to a rental lot, which had
always been his custom.

It felt strange to be here without the girls. Katie had been sad,
almost tearful about his leaving. Elizabeth appeared concerned, but
also seemed to be learning about the importance of the call of duty
by seeing him interrupt his beloved vacation. He checked the television monitor for his flight status. He had his boarding pass and was
traveling light, so he headed up the escalator for the gate.

Dave and Barb had asked June to close the shop so they could
take Laney and the girls to the Mucky Duck Restaurant. The rain
had stopped, the sun was breaking through the clouds, and Dave
thought Meamo's sense of humor would lift the girls' spirits. They
had seen his mustard routine before, but it was always good for a
laugh—unsuspecting first-time visitors recoiling in fear as Meamo
pointed a container toward them and squirted out a gag stream of
mustard, really only a yellow string.

As Barb and Dave walked toward the door, the phone rang. Barb answered it, but was greeted with only silence and then a click. Dave came in from patio in time to see Barb replace the phone on the hook, an annoyed look on her face. "Darned crank callers," she muttered. As Dave headed for the bedroom, the phone rang again. This time he answered it. "Good afternoon—Hocketts," he barked.

"David, this is Valmer. Meet me this afternoon on the beach just north of the crowd at the Mucky Duck. I'll be there at five thirty."

"Why don't we just come by…." The line went dead. Dave was puzzled. He had never known Valmer to like crowds. His dining preferences leaned more toward intimate settings like the Nutmeg House or the King's Crown at South Seas. "Why did he just hang up? Why didn't he close with a joke, as he usually does?" Dave wondered aloud.

"It's strange" he told Barb when she asked who had called. "That was Valmer. He wants to meet us at the Mucky Duck."

"Really?" she too sounded surprised that such a private man had chosen such a public spot in which to meet.

"He sounded weird. He didn't say anything about Jane coming with him. He just hung up."

"Tim said he had been working all night. Maybe he's just tired."

* * *

Tim enjoyed the leg-room and service in first class on the flight to his first assignment, the meeting with the Moslem cleric in Chicago. He usually flew coach, where he barely had enough space to open his shoulder bag attaché, but here he had space to spread out and pore over the briefing papers prepared by the old operations director. Valmer may have retired years before, but it was apparent that he had kept his hand in and was still up to speed. Tim thought that if he could have had text books in school that were written as well as these papers, he probably would have been a much better student. He was amazed at how much he was absorbing. By the time he got to Chicago he would know a great deal about Professor Juni Khadija and her somewhat cloistered mentor, Dr. Abu Shaker Haji. He read over the neat, concise report:

>   *Juni Khadija, Egyptian from a wealthy upper-class family. Dr. Haji, born to a Turkish father and an Iranian mother—a devout Muslim and brilliant scholar. He is a full professor at the University of Chicago, and she is a research fellow. They are collaborating on a new text about Abu Bakr, the early follower of Mohammed who recorded Mohammed's revelations and teachings and compiled them into the Koran. They are an unlikely combination for this type of collaboration: Khadija being modern and considerably more secular than religious, not to mention being a woman. Haji had once been a counsel to a powerful mullah, but despaired of the inherent politics involved. He is a Shiite fundamentalist who specialized in the study of the writing and translations of the Koran, the holy book of Islam. Haji and Khadija are united in their interest in the first manuscripts of Koran, and the beginning of Islam. Dr. Haji is member of an international study team commissioned by the United Nations to explore how to resolve disputes over documents and artifacts claimed by Muslims and/or Christians and/or Jews.*

*   *   *

As the Hockett van headed for Blind Pass between Sanibel and Captiva the passengers looked to the left, while Dave slowed and honked as they passed the Mad Hatter. Brian and Jayne's car was parked at the side. "I can hardly wait until our Saturday-night dinner there," Dave said, glancing around at the Calvin women in the back seat. "Tim should be back from his whirlwind research mission by then, and a grand celebration will definitely be in order. Right?"

"Right!" was the resounding chorus in response.

Elizabeth was explaining to Katie and Cee how the beach restoration project on Captiva had worked. Cee, ahead of the curve however, informed Elizabeth about the controversial and potentially damaging aspects of the multi-million-dollar dredging operation. They discussed the almost-futile attempt to stop the natural shift of the barrier island. Sand from the western beach was eroding while the eastern shore on Pine Island Sound and San Carlos Bay was actually growing. In a sense the island was "walking" toward the mainland. Captiva beachfront real estate was expensive and worth extending great efforts to preserve. One of the prime spots was occupied by the popular Mucky Duck English Pub, which directly overlooked the gulf. Traffic from the Mucky Duck and Bellini's elegant Italian restaurant choked Andy Rosse Lane each afternoon, from four o'clock until the last diners finally retreated to their lodgings. The narrow street was also full of walkers who parked out a couple of blocks.

Reservations were not taken at the Mucky Duck, and a two to three-hour wait was not unusual. Dave and Meamo, the manager, were old friends and practiced the unwritten code of the resort island: residents took care of each other. Dave had called to give him an idea of when their party of six or seven would arrive. "Hey, Meamo, you've got another crowd," Dave said as he walked toward the bar.

"So your business is bad? I saw how many cars were in your lot today, Hockett," Meamo shot back.

Dave ordered three bottles of beer, adding to the land-office business the Mucky Duck was doing this evening. Having a cold brew was part of the drill for the scores of people waiting on the porch and deck or beachfront for their names to be called on the loud speaker.

The gals walked down to the water's edge and watched for Valmer.

"It must be something really important to get Valmer out into this throng of tourists," Barb said to Laney.

* * *

Tim watched the early evening lights twinkle on in the city below as the plane circled in a holding pattern over O'Hare. He thought of the many great weekends he and Laney and the girls had spent enjoying the Second City. Elizabeth loved the shopping on the Magnificent Mile, so while she and Laney went off in pursuit of bargains, he and Katie would stroll to the Oak Street Beach and spend the afternoons. There had been wonderful trips to the museums and the Shedd Aquarium, excursions on the lake, and dining in Chicago's many superb restaurants.

He did for his daughters as his parents had done for him, making sure the family stayed in the Palmer House, now restored to its former grandeur, or at the historic Conrad Hilton. Now as they prepared to land he thought fondly of his favorite, the Whitehall, saddened that it was being converted to something other than the quiet and elegant hotel he had come to love. Tonight he would stay in the Whitehall's companion, the Tremont, also a place for discerning travelers, with the warmth and charm of an English manor. The hotel was in the heart of the great dining district, on east Chestnut, between Rush and Michigan Avenue.

"Here are a couple of cold ones for you," Dave said, handing beers to Barb and Laney as they stood on the beach in front of the Mucky Duck, watching the scores of people come and go from the deck porch of the pub. Dozens more sat at the picnic tables arranged for the comfort of the waiting crowds. "I'll take Cee and Katie with me and we'll scan the beach for Valmer. I wonder where he could be?"

"See ya, darlin'. Laney and Liz and I'll watch for him here and wait for Meamo to page us for our table," Barb said in her slow and relaxed manner.

Dave and the girls scanned the beach north of the Mucky Duck. They walked up the beach and even looped down south below the area where the wave riders were allowed to run. Dave saw no sign of Valmer anywhere. In the meantime Barb, Laney, and Elizabeth heard Meamo's call over the speaker and they took their table by the window.

After a few more minutes of searching the parking lot, waiting deck, and beach Dave and the little girls headed for the pub's entry. There they were greeted by Meamo, a big and robust fellow who orchestrated the throngs of patrons from behind his podium. As the crowds gathered in groups waiting to be taken to their tables, he entertained them by dispensing quick one-liners, gags, and good cheer, which he did with the flair of a maestro conducting an orchestra.

"Mr. Hockett, you are not a happy camper tonight?" Meamo chided Dave as he walked around and through the crowd waiting to place their names on the seating list.

"I was supposed to meet someone here a while ago and he didn't show up," Dave said exasperatedly.

"Well by my count, there are roughly two hundred people out there or in the environs."

"I don't think he made it; we would have found each other. But if an older gentleman with a formal manner shows up will you please send him our way? His name is Valmer," Dave said heading for the table, following Cee and Katie who had spotted their mothers and Elizabeth sitting by the window.

"Not to worry, Mr. Dave! Its just another Mucky meet," Meamo said as he quickly directed his attention to another crowded group of waiting diners.

* * *

Tim felt a twinge of longing as he navigated O'Hare. The kids had always gotten a kick out of the people mover and its pop neon, high-tech feeling.

The Tremont was just thirty minutes from the airport and he enjoyed the cab ride watching the hustle, as evening and the beginning of the nighttime social life, ushered out another city working-day.

"You know, there is a different pace in people's step, a different mood in a city as a business day turns to evening pleasure, don't you think?" he said probably as much to himself as to the cabbie.

"Yeah, sure, buddy," the driver said, giving Tim a sideward glance.

The ornate stonework framing the Tremont's windows and main door were elegantly accented by stone and brick landscape boxes. Neatly trimmed conifer trees and bushes were highlighted by the delicate blooms of the redbud and dogwood trees, and the street possessed a quiet European flair. The doorman, bell captain, and desk manager were gracious and attentive.

"Mr. Calvin we know this is your first stay with us at the Tremont," the manager said as he looked over Tim's registration. "I am sure you will come to love the Tremont as much as you enjoyed the Whitehall." The manager smiled at Tim with pride. "Our concierge is also quite accomplished at handling all manner of requests, and as at the Whitehall, our staff is multilingual."

"Thank you. I've heard very nice things about the hotel," Tim said, impressed.

"I know that at the Whitehall you preferred the corner room, number 1703. I have situated you in similar quarters here."

It was the crowning touch.

The meal had been splendid and the sunset spectacular. The Hockett-Calvin party walked to the van noticing that some of the people who had been waiting when they arrived were still waiting. For many devotees of the Mucky Duck, the wait around the restaurant at the picnic tables or on the deck or strolling the beach was part of the fun.

Dave wasn't having any fun now, though. He was troubled by Valmer's failure to show and decided he'd better stop at his house on the way home to learn what had happened.

As he turned off Tarpon Bay Road onto Valmer's long drive-way he noticed a telephone service truck parked at the roadside, but he didn't recognize the "SouthCom" logo on the truck as one he had seen before.

Valmer was sitting on the porch reading. He seemed surprised to see Dave drive up. As Dave, Barb, Laney and the girls got out of the van, Valmer called to his wife.

"Put on some coffee. I'll get brandy snifters. We have company." Jane was a successful artist of some acclaim. She had been very taken with Cee practically from the child's birth. Her own children were grown and when Cee had been younger, Jane had often volunteered to babysit. She greeted Barb affectionately and extended a warm welcome to Laney while Valmer offered Dave a brandy and invited him to a far corner of the massive porch.

"I've not heard from Tim yet," Valmer said. "We are staying in tonight so I can be here to receive his call. He was to meet with a man with whom I have some familiarity, and whom I have known since he was a young student. I am hopeful he can help us interpret the plate. What brings you by here tonight? I'm surprised to see you."

"Not as surprised as I was earlier *not* to see you," Dave replied, describing the phone call and his puzzlement over the location for the arranged meet, and then the no-show.

Valmer's response to the story caught Dave by surprise. He stiffened and his eyes narrowed; his color turned almost ashen.

"Dave, please be very precise. Tell me exactly what I said on the phone and how I sounded to you."

"What?"

"Humor me, Dave. It's important. What did I say?"

"Barb and I both thought it was weird. I think you said 'Dave,'—no, David—'this is Valmer. Meet me on the beach just north of the Mucky Duck. At five thirty'—or 'I'll see you at five thirty.' That was it. I started to ask you something and you just hung up. No good-bye. No Valmer joke. Click. It was just weird."

"Did I answer you directly? Did we actually talk—I said something, you said something back?"

"No. It was real short. Like I said, you said your thing and hung up. Why? What are you after?"

"Did you hear any background noise? Was there anything out of the ordinary?"

Dave was completely puzzled by now. "What in the blazes are you getting at? Are you telling me you didn't call?"

"David, I absolutely did not make that call." Valmer rose and started into the house. "Excuse us, ladies. Dave, come with me."

Valmer led Dave up to his office where he unlocked a desk drawer and produced an old packing box. From the box he pulled out an electronic device with meter, wires, and alligator clips. He proceeded to "crack" his telephone, unscrewing the mouthpiece pulling out the perforated disc, while keeping the cradle posts depressed so as not to activate the line.

"It's tough to do this on the new phones, that's why I keep this receiver around," he said to Dave as he worked with his device. "It's like looking under the hood of a car. Give me an old V-8 or a straight six and I can tell you where I am. This new technology is for younger men and their contrivances."

After connecting the device to the telephone receiver, Valmer dialed the South Seas Plantation on Captiva and asked whether "the party of Edward Earl had arrived yet. Not until tomorrow?" he said into the receiver, all the while watching the meter on his device. "Thank you. Good evening."

"David, we appear to have water in our lines," he was looking at his meter, "and I think it's rather close." He saw Dave's confusion and explained to him how someone had tapped his phone line, enough so to record and rig a conversation, a one-ended conversation. That explained the odd call Dave had received.

"Someone is interested in the connection between us, David. I'm sure the plate is the reason."

Tim leaned against the pillows propped behind his head as he lay on the hotel bed reading another of Valmer's files. The phone rang. It was Juni Khadija's undergraduate assistant, calling to tell him that Juni would meet him at Cricket's Restaurant in about an hour. That's a break, he thought. Cricket's was right downstairs in the hotel, an incomparable old dining spot whose four stars had been earned through years of exacting attention to detail and continual evolution of an excellent continental menu. Tim had eaten there before. It was a favorite of the business crowd on expense accounts. The club-like atmosphere was unlike anything else in the country, the decor featuring a display of Chicago-area corporate logos, designs, and memorabilia combined with wood beams and warm panelling.

Corporate high-rolling was evidently nothing new for Juni Khadija, if the information in Valmer's file was accurate. Her family was one of Egypt's wealthiest, with wide international business ties, and her father had been an advisor to Presidents Nasser, Sadat, and Mubarik. Juni had forsaken the family business, leaving that to her brothers, and had become an academic. From Cairo she went to Oxford, then on to Yale for another advanced degree, and finally to Berkeley. Some of her personal fortune endowed the research being conducted by Dr. Haji and herself. Tim set the brief aside and rubbed his eyes. He wondered what kind of woman he was about to meet. Would she be able to throw some light on the Moslem view of the mysterious plate? Or was she simply a buffer, a line of defense that he would have to get past to get to Valmer's contact, the Imam.

Valmer pulled another small box from a desk drawer. From a styrofoam packet about the size of a ring box he removed something that looked like a cross between a bottle cap and silver dollar. He placed it over the mouthpiece of the phone and tapped a button on its back side, producing a small, high-pitched tone. Valmer's dogs, which were out on the porch with the girls, began to howl, and he chuckled.

"This is an old tool, but it still works. It'll blow that water out of the line quite nicely."

"When I drove down your lane, I saw a telephone truck. But it wasn't anyone I had seen before. I didn't recognize the name. SouthCom, I think."

"I can assure you they will be gone when you leave. And I imagine someone inside will be seeking medical attention for a perforated eardrum," Valmer said, relishing the knowledge that his vintage gear had vanquished some new high-tech snooper. The thrill of victory was short-lived, though. He found no delight in knowing that someone had been hired to monitor his calls, and thus placed the call for the fabricated rendezvous.

"Dave, it occurs to me that there's probably more that's been done. They obviously wanted you away from your house."

Dave shot Valmer a quick look; he felt suddenly ill. Immediately the two of them started down the stairs. Jane, Barb, and Laney were watching the news on TV, and the girls were with the dogs on the porch.

"Barb, we need to get home. Pronto."

She responded to the urgency in his voice. "OK. Let me round up the kids. What's wrong?"

Dave cut off his answer and their attention became riveted to the television. Natalie Simmonds was updating her story on the man Tim and Katie had found on the beach. "He has refused to talk with authorities," she reported. "But the two men wanted in connection with his beating have been arrested and are being held by federal authorities in Miami. They have been cleared of any involvement in terrorist bombing incidents, but are undergoing further questioning by Miami police. Both men are former military intelligence officers for Libyan President Mohammar Khadafi."

The attorney for the two was shown claiming his clients were being mistakenly held and should be released. Simmonds came back to say "the Libyans' attorney had been hired by internationally renowned art collector Aoki Pasotti, adding further to the mystery surrounding the affair," Simmonds continued as a picture of Tim from the interview came on the screen. Everyone in the room held their breath. "We have learned that Tim Calvin, the vacationer who found the badly beaten man has left the country. My source says Calvin's departure has a direct connection with this affair. We'll keep you posted."

As Barb and Laney and the girls went out to get in the van, Valmer stopped Dave at the door.

"Caution, my friend—great caution is urged. Keep an eye open. Even before we learn more about plate, I can tell you we are at the edge of an old mystery. Old mysteries can bring with them great darkness. Call me and let me know what has happened. Peace."

The old boy was right, Dave thought as he drove past where the telephone truck had been parked. It was gone. But where to, he wondered, and who ordered them into action in the first place? Troubling thoughts plagued him as he sped toward his home.

The moment Dave drove away, Valmer returned to his office and contacted his source in Langley. He learned a great deal. As he had suspected, duty desks in watch rooms in Langley and Tel Aviv had taken notice of the arrest of Pasotti's men, whom he had arranged to have flown to Miami with an advance call to both State and Immigration Department officials. By now background files had been spewed out of databases, situation teams had huddled, and the management level of appropriate directorates had signed on. The arrest in America of men with such backgrounds was news which traveled quickly through police and intelligence circuits. Valmer's contact informed him that secure communication between the CIA and the Israeli Mossad had begun. Input from Valmer had been assessed and added to the analysis, and the information was shared. Tel Aviv reported they had monitored communication coming from Teheran about the arrested men. They were Libyans, but Iran was nevertheless quite interested in the situation. Since the media had linked Tim Calvin's trip to the arrest, and since he had discovered the beaten man, Iran had dispatched a team to follow him, thinking he might hold some sort of key to the significance of the plate's inscription. Valmer frowned. According to his contact, analysts in both the United States and Israel wanted a look at the metal plate itself. In the meantime, the Israelis had begun an effort on their own to locate Dr. Benjamin Stroutsel, the academic specialist in ancient artifacts. Valmer's associate in Langley noted that the Israelis thought Stroutsel was somewhere on sabbatical in Europe. "I could have told them that," he muttered to himself. "We're still ahead of the game on a couple of points. I think Calvin will reach him first. But good Lord, the fellow is out there by himself soon to be trailed by Iranians." Valmer clicked off his contact with Langley, feeling defensive and anxious.

Tim snapped off the television and watched the image of anchorman Bill Kurtis fade from the screen. The report detailed plans for Chicago's annual summer media blitz to attract tourists. The city was one of his favorite play spots, with its blues and jazz clubs, after-hours spots, neighborhood sidewalk cafés, pubs and pulsating energy. Chicago had a big-city vibe but was more friendly and less hostile than New York. Odd that in this city of good times he was about to meet with a Muslim woman to attempt to convince her to get him an audience with a holy man. It pained him to be separated from Laney with whom he had shared most of his Chicago good times. But now it was time to go downstairs for the dinner meeting at Cricket's and whatever revelations about the plate he might discover.

Dave became increasingly uneasy as he sped along Periwinkle, heading toward the house. His distress had been amplified by Valmer's odd mood and admonition. Valmer always frightened Dave when, occasionally, he slipped into that foreboding mode. Only rarely had Valmer opened that dusty volume of his life which constituted his time as an intelligence man to give Dave a glimpse into the netherworld and hellish existence of a "field man" or "operations talent." Dave shook his head, wondering at Valmer's strength. Being alone on a hostile plain, in a wilderness of deception where information and misinformation are currencies of controlled madness must take its toll on a man, leaving him spent, thirsty, shadowlike. Tonight he had seen Valmer flung back onto that fearful plain, and worried that his good friend Tim had become another drone in this strange game played by nods and winks, brutality and stealth. Tim was a good and gentle man, with a quick and sharp mind, who loved his family and friends. He was at home with businesses leaders and creative thinkers. He was not a clandestine operator, accustomed to cryptic nighttime pursuits around the world. His fields of contest were friendly ones, basketball courts and golf courses—certainly not a bloody beach where hands are severed by minions of greedy and vicious men. As Dave drove on through the darkness he felt a deepening darkness of his own spirit, and dread began to knot his stomach. The feeling was a correct indication of what was to come. As soon as he turned off the street into his driveway he could see that something was terribly wrong. Barb and Laney gasped, and the girls cheerful chattering stopped abruptly.

"Stay here!" he barked as he jumped out of the van. From someplace deep inside this gentle giant, the softspoken and easygoing potter, the tough master sergeant and brawling drill instructor he had been long ago was emerging again. His home had been broken into and ransacked. The anger at seeing the destruction that had been done to it sent energy coursing through his blood.

"David, be careful!" Barb cried as Cee first and then Katie began to cry. The little girls weren't sure what was wrong, but the fear communicated itself to them.

Dave cautiously approached the house and peered from the lawn through the open front door into the living room, instantly relieved to be greeted by Maggie the dog and Bart the cat. Maggie ran to him, wagging her tail and whining, as if in apology for not adequately protecting the house. If the animals were there and unharmed, Dave reasoned, the intruders surely were gone. He stepped gingerly into the house. The living room was a shambles. The couch had been shoved out of place, lamps and tables tipped over, records and CDs scattered around, drawers dumped, and books and plants swept from shelves. As he proceeded, he could also see that the kitchen cabinets had been rifled through and their contents scattered. He grabbed the kitchen phone and hit the auto dialer for the police; three rings later he was telling Phil, the night-duty officer, to come over quickly. Phil told Dave to get out of the house, to go to a neighbor's and wait, even though he knew his warning would go unheeded.

Dave reached into a pile of silverware dumped on the kitchen floor and grabbed a filet knife and a meat cleaver. Pumped up with pure adrenaline and rage, he started down the hallway to investigate the rest of the house.

* * *

Because it was such a warm spring night Tim decided to go outside the hotel and enter Cricket's from its street side. He was greeted by a tuxedoed maître d', gracious and professional, neither snobbish nor unctuous. A weeknight dinner crowd of business people were scattered throughout the warm, mellow room. Tim ordered a Stoli martini, extra dry, hoping the alcohol would not offend his dinner companion, but instead would have the effect, as Dean Acheson was quoted as saying, "of providing the desired courage" for pursuing his part of this odd quest he had undertaken. Although an introduction to Islam had been part of his curriculum in medieval lore in college, he felt uneasy at the prospect of meeting the two Moslem scholars. He worried that his Presbyterian background would automatically be seen as the mark of an infidel when he met with them, and feared that his knowledge of his own holy book, the Bible, would be quizzed and measured and found to be inadequate by these students of the Koran.

He glanced up to see the maître d' bringing someone across the room and soon an elegant and sophisticated woman stood before him, beautiful and smiling. Calvin was stunned by Juni Khadija. She seemed to read his mind.

"I disappoint you Mr. Calvin? I am not what you expected?" She extended her hand in greeting to him, palm down.

"You are not who I expected. I'm sorry," he stammered. "I don't mean anything by that. I guess I was expecting…well to be honest, I didn't know what to expect."

"Perhaps you expected a somber figure in black robes and a veil. But I am an Egyptian first, and then a scholar. My interest is history. Although I encounter difficulty in some places because I am not devout, my money succeeds in opening many doors and minds. You see, Mr. Calvin, the Arabic people are quite deft at pragmatism. Long experience has taught us to be realists."

"And to get right to the point," he added. And they can be disarmingly charming, he thought to himself, lifting his martini and searching her eyes for a reaction. "Would you care for a drink?"

"I think that would be quite lovely, thank you," she said as she continued to take measure of him, meeting his gaze with her own, tilting her chin up and cocking her head slightly to the right, the hint of a smile playing on her lips.

"You're a damn fool idiot, Hertt! How hard could it be to find the only metal plate there is. Why the hell am I paying you?" Ivan Wasser sputtered furiously into the phone from his New York apartment. "I lost this damned thing once—I don't intend to lose it again!"

"I went through the potter's house, top to bottom," Hertt replied. "He ain't hiding it there. I swear to you." He paced the floor of the house where he was holed up, one of many such private and "hidden" beach homes situated around Captiva Island.

Hertt was Wasser's fixer, thug, and expediter. Ivan Wasser was wealthy and influential, though in New York financial circles he was more tolerated than respected. As he often did when his boss gave him a rough time, Hertt pulled out of his wallet a frayed and yellowed clipping he had saved from *The Wall Street Journal*. It described Ivan Wasser as "a bottom feeder in a world of sharks. His style has always been to pick over the remains, the entrails, to hover near financial disaster and to move just as a moment of opportunity presents itself. Failure or collapse is the beginning of his financial day. Even those who knock him admit Wasser gets what he wants." Hertt smiled as he read the clip, fingering it with a retaliatory pleasure. You little lout, he thought to himself. Refolding the clip Hertt realized in this case the article was wrong. This time Wasser hadn't gotten what he wanted, and as a result he was roiling in a profane, self-indulgent torment.

"First I rent that house just to get the plate, then the man who's supposed to bring it to me gets whacked. Some little girl finds the damn thing, and you spend my money to set up a wild plan to get it from some local yokel potter and you get nothing! And then the crew you hire splits on you!" Wasser's voice cracked with rage as he yelled in his small raspy voice.

"The crew was worth the money," Hertt insisted. "They picked up real quick that the potter and the tourist was taking their moves from the weird old man. I worked with 'em before. They did all right. They got the potter out of his place. Ain't their fault the plate wasn't there. One of the guys got a busted eardrum out of the deal. He's hurtin' real bad."

"Yeah? Well I hope it hurts so bad he shoots himself. Stupid bastards! I'm going to get that plate! You hear me, Hertt? I got outbid by Pasotti before because I didn't move strong enough. So Pasotti's Arab gets a dose of entrepreneurship and calls me. That's a sign. You hear me? The treasure's supposed to be mine—it's mine! You got any idea what I can get for something like that? I'll have collectors like the mighty Calamari Pasotti drooling on their shoes. I'm moving strong this time. And that's what I'm paying you to do." Wasser's voice reminded Hertt of a hiss.

"Them other Arabs ain't got it. They got popped in Miami by the feds. The tourist ain't got it, cause the TV said he's leaving the country. So it's still got to be down here, man. The potter either has it or knows where it is and can get it."

"Then get off your butt and get it. Or I'll fly down to that stinkin' buggy little sand pile and do it myself!" An abrupt click ended the conversation.

Hertt knew Wasser had bid on the rare artifact, not because it might be a sacred relic, but because it was a commodity he could exploit. When Calamari Pasotti's Libyan agent contacted him, Wasser had moved quickly to close the deal. But Pasotti's henchmen squirrelled things when they made their attempted hit on the beach. Wasser had sublet the Captiva home and had sent him, Hertt, to make arrangements. Not altogether a bad deal while he was waiting—plenty of booze and babes on the beach outside his window. But when the original plan fell through, Wasser had ordered Hertt to get the plate from the tourist, Calvin, who discovered it buried on the beach. None of it had gone according to plan and now Wasser was on his case.

Hertt often thought how he would like to kill Wasser. So many times this shark of a man had shredded him, humiliated him. He wouldn't kill him, though, because Wasser was a goldmine. He now knew too much about Wasser's deals and his money to snuff him. He was going to ride this one as long as he could. Hertt knew in his gut that he never wanted to go back to doing stretches in prison, so he was always careful. "Careful" is why Wasser took him on, because he could "crunch" when he had to, and because he knew people. Hertt had come to realize Wasser also hired him because he would take the man's abuse. Not many guys would put up with Wasser's stuff, but Hertt didn't mind. He'd had it worse in the joints, worse from his abusive and drunk old man, and the whole scene was worse when he was in Nam.

"Screw 'em," he said as he poured a tumbler of Makers Mark. "Ain't nothin' in my face tonight," he said to the glass as he walked onto the porch to watch the surf glimmer in a bright moon. Hertt had a million dollar beach home to himself, and a full liquor closet. He was going to just sit here and drink and think about that sexy redhead he saw singing the blues the other night at that place in town.

* * *

Captive on Captiva

Dave walked to the van and told Barb to take Cee, Laney and the girls to a neighbor's house.

"I've cleared the place," he said. "Been all the way through it. Whoever was here is gone now but they made an awful mess. Everything is trashed. I don't want Cee to see this. Just stay next door with them while I wait here for the police."

Barb patted his hand, and she, Laney, and the girls walked away as Dave headed back toward the door and the pattern of light coming from their front window. He'd asked the police to run by and check the shop first. He prayed that his security locks, sentry system, and the routine patrol along Periwinkle had kept it safe. He seethed as he surveyed the mess his home had turned into.

This was all useless—the damned piece of metal was in a safe deposit box at the bank, he thought, frightened that someone he didn't know, some mysterious force could strike so close to his heart. As he searched around his ransacked home, his mind began a survey of defensive perimeters and counter strikes and spotter positions—a flood of images. He hadn't thought of these things since leaving Fort Leonard Wood, the last day he'd worn a uniform. He felt an old, familiar, but distant sensation that he recognized as something he had long ago worked to develop: a soldier's anger, part of the preparation for battle. He'd used to tell his trainees it was "the warrior's intensity." Well, he certainly felt it now.

He picked his way through the debris of the guest room and found his service plaque and the award from his unit buddies—"The Rowdiest Mad-Dog Mother." He picked them up and gazed at them. "I thought I had changed, got away from those days," he said to himself. "I've got Barb and Cee, and I love them. I try to be sensitive— I'm into art, not anger. I don't want this. I just want to be a good ol' island boy and run my pottery shop."

He put the plaques down and began to move some of the furniture back into place. What was happening? His friend Tim was off on a wild-goose chase, his family vacation in shambles, and now his own house had been trashed, attacked by someone who wanted an old metal plate. Some strange Arab had lost a hand and been nearly beaten to death. Valmer said governments were becoming involved, and even with their power they worried about what was going on. This whole situation was spinning out of control, disrupting his life and throwing him completely off balance.

The flashing red and blue lights of Lew Stiner's squad car pulling up in front of the house snapped Dave out of his thoughts. He met him on the front stoop.

"Everything's fine at the shop. Locked up tight. You ought to send Cee to a friend's house tonight. We'll be here for a while. Detective Waddell should be here in a few minutes—I think you know Ross. He'll help figure this out." Lew was an old friend and fellow member of the PTA, and he was obviously disturbed by Dave's predicament.

"Since Tim is out of town, they're all a little lonely, so we thought it would be nice if you stayed at the condo tonight, sweetie," Barb told Cee as she carried her overnight bag out to the van.

"You can swim first thing in the morning too," Laney added getting a quick smile from her freckle-faced goddaughter.

The ploy worked. Cee's excitement about the overnight at the condo on the gulf immediately supplanted her concern over why she couldn't go into the house.

"I don't think she can see you guys are worried," Laney whispered to Barb. "She's a sharp kid, but Mom outflanked her on this one."

Tim found Juni Khadija's charm and straightforward manner captivating. Her intense brown eyes, midnight black hair, delicate chin, strong nose, and perfect lips made her a beautiful woman, but her precise and deliberate manner of speech and her deep intellect made her intimidating. They had agreed there was no need to rush into a discussion about the plate or Tim's mission. She had suggested they first take some time to "get to know each other since we come from such different places." As they talked she would jab directly at a notion he held or a preconception or misconception he might reveal. She would then soften the thrust with her incredibly warm smile, or wink, seeming to veil herself in a soft feminine mystique, thus coaxing him into further conversation. In essence she was testing him to discover his depth of knowledge and level of understanding. By the time the salads had been served, Tim was almost woozy from the pace of this verbal dance of revelation.

They ultimately concluded that Tim's knowledge and grasp of the intricacies of Islam was considerably better than that of most Americans.

"I think you are correct in your assumption that most of your countrymen perceive us as a primitive people—radical ministers and armed hostage-takers, fundamentalists flailing their backs as they march and chant. Middle Eastern practitioners of Jihad or Holy War. But what do you know of the essence of Islamic thought?" she asked.

"Well, I know some of its history, beginning with Mohammed of the tribe of Qureysh. He was born in Mecca around 570, reared by his grandfather and later his uncle." Juni nodded, and Tim continued by discussing Mohammed's "travels in merchant caravans," and of "his marriage to a wealthy widow. That raised some eyebrows."

As he went on, Juni seemed a bit uneasy, put somewhat on the defensive by his knowledge, some of which he had learned years earlier in college but most of it from the background files he had read only hours before. She seemed most reactive to his narrative of how "Meccans claim descent from the patriarch Abraham through his son Ishmael. They believed their temple, the Ka'bah, had been built by Abraham for the worship of the One God, though most people worshipped idols in the temple.

"I always though Mohammed was a meditative type," Tim mused. "Apparently he got that from his clan. They didn't go in for idol worship. They were Hunafa, right? People who preferred to seek truth through the light of their own consciousness?" He paused, and she nodded affirmatively.

"They would retire for a month every year to meditate in a cave in the desert, or so it is said. Mohammed chose the month of the heat, the Ramadan. As I recall, it was there in his retreat, the Hira, that he was either asleep or in a trance when he heard the call to 'read.' " Tim paused, sipping his wine.

"But we're not all religious. What of Arab secular history?" she asked. "What do you know of the culture and enlightenment we produced?"

"Not as much as I would like to, and considering what I studied in college, not as much as I should, either. I am probably too ethnocentric, too Occidental in my thinking, but that is my lineage—the way I was raised.

"It's unfortunate, but I'm afraid that too many people don't know enough of their own history, much less that of a people on the other side of the world whose way of living they little understand," he said, stepping up the tempo of their dance of mutual revelation.

"There is so much to know," Juni's voice was firm, definite. "Moslem culture developed a highly scientific method of agriculture. We refined and manufactured high-quality metals and produced the finest wool and leather products. When your European ancestors were still barbarians, huddling in fear of the nighttime darkness and the evil spirits they thought brought the plagues that claimed so many lives, my people were pioneering the building of sanitary sewers and safe public water supplies. While Western physicians relied on the use of leeches and superstition to cure illnesses, our doctors studied anatomy and performed intricate surgeries. We contributed much to the knowledge of chemistry, and our system of mathematics provided a standard still used throughout the world today."

"Yes. Yes, I know." Tim said, feeling somewhat humbled.

"Our schools and universities provided education for the masses, while Europe lingered in ignorant darkness in the grip of tyrants." She was forceful and eloquent. She appeared somewhat more comfortable and articulate with Arab history than the Muslim religion.

"Of course our religion today is quite similar in some respects to Christianity and Judaism. We have different denominations and sects, such as Zuni, Shiite, and others, just as Christians are Catholic and several types of Protestant, and Jews are Orthodox, Conservative, or Reform. We have fundamentalists and zealots just as you have snake-handlers and cults who store weapons and prepare for a holy war." She sighed and leaned back in her chair, seemingly spent by the force of her speech. She gave him a somewhat sad smile. "Are we really so different, after all? Evil forces sought to destroy your prophet, just as evil forces seek to destroy all prophets. It is the way of the world. Does not good often perish because of its own goodness?"

Tim returned her smile. "You're right," he said.

It grew late and most of the other diners had left the restaurant, but Juni and Tim had been so engrossed in their conversation that they hadn't noticed.

"I feel as though we've traveled through time across cultures tonight—like we've been down a long and ancient road," Tim said, trying to express the feeling he had. It perplexed him. He felt a closeness to this woman he had known only two hours. But it was more than a simple familiarity.

"Odd, yes, that we should do so here in Chicago in the heart of the place they call the Gold Coast. But here is as good as anywhere to discover."

There she goes again, he thought. What did she mean by that? He paused for a moment to gather his thoughts, and then looked at her directly.

"I don't know. It just seems as though we've been through some kind of...process together., a kind of sparring match, or..."

"Have I been so tough that you feel beaten?" she asked sweetly, giving him an enigmatic smile.

"No, not at all. Maybe like we've been through a dance marathon, but not a fight." Tim was having trouble defining what he really felt, this sense of emotional intimacy, in appropriate terms. He flushed. The back of his neck and his ears seemed to be on fire, like a shy schoolboy asking for his first date. He felt ridiculous. "Do you understand what I'm trying to say?"

She stared at him for a long moment without speaking.

"Please excuse me, I need to make a call," she pardoned herself and left the table.

Tim sat there feeling embarrassed. Then it began to sink in that he had really blown it. He was sure now that he would never get to see the Imam. The whole point of the trip was shot, just because he had gotten in over his head. What in the world had he been thinking? Some sort of intellectual, sensual dallying? How humiliating! He had come here for answers about the metal plate. Instead he had succeeded in making himself look like a world-class jerk. How could he explain to Valmer that he had let an infatuation with a major contact, of all people, mess everything up? He took a ragged breath and closed his eyes, trying to figure what to do next.

Hertt was already upset by Wasser's first call, but the second one threw him into a fit of outrage. He had been two tumblers into the Makers Mark, when the old man called back. He had shouted at Hertt about having a plan, then put him on hold while he took another call. Now as he stood with the cellular phone in his hand, looking at the surf, he was ready to yell back.

Wasser came back on the line.

"All right, now listen to me and get this right. Don't screw up this time or you're through. You listening to me?"

"Yeah, I'm here." He growled. Hertt was close to losing his temper.

"I'm only saying this once, so you *better* listen good. Get the women—got it? Get the women and hold 'em. Make it clean, no bloodshed—none! *No one* gets hurt. I trade them for the plate—it's beautiful! Just don't screw this up. Make sure they can't recognize you or the house. Got it? Clean—no mess-up. Don't say a thing about why we grabbed 'em. I'm working on the trade now. We'll do it down there—make the trade, everything hush-hush, then a quick flight to Mexico. I have it all arranged down there. They get the broads when I get the plate. I'll fill you in later. Oh yeah—do this one by yourself. You don't need help. It's only a woman and couple of kids. There might even be a healthy bonus in it for you if you get everything straight. Yeah, I think even you can do it—just do it quick." Click.

"Only a woman and couple of kids? *Only* a woman and couple of kids?" Hertt thundered, slamming the phone down so hard he cracked the case. "How the hell am I supposed to do that? How the hell am I gonna grab 'em—how the hell am I going to keep 'em?" He tossed down another swallow of the whiskey and began to calm down. Hertt could cool off as quickly as he could blow up. He'd always had that ability. That's why he had been such a good leader back in school at Saint Thomas, where he started as an altar boy, and ended up as a quarterback.

People had been able go to Hertt with their problems and count on him to help. They did at Saint Thomas, before his own troubles began. They did again in Vietnam, where there were no rules. Even later when he was in the joint he could be cool when he had to be.

He checked the clip on his nine millimeter Beretta, and tucked it back in the holster. He would have to play this one by ear. He didn't want to have take them out of the condo. Maybe they were still back at the potter's house, helping clean up the mess. He'd have to move quickly.

As he drove the convertible along San Cap Road, he worked out his plan. He would wait until they were on either Rabbit Road or Tarpon Bay Road to make his move.

Traffic was light and he made very good time. He could see the potter's house from about two blocks away. The rental van was still in the driveway. He parked to wait.

It didn't take long. Laney Calvin and the girls came out of the house and got in the van, the older one climbing in the front passenger seat. Another little girl, whom Hertt thought must be the potter's kid, was with them. The potter's wife brought out an overnight bag which she placed in the back of the van with the two little girls.

Hertt slammed his hand against the steering wheel. "That's all I need—one more damned person to baby-sit," he fumed. He started thinking again about he was going to handle everything back at the beach house, as he watched the van back out of the driveway.

*   *   *

By the time Juni returned to the table, Tim had regained his composure a little and cleared his head. He wanted to offer an apology for getting "too heavy," but she spoke first.

"Mr. Calvin, the Imam will meet with you. I told him you are a sincere man of good intention. He is the man who can answer the questions you have come with. Your Mr. Valmer must have told you it is the Imam and not I who has the knowledge you seek."

"Yes. He told me you were his associate. I understand that to mean that you act as his 'palace guard' or chief-of-staff, if you will."

Tim was relieved that she had not taken him for a fool who had gone completely off the deep end.

"You understand correctly. The Imam is an important man, and he needs someone to screen visitors for him. Besides, your friend Mr. Valmer said you were a sensitive and intelligent man. I wanted to see for myself," she said with a smile. "Before we go, may I suggest the Turkish coffee. The Imam will meet us later. He is finishing a meeting."

The remainder of the conversation was less stressful, more warm and cordial, like an afterglow to the intellectual and emotional exertion of the past couple of hours. Juni's manner was less assertive as she spoke of the mounting prejudice and fear of Muslims and Arabs in America, even as the religion continued to explode in numbers there.

"You think of the mysterious plate as an ancient or regional thing from the far-away Middle East. But you should remember there are some eleven hundred mosques in the United States, and eighty percent of those have been started since the 1980s. Do you realize that about a billion people, a fifth of the earth's population are Muslim, and soon there will be more Muslims than Jews in America? You can see why the mystery of the plate and the tradition of the code can be so important to these Muslim Americans. It is not just people of the Middle East who might care. And not all Arab-Americans will react the same way. But this is something Dr. Haji will discuss."

As he listened Tim realized that had it not been for the crash course provided by Valmer's background briefs, there was very little he would have known about Islam, or the Arab people and their history. "We've got to get beyond stereotypes and media images," he said, thinking about his own role as a communications expert.

Juni nodded. "What America sees on its television screens and reads in its newspapers and magazines is usually the news generated by radical fundamentalists of both political and religious stripe, people on a mission of revanchment."

"We need to better understand the wealth of diversity that

exists in this country," Tim opined. "The next century will bring even larger changes. I wonder how well my daughters are being taught."

"I am sure they are being taught well, not just at school, but at home too. I mean, if their father willingly sacrifices a vacation to seek answers to a riddle that plagues all religions...."

She was so gracious, and for a moment he felt comfortable. In that instant his mind wandered to his family back on Sanibel, continuing their vacation without him. The distance between them, along with his appreciation for the seriousness of his mission, heightened his sense of duty. He thought of the knights who had brought the plate back from the Crusades, and of the knights carved on the lid of Valmer's special liquor chest. With this incredible woman from distant shores, intoxicating in personality and intellect and stunningly beautiful, sitting across the table from him, it was easy to empathize with those knights. He saw himself as being on a quest, far from home, a quest which he sensed would lead him far along the twisted alleys and infrequently-trodden footpaths. And this woman, for now, was his guide.

*   *   *

Hertt pulled his Mustang in behind the van as it turned onto Periwinkle Way. There wasn't much traffic at this hour; only a few headlights broke the darkness that was deepened by the canopy-like cover of trees along the roadside. As they drove past the Tahitian Gardens and the Periwinkle Shops , the dramatic lighting bathed the surrounding lush foliage, wooden bridges, and shopfronts, emanating a quiet splendor.

The parking lot at Jerry's was about empty. One car sat in front of the Pirate Playhouse. Hertt dropped back and slowed almost to a stop as the Calvin van approached the intersection where Periwinkle crossed Tarpon Bay and where Bailey's Market stood. The van turned left on Tarpon Bay and he let it move a few hundred feet down the road before he began following it again.

No cars were approaching on Tarpon Bay from the gulf. There was no one behind him, and the Bailey's lot was empty. This was the moment. He flipped the headlights on bright and flashed them on and off several times, then turned them off completely. Then he floored the accelerator pedal, and the Mustang responded with a roar and surge. He zoomed up behind the van, feathered his brakes, and nudged the van's bumper.

Laney had seen the flashing lights and was confused. She screamed as the van jolted from the rear impact, and she fought to control it. "What...?" yelled Elizabeth, bracing her hands against the dashboard.

"Mommy!" Katie cried. Cee's eyes widened in fear.

Hertt tapped the van again, and pulled alongside. Terrified, Laney looked down at the car and saw a man in a ski mask pointing a gun directly at her. He waved the gun to the right, motioning her over to the side of the road. Desperately, she looked ahead down the road, hoping for help. They were near the open wetland expanse known as the "Bailey Tract" and there was nothing—no lights, no cars, only the island darkness. Afraid the man would shoot if she tried to out run him to Gulf Drive, she pulled over and stopped the van.

Tim was beginning to realize that the Egyptian woman was even more complex than he had thought. She further mystified him as they waited for the valet parking attendant to retrieve her car for the drive to their meeting with Dr. Abu Shakir Haji. She stood close, with her arm entwined in his, her shoulder and hip resting against his. Her warmth, and the contact of skin on skin, contrasting with the cool breeze from Lake Michigan, filled him with sensations, a rush of emotion and a stirring of passion. He tried to dismiss it from his mind, but her gentleness and fragrance only compounded his confusion. He felt an almost overwhelming desire to hold this woman in his arms, to bury his face in her hair, to press her body against his. Tim knew that what he felt was in no way consistent with the seriousness of his assignment, and was at the least terribly inappropriate, but the urge was strong and primal. As he struggled with his feelings he trembled, more from nerves than the chill.

"Tim, you are freezing," she said, putting her arm around him, pressing her warm body against his. "You are not used to these Chicago spring nights. The lake breezes are much cooler than those from the Florida gulf, yes?"

Just then her red Mercedes arrived, and doorman and valet assisted them into the coupe. "Let me warm you up," she said, tilting her head down and looking at him with a wry smile. She turned on the car's heater and slipped a tape into the deck. The musical sounds of U2's *Joshua Tree* filled the car as Juni drove toward Michigan Avenue. She cut over to Lake Shore and headed north. The city was beautiful: stars glimmered over the lake, and the lights from the high-rises along the Gold Coast twinkled brightly. The warmth from the car's heater penetrated his chill and he stopped shivering. But his mind still swirled as he struggled to focus. Here he was with a wealthy Egyptian scholar of the Koran, riding in her Mercedes along Lake Shore Drive listening to an Irish rock band on the way to meet a Muslim holy man, all as part of a weird research mission to unravel the mystery of an old metal plate. What an odd set of circumstances.

It seemed unreal to him, like a scene from a movie, but he was all too aware that he was no passive viewer. For an instant his mind flashed on a picture of his family sleeping peacefully—little Katie curled up with her stuffed "rabbie," Elizabeth in the other bed, arms wrapped around her pillows, and Laney alone in the king-sized bed, as the surf rolled in with the warm gulf breeze. At that moment he wished he could stop things right where they were and return to the Tremont, lock the door and get into bed and turn off this strange drama.

Laney's heart was racing, her eyes wide; she opened her mouth to speak but was unable to. The car had cut in front of the van, forcing her to stop at the side of the road. There was no sound in the van, as all eyes watched the man darting toward them from the car. He wore a ski mask and all they could see of his face were the fierce eyes reflecting the van's headlights. He jerked the driver's side door open and shoved the gun against Laney's ear. The hard metal hurt; she smelled liquor.

"Do what I say!" he shouted loudly. "You kids in the back there, lay down on the floor—lay down now, both of you!"

As they did so, Katie started to voice her fear. It was neither a cry nor a scream, but a kind of pathetic moan, a small wail. "Shut up! Not one sound!" Hertt barked at them.

Laney and Elizabeth, immobilized by fear in the front seats, could do nothing. "Oh, please," Laney moaned. "Please don't hurt us. My babies..."

"Just cooperate, lady, and won't nobody get hurt." With that, he rapidly pulled off strips of gray duct tape from the roll that he had looped over his wrist. He grabbed Laney's hair and jerked her head back against the door jamb as he covered her eyes with the tape, extending the strip into her hair. Another strip was pulled over her lips, smashing them into her teeth and distorting her face as the tape wrapped around her cheeks to the back of her neck. Fear and the ability to breathe only through her nose made her breathing labored. As he shoved Laney forward and down into the seat, her hip struck the steering wheel. He yanked her arms behind her, wrapping them in tape too. She lay contorted on the front seat, her aching muscles straining. She could hear Katie in the seat behind her trying to control a whimper.

"You, blondie!" Hertt yelled at Elizabeth as he stormed to the other side of the van. He pulled off a strip of tape, yanked her hair, and covered her mouth. He shoved her over and forward into the seat, her face inches from her mother's.

"OK, blondie, put your hands up way high in the air. I want to see 'em all the time," he growled. Elizabeth twisted and put her hands up as high she could. "Higher!" he yelled. She struggled to stretch and, mumbling through the tape over her mouth, tried to tell him she couldn't go any higher. He grabbed her by the hair again and jerked her upright. The pain was intense and she thought he would pull her hair out. He straightened her up, jerking her like a rag doll, and shoved her head down between her knees.

"Now put 'em on the dash and leave 'em there".

Laney felt sick and helpless when she heard Katie begin to sob. Then to her surprise she heard the man say soothingly, "Don't worry, little darlin', I'm not gonna to hurt you. I'm just putting tape on your face so we can take a ride."

"Why are you doing this?" Cee demanded with haughty tone.

"You shut up or you're 'gator bait, kid," he snarled. "Who the hell are you?"

"I'm Celia Hockett. My father is Dave, and he will get you."

"Didja see what I did to yer house, Miss Celia Hockett? I'm keeping you for a trade," he sneered, ripping off strips of tape and pulling them extra tight over her mouth and eyes.

Juni guided her car onto the down ramp of a parking garage beneath a modern art deco-style high-rise overlooking the lake. A green space, a mini-park with neatly trimmed budding trees, formal garden, and elegant lighting gave the building the atmosphere of an oasis. She parked near the garage elevator which they rode up to the building's lobby. The building's entrance, all marble and polished wood and glass, overlooked the garden and across Lake Shore Drive to the vast expanse of Lake Michigan itself, giving it an airy, open feeling. Beyond the doorman and security guard position another set of double doors opened into an oak-paneled lobby richly appointed with oil paintings, gallery lights, magnificent oriental rugs, and deep leather chairs. A mahogany marble-top table set against the end wall, a gilt framed mirror above it, was flanked by a stairwell door and elevators. Looking around the magnificent setting, Tim knew this was serious money—the glitter of the "Gold Coast."

"You approve?" Juni asked with her enigmatic smile as they entered the elevator and she pressed the top button.

* * *

Hertt grabbed Laney by the hair, pulled her out of the car and half-dragged her along Tarpon Bay Road. Her knees struck something hard when he shoved her forward. With horror she realized she was being pushed into the trunk of a car. He carried Katie and shoved her beside Laney, and then he crammed Cee in on top. Their bodies were mashed together. Laney tried to rub what felt like Katie's face with her own. The trunk lid slammed shut. They smelled oil and gas, and despite the warmth of the night the compartment felt close and clammy. Muffled by the car's metal, they could hear the man yelling at Elizabeth.

"You follow me with no tricks or they're dead. You got it, blondie?" Elizabeth was shaken and near shock. Her mouth taped shut, all she could manage was a nod yes. Her only experience with violence of any sort had been on TV shows and in movies. With her mother and baby sister in the trunk of the car of a madman with a gun, she resolved to do everything she could to keep them safe. Hertt saw the fear in her eyes and grinned.

"You follow me, three car-lengths behind. No funny stuff or Mama gets it. Understand?" Elizabeth nodded again. He seized her shoulder, digging his fingers painfully into her muscles, and pulled her over to the driver's seat of the van. Grabbing the back of her hair, he pulled her so close she could smell the sourness of the whiskey on his breath through the ski mask. He stroked the barrel of the gun down her face and throat until it tugged slightly at the neck of her T-shirt. Her eyes bugged with terror.

"You're a real beauty, ain't ya?" he said with a chuckle, then shoved her away. He slammed the door, and waved the gun at her. "Now follow me and stay in the car till I tell you to get out."

Valmer was achingly tired, but his mind was so fully engaged it refused to acknowledge its need for rest. He had often felt like that while he had been with the CIA.

How far this had all advanced since a few days before when a former junior colleague called to tell him they had picked up reports that three of Khadafi's former intelligence officers were headed for his quiet little island. Ever since Calvin found the first Libyan, Valmer had been "operational." It had been a long time since he had been so into the game, and now he needed to reflect on the status of his mission. Calvin was in Chicago, Dave Hockett's house had been ransacked, and he himself had been under surveillance. Meanwhile Langley and Tel Aviv were ratcheting up their interest, Iran was sending a team to follow Calvin, and nobody yet had any idea what the plate was or what it meant. He sat looking at the print-out of the plate's message, reading and rereading.

Warrior of light who guards the south where Christ rules and judges enthroned to the setting sun. A second house on early spirit ground. Two sisters now reach for heaven.

For the love of God and all earthly issue. King of Ages here resides true light on sin.

Valmer's mind was on full scan. He considered old crypto systems, ciphers, and looking for a rhythm he reached back into dusty corners of his life.

All he could do was read the strange message, possibly a code, which had come down through the centuries—how many he was not sure—and ponder. Who wrote it, and what were they trying to say?

* * *

The elevator stopped its ascent, and the doors opened to a small private lobby. The top floor of the high-rise had been divided into two penthouse apartments.

Juni walked to one side to a key pad that operated the lock on the door, tapping in the combination. She opened the door for Tim and led him into the foyer, a two-story arrangement with a spiral staircase leading to a loft, a hallway, and what appeared to be a terrace.

"If you please, you must excuse me for a moment," she said. "If you would like to freshen up before meeting the Imam, there is a bathroom down the hall."

Tim welcomed the opportunity for a little privacy so he could steel his nerves before meeting the important holy man.

He was startled by Juni's dress as she returned. She was wearing a headcover and long white gown. She read the question in his face.

"I wear it out of respect for the Imam, and his wife and daughter who often are with him. They are not Western in their thinking and attitudes, and rather than confront and offend them with what they might consider to be my improper dress, I try to accommodate them. It's not such a hard thing to do."

They entered the large living room. Massive picture windows filled three of the walls, with the panoramic skyline of Chicago visible on two sides. A commanding view of Lake Michigan dominated the third, and Dr. Abu Shakir Haji and wife and daughter stood there, gazing out into the night sky. As Tim and Juni approached, Juni spoke and Haji responded in a Farsic dialect. His wife and daughter nodded to them both in silent acknowledgment and left the room.

"Beautiful stars tonight," Tim said, looking for an opening line of conversation.

"A mansion of stars, Mr. Calvin, as the Koran teaches, in the name of Allah, the Beneficent, the Merciful." Haji smiled and nodded his head in welcome. " 'By the night enshrouding, and the day resplendent, and Him who hath created male and female, Lo your effort is dispersed.' So Mr. Calvin, you have been recruited by Valmer. Years ago, when I was a young man, he also recruited me. He is a strange man is he not?"

"I've only recently met him. He is fascinating," Tim said, studying the cleric, who displayed no sign of emotion.

"And in only a short time he has you delving into matters of profound moral implication. Someone has been very acquisitive, and he has greatly dishonored Allah. In the Koran our blessed Prophet spoke of such things: 'As for him who giveth and is dutiful and believeth in goodness, surely he will ease his way unto a state of ease. But for him who hoardeth and deemeth himself independent and disbelieveth in goodness, surely he will ease his way into adversity. His riches will not save him when he perisheth.'" Haji turned to Tim and looked directly into his eyes. "Are you aware of the eternal consequences of hoarding and disbelief, Mr. Calvin?"

"By my tradition, it would be final judgment," Tim replied, wondering where the conversation was going.

"The Prophet warns us of the flaming fire," Dr. Haji spoke in a carefully modulated voice. He fixed Tim with a grave and solemn look. "I have been told of this Mr. Pasotti, vain and vile and a disbeliever. Tell me what you believe in, Mr. Calvin. It is important that I know before we can consider this old mystery you bring. Acquaintanceship is like a spreading tree. I must know your tap root before I can branch into the matters of faith."

Tim had prepared himself for this moment. He took measure of Dr. Haji, a serious man, dark eyes, full beard, and thin, the very opposite of corpulent. He saw before him a man for whom humor seemed to have no place.

He spoke of his life, of being brought up as a Presbyterian, at a time when school children often began the day with prayer, and of his knowledge of the religious history of America and the running issues of separation of church and state. Tim tried to impress upon the cleric his sincerity, and his full appreciation of the seriousness of the mission he had undertaken.

"It is important to me that you know I am not some flip Western unbeliever, interested in only temporal pleasures. I have more than a token faith, more than something which is turned on and off for convenience, like so many of the fads in our culture. I think these so-called new age religions are so popular because they require no real commitment. They have no theology, no solid foundation, no real history."

Well, he'd said it, and it was the way he felt. He could read nothing in the grave cleric's expression. The man merely listened passively, betraying neither agreement, disapproval nor understanding.

"It's a serious challenge for America," Tim added. "We seem to be falling away from our religious heritage. It's become a matter of priorities—most people don't give religion or faith much thought."

"I am not so sure about that, Mr. Calvin. I see Americans stamping religion on many matters. Abortion, sexual politics, cults, relationships of men and women. It seems to me that these are all matters of religion."

Tim recognized that discord and divergence were certainly parts of the reality of religion in modern America. "Well, there are people whose politics are motivated by their faith and whose faith may be very political."

"By their faith or by their religion? You are a Presbyterian, Mr. Calvin. Do all Presbyterians think alike?

"By no means."

"But you have similar beliefs on all matters of faith?"

Dr. Haji was forcing him to define what it was he truly believed.

All he had wanted from this man was information about the old metal plate. Some answers, clues to what it might mean. Instead he was being analyzed, tested.

"I'm sorry, sir. I am not a theologian. I'm just a guy who was on vacation and who was asked to help solve an old mystery. To do some research."

"Do not be sorry. You are not a theologian, but you are a believer are you not? I simply want to know what you believe. How do you see Jesus?"

"We see him different ways. That's why there are so many churches."

"Yes, of course, Mr. Calvin, but do not evade my question. This has much to do with what I have to tell you. How do *you* see him?"

"As an uplifting, wonderful teacher. He loved children, in

fact, he admonished adults to be more childlike. He was a joyful servant of the poor. A Redeemer and Savior." Tim was realizing, more than he ever had, that despite doctrine and theology, the perceptions and acts of faith themselves were very personal.

"Yes?" Haji said, indicating by raising his eyebrows slightly that he wanted Tim to continue, but otherwise remaining expressionless.

"I really haven't thought about it that much until now. I guess by comparison Americans are more casual, less serious about religion and belief than are the Muslim people."

"Which is perhaps why our friend Valmer has sent you to a student of the Koran, even though your mysterious plate is inscribed in the Latin and Greek languages of the Christian church. You see, Mr. Calvin, I know so many of you Americans see us—see Islam—as gray, strict, or as I heard one of your television ministers say, overly devout and too harsh. But, Mr. Calvin, we consider ourselves people of the Scripture, readers of purified pages in a world of disbelievers and idolaters. It is, in your vernacular, a serious business; we are about the work of Allah, the Beneficent and Merciful."

"You seem to be more devout, at least more stern. But it's undeniable," Tim said, "that among practicing Muslims there are no drug or alcohol problems, and you deal with crime harshly; people pray five times a day, life seems centered in belief. You know full well what is happening to the quality of life in the west."

"It seems so," the Imam said.

"You have asked me about my faith," Tim said. "In light of all the world's troubles with violence, and with all due respect, why are war and acts of violence so prevalent among Moslems? I would like to hear you explain why a messenger of God can and does advocate battle."

* * *

Elizabeth was in a near state of shock, but she followed the Mustang at the proper length, desperate not to get too close or too distant. She tried not to cry, but it was hard. She almost lost control as they passed the Mad Hatter, the source of so many fond memories and one of the great joys for her mom and dad. Tonight it was just another building on the side of the road that was leading her deeper into terror.

Many times she, Katie and her parents had driven past these secluded driveways on Captiva, wondering what kind of home stood at the end of the lanes. Now she was driving down one of those lanes, past thick foliage, curving around until the lights of the Mustang and the van shone on a magnificent modern new beach house. So this was where he was taking them. The place was bordered on both sides by Australian pines and surrounded by a high wall, boldly set on the gulf and affording a lot of privacy. The man stopped the car and got out and walked back toward the van.

*   *   *

Tim and the Imam had covered a great deal of intellectual and spiritual territory. Haji spoke of his admiration for Jesus as a "prophet and teacher, who was betrayed and murdered," and cited Old Testament evidence of "travail and pain." It was on the point of holy war, though, that they debated most intensely. For Muslims, Haji said, the revelation of holy war came when the clans of the Qureysh Tribe plotted to attack the Prophet Mohammed. He received a revelation ordering him to "make war on his persecutors until persecution is no more and religion was for Allah only."

"You see, Mr. Calvin, from the beginning Mohammed and what has come to be Islam was forced into times of what you call violence. The Prophet would have preferred to be just a teacher, to lead people in the ways of Allah and in peace. But the world forced warfare upon him. History has at many times forced warfare upon the people of Islam. Yes," he continued, "we would like to live our lives in peace. But peace as passivity leads to ends like crucifixion. This became clear to the blessed Prophet when his own people began to turn on him as the Jews had turned on their prophet Jesus."

Haji paused to study Tim and to center his attention. "It was then that Abu Bakr, whom I study, and the Most Holy Prophet fled Mecca for Yathrib, June 20 in the year 622 of the Common Era. It was the Hijrah, a clear dividing line in the course of the Prophet's mission. The years of humiliation and persecution were over. Until then he had been only a preacher. From that day on, however, he became the ruler of a state, small at first, but which grew to be the empire of Arabia.

"Here, Mr. Calvin, we begin to touch on events which could have some significance in your search for the meaning of your artifact, and for you personally. Even in his first year the Prophet made treaty with some Jewish tribes, giving them security, citizenship, and religious liberty in return for their support of the new state. But some among them wanted only a prophet who would give them dominion."

Tim was amazed at this man's depth of specific knowledge of battles and campaigns, expeditions and truces and conquests, of the Prophet's ideas of warfare and skills as commander. He tried to retain as much as he could of what Haji said as he spoke in intricate detail of the nine years of the Hijrah, the year of the Deputations, when tribes came from all over Arabia to swear allegiance to the Prophet and to hear the Koran. As Haji spoke of Mohammed's final pilgrimage to Mecca, of his death and the refusal of Omar to tell the followers, he began to show signs of grief. It was the first emotion of any kind that Tim had seen the holy man display. The piercing eyes were damp with tears as he recounted Abu Bakr's telling the Prophet's followers of the death of their beloved leader.

"Alas," he sighed. "The followers of Islam are still persecuted, and there are still unbelievers and idolaters and the force of evil still rules in many hearts. Where there is evil, there will be the violence we call war. Warfare against evil is a human condition. Did your mother and father not sing 'Praise the Lord and pass the ammunition' in the second world war?"

Haji's verbal skill had drawn him in, and Tim had to grudgingly nod agreement with a rueful kind of "you got me" smile.

"Dr. Haji, it would be impossible for us to see things the same way, in the same light. But we do both share a belief in a higher order."

"Yes, it would seem so."

"I think we both understand the human desire to reach for the divine, though we experience that force through separate cultures."

"I would say different cultures, but the primal human instinct remains the same, does it not?"

Tim smiled and thought he detected a hint of a smile on the Imam's face as well.

"So we have a common ground on which to meet as we worry about this old mystery, this arcanum, of yours. Mr. Calvin, I think we also both agree that sacred relics and artifacts do not belong in the hands of evil men like Pasotti." The Imam rose from his chair. "Please pardon me, Mr. Calvin, I must excuse myself for a moment. When I return we may resume our discussion."

Tim stood out of courtesy and thanked him. He watched as the old man leave the room a peaceful contentment filled him. Juni came to his side and quietly asked if his interview was proceeding satisfactorily.

"The Imam has answered questions I never even thought to ask," he said. "I think we can turn to the actual work at hand now.

"Can the girls at least use the bathroom, please? They're scared, and they're only little girls," Laney pleaded as they sat on a couch in the sunken great room of the beach house. Hertt, still wearing a ski mask, stood across the room, his gun pointed at the girls.

"First we're gonna get some house rules set up. One of you is going to be my collateral. If any of you tries somethin', the one I got is gonna be dead quick. You understand? Louder, dammit!" he yelled when, in their fear, they responded weakly. "You understand what I'm sayin'?"

"We understand," they cried in unison.

"All right now, all of you into this bathroom," he motioned to a room just off the great room, "and stay in there till I tell you its time to come out. Now move."

Inside the white marble bathroom, which had more than ample space—a gesture to the grandeur and extravagance of the house—Laney and the girls huddled together for comfort. They were all shaken and on the verge of tears, but Laney tried to appear brave and calm. Katie seemed dazed and hugged her mother's waist, burying her face against her. "Say a prayer, Mommy," she begged.

Laney did that, embracing the three girls and trying to maintain her composure. From somewhere in the house they heard a racket, a banging, like a hammer.

"Mom, he's just trying to scare us. It's part of the psychology of taking hostages. He wants us to feel helpless," Elizabeth offered.

"My father will take care of this. He will notice I am missing and he will take care of us," Cee said with an obstinate, pouting expression, and an assurance the others wished they felt.

"Dave, do you want to call Calvins to say good night to Cee?" Barb asked.

He checked the clock, and reacting to the lateness of the hour, answered, "Nah, they're all probably be in bed and asleep by now."

They continued putting their house back together, cleaning up the mess. Although he had calmed down and his rage cooled, Dave was aware that he was being driven to the state of mind acquired while he was in the Army—that of a warrior.

The old cold warrior Valmer clicked off the computer and moved to his leather chair. His shoulders sank back into the pocket formed by his body over the years, and his head dropped back in exhaustion. How much of my life have I spent here? he asked himself. How many nights like tonight, driven to the edge, an operation running, forces moving, and with a mystery clouding it all. The permanence of uncertainty.... He sighed deeply, trying to sink into an operative's nap, a quick respite from pursuit. Perhaps he could hide in a brief slumber—at least until the phone rang.

* * *

Once the intellectual bartering over issues of faith was completed, Dr. Abu Shakir Haji became a compliant source of information for Tim. He told him that in addition to the call from Valmer he had been contacted by members of the Iranian security agency. They too wanted to know what he thought the mysterious metal plate might be. Dr. Haji recounted that the UN commission he had served on had encountered stories of the discovery of artifacts and relics in an old chateau's burial catacomb in Normandy.

"Because records were poorly kept, and much of the find plundered, carried away by souvenir-hungry soldiers, there is no exact data on what may have existed there. But the photos you bring would lead me to believe the plate is the same relic described in the legends and tribal tales. It is reported to be an artifact of some power. Exactly what power, though, we do not know," Dr. Haji said. He and Juni told Tim there was no certainty as to the plate's meaning, but they revealed a list of possibilities.

Tim felt the same surge of excitement he had known long ago as a reporter. Only this time the notes he made were of something close to his heart—a historical mystery. As they spoke, he felt his adrenaline pumping. He made specific notes:

Haji/Khadija Theories—
1) A map giving location to
    a) gold/diamonds/jewels—some ancient treasure trove
    b) location of important religious artifacts, i.e., the
       Ark of the Covenant (these possibilities are endless
       according to Haji)

2) *A cipher plate to an ancient code used by a ruler or powerful religious figure.*

3) *Possibly an artifact from Justinian-the greatest of the Byzantine emperors. (Note: During his life from 527–565 the Greek Orthodox ruler compiled a written code of law; the plate could be part of that. Greek was the language of the Byzantine empire.)*

4) *Destination plate, an "address" indicating where important documents are stored. (A prevalent theory—the plate describes the location of a manuscript of great importance hidden at Mt. St. Michel.)*

5) *A burial plaque of someone of great importance.*

Tim had hit the wall, he was wrung out. His encounters with Juni and Dr. Haji had been torturous intellectual ordeals. He still had no definite answers, and leaning his head back on the sofa and sighing, thought about what he would tell Valmer. Iran was on the case, they had called Haji; Valmer might know what to make of that. And yes, the plate was indeed a priceless relic. He would have to go on to France after all, to Mont Saint Michel and meet with Valmer's other contact, Dr. Benjamin Stroutsel. Now, however, he just wanted to sleep.

Tim thanked Dr. Haji for the information and said good-bye as the Imam escorted him and Juni to the door. What a man! Tim thought. And what a night it had been. Like a spelunker in a wild cave, Tim had explored the deepest regions of his very being, and discovered intellectual and spiritual depths he had not known.

"You look very tired," Juni said as she studied Tim's face. "I can understand that your ordeal has deepened now. Let me get you back to your hotel so you can rest."

She drove in silence. Tim sat rolling his neck trying to ease his tension, and to clear his mind. She put Eric Clapton's *Unplugged* tape into the deck. As the song "Tears in Heaven" played through its emotional strains, the Chicago night passed by outside. The city was quiet now; few other people were out. The lake shore and Gold Coast slipped by, choreographed to Clapton's voice and music. Tim knew that this was a moment that neither one of them would forget. Their lives would probably never again cross, yet they both seemed to know this moment had become an indelible impression for both of them, belonging only to them.

The doorman at the Tremont waited at a discreet distance as Tim and Juni sat in the car. Unable to find words, they merely looked at each other for a long moment.

"What can I say?" Tim finally asked.

"Nothing," she replied.

He reached his hands to cup his fingers at the back of her neck, his fingers entwined in her jet black hair. With his thumbs he gently caressed her face from her cheekbones to her ears. He gazed deeply into her eyes with tenderness, wonder, and appreciation. She was so very beautiful.

Slipping her hands behind his head, she drew his face to hers, and pressed her lips against his.

She pulled way. "God bless you, Tim Calvin. Go in peace," she said as he got out of the car. He watched her drive off into the night and then turned to go into the hotel, thinking about the call he should place to Valmer, and the trip he would have to make to France.

"*Merci, merci!*" Valmer said, and hung up. The call had come from western France, where it was early dawn. Dr. Benjamin Stroutsel had been located at the Hôtel du Commerce in Carentan.

Stroutsel made occasional pilgrimages to the area of the D-Day invasion, and as he aged, his trips became more frequent, due in large part to his friendship with Marie Fouquet. Marie and he had a unique relationship, forged by the hardships and grief brought on by World War II. Stroutsel's entire family had perished in the Holocaust, with only himself and his cousin Golda managing to survive. Fate and the war had carried them to the west of France, where they became a part of the underground resistance, and where illness and exhaustion had taken their final toll on Golda, and she too had died. He had been seventeen, with a foot crippled by an SS bullet, and found favor with Marie's family which had for generations owned the hotel in Carentan, and who passed him off as a nephew in order to conceal his Jewish identity. Marie had been just sixteen when she befriended the young Benjamin. She became his best friend, his sister—no more, no less. The two young people, a Jewish émigré and a vivacious young French maiden, played a role by helping the invading allied troops. Their task was to listen for shreds of conversation or pieces of information, which they passed along to sources in the underground and a network of undercover operatives, one group of which had been headed by a young intelligence officer named Valmer. Benjamin and Marie finally met Valmer after D-day, after the German troops had been routed.

Today Marie still ran the family hotel, as she had since the end of the war, and Stroutsel frequently took breaks from his university position and UN work to return to Normandy and Marie, the only family he had.

As Valmer reminisced he could picture Marie and Benjamin, as he had known them during the war. He could envision them in the dining room of the hotel which her father had turned over to the intelligence officers of the Allies after D-Day, Benjamin so eager to help, and Marie imitating the manner of the officers to whom she served meals and pretending to be tough. She was the hotel owner's daughter, and that meant her orders were to be followed, especially by Benjamin. By the end of the war Benjamin had grown into a tough-minded young man who played a major role in the resistance. Marie had become a beautiful young woman, and Valmer had been smitten. There had been a brief romance when Valmer had been posted back for a week, to do some clean-up work after V-E day. For those six days and seven nights, the haze of the war and the devastation of Europe disappeared in Marie's beautiful smile and hearty laugh. So long ago it has been, he thought, but he could still hear the music of that laugh.

Soon Tim would see Valmer's friends and learn if the now-eminent Dr. Benjamin Stroutsel could help unlock the mystery of an even earlier time. He was certain that the Chicago trip had provided only a beginning for Tim's search.

The hotel manager smiled as Tim entered the lobby. "Good evening, Mr. Calvin. Is there any thing we can do for you?"

"No, thank you. I think I'll sleep pretty well tonight." Tim replied, getting on the elevator.

The bed had been turned down and a Suisse chocolate had been placed on the pillow. He thought of Laney and the girls as he put the candy in his travel attaché case. He thought about calling them, but a look at the clock told him he'd probably wake them. Instead he flopped on the bed and lay his head back on the propped-up pillows and sighed. Groaning, he realized he wasn't through for the night, though. Valmer would be waiting for his call.

He was so tired he thought he might just drift off, and call Valmer in the morning. He lay in a kind of reverie, astounded by all that he had done in this short day. Just that morning he had awakened with a bit of a hangover after the bizarre meeting with Valmer last night. Then there had been the canoe trip, the visit with Valmer, the successful hunt for Elizabeth's ring, and the departure and flight to Chicago. Topping all of it was the meeting with Juni and Dr. Haji which seemed now like it had been a week-long ordeal in itself. Yes, he would give the old boy a call right now, while the meetings were still fresh, and he could recall details about the Iranians and the theories. He would need to talk with Valmer about his plans for France. But he was so tired, so tired....

The liquor had begun to wear off and Hertt realized he was in the middle of something which could lead to a kidnapping charge. A federal charge—the Lindberg Law. He wasn't sure who knew this group he had was gone. If he were lucky it would be morning before they were missed. He didn't like the idea of being busted for kidnapping, but he had been quick and the snatch was clean. If they didn't figure out who he was, he would be all right. Still, he needed to hold these gals until Wasser was able to get here for the swap. The plane would get them out of here then. The thought of the bonus Wasser had offered him spun through his brain. This caper would be worth the risk—maybe.

Hertt was beginning to think he might just be able to pull it off after all. The captives were sitting on the large couch in the great room, and he could see they were terrorized by the ordeal.

"You—blondie! What's your name?"

"Eliz...Elizabeth," she stammered, clearing her throat.

"Take off your pantyhose," he commanded.

Laney's protective-mother instinct overcame her fear and she leapt to her feet to stand defensively in front of her daughter.

Hertt rolled his eyes. "Relax, lady, and sit back down. I ain't gonna hurt any of you. I got a job to do and it's got nothing to do with you. You're just part of a deal. You stay here until my boss gets that piece of metal your kid found. Now go in the bathroom and get your pantyhose off, kid. This mask is too hot and it makes me mad—and you don't want me to get mad."

"Why don't you just let us go and negotiate a price?" Cee asked matter-of-factly in her precocious way.

"And why don't you keep your mouth shut, freckles?" Hertt blazed back. "Or I'll find something to stuff it shut."

She crossed her arms, puffed her cheeks, and exhaled, giving him a look that was the equivalent of a round-house punch.

When Elizabeth came back into the room and handed him the hose, he pulled out a long knife and ripped them. Ordering the four of them to remain on the couch, he stepped up out of the greatroom and around the corner. When he reappeared, he wore a layer of nylon which smashed his face and contorted it beyond recognition. Katie fearfully moved closer to Laney.

He ordered them to the guest bedroom suite in the house. As they entered the room they saw the product of his hammering: the windows had been boarded up, keeping the captives from seeing outside. There was a large bathroom and small sitting room that contained couch, a television set, and a VCR. There were twin beds and a couch in the bedroom.

"You ought to be comfortable here. One of you will cook. You can all use the pool in the day," Hertt said as he started out of the room. "Relax, this ain't so bad. You got your own vacation house here." He shut the door, and they heard the sound of a dead bolt sliding closed.

* * *

"Yes, I have heard that Iran has taken an interest. I suspect it is only because of the Libyans, the man you found on the beach and the two who were after him and the plate. I can't imagine they'll do much now," Valmer said, knowing he wasn't telling Tim the whole truth. He didn't want to unduly alarm him. Tim was no professional in the world of international intrigue. "Tell me what my old friend Dr. Haji suggested about the plate."

"Several possibilities. It could be a map of some sort to an ancient cache of gold and jewels. Another option is that it's a cipher plate of a code used by a ruler, or pope. Close to that is the idea it's part of the codification of law that Justinian ordered for the Byzantine empire, which might explain the Middle Eastern interest. You had mentioned Mont Saint Michel; well, we got a hit on that, too. Haji said the inscription could be what he called an address, in code, to where some other documents are located. He suggested Mont Saint Michel. And he said it might just be a burial plaque. So we've got five possibilities. I figure the Greek and Latin are definitely some kind of old code." Tim closed his notebook and laid back on the pillows.

"That is quite an adequate list of possibilities," Valmer said. "But they are like Chinese boxes at the end of a maze. Dead ends to be avoided or navigated, puzzles to be pieced, unpacking to do. Tim, I've booked you on a 6:00 A.M. shuttle to Dulles."

Tim's heart sank when he heard the word Dulles. The thought of flying anywhere as exhausted as he was filled him with dread.

"From there you'll take the Concorde to DeGaulle International," Valmer continued. "I'm still working on your ground package. I think it might be best to put you on a bullet train rather than renting a car. Call me from Paris."

"What am I after first?"

"I don't know which makes the most sense, for you to head to Mont Saint Michel to check out the records there, or to go see my old friend Dr. Stroutsel to get his analysis. As another member of that UN antiquities commission I'm confident he will be able to help us open these Chinese boxes. And he'll be able to give us a view different from that of Dr. Haji. Let me think about it. But you'd better sleep now. In less than four hours you'll be starting a sprint race." Valmer clicked off.

The Atlantic Dash

The boards on the windows blocked the morning sun, and the girls slept later than usual. On one of the twin beds Katie slept in the protective curve of her mother's arm. Normally she was up and full of energy by seven, but the late-night ordeal and the overriding fear and paranoia of being held captive found her this morning retreating into a deep sleep, curled in a fetal position. Cee huddled on the couch in the sitting room and watched a program on PBS, while Elizabeth slept in the other bed. Laney lay staring at the ceiling and thought of Tim, far away on his trip. She wondered if he knew what had happened to them.

"I'm not getting an answer," Barb said to Dave as he brought cups of coffee to the table. "Knowing Laney, she's probably got them shelling. The storm brought a lot of stuff in."

Dave nodded as he sipped his coffee, looking around the house, back in order now. He was still angry at the thought of someone invading it. Why had he involved himself in this whole plate thing? Why had he let Valmer talk him into dragging Tim into it? It had seemed simple at first: figure out what the old plate was. He should have known, if the government couldn't get involved publicly then he and Tim should have stayed away from it too.

* * *

It was the fifth morning of his vacation and Tim Calvin was flying into the sunrise. He felt almost out-of-body. His sleep had been a fitful process of sorting through images; the lightning arcs across the eyes of the Thomas painting in Valmer's office, the penetrating eyes of Dr. Haji, the beautiful eyes of Juni with whom he had felt such a bond in so short a time. These images had all tumbled and clashed with his confusion in comparing the American concept and practice of religion to the devoutness and seriousness of Islam, the metal plate and its foreign inscriptions, and the images of Elizabeth in the mangrove as though behind bars and Katie's frightened eyes as the men on the beach ran and yelled. He was tired and sleepy, but he refused coffee on the flight trying to nap instead. It was difficult; his mind dashed around on a schedule of its own.

* * *

Laney was surprised that the girls had any appetite. They had been released from the bedroom and were gathered around the ultra-modern white kitchen bar, drinking fresh juice and eating toast. The elevation of the room, above the greatroom, gave them a commanding view of the gulf. The glass doors to the deck and pool had been pulled open and the fresh morning breeze blew in. Hertt was not in sight, but they knew he was near. The phones in the beach house had been removed, the unit in the kitchen pulled from the wall, leaving screws and wires exposed.

"After breakfast we'll go out to the pool," Laney said looking at Katie and Cee. She was trying to force a little normalcy into this crazy situation. Despite the beauty of the luxury home and the bright sun of the morning, she felt the fatigue of despair threatening to wrap her and the girls round like a blanket. The realization they were hostages filled her with unshakable dread, even though, ironically, the beauty of the island paradise met her eyes in every direction.

* * *

Tim picked up a bag of almonds, a couple of bottles of water, and copies of *The Washington Post* and *The New York Times* for the dash across the Atlantic on the Concorde. He hadn't noticed the two men who had left the Tremont right behind him. They had been on the flight from O'Hare, and were now at Dulles, remaining at a discreet distance. The middle-aged man had short brush-cut hair and was light-skinned. The younger was olive-skinned, and wore a close-cropped mustache and longer hair. Thoroughly occupied in watching Tim, they for their part failed to notice they had picked up a shadowing tail of their own as they hustled through the expanse of the terminal.

"I'll not trouble him with these complicating details," Valmer said over the phone. "The poor man is not a professional. His mind must surely be a jumble as it is and I want him to remain focused." He listened to the voice on the other end. "All right, Brooks, very good," he replied, and hung up the phone.

He rubbed his temples and forehead with his fingers, trying to assimilate the details of the phone conversation with Brooks, a former colleague at Langley. He had called to say an Iraqi free-lancer, a cousin of Saddam Hussein who was sometimes in and sometimes out of favor and power, had joined the chase and was now following the Iranians who were following Tim. An operations group monitoring phone traffic out of Baghdad picked up that piece of intelligence. The Iraqi operative, Tariq Abel, had been the target of interest of several security agencies and police forces for some time now. Abel was thought to have been a major player in assorted acts of terror, attempted assassinations, and extortions. Brooks had told Valmer that the analysts said Abel's cousin Saddam was a picture of sanity compared to Abel. A playboy, heavy drinker, and lover of fast cars with a possible cocaine addiction, Abel was quite adept at moving in the underworld of international terror and crime."

"And his assignment?" Valmer asked, knowing the answer.

"To determine what the Iranians are after."

Should he inform Tim? No, he had already decided. It was best to let Tim continue his course of action without further worry. If he mentioned any suspicion that he was being followed, then he could be told. Valmer tried to rationalize his decision by thinking that Abel was interested only in the Iranians and their mission. With any luck he would never clear that hurdle to move in on Tim.

Again there was no answer at the condo as Dave listened to the monotonous ring. He assumed the gals were at the beach, or more than likely at the pool where Cee was working on overcoming her fear of the drain. Elizabeth had offered to help her practice swimming in the deep end. He hoped Cee, who had inherited his fair skin, was well protected with heavy sunblock. After letting the phone ring a few more times, he hung up and decided he'd try again later.

Tim was baffled that Laney had not been in to take his call all morning. This was the third time he'd tried since getting into Dulles after nine. Probably at the pool, he concluded. He checked his travel schedule and decided he still had a few minutes before he needed to go to the gate. Maybe he would get a snack.

The pool was to the right of the large deck as you faced the gulf, and it was completely under screen. Hertt had ruled that the girls could play in the pool or sun on the deck but they were not to stray beyond those limits. The beach, and its access to others, was strictly out-of-bounds. Little Katie would be his "collateral," he said. He had told the girls if one of them tried anything, like making a run for it, Katie would "pay the price."

Elizabeth managed to get Cee and Katie interested in a game of splashketball. Laney joined in the fun, her attempt at assurance that everything would be OK. Hertt sat on the deck, cleaning his pistol and drinking coffee. He waited to hear from Ivan Wasser about the next move, and hoped it would be soon.

The flight was scheduled to leave at 11:00 A.M., and Tim was anxious to board. He tried dialing the condo again. After several rings he hung up and dialed the shop, where Barb answered.

"Good morning, a Touch of Sanibel."

"Hi. How are things down there?"

"We're fine, Tim. Where are you?"

"I'm at Dulles. Ready to take the Concorde."

"Wow!"

"Yeah. It'll be my first. I just want to get over there, talk to Valmer's people, get some answers and get back to sunny Sanibel. Still, it's kind of fun—in a wearing sort of way. Is Dave there?"

"No, he's on his way out to the condo. He's taking Cee her dress for dinner," she said. "Somebody will have to order the 'all you can eat' shrimp for you at McT's tonight. Sorry you're going to miss it. We'll go again when you get back."

Talking to Barb eased his concern and made him feel a little calmer. Still, he was a little miffed Laney didn't make a point of being at the condo when he called. He would have thought she'd be curious, that she'd want to talk to him. He heard his boarding call, so he said good-bye to Barb, telling her to tell Laney he'd call later, and hung up the phone. He walked to take his place as he and other first-class passengers lined up for boarding.

The middle-aged Iranian with short hair sat in the lounge area reading a newspaper and watching his young colleague follow Tim away from the phones. Tim had been so absorbed that he hadn't noticed the mustachioed, olive-skinned man on the phone next to his had said nothing, but had instead been listening to his conversation with Barb. On the other side of the lounge, Tariq Abel chuckled quietly to himself as he watched the watchers and their target.

* * *

Bright sunshine illuminated the island, its green mantle vibrant and fresh following the heavy rain of the day before. Dapples of sunshine broke through the lush overhead wispiness of the Australian pines, and Periwinkle Way was speckled with sunshine and shadows. Sweetness was heavy in the air, the blooming flowers and plants rich with the warming sun after the revitalizing showers. As Dave drove toward Tarpon Bay Road, the absolute beauty of the day began to ease his anger and tension.

This will soon be over, he thought. He'd return in a short time to his normal island state of mind. Life was too short for this induced anxiety. He stopped to allow a group of bike riders to cross before he turned off of Gulf into the condo area. It struck him as being odd that the Calvins' rental van was not in its usual spot. Why would they be gone in the middle of the best time to get the good morning sun? Laney must have had to run an errand and the girls might be in the apartment or at the beach.

The outside night-light was on at the third floor unit and there was no answer when he knocked. He took the elevator back downstairs and walked out to the beach. He looked north and south but saw no sign of the girls. He was perplexed. He couldn't imagine why they would be off somewhere, and he made a mental note to keep an eye open for them as he drove back to the shop.

For a thousand years pilgrims and tourists had journeyed to Mont Saint Michel, and for the last eight hundred years they had beheld with the awe the Marvel—*la Merveille*—the Gothic monastery crowning the granite mountain which rose out of the sea a couple of kilometers out from the Normandy and Brittany shore. Valmer's brief added to Tim's own personal knowledge of the place. Years before he had visited the magnificent spot, one of the locations on the planet which evoked an overpowering sense of grandeur and spiritual timelessness.

The Archangel Michael, general of the armies of heaven, celestial avenger, dispatcher of justice in fire and death, was the object of reverent homage paid in the architecture of the massive structure that towered out of the mountain. It erupted from the water with a power bespeaking the awesome force of nature. Saint Michael, God's warrior angel, pure spirit, and part of the inner court of heaven, was the angelic potentiary who had defeated Satan.

"Build me a shrine," tradition said he had commanded to Aubert, bishop of Avranches in 709. A century later, a church was built by Norman dukes. A Romanesque abbey came in the mid-eleventh century, and another in the thirteenth century, Gothic and lighter in style. The fifteenth century brought more building in the Gothic style, and so it continued through the ages. It had become an act of faith carved in stone.

This place had come immediately to Tim's mind when he had first read the translation on the plate. Valmer and Dr. Haji apparently also considered it a key element in his pilgrimage to solve the riddle. During his years as a history student he had come to know Mont Saint Michel as a place where ancient monastic records were stored, and where much of the essence of the middle ages had been incorporated in stone.

Now as Tim sped high above the clouds in the supersonic jet towards the past, he carried an ancient riddle which he hoped might be solved at *la Merveille*. He pulled the computer printout from his attaché and again read the translation of the inscription on the metal plate:

> *Warrior of light, who guards the south, where Christ rules and judges, enthroned to the setting sun. A second house on early spirit ground, two sisters now reach to heaven.*
>
> *For the love of God and all earthly issue, King of Ages here resides true light on sin.*

Tim held the translated text in his left hand, the picture of the plate in his right, and stared beyond both, contemplating. If any place could help decode the riddle and solve the mystery then surely this thousand-year-old masterpiece of architecture and devotion might. Mont Saint Michel had survived bloody wars between kings and dukes and had preceded and outlasted centuries of Crusades. It had endured the French Revolution and the ousting of the monastic order, which returned after the sacred monument had been defiled in its use as a prison under the tyranny of Robespierre. Finally, it had come unscathed through the modern evil of two world wars and their bombs, as though truly guarded by Michael the Warrior Angel himself. Could Michael be the 'warrior of light'? Tim wondered. The rocky mountain island faced the setting sun, the church, altar, and Benedictine order of monks had persevered for eight hundred years. Couldn't this be the house of the Lord to which the plate referred, where Christ ruled? The original church had been added on to, 'a second house on early spirit ground'; or perhaps the whole abbey itself could be the second house on the granite outcropping—perhaps the early spirit-ground as selected by Michael? But what of the sisters reaching to the heaven? And why would the Muslims care anything about this? Valmer had said they would be interested at the international level. That must be so, Tim decided, because clearly the holy man in Chicago was not surprised by his interest in the plate.

Tim's mind raced, but it was also tired. He returned to reading the briefing papers, hoping some sliver of information might provide the "Eureka moment" and reveal the answer to the mystery. By now the need to know was compelling. He had been captured by whatever drive it was that sent archaeologists and anthropologists on the quest for knowledge of the mysterious past. He knew this feeling of being obsessed all too well, and he knew he could not abandon the quest until he had the answer.

* * *

Laney was worried about Katie. The child had eaten almost nothing and was becoming listless. She had only half-heartedly participated in the splashketball game earlier. Later, rather than swimming with her usual vigor and playfulness, she had just stood in the shallow end of the pool looking out either to the beach or down at her feet, her small face devoid of expression. Once out of the pool she had curled up on one of the chairs and slept or simply stared blankly off into space. Attempts to soothe or reassure her set off a flow of tears and sobs. The little girl was clearly troubled and distressed.

From the time this child was born, Laney and Tim had known that Katie was a much more fragile child than her older sister Elizabeth. Whereas Elizabeth had always been a scrappy and assertive youngster, Katie was more passive. She was gentle and trusting and extremely sensitive.

Cee's attitude, on the other hand, had been more accepting of their situation, treating it as a nuisance, a minor irritation. Elizabeth had ingeniously engineered activities that at least kept Cee focused and engaged. By keeping her busy, Laney and Elizabeth hoped to stifle her smug and indignant sense of outrage, and bold proclamations that "her Daddy would get even for this." Her attitude and remarks could prove to be dangerous. Hertt made only periodic appearances, often from the window of the master bedroom overlooking the pool and deck, but they were unsure as to how much annoyance he would tolerate from the child.

Following a second call to the condo with no answer, Dave found his concern deepening. He tried to dismiss it, but it nagged at him that he hadn't been able to hook up with Laney all day. Surely it could be nothing more than coincidence. As he loaded his kiln shelves, he decided he would drive back out to the condo to check the beach and pool if his next call went unanswered.

* * *

Valmer, through his extensive electronic network, had learned that Israeli security and intelligence had been unable to locate Dr. Benjamin Stroutsel. However, there was new information on the Iranians and their Iraqi stalker. Israeli security had decided to send a field operative team to keep an eye on the Iraqi who was watching the Iranians, who in turn were following Tim. Valmer found this sort of old "cat and mouse" game amusing. Tim, of course, would lead the Israelis to Dr. Stroutsel, but Valmer decided to keep that close to his chest for the time being. It might give him an advantage down the road, he reasoned. He sighed and looked up at the El Greco oil of Thomas and his haunting eyes. How many times before had he sat in this chair, staring at that painting, though in other homes or offices in other cities, puzzled by details of intelligence or an operation. For all those years he had lived through, all the moves and their accompanying hassles, and now in retirement, as an old man, a mystery held him in its grip. Analysts and crypto experts had been unable to crack the meaning of the inscription, although theories were circulating in both Washington and Tel Aviv. Tim's "operation" was vital. The answer lay somewhere out in the field, near where the plate originated, perhaps Europe. Valmer knew by the building interest from Jerusalem to Baghdad to Washington that his inexperienced and amateur man in the field needed to find answers—fast.

* * *

Tim found traveling on the Concorde comfortable. He was mildly interested in the other passengers who could bear such expense on this supersonic shuttle, but he had no time to examine his travel fantasies. He had a job to do, a mystery to solve.

Even though Tim's original dream of doing doctoral research in the ancient monument's archives had been thwarted, he had been able to visit Mont Saint Michel with Laney while they were on their honeymoon. He remembered the majestic setting of the mount, sitting out in the water connected to the mainland only by a causeway, built by the French in the 1800s. At certain times of the year even the causeway was underwater and the only route to the island was by boat. Over the centuries, the sea had claimed, then subsided from, the small land bridge. The towering spire of the massive structure clinging to and claiming sides of the mountain was an awesome sight. Tim remembered the intricate, castle-like maze of chambers, chapels, refectory, and halls, as well as the winding stairs and roadways up and around the mountain to the Marvel and down through the village.

Valmer's brief noted that songs of Charlemagne's victories against the Moors had been sung of in the abbey. In fact, William the Conqueror's own minstrel had sung the tales while his master and Harold the Saxon broke bread together. They had gone to the mountain to seek the blessing of Saint Michael, which, of course, William later betrayed. Over the course of a millennium, kings and knights had journeyed to Mont Saint Michel. Now one lonely traveler was on his way to the Marvel, seeking the mystery of the "warrior of light." But not for a while. For now, the seeker sought only to slip into a nap, a respite from his self-induced expulsion from his island paradise. As he tilted his seat back and closed his eyes, he derived some satisfaction from the knowledge that Laney and Elizabeth and Katie were out enjoying the warmth of the sun and the Gulf of Mexico on the tranquil little island.

Island Darkness and
a Norman Midnight

Tim cleared customs quickly, carrying only his attaché and an over-the-shoulder bag. DeGaulle Airport, he thought, represented modern French technology. The domed satellite buildings and tube transit tunnels were like a cluster of nerves feeding a larger bustling main terminal and entrance to France. He found it surprisingly easy to get a cab to the Hôtel Georges V, or le Georges Cinque, as he directed the driver in his poor French.

The Georges V was an elegant hotel in old Paris, located in the heart of old French money. The Avenue Georges V was a short street, extending just from the Champs Élysées to the Seine river, a few blocks of classic and traditional Paris near the Arc de Triomphe.

As the taxi maneuvered through the crowded streets, Tim felt humbled by the beauty of the Paris spring night, but he couldn't resist the excitement that emanated from the lively boulevards and avenues. For the moment he was able to put the quest out of his mind, and he was grateful just to be a tourist in this beautiful City of Light. Coffee shops and sidewalk cafés bustled vibrantly, and cars sped by at a dizzying and sometimes alarming pace through the crowded streets. Lovers and sightseers strolled the lanes and avenues among the centuries-old buildings which were breath-takingly illuminated for the nighttime. The magnificent panorama of the Eiffel Tower with its plaza of fountains could be found just around the corner from the Georges V.

The doorman ushered Tim into the opulent palace that was the hotel. A high marble arch provided a grand entrance to a gallery lobby hung with massive oil paintings and tapestries acquired from various chateaus and castles. A private sitting area, small and elegant, was off to one side, and beyond that was Le Bar. The scene brought to mind the unwritten law of status practiced at the Algonquin Hotel in New York, and at others like it. In these certain important hotels, only the "right people" were permitted to inhabit these small private sitting areas. Here among the overstuffed velvet chairs and polished settees, the wealthy and powerful chatted and discussed their affairs in low, hushed tones, insulated from the general populace by unspoken codes and unseen boundaries. Tim didn't want to appear to gawk, so he stopped to rub his neck, rolling his head back onto his hand, in order to appreciate the decorated beauty of the lofty ceiling, its gilt chandeliers bathing this scene of grandeur in a regal glow.

He needed to call Valmer for instructions on how to proceed. As it now stood, he would first go to Mont Saint Michel, then rendezvous with Benjamin Stroutsel. In the meantime, he figured he might as well relax from the flight and enjoy the evening. He took a dimly lit table at the end of the bar and began to read the menu, chuckling to himself as he read that cognac ranged in price from 80 francs to 135 for the *cognac exceptional*. Tim wondered how a Vielle Chartreuse for 120 francs might taste. Some of the champagnes listed in the upper right of the fold-out menu ran as high as 900 francs. For a moment he thought of Laney and how much she would enjoy the beauty of this bar and the sophistication of its menu. Sighing, he ordered a vodka dry martini and asked for a phone. It was time to get his marching orders.

*   *   *

By late afternoon Dave's concern had turned to worry. His second trip to the condo, and the beginning of evening without hearing a word from Laney were troublesome to say the least, especially in the wake of the break-in. He could tell that Barb was worried too.

"You guys go over to the condo and figure this out. I'll close for you," June offered.

"Something is wrong. I can just sense it," Dave fretted.

"Well, let's try to not worry. Let's just go see. There may be a perfect explanation, sweetie," Barb said in an attempt to reassure herself as much as Dave, though she too was beginning to fear that the drive across the island would bring bad news.

*   *   *

The waiter handed Tim a menu from Le Princes, the Restaurant Gastronomique, "in case Monsieur might care to dine." The overseas call to Valmer had been delayed by a loaded circuit. Tim browsed over the incredible offerings on the menu as he continued to nurse his martini.

Laney was increasingly concerned about Katie, who had been moving slowly and refusing to eat. Elizabeth and Cee had used what few canned goods and frozen items they could find to put together a buffet-style meal, but no amount of coaxing could get Katie to take more than a nibble.

Hertt in the meantime had been busy on the phone with Wasser, setting up the details of making contact for the ransom. He was busy planning for Wasser's arrival later as well.

"You're hitting me with a complication here," Hertt complained. "I can't pick you up."

"I want you to meet me at the airport. It's that simple—you know I don't drive, so you've got to do it. But I don't like the idea of leaving the women there alone either, dammit!" Wasser snarled.

"It'll be all right. I got a room fixed up they can't get out of. And I know how to make sure they won't do nothing funny," Hertt said, thinking how he would take the little one along for insurance.

"Well, dammit, don't screw this up. Somebody's sure to have reported them missing. We'll have to handle this fast and get out of the country, got it?"

"Yeah. I got it. I'll see you at the hangar."

As twilight deepened, so did Dave and Barb's panic. No one around the condo had seen Laney or the girls all day, nor could anyone remember seeing the van. The porch light had remained on, and there were no signs of life around their unit. The Hocketts came to the sickening conclusion that something terrible had indeed happened: the gals had vanished, disappeared, and no one knew when. They could only speculate that they had probably been gone for quite a while. And to compound the situation, Tim was gone, virtually unreachable and unable to be informed. Barb and Dave were the only ones who could respond.

"Oh God, oh God!" Barb kept repeating. Dave was too worried to speak. Numb and sick with fear they headed toward Valmer's. He would know what to do.

Tim didn't know how he did it, but Valmer had called up a Rail Europe and a France Rail-and-Drive schedule on his computer. His dependence on Valmer was now absolute. He was in Paris, but his itinerary was being made on a computer screen on Sanibel Island.

During the course of their trans-Atlantic phone conversation, Valmer admitted that he was unsure about which would be the best route to the mountain monastery. He could either take Tim through Rouen to the north and west, where there were more frequent departures, or he could book him on a south and west course on the TGV bullet train to Rennes, where he could pick up a car for the drive to Mont Saint Michel. Yet another option would involve sending him to Caen for the drive to the Mont, then on to Carentan. Valmer read the times and prices and schedules out loud, more for his own information than Tim's.

"I've been quite preoccupied, Tim. I apologize for not having this sorted through for you yet. Just bear with me. But let's change our original plan just a bit. I think it best that you should meet with Dr. Stroutsel before you go on to Mont Saint Michel. Our 'friends' are still trying to locate him. Before you go any further, let's hear what he has to say."

"Locate him—by the word 'friends' do you mean the Israelis?"

"Indeed. Their interest has been piqued by the Iranians' curiosity. Maneuvers in that region always prompt an immediate shadow response. Each needs to be aware of what the other is doing, and both want to reach Stroutsel because of his expertise. Perhaps he can tell them the significance of the artifact. This is, after all, his area of expertise." Valmer hedged on telling Tim that the Iranians had picked up another shadow—Tariq Abel, the Iraqi—whose appearance on the scene had, according to Valmer's sources, particularly stimulated the Israelis' interest.

"Why don't you just tell them where the man is?" Tim asked, curious about Valmer's reluctance to divulge Stroutsel's whereabouts to the Israelis.

"It's better this way," Valmer reassured him.

"Have the Iranians made a move yet?" Tim queried, wondering if they might be following him.

"I think they are probably rather slow in catching up. Just keep your eyes open," Valmer replied noncommittally, evading Tim's question. "Ah yes, this will work," he said, quickly changing the topic. "Tim, you can catch a train to Caen, and pick up a car just a couple of blocks from the terminal. All of the sleepers are booked, but I can get you a couchette, an open bunk in a compartment in second class. You get a pillow and blanket, but they accommodate up to six. Or there are some first-class compartments open. I would imagine, with the sleepers booked, you would have greater privacy in a compartment."

The connection began to fade a bit and Tim was forced to speak more loudly, decidedly pleasing the Iranians sitting at the table behind him. Tariq Abel loitered just outside the hotel, admiring the exquisite furs displayed in the windows of the elegant furriers along the Avenue Georges V, the cab which he had hired waiting nearby. Like many of the wealthy Parisians who composed the clientele of the stores, Abel cared nothing for animal rights nor the arguments of the activists parading with signs and distributing pamphlets along the street. Unlike most of the stores' patrons, though, Abel had no regard for human life, either.

Valmer's dogs bellowed their welcome to Barb and Dave, alerting Jane to their approach. As soon as she saw their faces, she knew instinctively that something was dreadfully wrong. She led them into the greatroom and called up to her husband's office, "Come quickly! The Hocketts are here—something has happened!"

Too upset to wait for Valmer, Dave bounded up the stairs two at a time to the office. He got there in time to catch the tail end of the conversation with Tim.

"Call me from Caen or Saint-Lô—yes Caen or Saint-Lô!" Valmer repeated loudly as he and Tim gave up the fight with the fading overseas telephone connection.

Valmer had been too engrossed with his conversation to hear Dave's entrance, and he was now startled when he charged over to his desk. He was even more startled by the news Dave carried.

So Tim's first French rendezvous would be in Carentan with the old Jewish scholar, Dr. Benjamin Stroutsel. Perhaps he could shed some light on this dark mystery and expedite his research at Mont Saint Michel, or wherever else the quest might lead. The first move was to take a cab to Roissy terminal. There he was able to find a ticket clerk who, after admitting to speaking a little English, helped Tim purchase his rail and auto pass. About three hundred dollars bought him three days of rail fare and three days of small-car rental. The clerk had been positively effervescent in describing the five hundred and twenty Avis rental locations around France. She had also made a point of getting a signed acknowledgment from Tim that he understood he had paid local tax in the price of the ticket.

That business transacted, Tim paused to buy a copy of *The International Herald*, and then decided to grab something to eat in the terminal's restaurant while he waited for his departure. The pictures on the plastic menu helped him figure out the selections, and ordering a café au lait and croissant, he unfolded his paper and began to read. Out in the pavilion the Iranians, who were becoming increasingly interested in Tim's mission, also unfolded a newspaper and pretended to read. Tariq Abel walked right past them into the restaurant and took a seat.

Laney was beside herself with panic. Katie's terrified crying ripped through her, and Elizabeth clutched Cee, who seemed near shock. Hertt, who had told them he needed some "insurance" while he ran an errand, ignored Laney's frantic pleas to take her instead of Katie.

"Mommy—Mommy—Mommy—" Katie whimpered in metronomic desperation. She sounded like a child much younger than her seven years. Robotic and listless, she was already in terrible shape, and now was being ripped from what little security she had left. She could not begin to understand the evil and madness which had exploded so harshly into her life.

Laney continued to beat on the bedroom door after Hertt locked them in, begging him to return her child. As they heard his car drive away she collapsed, sobbing, into a heap of exhaustion and despair. Elizabeth sat by her side and curled her head onto her mother's lap. Cee huddled against them, wiping the tears from Laney's face.

"Don't worry. We'll get out of here," she said, but even her confidence was somewhat shaken now.

*   *   *

"The only reason the girls are gone is because someone intends to use them. They are a bargaining tool," Valmer said. "What worries me, David, is that they might be in the hands of an amateur. That would be dangerous."

"Why?" Dave demanded in a tight voice, his eyes fierce.

"A professional more than likely will deliver them safe and sound in exchange for the object." He was not altogether certain that was true, but felt he had to say it anyway. "I must think, however, that whoever is holding them has the skill to know the girls are good for barter only if they are well. That someone will have to contact us. When that happens we can prepare our response."

"Isn't there anything we can do now?" Dave asked.

"Nothing but wait. The girls are pawns. What I intend to learn is upon whose board they are being moved."

"How?"

"An associate of mine, Edward Earl, is flying in. He is a collector of antiquities and artifacts, but more importantly he is a collector of information. His is one of the sharpest legal minds in the country. He is a former prosecutor, and in his youth one of my 'boys.' I believe that Edward has the requisite skill to determine who may have sought to undercut Aoki Pasotti. There is no reason to believe Pasotti has a hand in this; it is not his style, nor would he be able to do much now while one of his men is in the hospital minus a hand, and the other two are in custody in Miami."

"So who could have Cee and Laney and the kids?" Dave persisted.

"Who indeed? Who arranged for the nefarious meeting on our gentle Island? That 'who' is probably behind the abduction of your daughter and the Calvin family. Edward will be able to gauge the depths of this. He will also be able to work with the Chief and the officers of the Sanibel police. I am sure they will remember him from his days as a U.S. attorney and will probably be relieved to have him take control, so to speak."

"Shouldn't we call them now?" Dave was urgent.

"Not yet. I am sorry, but all we can do is wait. You must trust me on this Dave," Valmer said with an increasingly heavy heart.

* * *

"Hush now baby don't you cry, momma gonna buy you a punkin' pie..." Hertt wasn't sure where the words were from or from what part of his life they echoed. It puzzled him, and as he thought he hummed and sang and patted the head of the little girl in the passenger seat, restrained by a seatbelt, but slumped over, sobbing and moaning.

"Now, now, baby girl, shush, shush, you little pearl." For the first time since Vietnam Hertt was experiencing an almost foreign emotion, tenderness and concern for another person. As he drove toward the airport, he felt compelled to protect and care for this frightened little girl. He was confused, and the nonsense rhymes he hummed were the only way he could think of soothing the child. "Now, now, you sweetie pie, your unca gonna take care of you, don't you cry..."

What the hell's going on here? he asked himself. Sometimes lately he felt like he was getting weird. These last few months with Wasser had been especially rough. When he'd first gone to work for him, he'd enjoyed the money and the power, the great car and the fancy townhouse. He could buy anything he wanted. But lately Wasser had become a screaming s.o.b., almost more than he cared to put up with. Wasser's abuse made him feel less than a man.

Hertt didn't mind the threats and the strong-arm work he did, but how the hell did he get where he was now—scaring little girls and setting himself up for a kidnapping charge? He sang a snatch of a song again—where did these songs come from? Something about them tugged at his mind, and he searched his memory as he drove into the Florida night, skirting Fort Myers, heading to pick up the boss.

Dave had occasionally wept for joy, but never had he cried from raw, paralyzing dread and worry. Barb's reaction was to withdraw into herself, quietly, almost inaudibly murmuring prayers. Dave drove along, wiping the salty moisture from his face. He felt helpless, but worse, he felt an awful sense of responsibility. He had been the one who had provided the connection between Tim and Valmer, thus turning the terrible find on the beach into an even more terrible, life-wrenching nightmare. And it was to him, as brother-best friend, that Tim had entrusted the care of his family while he was away.

He abruptly pulled the van off the road and into one of the residents-only parking cutouts along West Gulf. Turning off the ignition, he leaned his forehead against the steering wheel for a moment. He turned to his wife and lightly stroked the side of her face.

"Barb, I need to walk a while, to think," he said. She leaned over and gently kissed his tear-streaked cheek.

A gentle surf lapped, and its tranquil sound soothed him. As he walked along the darkened beach, the salt breeze brushed his face and filled his nose and lungs, acting like a tonic. He stood looking out to the horizon as a distant ship's light danced on the waves beneath the lowering sky. Dave rarely came to the beach at night. In fact, only vacationing friends from up north, or occasionally Cee, got him to the beach at all. He rarely saw the pink and purple glow of the sunset reflected over the gulf, or the twinkle of the early evening stars. One of the ironies of living in this paradise was the lack of leisure, of the play time to which visitors devoted themselves. He promised himself when he got Cee back he would make more time for the beach, for evening walks to listen to the whisper of the surf and tell tales of pirates long ago.

"We'll walk the beach together, Cee. I promise. Daddy promises you—we'll come here and walk and be together, sweetheart. I promise you."

Tim was impressed by the streamlined look of the TGV trains. He stood on the platform watching them come and go, thinking how unfortunate it was that American rail travel couldn't match up. Here French people of all economic classes could travel in convenience, and in comfort and style.

The bullet train would get him to Normandy much more quickly than he could drive there in a car. As he prepared to board his first class compartment, he made eye contact with an attractive young couple, the girl of medium height, perky with a cap of short, curly brown hair and a bright smile. Her companion was a tall man, with wavy red hair, a prominent nose, and intelligent-looking blue eyes behind round, wire-rimmed glasses. They both were dressed in khaki shorts and carrying backpacks and appeared to be in top physical condition. Probably hiking through Europe, he thought. He stopped and stepped aside to let them board before him.

"No, please, after you," she said. "We'll follow," the man added courteously.

"Thank you," he nodded, trying to determine the nature of their accent. Something about them struck him as out of the ordinary. They exuded familiarity, with an unspoken friendliness he found most unusual.

Katie had stopped crying and had fallen into a fitful nap as Hertt pulled the car up next to the private arrivals hangar. While he waited for Wasser's small jet to taxi in, he sat looking out at the action of the airport, now and then reaching over to pat the child's head. Occasionally she would whimper and sigh in her sleep, exhaling shakily as a child does after a long cry. Hertt gazed beyond the lights and planes on the runways, looking deeply into his past.

The realization was so powerful it caused him to jerk. It was as though his emotions, long numbed by war, prison, and violence had suddenly snapped back to action. He thought of Royena—Aunt Roy, his mother's older sister. He remembered himself as a sobbing child, curled in her lap. More nights than he cared to remember his mother, bruised and bloodied, would flee with him and his sister to Aunt Roy's. When his father, in a drunken rage, pounded the door and screamed and rattled the windows, Aunt Roy stood up to him, sometimes threatening him off with her shotgun. She had been a member of the Women's Army Corps, and in happier days the family had affectionately called Roy "the Sarge." She had spread her wings and protected her younger sister and her children with loving force and power. She would sing to soothe him and his sister, nonsense tunes and lyrics. Roy and her songs had become an escape from a cruel world, a lullaby retreat from a mother in pain and a father who hated. Tonight after years of a life of pain and misery, this little girl had forced him to go home, and again he had heard Aunt Roy's songs.

"*Hush, hush, little baby now, don't you cry...*" For a moment this poor little delicate child whom he had frightened beyond reason had suddenly become more important than Wasser or the artifact or his job.

Tim had the compartment to himself. Valmer had been right: the departure was late enough that most travelers opted for a sleeper or couchette. Tim guessed many of those people were probably bound for farther down the line, perhaps Cherbourg or the southern loop back toward Coutances, Granville, or Avranches.

If anything could be positive about this intrusion into his dream vacation, then the fact that his research mission was taking him to Normandy might just be it. A hale and hearty region, Normandy had a native population that was full of life and history. The province owed part of its greatness to the reign of William the Conqueror, an illegitimate child who grew up to be not only duke of Normandy but, after his invasion, king of England. A man whose thinking was advanced for his time, William had created the first system for ownership of property, and a legal system for settling disputes. As Tim watched the lights of Paris slip away, he thought how ironic it was that a cryptic and ancient metal plate of mysterious origin, an object of great lust by the lawless, as the Imam Haji had said, had sent him on a journey seeking resolution to its mystery in this land of early law. How long would it take him to get to the inn, he wondered. What will this Stroutsel be like? He hoped he could also give him some insight into Mont Saint Michel itself. The place was a history buff's dream, and that alone could make it worth his coming half-way around the world, leaving his family and vacation behind. He settled back and continued to watch the passing scenes of the outskirts of Paris as the train headed north and west.

Tim and Laney had visited Normandy, and he remembered the windswept land and its beaches. He hoped the light along the train route would be sufficient for him to see some of the magnificent architecture along the way: abbeys and cathedrals, fortresses and walls, châteaus and manor houses, and homes and cottages. Throughout the centuries Norman builders had exacted their own unique look and style. Brick and flintstone set in geometric patterns between half-timbered supports, massive sandstone buildings, thatched roofs, tile roofs, decorative tiles, stone walls, neatly trimmed hedges, and towering spires all came back to him as memories of this region. He sighed, unsure about what this visit to Normandy would produce. But he knew it would be close to midnight before he crossed into the province, and that he would miss the evening meal. And that would be a great loss indeed.

Meals in Normandy, he remembered, were a delight, because the Normans consider eating to be something quite special. The sea, the dairies, and the orchards were the natural resources from which Norman chefs create specialties like Dieppe sole with Normandy oysters, delicate saltmarsh lamb, creamy chicken *à la Vallée d'Auge*, Vire andouille sausages, boudin sausages of Mortagne, world famous cheeses—Neufchatel, Pont-l'Éveque, Livarot—and the incredible desserts—bourdelots, teurgoles, and Isigny toffees and apple sugars from Rouen. In their years of traveling, he and Laney had developed a deep appreciation for the many wonderful ways of preparing and serving food. He saw no reason why he should not enjoy the culinary pleasures of the region while he worked to solve the mystery. After all, it was one of the recreations of his life. He might be considered a good communications consultant and a fair tennis or basketball player; but as a fan of chefs and the culinary art, he was a blue-ribbon winner—one reason he was always battling his waistline. But now as thoughts and visions of Norman delights teased him, he pulled the bag of almonds from his shoulder attache, and opened another of Valmer's files on Dr. Stroutsel and Marie.

The last colors of the sunset had faded and the sky was star-filled as Dave and Barb walked away from the beach. She had joined him, and they had walked, arm in arm, remembering when they had first come to the island.

"This is where we used to walk when I was pregnant with Cee. Remember? Until I got too big," Barb said, looking up at Dave.

"Then we would bring the beach chairs and just sit and listen to the surf."

"It was such a release, after all the building you did, and the clay you were throwing. I remember how some nights you would fall asleep out here in the beach chair."

"I think that's why Cee is such a beach lover. She was used to hearing the surf even before she was born," Dave said, blinking away tears. "We're going to get her back, Barb. We have to."

She put her arms around him and held him close. "We will, Dave, we will," she said. "It's going to be OK. Things will work out—I'm positive." Her quiet assurance calmed him.

They drove to the Mad Hatter, where their dear friends Brian and Jayne were in the process of greeting the first group of the evening's dinner customers. Barb waited in the car, while Dave walked back to the kitchen entrance and signaled to get Brian's attention.

Brian's ready smile dissolved as he listened to Dave's story. Jayne, darting into the service alcove between the kitchen and dining room, caught a glimpse of Dave and her husband huddled in conversation. She joined them, her cheerful expression turning to one of concern when she saw their grim faces.

"Have you seen or talked to Laney Calvin today?" Brian asked her.

"No. Why?"

"Laney and the girls are missing. Cee was with them," Dave said. "They're gone—vanished. We've looked everywhere and can't find a trace."

Jayne's face turned chalky. "Where could they be?"

"Dave thinks they might have been kidnapped," Brian told her gently.

"Oh God, no!" Jayne's gasp drew quizzical looks from the kitchen staff. She ran outside to where Barb waited in the car, and the two women held each other and cried.

Katie woke up when the car door opened. She sat up and rubbed her eyes, looking sleepily around, puzzled by her surroundings. As memory returned, her face became masklike, emotionless, and she stared blankly out onto the airfield. While Wasser put his bag in the trunk, Hertt spoke gently to her.

"Little darlin' I want you to ride in the back seat, OK? I'm going to take you back to your mommy." This drew a response, and Katie looked at him inquisitively. She had not seen the man who held them captive without a mask on his face, but she instinctively knew that this was he. But that man had been so mean, and now he seemed nicer.

"You damned fool! I don't want that little bitch to look at me. She can identify you now!" Wasser shouted from behind the trunk lid.

"I can't sit here outside a public airport with a mask on, can I?" Hertt barked back. "Besides, she's only a kid and she's scared to death. She's not going to hurt us."

"Well, cover her damned face, then. She's not going to see me, you idiot." Wasser turned with his back to the car and waited as Hertt gently lifted Katie over the back of the front seat and into the back.

"Now, Katie, we're going back to Mommy. But we gotta play a little game. I'm going to cover your eyes, and you see if you can tell

me when we get back to the beach. OK?" He was becoming concerned by her appearance and her lack of response. She is just in a
kind of shock, he rationalized, she's OK. But the distance in her eyes,
the way they seemed to look beyond him, worried him. She also
seemed terribly weak, and her breathing was heavy.

"Mommy? Rabbie?" She whimpered as he covered her eyes
with the tape, gently this time, pressing just enough for it to stick to
her temples. He wanted to be sure it wouldn't hurt when it was
pulled off later. The little girl lay down and curled up on the back
seat, gathering some of her T-shirt up around her face and mouth,
almost as though she wanted something to suckle.

"I want to get her back to the beach. I shouldn't have brought
her. She ain't doin' too well," Hertt said, sliding in behind the steering wheel.

"I don't care what the hell you do with her. All I want is that
piece of metal. Once I get it I'm outta here. Then I'm going to name
the price, and if Pasotti doesn't pay, I know who will," Wasser said.
"You got any booze left or have you cleaned out the closet?"

"There's plenty," Hertt said, looking over his shoulder at the
pitiful sight of Katie, huddled in fear, her eyes covered by the gray
tape, and clutching the wadded front of her shirt as though her life
depended on it.

    The tight comfortable, thickly-cushioned seat and the hum
of the rails lulled Tim to sleep. Since he had the compartment to
himself, he propped his feet up on the facing seat and lay his head
back. His last thought before drifting off was to wonder why Monet
had chosen to live in this part of France, in Giverny. When he
awakened, he figured that must have been the reason why he had
just dreamed of Monet's garden as it had been painted by the master.
It must be a kind of defense mechanism against his somewhat self-
imposed exile to the inside of planes, terminals, cars, hotels, and
now this train, all of which had been his reality since his departure
in the rain from Sanibel. The nap did little more than make him feel

groggy and sluggish, and as the train stopped, he was also feeling a little sorry for himself.

The walls of the terminal at Caen were festooned with posters and advertisements celebrating the history of this capital of William the Conqueror's Normandy. Visitors were invited to see a variety of sights including a feudal castle, the fine-arts museum, the museum of Normandy, and the war memorial. Then there were the churches—Saint Peter, Saint John, Saint Michael, the eleventh-century church of Saint Nicholas—and the mansion of the Hôtel d'Escoville, ancient abbeys, gardens and other notable buildings and sights. It was late and the station was nearly empty, but the brightly-colored posters gave the stairs and walls a touch of light and vitality. Tim noted a wall display that mapped the short route to the car rental counter.

As he walked, he sniffed the drifting aromas from nearby bistros and restaurants. Caen, just a few kilometers south of the English channel, had a feel and fragrance heavier than that of Sanibel and the Gulf of Mexico, and he noticed a different kind of scent on the sea breeze here. He looked at his watch and calculated the time difference. Well, Laney and the girls and the Hocketts had probably just finished a dessert of mud pie at McT's and were sitting on the patio having a nightcap. He decided to them call from the car-rental agency.

Katie acted almost as if she were in a trance, or sedated. Her movements seemed labored, and she struggled just to walk. She said very little and would not respond to Laney's repeated attempts to engage her in conversation. She simply clung to Laney, or lay next to her. Katie still refused to eat, and Laney feared she would become weak, possibly dehydrated. Thankfully, Laney had been successful in coaxing her to drink a bit of the fresh-squeezed orange juice Hertt had given them.

Pressing her ear to the door, Laney could not make out what the two captors were saying, but she could tell by their shouting that they were arguing. She guessed the man who had come back with Hertt was the one in charge, and she figured things would really begin to happen now. If what Hertt had said was true, then a swap might take place soon. But judging from the sounds of the argument her apprehension grew that the new man might become violent. That frightened her.

* * *

As Tim approached the rental agency, he could see through the glass door that the clerk was watching television. The staccato dialect and laughter from the set mixed with the clerk's laughter. Tim couldn't understand the punch lines, but he could tell by the sounds that a comedian was working an appreciative crowd. The clerk, tall and looking to be in his late twenties, wore a name tag identifying him as Jean. He eyed Tim somewhat grudgingly, then looked past him at the door. Tim turned to follow his gaze and noticed several other people coming in to line up at the counter as well.

"*Merde!*" Jean muttered. Tim didn't know what that meant, but assumed it to be an expletive of some sort, in response to the sudden rush of business from the train just in from Paris. Tim recognized the young backpacker couple who had boarded the train with him. They smiled in greeting and took a place in line behind him. They also carried a France Rail-and-Drive pass. Behind them stood a middle-aged man in glasses, a young man with a dark complexion and mustache, another middle-aged man, also dark, a woman with two children, and another man whom Tim thought looked amazingly like Saddam Hussein.

Jean was becoming impatient with Tim's attempts, using a phrase book and map, to tell him where he wanted to go. Fortunately the young woman standing just behind Tim could speak French. "Please, perhaps I can help," she said, as she intervened and translated for him. She told Tim that she and her husband were also traveling through what she called "D-Day country." He thanked her and they wished each other well, and Tim walked over to the nearby bank of phones.

It took some doing, but he was able to get an operator who spoke a little English and they placed a call to Sanibel. There was still no answer at the condo. Disappointed, he figured they must not be back from dinner yet. What tough luck, certainly an odd set of coincidences, they had not made contact yet. He asked the operator to try another number in the same area code and gave her the Hock-etts' number. After a few moments of clicks and other noises she informed him that all the circuits were busy and he would have to try later. He sat for moment thinking about his next move. The olive-skinned, mustachioed young man was talking loudly, almost excitedly, on the phone next to him. Tim glanced over and noticed his young car-rental rescuer's husband listening intently to this end of the conversation. If she could speak French and English, as well as her native tongue, he thought with some amusement, and her husband could interpret this apparently Middle-Eastern dialect, they were quite an accomplished couple.

Brian and Jayne went back to work at the restaurant, trying to act normal and be gracious hosts. It was very difficult for Jayne, who was unusually close to Cee, almost like a big sister. Barb and Dave drove home to wait in case the kidnapper called. He knew he couldn't go to the police until he had a full scope of the situation, and had dealt directly with whoever was responsible. But he couldn't wait forever. They'd have to call eventually, and he hoped it would be soon.

Dave wondered if he would have trouble controlling his anger, but he knew he must. Cee's well being, and that of Laney and Elizabeth and Katie, depended on his self-control and alertness.

Tim gathered his bags and headed for his rendezvous with Dr. Benjamin Stroutsel, and what he hoped would be some light on the long, dark mystery attached to the plate. He flipped open the Michelin map to chart his route. He could take Highway D-9 south through the little villages of Tilli and Balleroy to Saint-Lô, and then up to Carentan, or he could take the main highway up to Bayeux. An ancient city with many houses and mansions, it was built between the fifteenth and eighteenth centuries. The young backpacker had told him she and her husband were planning to visit the famous Bayeux Tapestry embroidered by Queen Maltilda in the eleventh century. One of Valmer's notes had made mention of Bayeux's ancient religious heritage and the museum of the 1944 Battle of Normandy located there. The old urge to see these particular relics of the past drew him, even though he figured it would be too dark to see much of anything unless some of the famous châteaus were well lighted. Still, it looked to be a quicker trip from Bayeux up to Carentan. He made a note to backtrack to Isigny to buy toffees for the girls.

He found his rented Renault V in space number seven. It was a smaller car than the one he drove back home, but it would be perfect for driving along the cramped roads and through the narrow-streeted villages of Normandy. As he backed out and turned toward the roadway, he saw the young backpackers, who waved to him as they walked to their car. He was mildly curious about them, some of his old reporter's instincts kicking in. They must be newlyweds, he thought, trying to avoid acting too romantic. Maybe it was their culture, which he guessed was Near or Middle Eastern, judging by their accents when they spoke English. They were certainly in good shape—it must be the hiking.

Tim followed the signs to the highway and began his night-time drive through the historical countryside, toward the area and towns of the D-Day invasion. Valmer said he had known this area as a young intelligence officer in the war. It was a history lover's dream. In the centuries after William the Conqueror, it had been the land of the knights of the Crusades. And even before the Conqueror, the scene of fierce battles between Norse invaders and half-Romanized druid warriors. After June of 1944, although much of this area had been devastated by world war, a sense of the ancientness of this land prevailed. The past was an almost tangible presence to Tim as he drove through the blanket of darkness. Speeding on toward Carentan, he hoped Dr. Stroutsel held the key that would unlock the ancient arcanum that had brought him here.

As tired as he was, the drive both calmed and relaxed him, and he drew some strength from the silent journey past the neat and linear stone farm walls and lines of trees. Along the country highway, over gentle hills and past sleeping villages, the look and feel was so unlike anything he knew at home. He began to reflect on issues of eternity, aspects of human ascendancy, and the monumental fragments of history that had been played out or undertaken on this terrain. He felt himself being swept into an even deeper historical vortex. Why was he, a lifelong Presbyterian with what he believed was a deep but nonetheless relatively simple faith, trying to decode some ancient analog of Christian theology, an arcane riddle? Wasn't it preposterous that a middle-class Midwesterner, born in the middle of the twentieth century, was now like a pilgrim on a medieval backroad seeking help from an Islamic holy man and a Jewish scholar in hiding? His only rationale was his burning curiosity and a desire to convey the significance of the past to the present day, the same urge which had drawn him as a kid to museums and issues of *National Geographic*, and driven his study of history throughout college. He discovered with a shock that he was finally coming to terms, a kind of truce, with himself. The passion had been unbridled, and the regret he'd nursed since the demise of his academic career evaporated as he drove through the darkness.

Another night of vacation merriment on the islands of Sanibel and Captiva found restaurants full, and couples and families strolled the night beaches. Swimmers lolled in illuminated pools and spas, getting in the last soak of the day, and blissful vacationers idled on screened porches. Conviviality was the order of the day.

But the moods in a secluded beach house on Captiva and a low-slung bungalow on Sanibel were neither blissful nor cheery. The fate of a woman and three girls was the preoccupation in both places. Wasser had decreed that the potter would be called first thing in the morning. It would be a simple exchange—the metal plate for the females—somewhere near the airport, maybe at the hangar itself. He toyed with the idea of having the captives on the plane. If the deadline passed, he could simply fly them away and up the ante, but that would increase the risk and hassle. He sat on the deck, drinking Chivas over what he called "foul tasting" ice and continued to work over the details in his mind.

Hertt was deep into the Makers Mark again, though twice he had excused himself to ask through the door about the "little darlin'." He had been told she was sleeping. The second time he asked there had been no answer.

Barb was pretending to sleep, Dave knew, hoping somehow that would put him more at ease. But he was nowhere near sleep. He lay there feeling helpless. If only he could see the enemy's face, know his location, gauge his strength—then he could do something. Instead he was prone, forced to merely wait for the attack, without defense.

He got up and walked to Cee's room. He looked at her wall of pictures, a montage of her life: her first nursery picture, the little stroller, her first preschool play; sandcastles on the beach, the little red jumpsuit, her first day to throw clay, with Grampa John on her bike. Emotions overwhelmed him as he studied the smiling pictures of Cee and Katie, young and vital and unsuspecting of evil in the world. Evil which now held them prisoner somewhere—where, only heaven knew.

Tim had seen only a handful of other vehicles on the night drive. His had been the only car on the curves and winding stretch from La Cambe, around the bends and down across the river at Isigny-sur-Mer. A full moon had risen, and its luminescent glow made the drive along the otherwise unlit road a pleasure.

Just outside the picturesque fishing port, as the road stretched up through rich dairy country, he looked in the rearview mirror and noticed two sets of lights some distance behind him, or at least he thought he had seen two. From the crest of a hill looking down on the channel where the fishing boats were docked, he could see the ribbon of road wandered down into the port town from the north and east. From this hill he saw a set of headlights coming from behind, making good speed. He stopped so he could look back more carefully, and what he saw gave him pause. Indeed, further back on the road, around a hill and a bend, not visible to the speeding car, was another, also moving with some haste. But it was running at a distance and without its headlights on. Now and then the lights would flash on and then go dark, only for the car to reappear farther up the road with lights back on for a moment, and then disappear again into the darkness. He felt a warning tingling on the back of his neck, but shrugged and gave it little more thought as he drove on to Carentan.

Tim had found the brief on Benjamin Stroutsel and Marie Fouquette fascinating. He had detected an uncharacteristic fondness in Valmer's notes about these two people. Tim wondered if perhaps Valmer had been overly sentimental in sending him here. He hoped Valmer hadn't overestimated Stroutsel's ability to understand the meaning of the plate and its inscription. At least the man might be able to direct him to whichever dusty old library of antiquity might hold the answer. Despite the thrill of the enterprise, Tim was eager to get the answer and get on with his life.

As he slowly drove through the deserted streets looking for the hotel, Tim took note of the village. Constructed mostly of stone, in a variety of colors and textures, the buildings all shone with the soft, pale glow from the streetlamps and opaque-glass lantern-style lights which hung from many of the old buildings on iron and metal supports. The lights had been converted to electric, but with a little imagination he could envision the original gaslights, the flare from the lamp lighter's wick igniting the Norman midnight. The shops were dark, the windows bare or shuttered, and wooden signs hung overhead like sentries, their occasional creaking in the night breeze the only sound.

What looked like a hog's carcass hanging on a hook in a butcher shop window cast an eerie shadow in Tim's headlights as he steered around a gentle bend into another row of shops and homes. Lights burned in the windows along the narrow lane. The ancient street wasn't much over a car's width across, and a stone sidewalk, only inches wide, was the only buffer between the stone pavement and the sides of the buildings. Tim felt as though he could reach out of the car window and touch the walls. If two cars were to meet head on, one would have to hug the curb or even pull up onto the sidewalk in order to pass. He passed a brightly-lit building and sniffed the enticing aroma that came from it—the bakery, and someone was at work so the village could wake to fresh loaves. The village resembled a tourist poster with its well-scrubbed look, decorative flower boxes, iron fences and gates, and neat lawns and gardens.

The Hôtel du Commerce was just off the center of the village. Bounded by a small gravel parking lot, iron fence, and stone wall, the gate opened onto a stone walkway which wound to a large wooden porch, up just one step from the walkway. Windows with small wood-framed panes were hung with lace curtains, and featured window boxes and planters full of blooming spring flowers. The building was pure Norman architecture, stone and wood. To Tim, the hotel was the very picture of charm. A metal shield was attached to the wall next to the heavy wooden door, and he noticed that it was the Gourmande Shield, an indication that great things happened in the kitchen of the Hôtel du Commerce.

Would others show up here in Carentan? He knew the Mossad was looking for Stroutsel, and he figured it probably wouldn't take them much longer to learn where he was. There were also the Iranians. He remembered the two cars on the road behind him, one with off-and-on headlights, and wondered if they might be connected to the Iranians and the Israelis. He also couldn't help wondering if and when their paths might all cross, and whether he would recognize it when it happened.

What he could not know was that other travelers did indeed move into Carentan that night. The young couple Tim thought were backpackers had taken a room at a bed and breakfast only a couple of blocks from the Interhotel, which now in actuality lodged the two Iranians. Before retiring for the night, the man and woman had watched from a safe distance as the two men made a circuit of the village, pausing for a moment when they spotted Tim's car at the Hôtel du Commerce. They then followed the men to their hotel and took up an observation point behind a low stone wall. The two became especially alert when a man on a motorcycle stopped his bike in the shadows of the Interhotel parking lot and produced something from his pocket which he appeared to tap as though it was a calculator. He looked around furtively, despite the late hour, as though checking to be sure no one was watching, and went to the car the Iranians had driven, scooted under the trunk, and lay there for a moment. The young woman caught a good look at the man's face and her companion was able to capture it on film; they stared at each other in wide-eyed recognition, then continued to watch as he remounted his motorcycle and rode off. It was Tariq Abel, a terrorist on whom they had plenty of intelligence. He had a peculiar penchant for the baser pleasures of the of the flesh, and they presumed he was off to someplace near where liquor, drugs, and women could be found. They retired to their room to contact Tel Aviv with their news on the location of the much sought-after terrorist.

Tim walked into what looked as much like a parlor as a hotel lobby. Standing next to the front desk, he heard a male voice speak briefly, and what sounded like shuffling steps upstairs. The sound of a woman's voice singing in French drifted from another room, on tape or a record perhaps. A small lamp glowed at one end of the counter, and more lights illuminated a step-down room to the left, apparently a sitting-room, with couches and chairs, and tall windows that opened to the grounds hidden behind the tall stone wall out front.

A lamp with an old, dome-shaped, etched-glass shade burned at the top of the stairs, which began on the wall that divided the lobby and the sitting room. An arched entrance next to the counter drew Tim's attention. Heavy velvet tapestry-like drapes, their braided tie-backs looped on hooks, hung down across the arch, blocking the room from view. Light crept out over the top and beneath the curtains, as did the singing voice.

Tim moved close to the curtains and parted the opening slightly so he could peek through. He saw what looked like a dining room, or rooms, with tables set with linen cloths and silverware. Antique chests and cupboards lined the walls.

A woman came into the room from around the corner beyond Tim's view. This was surely Marie, he thought. She was a big woman, buxom, wearing black slacks, high heels, and a silky-looking white blouse. Her full, thick hair was a champagne blonde, tinted probably. By Valmer's calculation she was in her mid- to late-sixties, though from this distance and in this light she looked younger. She turned, facing the curtained arch, and set a bottle of brandy on the table beside her. With her right hand on her hip, she tossed her head, causing her hair to undulate softly, and stood looking over her left shoulder as if posing. She was a beautiful woman, big, strong, and full of energy. He sensed, in just this glimpse, that she had indeed been vitalized by the life she had led. What stories she could tell, Tim thought—a beautiful French teen-ager who had fought in and survived the war! Nevertheless, it must have taken a toll. He watched as she lifted the bottle, poured the liquor into a snifter on the table, and downed the drink in a single gulp.

Feeling somewhat guilty, as though he had been spying, Tim

retreated to the front desk and tapped the service bell. The small tinkle was lost in the plaintive singing coming from the room behind the curtains. He waited for a pause in the singing and tapped again a couple of times.

"*Oui, oui—un moment,*" came from the room. The curtains parted and Marie emerged. Hands on her hips, she stood looking at Tim as if appraising him. At this closer range he could see that her face bore the record of an often difficult life. Still, she was a lovely woman, and her eyes flashed with zest.

"You must be M'sieur Tim," she said with an accent that captured the poetic ring of the French language. "Valmer phoned to tell me of your arrival. Please, come into the light where I can see you—let me make you comfortable," she said extending her hand and leading Tim into the dining room.

Her perfume attacked his senses with a hypnotic power. He was either overwhelmed by this woman almost old enough to be his mother and the environment of low light and haunting French melody, or he was simply spent from his exhausting ordeal, begun some thirteen to fifteen hours earlier. The short night of strange dreams following the experience of Juni and Dr. Haji, along with flights and airports, customs and train stations, the rail trip, the drive, little sleep, little food, and the strangeness of the mission itself, all were compounded by the lack of phone contact with Laney or the girls, and now he felt as though he was about to come unraveled.

This aging but glamorous former war heroine seemed to read his thoughts. He felt a hollowness in his stomach and his mind went blank. He remembered feeling this way as a schoolboy when he tried to talk to Jane Gustafson, a popular cheerleader, and later as a fraternity man at a college mixer and found himself next to stunningly gorgeous sorority president Judy Figel. It seemed like every time he was in the company of a beautiful or popular woman he didn't know well, he was seized with this blankness. He felt somewhat inadequate, shy, and unsure of how to make a proper opening, which seemed ironic to him; after all, he made his living as a communications consultant coaching people in effective methods of human contact. But now, with the fragrance and enchanting power of this woman swirling around him, his brain seemed to be put on hold and he felt like a kid of eighteen, awkward and inept.

"Let me fix you a snack," she said. "The kitchen is long closed, but I can find something." She disappeared around the corner, and Tim took the opportunity to observe his surroundings. He was in what he assumed was the main dining room. Wooden beams arched the ceiling and spanned the walls, and the dark hardwood floor glistened with years of oil polishing. Small-paned windows like the ones in the front of the hotel edged the room. Two other rooms led off the main room; one looked as though it could be a banquet or meeting room, and the other was too dark to see. He noted the bottle that Marie had set on the table contained Calvados, the apple-cider brandy for which the region was famous. Glancing at his watch he saw that it was almost 3:30 A.M., local time.

Marie returned carrying a plate toward him. "This will give you strength," she said with a hearty laugh. "I like for my men to be strong, M'sieur Tim." She set before him an array of meat and cheese, with thick slices of crusty bread. "The sausage is andouille, the tripe is cooked *à la mode de Caen*, and the bread is, sadly, yesterday's, but it should do. And this is our Calvados. You must have a drink with me—I insist."

The "snack" was perhaps the best he had ever eaten. To be sure it was the first food he had all day. The Calvados was powerful, but it warmed him and the aftertaste was magnificent. It helped him gain his sense of self control.

"Tell me about Valmer. How is he? How does he live there in Florida, where it is always August? Is he well? Does he seem to be happy?" she asked, leaning on the table with her elbow, her chin in her hand and gulping more than sipping at her snifter of Calvados.

Dave walked to the fence at the back of the yard, and he looked over onto the lake. Maggie the dog seemed confused by her master's behavior; a nocturnal walk was unusual for him. She sat beside him as he stared at the stream of moonlight reflecting off the small lake. A splash out in the water brought a bark from Maggie, but it hardly drew Dave's attention. He was in the midst of formulating a plan of action. The girls surely had to be near, perhaps even on the island. If he could just learn where, he might be able to figure out how to free them. But it had to be done properly. Valmer had said it was best to let his friend Edward Earl work arrangements out with the kidnappers. It was not as though he couldn't trust the local police, but they had never been up against something like this. Dave knew the police chief and officers Stiner and Waddell well enough that they would give him some room, but they didn't need to know about Laney and the girls just yet. It would only be counter-productive if they were indeed dealing with international plotters. Not a word so far, but soon....

He stood and stared and thought.

Wasser had gone off to bed, telling Hertt they would make the call at ten the next morning, right after the pottery shop opened. He would fill him in on the details later.

Hertt didn't feel like sleeping. He roamed the house and deck and found himself looking out into the white foam of the surf shining in the moonlight. He was still thinking about Aunt Roy. He hadn't seen her since his mother's funeral. Was she all right, up there in North Carolina? Did she ever think about him? He took a long pull of Makers Mark. This life was the pits. No one to get close to, to care for or have care about you. No one you could really trust.

He thought heard a sound from the bedroom. He tapped softly at the door and asked if everyone was all right.

"Yes. Katie woke up," Laney said from their luxury-room prison. "She wanted me to say a prayer, that's all. Please go away. I want her to sleep." He heard her walk away from the door.

* * *

The two Israeli "backpackers" were on tricky ground. This was their first field assignment, and what made it rough was the cover they were using, posing as a married couple. Moshe and Anna had actually had been attracted to each other since they been through training together. But such involvement was strictly prohibited; they knew the reason was good, because it could interfere with their effectiveness. But that didn't make being alone together, especially in a bedroom posing as husband and wife, an easy thing to do. Despite their separate sleeping arrangement—she on the bed, he on the couch—they remained acutely aware of each other.

But for now, though, the surprise appearance of the wanted Iraqi terrorist gave them something else to worry about beside remaining "appropriately professional." They had worked quickly to develop the film. This small camera was an amazing invention. Moshe pulled the exposed film from the small chemical bath in the drinking glass provided by the hostess of the bed and breakfast.

"I knew it!" he cried, waving the photo to dry it. "Anna, look it is him—Tariq Abel!"

"We can send it soon," she said typing onto a small laptop computer. Next to it on the table sat a miniature fax machine attached to a cellular phone. "Tel Aviv should like this," she said as she keyed in the message.

> ***T.C. has not seen the Iranian tourists. Tourists have not seen the beauty contestant who is following them. Photo sent. Do we remain with new contestant or with TC and tourists?*** —M & A

She keyed a series of numbers that would send the transmission to Tel Aviv, then sat back and gnawed her lip. While the appropriate senior directors at Mossad headquarters read the message, in Carentan Moshe and Anna anxiously waited for a response.

* * *

Dave dialed Valmer. "Have you heard from Tim yet?"

"No, I haven't." He sounded groggy. "Sorry, I was taking a bit of a nap. It's almost 5:00 A.M. there. I don't know why he hasn't called yet. There could have been some delay."

"I think you should tell him. I know he would want to be here," Dave said with some force.

"Which is exactly why I won't tell him. There is nothing he can do. He would simply backtrack, lose time, and probably arrive too late to help; it would serve no purpose. We must let him go forward with this. He may learn something which can prevent great trouble. It is the same reason you would not simply give over the plate. To do so blindly, before we know what it means, could result in something horrific. You do trust me on that, don't you?"

"Yes, of course. But I just think he ought to know—they're his wife and daughters. This is something personal. The plate is an abstract danger."

"Exactly what would he do at this moment about all this? He is three thousand miles across the ocean. Let's get our strategy together; then we can tell him exactly what is happening and what we are doing about it. After all," Valmer added, "your daughter is involved, too.

"David you must trust me. We must lead with our strength and avoid playing to our weakness. In this case emotion is weakness. Get some sleep. You need a clear mind."

Tim told Marie everything he knew about Valmer and his life since the end of the war. He also answered all her questions about himself and his family and what his life was like in the States. She wanted to know what he knew of her, what had he been told of her life? She pressed him for details about his knowledge of the war, the Battle of Normandy, and the D-Day invasion. The bottle of Calvados had been drained and a second one opened. It was sometime during the second bottle that he noticed her intense appetite for information and detail beginning to wane. She had become more whimsical.

He had, for his part, become intoxicated. His face and forehead felt flushed, his ears buzzed with a kind of hum, and he had begun to slur his words. And the giddiness between them was exciting. His mood was under the control of this enchanting woman and the music which she played, frequently changing tapes and thereby changing the ambiance.

A few times she asked if he thought she was attractive or sexy. She wondered, did she look like a "dried up old lady" to him?

"Not at all. You are...a beautiful woman," he had said in a variety of ways. With the Calvados controlling his head, he couldn't be sure how he answered all the inquiries.

As she went to change the tape she stopped in front of him, grabbed his hands and turned him around to the side of his chair. Clutching his hands to her bosom, she demanded huskily, "Do I appeal to you?"

"I think you would be a marveloush sheductress," he slurred.

She responded with a hearty laugh which rang against the walls as she went into the other room put on another romantic recording. He recognized the sultry, sensual voice of Nina Simone.

When Marie returned to the room she came up behind him and slipped her arms around his shoulders, pressing her full breasts into his back. She ran her lips over the back of his neck, and along his ear, lightly tickling with the tip of her tongue. She kissed his ear with a passion that surprised him and lightly nibbled her way to his jawline. Her body moved against his back, swaying and rubbing gently. Her hands massaged his chest, and worked their way toward his stomach. He was becoming inflamed, and against his will his body began to respond. He knew he should not do this, but he felt weak, and warm, and thrilled. This shouldn't be happening, he reasoned in some remote zone of his brain, but there was such intense pleasure in this intimacy with this older woman. Her sensuality had overpowered him almost from the moment he saw her. His heart raced. She came around in front of him and sat on his lap. From deep inside some fragment of morality sounded an alarm and momentarily chilled him, and he attempted to pull away. She pulled him back and began to unbutton her blouse, and his eyes became riveted on the exposed cleavage. He was indeed succumbing to her seduction, but it was a seduction he had more or less asked for. His hands groped for her breasts, and his lips met hers, when a sudden loud hammering sound vibrated through the room like a loud shot. Someone was pounding at the door. They bolted up and she looked at her watch and said something he could not understand. She looked back at him and smiled. She caressed his face, then pinched his cheek and laughed.

"M'sieur Tim, you are indeed a passionate young man, no? Your wife will be most glad to have you home." She gave him another pinch and a quick kiss. "*Mais oui*, such a delightful paramour to this old lady." She stood and gathered herself, buttoned her blouse, and walked into the kitchen toward the door. Tim exhaled raggedly and felt the adrenaline-rush of energy flow out of his body. His heart began to slow, and he wiped the sweat from his forehead with a napkin.

He could overhear Marie and a man speaking together in French. She came around the corner from the kitchen and he saw her swat the man's hand away from her bottom.

"M'sieur Tim, this is Enloui. He is our dairyman. Enloui, this is Valmer's friend M'sieur Tim," she said.

Enloui spoke very little English but managed, "Nice to meet you. I knew your friend Valmer during the war." Enloui was perhaps late fifties or early sixties, and looked every year of it. He was barrel-chested and his stomach bulged beneath his flannel shirt. His head was balding, and the large, full mustache on his weathered face was peppered with gray.

"M'sieur Tim, you will stay in room number three; the key is in the door. I'll see you tomorrow at lunch. If the dairyman is here, it is time for bed," Marie said, while Enloui grinned and tried to stifle a chuckle.

Rubber-legged and more than a little inebriated, Tim bade them good-night, picked up his bags, and started up the stairs. He turned to ask about making a phone call.

Looking downstairs he saw Enloui and Marie embrace, his hands on her derrière and her arms wound around his neck. Their lips were pressed together in a passionate kiss. Tim chuckled as he continued up the stairs.

Whew, he said to himself, the dairyman is about to deliver. He walked into his room, kicked the door closed, dropped his bags, and fell back on the bed.

* * *

At the bed and breakfast, a series of low beeps alerted Anna and Moshe that their fax was receiving a message. Groggily Moshe put on his glasses and shook his head to clear it, waiting to see if their mission was about to change. He pulled the paper off the machine.

****Lovely photo of new contestant. Make new contestant your top priority. Crown the queen. Tourists unimportant. Keep an eye on T.C.****

"Anna, Anna wake up," Moshe whispered loudly. She sat up, rubbing her eyes, and Moshe read her the fax from Tel Aviv confirming what they already knew: the interloper on the motor-cycle was the Iraqi terrorist, Tariq Abel, a wanted man, one whom they were now sanctioned to get.

Anna, instantly wide-eyed and awake at the news, looked lovely to Moshe. "Do you understand what this means, Anna? We can take him—we have authorization. 'Crown the queen,' it says. We need to stay with Calvin, long enough to see what he is after, but we can forget the Iranians. 'Tourists unimportant,'" he repeated. "Our first field assignment and we get a chance at a terrorist and criminal like Abel." Moshe was pumped up.

Anna found his enthusiasm contagious, and in the excite-ment of the moment, emotion got the better of them both. They embraced and Moshe spun her around. They kissed, and immedi-ately they remembered their training and code of conduct and quickly pulled apart, feeling self-conscious. The chemistry between them had to be controlled, at least while they were on duty.

"Abel doesn't seem to be interested in Calvin. Obviously he's just following the Iranians," Anna said as she straightened herself and regained her professional composure.

Moshe nodded agreement. "But I'll wager if he doesn't know yet, he soon will learn the end of this chase is something worth a lot of cash money," he said, an ominous, warning tone in his voice.

*   *   *

"Eh, bien—la menagerie," Tariq Abel murmured, looking down onto the bed at the two nude French prostitutes he'd picked up, a brunette and a bleached blond. His French was not the best, but it was enough to get by on. He sat down on the edge of the bed and took a long drink from a bottle of whiskey. "Quel est votre prix, eh?" he asked, wiping his mouth on the back of his hand. But before they could tell him how much they charged for their services he reached over and grabbed the brunette by her hair, twisting his fingers in it and yanking savagely.

"Ah, les cheveux—si beau—et votre visage, ma chérie," he said pulling the woman's hair until his rough face scraped against hers. Suddenly he flung her away and lunged at the blond, grasping her face and squeezing her mouth into a distorted pucker. She was bewildered and becoming frightened; she and her friend had had unpleasant customers before, but an element of madness they had never seen before glittered in this man's eyes.

"Les lèvres—ce n'est pas rouge," he brought his face to hers and pressed his lips roughly against hers, smashing them into her teeth. Then he savagely bit her lips; and as she shrieked in pain he danced crazily around the room, cackling and licking the blood from his lips and crying, "Maintenant, c'est rouge—maintenant!"

He grabbed the bottle and turned it up to drain the last of the whiskey from it, then smashed the bottle against the dresser. The women huddled next to each other in fear as he lurched toward them, brandishing the broken bottle at them. Tossing the glass away, Abel pulled a long knife from off the top of the dresser and waved it at them. He was no longer laughing.

"*Un souvenir, s'il vous plaît?*" he coaxed menacingly as he leaned over them. "*Le sein, peut-être?*" he said, cupping the brunette's breast in his hand, squeezing and pulling brutally. "*Quel est votre prix?*" he screamed at her.

"*Non, non!*" she cried, trembling in fear.

"*Ça ne fait rien*—it does not matter!" the other sobbed.

"*Un souvenir!*" he demanded. "*Ah, oui—le coeur?* The heart?" he pulled the point of the knife down the middle of the brunette's chest, making a thin red line beading blood that trickled down to her stomach. Too petrified to move, she lay with her eyes closed, tears trickling from under her lids.

"*Pitié, monsieur, pitié!*" the blond woman pleaded.

"*Mon souvenir—merci!*" Abel cried, waving the knife in circles over his head as he straddled the brunette, grabbing her by her hair again and pulling her head back to expose her throat. Her eyes rolled and she gurgled her terror.

"*Merci!*" he howled in a guttural and crazed voice as he stared at the women with wild eyes. He leapt off of the bed still clutching the brunette by her hair and hurled her across the room, slamming her body into the wall, and she lay crumpled and whimpering on the floor. Both women were paralyzed with fear, unsure what would happen next. Finally he waved the knife at them and then gestured at the door. He laughed at their puzzled expressions. He always loved to terrorize prostitutes and then cheat them out of their pay.

"*Au revoir, mesdames—dehors!*" he screamed as a warning for them to leave now.

"*Dehors—maintenant!*—get out!" He laughed maniacally as they scrambled from the room clutching what clothing they could grab from the chairs and floor as they ran naked into the hall. He grabbed the sheets from the bed and in one furious motion wadded them into a ball and threw them after the women running toward the stairs.

"*Je voudrais faire laver ce linge!*" he screamed at the darkened hall. In the next room a frightened business man wondered what the disturbance was and why anyone would be screaming to have his linen washed at sunrise.

Abel retreated back into his room where he poured a rock of cocaine from a vial on the dresser. He cut the rock on a small mirror with his knife, chopping it into a fine powder. Pulling a small glass tube from the pocket of his shirt that hung on the chair, he snorted the drug. He smacked his lips and lay down on the stripped bed, laughing at the memory of the frightened women running away from him.

At the Interhotel the two Iranians were on a late-morning conference call with the committee in Teheran. The middle-aged operative with the short brush cut had told the committee that they had been able to learn very little about Tim's mysterious trip.

"He's here to meet an old man, a professor. This Calvin reads a great deal," the operative said.

"This is waste—needless—when there is real work to do," spat one of the clerics on the Teheran end of the call, berating the group for spending money to follow a "Christian pilgrim on a meaningless mission, a man who is probably nothing more than a procurer for a wealthy American who seeks authenticity of this artifact. We waste our time and we waste our money on this."

As the voice squawked out of the phone, the agent held it from his ear and smiled. His younger partner with the mustache and longer hair mocked the stern voice with animated gestures and expressions. They listened as other voices on the Teheran end joined the chorus of debate. There was general agreement that any involvement of the UN team member, Dr. Stroutsel, probably had little to do with a national security matter.

"More than likely it is merely a matter of business," a young deputy minister of state affairs began. The two men in Interhotel room listened carefully. They recognized the voice as belonging to a man who directed the operations of their division.

"While our scholars can find nothing to substantiate an interest in this metal plate, Dr. Haji says it may be an important Christian relic, though he can not be sure of even that meager shred of possibility. Dr. Haji says this man Calvin seems to have a deeper interest. We suggest that you continue with the surveillance until it is determined whether there is nothing more than Christian history or merely the greed of a Western collector involved."

The men in Carentan nodded agreement. They waited for the committee of voices in Teheran to give them further instruction. The committee discussed it briefly.

"Stay with your mission. Watch Calvin until he meets with the old Jew, and learn what you can of his interest. If this is only some archeology and museum matter, we have no further interest," the young deputy minister of state affairs said.

"Yes. It shall be so. Praise be to Allah." The man in Carentan ended the call and smiled with satisfaction at his younger colleague.

As the conversation ended Tariq Abel also smiled to himself. The listening device he placed in the Iranian's bag in Paris was working well. If they were losing interest in Calvin, he certainly was not. The greed of a Western collector indeed. He began to think there might be more than one way to make a profit in this venture. He knew for certain of many ways to spend money.

* * *

A rich aroma pried Tim from his sleep. Nestling deep in the bed, he slowly opened his eyes and looked around the room. Floral wall paper topped by a border of crown molding was inset with a shuttered window that leaked a crack of light across the foot of the bed. An antique desk sat beneath the window, and an old armoire stood at the foot of the bed, a masterfully carved dark wood poster and headboard arrangement which in his deep exhaustion he had not noticed last night. A washbasin and pitcher sat on a small round table next to the bed.

He checked his watch—almost 1:00 P.M. He sat up, feeling surprisingly well considering the night before. The smell of sausage or bacon wafting up from the kitchen had his stomach rumbling in hunger. He opened the shutter on the window and the bright Norman spring day bounded in. A balding and bearded man in an open-collared white shirt sat on a garden bench beneath his window reading a book and smoking a pipe. He looked up at the sound of the shutters opening and spoke, startling Tim.

"So you survived Marie's welcome did you, Mr. Calvin?" he asked in a gravel-like voice. Reading Tim's surprise he continued, "I think you have been looking for me. Join me in the dining room, won't you? We'll have an opportunity to get acquainted over *le déjeuner*."

"Dr. Stroutsel? Yes, thank you. Please give me a little time," Tim said.

"I still have a bit of that to waste, Mr. Calvin," came the gravel voice, as Stroutsel tapped his pipe and returned to his reading. "We will take some time to get know each other. And you will be able to help me."

Help Stroutsel? How so? Tim was puzzled by that. As he began to pull in the shutters, he looked around, over the wall to the street and the portion of Carentan visible from his room. The village was picturesque, busy with foot traffic flowing in and out of the shops, people carrying loaves of bread, bouquets of flowers, and shopping bags. A group of older men were bowling on a grassy patch of lawn. Among several people sitting at a nearby sidewalk café, under an umbrella, he noticed the man he had seen earlier in Caen, the Saddam Hussein look-alike. "He must get tired of the comparison," Tim thought as he closed the shutter to go down the hall to the bathroom. For a moment he wondered about the man showing up here, but shrugged it off as a coincidence, not unusual in a tourist spot like Carentan.

* * *

"So, Mr. Calvin, you come with an old mystery burning in your mind, thinking that I can help," Stroutsel said when he met Tim in the sitting room at the bottom of the stairs.

"Valmer is confident you can do so. I am hopeful," Tim answered.

"A hopeful man, are you? Well you need to understand what I regard as hope. Certainly you are not in such a hurry that you can't indulge an old man in his need to explain. Later we shall take a drive, up to the Utah Beach. But come, let us begin over some food."

Lunch was the special of the day, Marie insisted. She teased Tim about drinking too much Calvados the night before, and said she was appointing herself his "chaperon," then she walked away with her laugh booming like an exclamation point. A salad of fresh greens with chives, radishes, and a house dressing gave Stroutsel an opening to talk of his youth in the spring of 1944.

"Those in the resistance, of which Marie's father was an important part, knew that an invasion would soon be launched," Stroutsel told Tim. "I had been hired by the hotel keeper to work in the kitchen and do odd jobs. Together Marie and I tended to the garden. It was a heady time, and filled with danger."

"Marie told me last night, you helped the resistance. You were good at listening."

"We had to pretend, all of us. Pretend we could stomach the loutish German officers and their arrogant ways. I had to pretend to be a retarded cripple. To have been seen as a Jew would have meant certain death. The garden was the only place Marie and I could talk freely without listening ears. It is still our favorite place, and that is why."

"I can't begin to imagine that kind of existence," Tim said, feeling a deep respect, remembering that Stroutsel had lost his family and fled Eastern Europe with a cousin who died here in Normandy.

"No, and the children of your generation have even less imagination of a world in flames," Stroutsel sighed with resignation.

The tone of the conversation and the mood brightened as the remainder of the meal was served. Daruda fish in cream sauce, green beans and squash, sautéed morel mushrooms, and a bottle of white table wine provided the context of this first meeting with the fascinating Dr. Stroutsel.

*   *   *

By the time they had eaten and were drinking their coffee Tim had begun to feel more comfortable, and he sensed Stroutsel felt the same way. Stroutsel had finally asked Tim to brief him on the evaluation of the metal plate he had received from his former UN colleague, Dr. Haji. Tim listed the theories Haji and Juni had outlined in the Chicago meeting: map, cipher plate, part of Justinian's code of law, destination code for other documents, burial plaque. Stroutsel listened with an almost impatient politeness before speaking.

"So Haji couldn't help much. Of course he would show more interest in implications for Islam." Stroutsel said, puffing on his pipe.

"Well, I certainly thought it was interesting. I ended up giving my views on his religion and its history. But all he gave me were those theories, nothing definite." Tim nibbled at a piece of the fruit Marie had brought them for dessert.

"My dear Mr. Calvin, you must realize that the history of this talisman, this artifact, is quite convoluted. In all truth, the stories of this plate were put aside as rumors and legend. Not until World War II could anyone in modern academia be sure it even existed. You are of course familiar with the story of the plate's being found in a burial catacomb here in Normandy. But the inventory of the artifacts found by the allied soldiers in the château was quite incomplete. That makes what you seek very difficult. It also makes the work of the UN commission very complicated. However, we know there has been some recent interest in those circles which trade in these items. And the man you found on the beach, and the metal plate your daughter found are quite real. So what should we make of this? What should we make of this cryptic message?" he asked from a cloud of pipe smoke.

* * *

Dave and Barb awoke and went through their morning routine with a gnawing emptiness. They went through the motions, but their thoughts were totally fixated on the disappearance of Cee and the Calvins. Surely they would soon hear, and then they would need to act—rapidly. Dave skipped breakfast and drove to the aviary to meet with his friend Dick about a plan he had an idea for, a wild and unconventional plan, but he thought it would work, if, as he suspected, they were still on the island.

Valmer and his associate Edward Earl arrived at the Hockett house shortly after Dave left. They had come from a meeting with the Sanibel police chief. Earl was a tall slim man, well-dressed, with horn-rimmed spectacles that continuously slid down his nose.

"We've worked out an arrangement. Because no one has formally reported Cee and the Calvins as missing, the police are not 'actively' involved. They know the situation, but they are giving us some latitude. Earl's reputation as prosecutor and skill as former intelligence officer also eased the police chief's mind," Valmer told Barb. Earl in turn said he was sure he would be able manage the investigative effort with more resources than the Sanibel police department had access to.

"I've done these cases involving abductions before and the chief knows that. These types of cases have their own sets of rules. I told the chief if things go well, he'll get a grand slam, catching the perpetrator red-handed. Try not to worry, Mrs. Hockett. We'll learn who the abductor is—it's only a matter of time."

Valmer had brought a recording device to attach to their phones, both at home and at the shop. "When the kidnapper calls, and he will, this technology will be of great value," he said as he attached it to the kitchen phone. "You and Dave won't have to do anything—it will start automatically. So all we can do is wait."

* * *

At the Captiva beach house, Hertt was up and pacing, listening for sounds from the bedroom. Wasser was still sleeping off his hangover. Meanwhile, behind the closed door, Cee watched TV and fumed that she was missing her riding lesson.

As Laney watched her younger daughter become more withdrawn and lethargic, her desperation and fear increased. Katie tended to stay curled into an almost fetal position, basically unresponsive, but reacting to any motion that seemed to take Laney away from her with a whimpering moan. The child's depression and reaction to their situation was so profound that Laney began to worry whether she would ever come out of it.

Elizabeth lay next to Katie, stroking her cheeks with her finger and smoothing her hair back off her forehead.

"Come on, munchkin," she wheedled. "This isn't so bad, kinda like a little vacation in a vacation. Besides, we're all here together, right?" Katie didn't respond, and Elizabeth's eyes burned, but she knew she couldn't cry now.

"Come on, Katie. Come back to us."

She'd never seen her sister, or anyone else for that matter, act like this. Elizabeth didn't know what deep psychological or physical chasm Katie might be ready to plunge into, but feared it was dangerously near.

Stroutsel had asked Tim to drive him to Saint-Mère-Église, and then on to Utah Beach, one of the beachheads of D-Day. It was an obligatory pilgrimage he made on each trip to Normandy, he told him, a "balancing of the ledger, a survivor's tribute, a chasing of ghosts." His family had perished in the death camps of the Holocaust, and his cousin and many of his friends had died in the resistance. He had himself with young eyes watched the bloody battles of Normandy some forty-odd years ago. Now he was an old man, convinced of his mortality, and he came here whenever he could to remember that rip in the fabric of life where so many had fallen through to death.

As they approached the village of Saint-Mère-Église, Tim realized that he had failed to phone Valmer. He jotted down a note as he drove to call as soon as he returned to Carentan. Now he was struck by the scene of the village and church steeple made famous by movies and history books. Saint-Mère-Église was the first French town liberated by the American troops who parachuted into the area on June 5, 1944. Stroutsel had been there at nightfall, waiting for the first drop. Some of the GIs died, dropping into trees; others came in gliders and some of them became casualties when their crafts tangled with the thick Norman hedges lining the fields.

"I hid in a barn. When I heard the planes I ran to the door and saw the sky lit with stars and filled with parachutes, truly filled." Stroutsel lit a French cigarette, and blew a thick blue smoke into the air. He titled his head back and watched the smoke as though it conjured the liberating troops descending from the heavens.

"Did you know, did you sense that was a turning point?"

"I knew many of the boys would die. I knew many of my friends would die." He turned to Tim, smoking with the automatic motions of one who has done so for years. "I even thought that perhaps freedom would mean death for me, that death had followed me from home.

"For a long time I was in despair: all of the death, the destruction of not only my family but every Jewish community in Europe…. In light of the Holocaust, I wondered, after I had served my purpose and the war ended, what right had I to live?"

Tim drove on in silence, absorbing Stroutsel's somber fatalism. There was pain in the man's eyes and in his lined face, an acceptance of the worst life can offer. But there was also a sturdiness in his small hunched frame, and the resolution that comes from survival.

"Does a person ever get beyond despair?" Tim asked after a while.

"Despair is something we must embrace and then throw off. Pain never really goes away, but it strengthens us and fortifies our resolve, and enables us to defiantly cry, 'never again.'" There was a long silence, as the countryside passed by. "Sometimes, Mr. Calvin, I feel that life has cheated me, cheated me the death that so many I knew and loved were able to acquire. Living itself brings its own pain."

As Tim thought over what Stroutsel said, he found his mind was, for the time being, freed from its own obsession with the plate and its meaning. In fulfilling Stroutsel's request, he had indulged an old man's desire to explain himself. Now he found he was glad to accompany the man on this pilgrimage to the beach of his memories, as a journey of redemption and, hopefully, a release from pain. Still, Tim realized he was an outsider, a neophyte, observing a man cross centuries of affliction and rejection and struggle. For Stroutsel, and his sense of history, this visit was an act of duty, showing respect for the death of warriors; and through that act, the old man tried to come to terms with pain for his people, who had been destroyed only because they had lived.

A few other cars were parked outside the Utah Beach memorial building and information center. The beach itself was windswept, large, and angry. The gray sky hung low over the rough, choppy water, and the surf pounded the beach with an intensity that seemed to border on animosity. An ominous pall seemed to hang over the place. Old enforcements and battle walls, pill boxes, and even strands of barbed wire were visible, while cattle grazed over the dunes in fields where one of the decisive engagements of mankind's warfare had been played out in blood.

"You can sense the terrible loss just standing here," Tim said, more to the wind than to Stroutsel, whose face was turned toward the beach, but who seemed to be looking beyond time. "Doesn't this bring back the anger, the hatred?"

Stroutsel cut the misty wind of the beach with his gravel-like voice. " 'Do not be eager in your heart to be angry, for anger resides in the bosom of fools.' Solomon, from Ecclesiastes, Calvin, it would do well for all of us to remember it."

They stood, wrapped in silence and reflection as if in a place of prayer, as sand and wind and salt spray assaulted them. Stroutsel faced squarely into the wind, and seemingly oblivious of Tim's presence, in a calm, still voice, recited a benediction.

"*Baruch atah Adonai*—Blessed art thou, O Lord, my Rock, who trains my hands for war, and my fingers for battle. My loving kindness and my fortress, my stronghold and my deliverer, my shield and He in whom I take refuge."

Tim stood transfixed by the moment, and the sweeping emotions which girded them against the ghosts of this killing beach.

"We are a mere breath, our days are like passing shadows," Stroutsel's voice began to fade, as he walked north his eyes cast on the sand or looking out to the sea. Tim let him go. He walked to the memorials and read the names of those young men who had fallen on this strip of sand and sea.

Only one of the Iranian surveillance team had followed Tim and Stroutsel to Utah Beach. In turn, only Anna had driven north, interested now in Stroutsel and Tim. Moshe stayed behind in Carentan, keeping watch on the Iraqi Tariq Abel who sat drinking a bottle of wine as he made calls on a cellular phone.

* * *

Edward Earl had set up his laptop and a cellular phone on the Hockett's patio and was making good progress, rapidly piecing together information on who the likely kidnapper or kidnappers were. "Come on, come on," he muttered while he waited for one of his contacts to get back to him with some information. He stared at the phone as if willing it to ring. The pressure was really on in this case, and although he was used to it, it wasn't helping his ulcer any. Valmer patted his shoulder in sympathy and went into the kitchen for a cup of coffee.

Meanwhile, Dave had returned from his meeting with Dick Munch and told Valmer the details of his plan of attack. Valmer in turn explained to Dave that the police chief had been filled in on Earl's reputation, and was giving Earl three days to run things before the police became involved. Dave's response to the news was halted when the phone rang. Earl hurried into the house and activated the tracking equipment and tape recorder. He nodded to Dave to lift the receiver.

Dave took a deep breath and said, "Good morning—Hocketts."

"Hockett, you've probably been expecting this call. I have something precious to you. You have something precious to me. We can trade them, and we both get what we want. We will make the…"

"I want to talk to them—each one of them, before we go any further."

"You aren't in much of a position to make demands, so listen to me. I'm telling you how this will work."

"No! Not until I hear the girls. I have to know they're all right or there's nothing to discuss."

"I'm telling you they are fine."

"Like I can trust you. I want to hear them myself. Put them on,"

"You're stalling for time. I'll call you later."

The line clicked and a dial tone came on.

"It's a cell phone," Earl said, examining at a panel of meters. "But its close. Let's hear it again."

Wasser was furious. He had counted on making the switch that afternoon and getting away from this humid island and the increased risk of complications. He wanted to dump the broads, get the plate and get on to Veracruz then down to Rio where he could lie low and work on finding a buyer.

He hadn't anticipated the damned potter throwing a wrench in the works. He chaffed at the thought that he might have to play into the potter's hands, delaying his move and upping his chances of being traced. It was baggage he didn't want. His mood darkened and he yelled for Hertt.

*   *   *

It was after 5:00 P.M. when Stroutsel and Tim arrived back at the hotel. Tim had grown impatient with the delay in his research when the old man insisted on the drive and pilgrimage; yet he was fascinated by the depth of Stroutsel's character. The drive back from Utah beach brought out another facet of Stroutsel's personality. He had been a friend of the author and famous lecturer Rabbi Joshua Heschel, and had condensed Heschel's considerable intellect and teaching to a simple adage—"celebrate life." That Stroutsel could go from what seemed the depth of depression to a discussion of theological Judaism, all the while fending off inquiries about the metal plate and his theories about it with a facile wit, both amused and frustrated Tim. Now, as they went up the step to the hotel, Stroutsel announced he was ready to "talk business and to drink a bottle of wine."

Tim was at the phone in the dining room, watching across the room as Marie and Stroutsel nibbled at cheese and bread and opened a bottle of wine. He waited for Valmer to come on the line.

Valmer opened the conversation. "You are bit overdue. I hope there have been no problems."

"I got in late and slept in. Stroutsel talked a bit this morning, then wanted me to drive him to Utah Beach. I hated to delay things, but I felt like I couldn't refuse."

"You've had a somber session, I'm sure. Old Ben can be a bit compulsive and somewhat depressive. Has he told you anything about the plate?"

"Not much. We're ready to have a go at it now."

"Good. He'll be ready to talk. You've endured his eccentricity, and now he may be able to tell us what we need. He's a great source, Tim."

"Any word yet on what the inscriptions mean?"

"You're with our best hope now. Tim, I feel obliged to tell you that Iran's state security agency is still interested. They possibly have some people in the region. Have you noticed anything?"

"Like what?"

"Anything or anyone unusual, who seems to keep showing up, as if they could be following you."

"I really haven't been watching that closely." He remembered the two cars on the highway last night. "I'll pay more attention in the future. What do you know about them?"

"Very little. They probably want to know what we're after. They want to satisfy their curiosity with more than what Haji could tell them or you, such as what is the source of the plate and its value, and whether it could be related to any of their holy sites. They probably would be interested in what the message means, too. Think carefully; are you sure you haven't seen anyone?"

"Well, there are a couple of cars that I think I've seen before; and I have seen one particular guy a couple of times. He looks like Saddam Hussein, a very strong resemblance."

"Poor bastard. What a curse! Wrong nationality for the Iranians, though. Well, you'd better get cracking with Dr. Ben, so you can get back. Give him my regards, and tell him I have a drink waiting for him in Florida."

"I have all evening with Stroutsel," Tim said. "But I haven't talked to Laney since I left. I'm going to call her as soon as I get off the line with you. I hope I can catch her this time before she and the girls take off for the day. You'd think they'd at least stick around until they heard from me," he grumbled.

"I'll be sure to tell your ladies you called," Valmer reassured him.

Tim hung up and went back to the table to join Stroutsel and Marie. Dejected by not being able to talk to Laney, he didn't notice the two dark-complexioned men examining the menus at a nearby table.

Valmer turned to Earl and Dave. "He's seen Tariq Abel. I have a rough feeling."

Dave was incredulous. "You flat-out lied to him!" he exclaimed. "How could you say you would tell the girls he called? I just don't see how you can do that."

"My God, David! Don't think it is easy! Of course I want to tell him what's happened—any man should know when his family is in jeopardy. But you have to understand there is nothing to be gained from his knowing, nothing constructive. It could only result in a bad outcome."

"We used to call it situational ethics," Earl interjected as he fiddled with the wires of the tracking device. "A lot of things we do in operations, in intelligence or investigation, don't look so good in the light of day. Of course, you don't do that kind of work in the light of day. It's a world all its own. Valmer's right about this, Dave. It would do a lot more harm than good."

"David, you must understand I spent a career in this kind of work," Valmer said. "Tim simply cannot know, if for no other reason than it would interfere with his concentration and possibly put him at increased risk. He is most certainly being followed, and being distracted could be disastrous for him, even cost him his life. For that matter, we must insure that anyone who may be following him does not know about the kidnapping either. The Iranians or Abel could use it somehow to their advantage."

"I just feel like an accomplice in this. He is my best friend," Dave fretted.

Jayne had gone to the restaurant presumably to work on inventory and menu planning, but mostly just to occupy her mind. She'd tossed and turned all night, and what little sleep she'd had was riddled with nightmares of her young friend Cee held captive, the girl's resilient spirit buffeted by something more powerful than her own childish toughness could combat.

The attempt at chores did little good. Her eyelids felt leaden, and her head ached and felt stuffy. She gave up trying to concentrate and decided to take a walk to try to clear her head. She stood looking out over the water for a moment, then headed north toward the stretch of beach than ran behind some of the Captiva beach homes.

Hertt himself had tried to convince Katie to drink more orange juice. Despite Wasser's rantings about their being identified, Hertt had abandoned wearing the stocking over his face by now, mainly because he didn't want to frighten the child anymore. He coaxed and begged, and even sang to her, but she was unresponsive and acted as though she couldn't move.

"You can see she's not well. You've got to do something. Let us go, or at least call a doctor." Laney's outrage was a mixture of anger and fear for her child.

"I can't do nothing, lady. The other man—my boss—wants to trade you for that metal the kid found. Soon, I hope."

Laney stared hard at him for a moment. "Then if you won't help us, you'd better pray she doesn't get worse—if you even know how to pray," she said through clenched teeth.

Hertt made no reply, but an inner spasm of conscience contorted his face. Laney hoped that his tortured expression was an indication of a relenting, that whatever was good in him might surface in time to help them.

*   *   *

After Tim and Stroutsel returned to the hotel, Marie brought them a late afternoon snack of bread, cheese, sausages, and another bottle of wine to sustain them, then took her leave. The old Jewish scholar kept his pipe lit, and spoke from behind a haze of blue smoke, his rough voice deepened by years of smoke and wine. Stroutsel described the UN commission's work, and the research they had compiled on the wealth of religious art and materials in dispute.

"From around the world there are thousands of pieces of sacred material, and manuscripts which, for almost as many reasons as there are objects, have been displaced, lost, bought, sold, stolen, smuggled, seized, and are now in dispute. The Elgin marbles are only one notable example. Schools, churches, temples, sects, individual collectors, historians, and governments all lay claim to them. It's the work of the commission to settle these disputes of ownership, or at least to make recommendations to the Secretary General." Stroutsel paused to sip.

"It sounds fascinating," Tim said, "especially to someone with a love of history.

"It is. You are at once detective, historian, art critic, anthropologist, and sometimes a theologian rolled into one."

"What about the plate, though? What do you think it is, or might mean?" Tim asked, trying to steer the conversation where he wanted it. "Any hunch on its origin?" He opened his notebook and was finally ready for progress.

Stroutsel titled his head to give Tim a long stare. "This plate with its message of a warrior, and its Christ enthroned? It may be an authentic piece of history, but it may not be accurate."

"You mean the Christian aspect?"

"Not at all. Nothing to do with the theology of it. Authentic, old, yes; but perhaps nothing more than just some man's musing. In other words, authentic but meaningless, at least to us now. It could have had meaning only during the life of its maker. Sometimes these artifacts are the work of cranks or schizophrenic visionaries, or may even be hoaxes. Not everything that comes to us from the deep past can be explained, nor should it all be revered."

"But what do you think it means?" Tim persisted.

"My God, Calvin, I wouldn't begin to know! Tell me what *you* think." Stroutsel emptied his glass and refilled it to the top as Tim began his tentative theory about the message describing Mont Saint Michel.

"Yes, yes, but please spare me the story about this warrior angel." Sarcasm drenched the gravelly voice coming at Tim through the heavy smoke. "I have no stomach for superstition, Calvin, only facts and your theories."

Momentarily nonplussed by Stroutsel's interruption, Tim regathered his thoughts, and referring again to his notes, proceeded with his narrative. Engrossed with the business at hand, he didn't notice that he also had the attention of the two men at the nearby table who were taking in more than dinner.

* * *

Wasser listened on an extension phone out of sight of Laney and the girls. Hertt had herded them into the greatroom for the phone call. On Wasser's signal Hertt held the cordless phone to Laney's ear and mouth.

"Dave, we've got to get out of here. Katie's sick, she's real weak." Hertt pulled the phone away before she could say anything more.

In the next room Wasser barked into the phone. "Enough! All right, Hockett, now do you believe I'm serious?"

"Let me talk to Cee, my daughter."

"All right, dammit. Put his kid on!" he yelled to Hertt.

Hertt moved the phone to Cee.

"Daddy, Daddy, get us out of here!"

"Celia, darling, are you all right?"

"Yes, but this is ridiculous, and besides, I'm missing a horse-back riding lesson."

Dave was unable to suppress a small chuckle at Cee's prioritization and spunk. "We'll make it up darling. We love you."

"All right that's it." Wasser's contemptible voice interrupted the conversation. "Now listen, Hockett if you want to see them again you do what I say. Like you've been told, no cops and no tricks, or the broad and the kids pay."

"I'm listening, but you listen to me: if anything happens to them—any one of them—I'll find you, and I'll get you. I swear it. There won't be any place you can hide. You'd better believe me!"

"Stash the hero bullshit, potter. My commodity is perish-able. We'll make the switch at seven tonight. Come alone and bring the plate to the third cross-over road from Treeline on the approach to the airport. Drive your shop van so you're easy to spot. Come in from the entrance road and stop right after you turn left onto the cross-over. Get out of the van and hold the metal plate in the air over your head. We'll get the plate and bring the girls. Then you all get in the car and leave and don't look back. Remember—third cross-over road from Treeline tonight at seven. Got it?"

Dave knew the location well. It was perfect for an exchange, a wide sweep of grass and palms. The approach to Southwest International Airport was like a scenic interstate highway, with a football field-like median and ponds to the side of both roads. There would be no way to sneak into the area, and there was no other access. From a vantage on the third cross-over the captor would have what amounted to the high ground and could easily tell if Dave wasn't alone. The place was also close to South Jet, the private hangar.

"I know where you mean, but it can't be tonight."

"What the hell do you mean? It will be tonight!"

"I've got to get the plate. It's not on the island." Dave stalled; Valmer and Earl nodded approval. "It'll have to be tomorrow night?"

"Too late. What's the earliest you get it and get there?"

"Three tomorrow afternoon and that's pushing it!"

"You're a stooge, you mudslinger! That's the earliest?"

"That's a push." Dave clenched his teeth, his voice nearly cracking with rage, but he felt some measure of success in the bluff. The plate was actually only blocks away, in a safe-deposit box in his bank. "Three tomorrow. That's the best I can do."

"Three tomorrow, you stinkin' bastard! And be sure you're alone. Do exactly as I said. If you want to see your little bitch again, don't even think about the police—I'll know if you do. This business is just between you and me. Got it?"

"Yeah, I got it, you son-of-a-bitch!" Dave snarled.

Both ends of the conversation clicked off in anger.

Stroutsel had waxed almost poetic as he reacted to Tim's theory that the Greek inscription described Mont Saint Michel. He had begun to say there was "something quite relevant to the idea I want you to know" when he switched gears and launched into a tirade against Aoki Pasotti and other private collectors of sacred artifacts, calling them "beasts."

"From Proverbs, Calvin: 'There are six things the Lord hates, yes seven which are an abomination to him. Haughty eyes, a lying tongue, and hands that shed innocent blood, a heart that devises wicked plans, feet that run rapidly to evil, a false witness who utters lies and one who spreads strife among his brothers'. These rich scum breed in their comfortable enclaves with desires and lusts for fragments of heaven. What do they think they can do? Buy divine grace by possessing the unattainable?"

"Aoki Pasotti must be among the worst." Tim had put his pen down on a notepad as he listened to Stroutsel's homily.

"Yes, sadly, this man holds what belongs to the devout of several faiths. Its all an obscene vanity. The fifth verse of Ecclesiastes says 'he who loves money will not be satisfied with money. This too is vanity.'" His pipe had gone out again and he paused to light it, doing so with flair. Tim thought the gesture had an almost dance-like quality. In a fluid sweep Stroutsel would add tobacco to the bowl, tamp it lightly, and then punctuate the finale with the flick of a lighter. The old man puffed contentedly for a moment, surrounding himself in a wreath of fragrant smoke. He lifted his wine glass, swirled it and took a swig, and watched the smoke spiral up in the light.

"I have my own sense of divine justice. I have found my beliefs within the hearts and minds of the people of the ages whom I study. They are the true proprietors of these sacred relics—they possess them with their hearts and with their faith."

"You were going to tell me something about my theory about Mont Saint Michel's being a connection."

"Yes, I will come to that, but now let me complete the list of possibilities regarding this plate for our Valmer. I trust my countrymen will have access to it and to Haji's list as well."

"I'm sure Valmer will share them," Tim reassured, eager to get to the list and continue with his quest, before Stroutsel drank himself into incomprehensibility. The old man was rapidly becoming verbose and deep.

Stroutsel again scanned Haji's list which Tim had given him earlier. He clucked his tongue and sighed. "Ah yes, it is best to leave this kind of sorting out to those who sit in small rooms and try to make sense of splinters and shreds. People like Haji and I make theories, Calvin, not sense."

As Stroutsel listed his range of theories, they were more detailed than those presented by Dr. Haji. One of Haji's postulations he dismissed as "fanciful murmurings of a superstitious heart"—that the metal plate might somehow be connected to the Ark of the Covenant.

Stroutsel pulled a folded paper from his shirt pocket and surveyed it.

"Calvin, what I have done here is hypothesize. I am not a definitive expert, but I am a man with considerable knowledge of history. I think this plate presents several possibilities. Perhaps, not unlike Haji told you, it is a code to where some relevant documents are deposited."

"Mont Saint Michel, perhaps?"

"Maybe. It may be part of Saint Augustine's *City of God*, dating from around 390 to 430. Or it may be related to another event of major historical impact, perhaps part of the Emperor Galerius' Edict of Toleration that recognized Christianity as a lawful religion. That would have been in 311. Or it might be from a year later, 312, the Edict of Milan. Galerius, Emperor of the East, confabulated with Constantine, Emperor of the West and they decided to allow the 'little people' to practice their chosen religion."

"These are world milestones? I always thought they were somewhat abstract."

"Perhaps to us they are. But to a world permeated—no, obsessed, rather, with religious practice as the reality of life...."

Stroutsel uttered his theories with only a half-hearted passion, but Tim zealously wrote them down anyway, unwilling to overlook any fragment, regardless of how insignificant it might seem, that could provide a clue. As Tim listened to the cynical old Jewish professor's ramblings, his historian's heart quickened. Stroutsel's words were tapping directly into Tim's memory bank, bringing sub-conscious thoughts and details swirling to the surface.

"Of course. This is more like it. The inscriptions could be elements of any of these," Tim said enthusiastically, his brain shifted rapidly into higher gear.

"Calvin, I think you find this more interesting than I do," Stroutsel said as Tim continued to scribble furiously. "Those possi-bilities stem from the same general time frame. My own radical idea is that the plate may be part of a code of law Charlemagne ordered set down in 812. He ordered that all laws be written, a milestone among milestones in an otherwise dark world full of anarchy. Did you get that?"

"Yes—let me finish here."

"But remember my prelude to you. This relic may be authen-tic but of no significance. Keep in mind that there were some learned people back then who had odd interests. This could have been the writing of some religiously intoxicated duke, or some such poten-tate, who thought he had touched the hem of heaven." Stroutsel seemed to be slightly intoxicated himself.

"But at the least it's old, which gives it some value. And if it is something more than a zealot's musings, then we have to face the prospect of its being of an even greater value," Tim said, finishing his note taking.

"I hope it is, my dear Calvin. By our standards the ancients seemed so full of piety and zeal. What from our age might provoke such inquiry a millennium hence? A video tape? A movie? No, we are dwarfs on the shores of time." Stroutsel sat back in the chair and rubbed his beard with both hands, his chin tilted up, his eyes study-ing Tim who in turn was studying and comparing the range of pos-sibilities with those he had compiled in Chicago with Haji.

He reviewed Stroutsel's theories. The plate could be:

1) *A code describing locations of manuscripts deposited at Mont St.Michel.*
2) *Part of St. Augustine's* The City of God*—dating from*

354-430. The writing strengthened Christians as Rome was falling to German barbarians. Its premise: God is present in all human affairs.

3) *Related to or part of the Edict of Toleration by Emperor Galerius in 311. The Edict recognized Christianity as a lawful religion. Galerius was Emperor of the East.*

4) *Related to or part of the Edict of Milan in 312 issued by Galerius and Constantine, Emperor of the West-allowed the right to practice a chosen religion.*

5) *Related to or part of an order of Charlemagne in 812. He ordered that all laws of nations under his rule be reduced to writing and codes. He allowed people to live by their national law.*

Haji and Juni Khadija's theories, however, presented different possibilities:

1) *A map giving location to*
   a) *gold/diamonds/jewels*
   b) *location of important religious artifacts, i.e., the Ark of Covenant (such possibilities were "endless," according to Haji)*

2) *A cipher plate to an ancient code used by a ruler or powerful religious figure.*

3) *Possibly a Byzantine artifact from Justinian circa 527–65 (could be part of written code of law compiled then— Greek was official language of Byzantine empire then)*

4) *Destination or "address" plate, telling where important documents are stored. (A prevalent theory—the plate describes the location of a manuscript of great importance hidden at Mt. St. Michel)*

5) *A burial plaque—of someone of great importance.*

By Tim's reckoning, Stroutsel had been more specific than Haji. But something told him he still didn't have what he needed, and the quest was not over yet by any means.

The two men across the dining room signaled for their check. The smaller of the two reached into his jacket pocket and quietly clicked off the recorder he had used to tape the conversation between Tim and Stroutsel. On the way back to their hotel the Iranians discussed the situation and determined that keeping tabs on the American and the old Jew would provide no advantage to their government. Allah would not be served by watching someone seek the bona fides of an old piece of metal written about Christ and sin or some epic of Christian civilization. They knew that Pasotti was a venal disbeliever of no value to Iran.

The Iranians, however, were unaware of the service they had provided for Tariq Abel. The bug he had planted on them had proven valuable indeed—he had been able to not only listen to their conversation and the play-back of the tape, he even listened to their call to Teheran where it was decided they should return to Paris. He removed his earphones, and smirking, he raised his bottle of whiskey in a mock toast to the Iranian agents who had saved him so much footwork.

Two can play this game, Moshe thought as he switched off the small radio he used to scan microwave frequencies used by cellular phones. He in his own turn had been able to tap in on Tariq Abel's calls. The Israeli agent had been half-dozing while no more than routine calls went through, but his head snapped up in surprise when he overheard Abel place a call to a new player, Aoki Pasotti. Moshe and Anna were alert when the collector called back to strike a deal with the terrorist. Abel tempted Pasotti by saying "the old Jew thinks the plate is not the real value, and told the American that it perhaps is a clue or map to something else at an old Cathedral." Pasotti slaveringly told Abel he would pay him well to stay with the American and acquire the plate. Another price would be discussed if something more than just the plate resulted.

Moshe and Anna digested the intercepted conversation and prepared a fax to Tel Aviv. Moshe stood behind Anna watching as she typed the message, and couldn't resist stroking her curls. She paused for a moment, and smiled up at him. She patted his hand and removed it from her head, telling him that "this is not an appropriate time—we have work to do." Pleased with the hope that maybe an "appropriate" time would come later, Moshe accepted the rebuff good naturedly.

As far as Anna and Moshe knew, Pasotti and Abel had never met, but the two were like sharks of the same ilk. Obviously Abel knew enough about Calamari Pasotti to get his attention and to stimulate his desire. The Israelis realized with a sense of dread that Tim was in deep water now, possibly way over his head.

"He is an innocent and inexperienced and he is after something which these two brutal, self-absorbed, predatory men want desperately," Moshe said.

"They'll stop at nothing. The stakes are incredibly high—in the millions of dollars—and that's going to make them even more dangerous than usual," Anna agreed.

"They will let him lead them and then they will take what they want—regardless of the cost." Moshe's words chilled her, and despite the warmth of the spring night, she shuddered.

Jayne found herself standing and staring at the foam of the surf as though she were searching for Cee's face. She and Brian had been too busy for children, and Cee occupied a special place in her life. This kidnapping had hurt Jayne deeply and today she felt tied in a knot of pain and tension.

The late morning sun glistened and the water sparkled in pools of blue and green, and frothy waves gently lapped the Captiva shore. The beach here took more wind than it did at Sanibel, so the vegetation was less thick, and that which did grow on the stretch carried a windswept, almost forlorn look.

* * *

Laney had carried a listless Katie to the pool deck, thinking the sun and water might help her come out of her zombie-like withdrawal. Elizabeth paced, trying to contain her own fretfulness and fear, and her stomach hurt from the strain of holding it in. She tried to remain as calm and upbeat as she could for Cee, hoping that it might also help her sister.

Cee sat by the pool playing with a powder compact she had found in the guest bathroom, catching rays of sunlight with the mirror and flashing them around. Hertt sat inside the great room, looking out while Laney tried to get Katie to show some interest in the pool, kneeling next to the lounge chair and dribbling water on the child's arms and legs, but Katie remained almost catatonic.

You'd better pray...if you even know how.... Laney's admonition rattled through Hertt's head and wouldn't go away. He was having trouble thinking straight, and any contact with Wasser was becoming an increasing source of irritation. He despised him more by the minute. Hertt wondered if he was having a breakdown. He didn't know what was happening, he couldn't understand the feelings he had. It was as though something inside was cutting him like a blade. He'd never felt like this in Vietnam or in prison. For the first time in his adult life he had the sensation of being scared and he didn't know how to shake it. Instead he sat there watching the little girl. He felt compelled to watch her. Her delicate face was kind of blank and her eyes didn't sparkle anymore. They looked hollow, like guys he had known who were about to die.

The way her mother bent over her reminded him again of his Aunt Roy, bending over his battered mother. Something welled up inside of him. It came like a wave of nausea, and a shiver along his back. His head felt kind of weird and tears trickled down his face. Damn! He was crying! He couldn't remember when he had cried last. He felt panic, like something was trying to leap out of his throat.

Father, forgive me, for I have sinned.... The memories and pictures came swirling at him, strange and unsummoned like the dreams when you're only half awake and thoughts tumble over each other like clothes in a dryer: the days at Saint Thomas', when he was an altar boy at mass. Things had seemed so much easier; he would go to confession and pour out his heart and his troubles, and the Hail Marys he would have to recite as penance afterward. He had actually enjoyed practicing his religion then; he could remember feeling like he started fresh each week, like a new person. He remembered how even he used to cross himself when he played ball.

But that new, starting-over feeling came harder as he got older, and he had begun to wonder if it was all worth it. He could almost hear his aunt Roy telling him not to waste his life, but to do something with it. Damn! He hadn't thought of any of this stuff since he was a kid. He couldn't get the picture of his Aunt Roy out of his head. Especially the night his mother died, the way Roy looked at his mother, dead and lifeless, and then at him. He had never wanted to think of that night again. Now he saw that little girl and her mother and he couldn't shake that picture of Aunt Roy and his mom. It was his fault; he should have stopped his dad. Now this— it was his fault again. This little girl could turn out like his mother had, and it was his fault. He did it. For what? Why was he crying? Why did he feel this way? It was his fault.

The little girl seemed to be looking at him, her hollow eyes boring right through him. Those hollow eyes like death. God, she looks bad he thought. How long could a little kid go on like this? He turned away; he didn't want to know, to even think about it. Then something forced him to look at her again. *Hail Mary, full of grace, pray for us sinners....* Could he still pray? Would anyone even listen?

"God, help this girl. I can't go through this again. Don't let her die. Please!" he heard himself say, and then he sat there, shaking.

* * *

Jayne walked north on Captiva, along the white strand of beach which had been rebuilt. The deep blue of the sky and the reflective water were beginning to calm her. A sudden flash caught her eye, momentarily blinding her. She stopped in her tracks and shielded her eyes, trying to locate where the flash had come from.

She scanned the area and saw another flash coming from the screened porch and pool of a large white house.

Some kid playing with a mirror, she thought, and remembered a day just a few weeks ago when she and Cee had been playing with Jayne's makeup mirror. They had pretended to be stranded on a desert island trying to signal planes and passing ships. She had taught Cee the signal for the S-O-S code using the flashes of light from the mirror. The child was so bright, she had learned in nothing flat.

Jayne studied the flashes coming from the house just yards away. Probably just random flashes from a hanging prism glass, or watch crystal, or glass. But no—there was a definite pattern. It was a signal! Three quick flashes, three long ones, then three quick ones again. Over and over. Each flash struck a nerve inside her, and Jayne soon was convinced that it was Cee sending the signal, and that the white beach house was where she and the Calvins were being held.

*　*　*

Hertt was still deep in thought, watching Laney and Katie, when he saw a figure coming from the beach, through the fence, and toward the patio.

"Hey! Get them girls and get 'em inside. Get to the bedroom. Hurry! Now!" Hertt's shouts startled Laney, and Cee jumped and dropped the compact, catching it on her knees.

"Move—now!" He dashed toward the pool deck from the greatroom and met Cee as she crossed the sliding glass door. He patted her shoulder and pushed her gently along. He reached for Elizabeth's elbow by stretching his other arm, while twisting his neck to watch a woman approach the back of the house.

"Leave the baby, let her lay there. You get out of here!" he barked at Laney. When she looked as though she would refuse his order he gave her another vicious yell. As Laney reluctantly pulled away, he softened his voice.

"Just for a minute. She'll be OK there, I swear it," he said.

She walked into the bedroom, glancing at her daughter's still figure on the lounge chair. Katie hadn't left her side since Hertt had taken her to the airport, and she was afraid what effect even a short separation of just a few minutes might have. If she thought about that, though, she would go crazy, and she couldn't afford to do that, not now. She wanted to believe—had to believe—what her kidnapper and tormentor told her.

Hertt, on the other hand, couldn't believe what he was seeing. It was the redheaded singer, the hot babe from the nightclub. He straightened his shirt and smoothed his hair with his hands, and sucked his stomach in a little before stepping outside.

"Oh man!" he said to himself, feeling a flash of anger that not only the woman and kids, but also Wasser, were in the house. The babe by now was standing below at the foot of stairs which led up to the screened deck and pool.

"Excuse me," she called up the steps, "I was just walking along the beach and saw some children running," her heart pounding, she flashed her most dazzling smile at him and started up the stairs. "One of them looked like the son of a good customer of ours. My husband and I operate the Mad Hatter restaurant. I thought I would just say 'hi,' since I was just walking by...." By now she had reached the top of the steps and stood on a landing set off by a rounded railing. The house was an immaculate white, with white accent on the cream and almost white screen. Visibility into the porch was good and what Jayne saw made her heart lurch. Katie! It was Katie on the lounge, but she didn't look quite right.

"Sorry, no kids here." He saw that her eyes were on the little one. "Just my sister's little girl. Poor thing's been sick, maybe the measles."

"Too bad. Probably while they're on a vacation, too," She wished she could strike out at this man, and grab Katie and find Cee and the others. Instead she must be calm so she could quickly return to the restaurant and tell Brian and Dave where the girls were being held. She felt flushed and her heart was pounding in her ears.

"You're a hot singer. I saw you the other night. You look real good up there."

Jayne tossed her hair and turned the smile on him again. "How sweet of you to say so. We'll be at the Porch again next week. Will you come? Maybe I can sing a request for you." Hertt grinned.

Jayne wanted desperately to run and get help, and it was a struggle to maintain the facade. She smiled apologetically and turned to go. "Well, I'm sorry to have bothered you, but it's always nice to meet a fan." She glanced over her shoulder as she started back down the steps and caught a glimpse of someone. It looked as though the person had begun to step out of the house, and quickly darted back inside, as though he didn't want to be seen. "In fact, I would love to have you and your sister's family join us at the restaurant as our guests as soon as the little girl is better."

"Yeah? We'll see." Hertt said with a bit of bravado as she turned to leave.

I found them! I found them! Jayne repeated silently to herself almost like a mantra as she walked down the steps, over the patio and through the gate back to the beach. She tried to walk casually, as though interested in the surf. As soon as she was out of sight of the beach house she broke into a run.

*   *   *

Tel Aviv wasted little time before sending on to Langley the new information from Moshe and Anna: Tariq Abel was making a deal with Pasotti. Langley in turn transmitted the message to Valmer confirming the old agent's worst fear that if something can go wrong it will. The time-tested adage of field operations was again proving itself correct: Tim was in danger and he had no skills in protecting himself from someone like Abel. Experience had taught Valmer that the unexpected, the sudden turn, was the reality in the field. At the moment he felt powerless to do anything but hope some rapid change would occur to improve Tim Calvin's odds. Now the situation would have to play itself out. It was almost as though the old plate had a power of its own, impelling people to alter their lives to seek its meaning.

* * *

Tim had acquired another priority in his quest. With the finesse of dropping a bombshell, Stroutsel imparted information that would change his plans.

"I can assist you only so far with your research. I told you I had information I thought relevant to your theory of Mont Saint Michel. But there is a man who may not be far from here, who can help you immensely, a Dr. James Millerkirk of the University of Edinburgh. Millerkirk is a UN Commission member and his specialty is ancient manuscripts."

In the haze of drink and dramatic talk, Stroutsel had almost forgotten to mention Millerkirk's name. It wasn't until late in the evening he spoke of him or the attendant good news.

As luck would have it, Millerkirk had called to tell Stroutsel he would be in France, at Mont Saint Michel, during the time of Stroutsel's trip to Normandy.

Tim couldn't suppress a surge of anger listening to Stroutsel speak about Millerkirk. Why had the old man waited so long to tell him this? A whole day wasted on a drive to the beach! Chagrined, Tim realized he had been tested, that he had had to earn Stroutsel's respect before being handed this nugget of gold. He wondered what other roadblocks Stroutsel knew about that he wasn't telling him, what other "tests" he might have to pass.

"At the last meeting of the UN commission Millerkirk told me he had read references to a 'riddle,' the existence of coded messages which were either to be taken together as total, or were in parts, pieces of a larger set," Stroutsel continued, oblivious to Tim's dismay and irritation.

"A riddle? From where? Anything like the writing on the plate? Are you saying this plate is part of a set?"

"Possibly. Our UN commission had a case involving a nasty

dispute over mosaics and marble work found in the château's catacombs, the last known location of your mystery metal. All these
years later there was disagreement over ownership, and so some of
the commission and staff made an on-site inspection. Nobody had
been down there since the war, when the government closed it off.
Aside from bones and burial crypts, commission researchers found
clay vessels holding old manuscripts and scrolls. Old books, even
these hand lettered papers, had been of little interest to the souve-
nir-grabbing GIs, and so they had been left behind nearly a half a
century earlier. Millerkirk, on the other hand, was fascinated by the
material and considered the soldiers' oversight a bonanza. Since
then he has had a field day reading and translating the old manuscripts. In reading those documents, and others he translated at
Mont Saint Michel, he found mention of a cryptic message which
was somehow related to another and extraordinary manuscript said
to be of profound importance. Or so he says."

"Could that be related the plate? Or its meaning?"

"It would be too damned convenient wouldn't it? I don't go
in for that kind of research, piecing shreds of information from centuries-old manuscripts and tattered remains of earlier social structures. Too much like archaeology. Still, Millerkirk's a bright thinker,
highly regarded, and so it would be foolish to discount his theories,"
Stroutsel said.

"I am not at all familiar with him or his work. Obviously
Valmer doesn't know him." Tim was curious to meet this Millerkirk.

"He's just coming into his own. He's a younger man, probably a few years younger than you. But he's got this theory of some
ancient 'super manuscript.' I don't know whether he's onto something or if it's just a wild idea."

"What does he say about it?" The idea of a mysterious manuscript seemed to Tim to be important.

"More theories, Calvin. Jim and I have discussed them over
a few pints. He thinks it might be an early translation of the Bible,
or something perhaps like the Dead Sea Scrolls. Tales of the talisman and inscribed artifacts like your plate might be something he

calls 'post cards' or 'post-it notes' or 'billboards,' maybe references to this famous landmark manuscript. Millerkirk says these messages were chiseled, carved, or cut as reminders of places and thoughts." Stroutsel was somewhat vague about the specifics of Millerkirk's theory and concluded by saying, "But that's it, and you should probably make contact with Millerkirk for more."

The more Stroutsel spoke, the more frustrated and angry Tim felt. This Millerkirk was the person he should have been talking to in the first place. Stroutsel had been a detour on his search, though he had to admit he would never have heard of Millerkirk or this "supermanuscript" research if it hadn't been for this boozey stop in Carentan.

Tim's fuse was growing shorter and his temper was about to flare. He had been trying unsuccessfully to get a telephone connection to his new contact. After several attempts and disconnects, the bilingual operator explained to Tim that a Dr. James Millerkirk had been booked into the hotel near Mont Saint Michel, but had since checked out. His heart sank. Gone. He'd just missed him. The operator relayed that the hotel clerk had told her that Millerkirk was traveling to either Chinon, Châtellerault, or Chenonceaux. She wasn't sure. It was an ordeal requiring all of the operator's patience just to explain to Tim how to spell the names of Millerkirk's possible destinations, and they were just guesses provided by the clerk who remembered only vaguely the mention of a town with that sound. It was getting late, he was tired, he felt as though his day with Stroutsel had been agonizingly long and needlessly frustrating. Now he found himself trying to locate a man he didn't know, who might or might not have the answer to a riddle which could be centuries old.

It seemed as if all he was doing was running into walls and placing calls to people who couldn't be reached. Including his family. He found himself becoming anxious about them. Why hadn't he been able to reach them? He sighed and rubbed his eyes. The fatigue and tension were getting to him; if something had happened back on Sanibel, Valmer would have told him, and at the very least, Dave would have found a way to get word to him. He couldn't let his nerves run away with him now.

But the more he stewed, the more he fumed, and the more the idea of this great quest and thrill of the research mission seemed stupid and ill-conceived. What in the world was he doing here? What was he trying to prove?

Brian told the restaurant staff to continue preparing for that evening's seatings without him. After a hurried phone call to Dave, he and Jayne dashed toward the Hocketts.

Dave's mind leaped into a high state of readiness. Edward Earl, through his network of contacts and cross-checking made possible with computer assistance, had deduced the Captiva connection was none other than the New York wheeler-dealer Ivan Wasser. The arrival the day before of Wasser's private jet and registered flight plans nailed it down. Still, they hadn't known where he was until Jayne's discovery. Now Dave knew who the enemy was, and could give the evil force a face. Soon he would have a first hand report of where the man was hiding with the girls. He began to measure, approximate, time, and shift around elements of the plan of attack he had developed. Valmer didn't care much for the idea. He thought it contained "unpredictable variables" which could lead to a serious escalation of violence. Valmer proposed that perhaps now was time for Edward Earl to bring in police assistance.

"Not a chance of that. It's too late—it's my turn now," Dave said, undeterred. He'd been through too much, and no one was going to take this element of revenge away from him. Besides, he was sure he could control the situation and get his daughter and the Calvins out safely. He didn't have the same confidence in the police, no matter how well-meaning they were.

He knew the kidnapper wanted to make a trade, and that the well-being of Laney and the girls was insured at least until then. Right now the sergeant in him was snapping to. He had been there before, when officers went more with head than gut, and had been wrong. Experience had taught him to trust his instincts, and this time he was more sure than ever his plan was right. He felt connected. Soon he would be on the attack, no more the prone victim. Instead he would be a warrior rescuing his daughter and seeking revenge.

A Medieval Memo

"M'sieur Tim! M'sieur Tim! Time to wake up!" Marie's voice pulled him from the depths of his sleep. Even before he opened his eyes he smelled her perfume, and felt her fingers on his cheek.

"Too bad you are in such a hurry." She sat on the edge of the bed and teased him, pretending she was about to unbutton her blouse. "You could make this old lady feel young again, no?"

He rubbed his eyes, sat up and smiled and sleepily shook his head. He reached for his watch.

"Eh, bien. Another time, perhaps," she said with cheerful resignation. "It is 5:00 A.M. I have brought you coffee and bread." She stood and reached for the tray she had set on the night table. Tim had finally dragged his exhausted body to bed the night before, leaving Marie and Stroutsel poring over a map and making a series of phone calls. Stroutsel had drawn an arc on the map from Chinon through Châtellerault to Chenonceaux—the towns where he had been told Millerkirk "might be heading." The arc formed a ring below the Loire valley city of Tours. Together the two former resistance compatriots once again plotted a strategy, making calls and crossing names off Marie's hotel-keeper's guide. Through a process of elimination they had at last found Millerkirk's hotel, and by late at night had reached Millerkirk himself. After a last toast of Calvados, Tim excused himself to bed, feeling less angry about the old man.

Stroutsel had arranged for him to meet Millerkirk at the "floating" château of Chenonceaux a few kilometers southwest of Tours early in the morning. Millerkirk was there meeting with a manager of the magnificent castle, and Tim could catch up with him by taking the 6:00 A.M. train from Caen, through LeMans and down to Tours.

Tim sipped the hot coffee and looked at Marie. Her fatigue was obvious, and he was sure it wasn't just from the late-night strategy session. The dark circles and rings around her eyes told him that she had once again spent the night tilting with old memories, dancing with old ghosts, and arming herself with Calvados against fleeting time.

"Do you still wish to call Valmer?" she asked.

"Yes, but I'll have to make it quick. I'll need to hustle to catch that train."

"Then be up, *mon cher*, and get out of the bed—do not be so modest. You have my promise not to jump upon you," she said, the old twinkle returning to her eyes.

"Enloui will be here soon, no?" He swung his legs over the side of the bed and stood. Marie winked and patted his cheek affectionately.

"Oui, Enloui is my morning coffee. He shall get me, as you say, 'jump-started.'" Her hearty laugh rang out as she left the room. "I shall begin the call. You hurry."

Tim was puzzled by Valmer's tone during their brief conversation; the man had sounded distracted, unfocused. It was late evening, going on eleven in the States, and maybe Valmer was just tired. His enthusiasm when Tim told him he would be meeting with Millerkirk had sounded manufactured. Tim decided perhaps he was over-reacting, reflecting his own anxiety and weariness. How long ago and far away Sanibel and his vacation seemed. As the French bullet train hurtled him along on his mission, everything else seemed distant and unreal, a memory of some sort. The only plus at this point was that his passion for getting to the bottom of the mystery had been revived by the night of sleep and the locating of Millerkirk. He would be in Tours in time to pick up a car and drive down to the château. His Drive-and-Rail pass had made that easy: when he dropped his car in Caen, the agent had relayed his reservation ahead.

He smiled to himself, proud that he had slipped out of Carentan without drawing anyone's attention. He had become increasingly suspicious of the couple who looked like backpackers or hikers. They were popping up too often, and he had come to fear that they could be the Iranian surveillance team of which Valmer had warned him. If the woman and man were spies, that would explain their considerable language skills, and why he had seen them so often. He was aggravated that he hadn't picked up on it sooner. But no matter now; he was sure that they had not been on the train when it left the station, and he felt as though he had achieved a field operative's success. Valmer would be proud.

Tim watched the sun rise on the Loire valley, over the lush countryside where kings and queens had come to play. This had been their region for recreation, along the banks of the Loire, Cher and Indre rivers. Along passages through wild wooded hills and golden fields of wheat, the gentle rivers reflected the graceful balustrades and grand castle-towers of architectural masterpieces. This was the land of the château and castle, massive monuments to grace and wealth and an age of extravagance which today seems almost unreal.

The Loire valley was also rich with historical churches and abbeys. The oldest church in France stood in Germigny-des-Prés, where it was built in the ninth century. The Gothic cathedrals of Bourges, Tours, Orléans, and Blois soar above their towns, and the magnificent cathedral at Chartres was acclaimed for its incomparable statuary and breathtakingly unique and beautiful stained glass. It was this religious art and architecture which had drawn Millerkirk away from reading the ancient manuscripts and early printed books in the museum at Avranches and Mont Saint Michel, and Tim wondered now if his new agenda would take him back to Mont Saint Michel, or if Millerkirk would have other ideas.

Dr. Jim Millerkirk was a charismatic man in his late thirties, tall, lean, with a thick head of dark brown hair which he wore in a casual manner falling onto his forehead. In Stroutsel's briefing the night before Tim had learned that Millerkirk was the product of prep schools and the Ivy League, where he learned to read Greek, Hebrew, Latin, and old English. He had earned his doctorate from Princeton Theological Seminary and had been a staff minister at a couple of churches before taking a position at the University of Edinburgh. Tim supposed that Millerkirk's quick mind, ready wit, and warm smile, would make him the kind of man to whom people would be attracted and whom they would trust.

It was that ease of Millerkirk's nature which had gotten him invited down to the Renaissance jewel of Chenonceaux, the lavish country palace built in 1513 by Thomas Bohler, comptroller of the royal treasury. Millerkirk had admitted to Stroutsel that he felt some twinges of anxiety and guilt, staying in a palace built by money ripped off poor peasants by royal tax collectors so the rich and powerful could have an elegant playhouse.

Chenonceaux was unique amongst the galaxy of châteaus because of its two-story gallery which "floated" above the Cher river. That part of the massive white stone castle, with its towers and turrets and long formal hall, was built up like a bridge. Towering over the rich green of the ancient forest, part of it overlooking the gentle Cher while another extension "danced" over the river, the castle offered a visual magic. The addition had been built and decorated by Henri II for his mistress, Diane de Poitiers. When he died, however, his widow Catherine de Medici took gleeful possession and forced the mistress into less grand circumstances. Tapestries and oils and baroque furnishings gave the palace a patina of splendor. Stroutsel had told Tim that this was the kind of break that Millerkirk needed after days of the tedious reading. It was indeed a far cry from the tight and sequestered world of dusty archives and ancient piety.

Tim was dazzled by the beauty of the castle and its approach past low-walled formal gardens with maze-like paths and hedges. The place seemed alive with the glorious color of the French springtime. He had never seen this part of France, and he was absorbed by the magnificence and splendor of the place. After announcing himself to a docent, he was ushered to a parlor and pointed toward Millerkirk, who stood looking at a massive oversized oil of Louis XIII. The haughty king stood with a smug and evil look, his opulent clothing and fancy hair ornately framed in gold. The portrait was a masterpiece not only of composition but also of incredible cost.

"His lavishness caused so many to suffer. It's hard not to feel angry, just looking at him now. Excuse me, I'm Jim Millerkirk. I got a little carried away."

Tim shook the proffered hand. "Hi, I'm Tim Calvin. This place is unbelievable."

They stood silently for a moment looking at the king.

"It's fitting, maybe even poetic, that a few centuries later he hangs there to face disgust, instead of praise." Tim offered.

"Oh, yeah. He has surely faced a tough judgment, don't you think? Even though he lived much too early to get his head chopped off like his descendent." Millerkirk chuckled as they headed toward the door to the outside. "Dr. Stroutsel tells me you are doing some ancient detective work. Old mysteries can be pretty tough. How are you doing, and what can I do to help?"

Tim started at the beginning, relating the account of the idyllic vacation interrupted, and continuing through the whole agenda to date. Millerkirk listened intently, occasionally interjecting questions, as they strolled the grounds, sat in the garden and wandered the flowering paths. Tim detailed the widening scenario of the mysterious artifact—the enigma of history, object of greed and lust, and apparent item of great interest to intelligence agencies and security apparatus of the United States, Iran, and Israel.

Tim described the metal plate and its twin inscriptions. "It almost seems like a piece of civilization floating through time, out of sync, out of context, disrupting life centuries later. It's a chunk of history tossed into a pool of twentieth century life, sending ripples from the middle ages." He stopped abruptly, embarrassed. "Sorry, I'm getting carried away, too."

"Well, I can understand," Millerkirk smiled. "These antiquities do cast a spell. But this plate is obviously more than a mere historical curiosity. As you say, there is an element of criminal activity involved in the United States. Furthermore, I think your friend Valmer might be right: there could indeed be international repercussions. Why else would the CIA, Mossad, and Iran be interested? As member of a UN commission, I can tell you that we definitely are interested."

"I hate to impose on your schedule but I am here for fast answers."

"I don't know how fast they'll be, but I want to learn more about this plate; I've been toying with an old mystery myself. But the only way we'll get anything done is to get started. Let's drive into Tours and see what we can find."

Once in the car, Tim gave Millerkirk photos of the plate and a translation of the inscriptions. Millerkirk's primary interest was in the inscriptions which he repeated aloud to himself, as though actually hearing the words might shake something out that otherwise would be missed. As they drove toward Tours, Tim had the feeling that although Millerkirk seemed to be immersed in the scenery of the French countryside, his mind was exploring its accumulated store of historic knowledge, searching for some clue to the mysterious inscriptions.

" 'Warrior of light who guards the south where Christ rules

and judges enthroned to the setting sun. A second house on early spirit ground. Two sisters now reach to heaven. For the love of God and all earthly issue. King of Ages here resides true light on sin.' " Millerkirk recited it over and over, and began to mumble rather than speak. Lost in thought, he was apparently wrestling with the meaning, just as Tim, Valmer, and analysts in Washington, Tel Aviv, and Teheran had also done.

Millerkirk seemed to need a break, so Tim explained his Mont Saint Michel theory. "It almost fits perfectly, but I'm stymied by the phrase 'two sisters reaching to heaven.' "

"Your 'early spirit ground' explanation and 'second house' theory sound very plausible," Millerkirk responded. "And Michael as the 'warrior of light' could work. But the business about 'who guards the south' doesn't fit in describing a granite mountain off the northwest coast of France."

As they drove on, pondering, the two men found themselves taking a new measure of each other. Millerkirk asked about Valmer, and the interest of Valmer's "friends at Langley" in the plate, and the chain of events which had set everything off. Tim responded easily, drawn to the way the other man spoke, listened, and reasoned.

Tim made his living teaching business men and women and corporate leaders techniques in sincere and effective communication, including listening. But Millerkirk did all of that naturally, demonstrating both sensitivity and keen intellect, and something else—something intangible: an ability to convey great depth and peace. He was at once serene and cheerful, and Tim thought his obvious compassion and strength would make him an ideal leader. He would be a calming influence in any crisis, capable of inspiring and motivating his followers. While Haji and Stroutsel tended to apply a linear and intellectual way of thinking toward the mystery of the metal plate, attempting to ground it in the concrete of lists and comparisons, Millerkirk seemed to welcome its inexplicable and puzzling nature with zest and enthusiasm. He told Tim he thought the government agencies' interest was odd, but concluded it merely added spice to the pursuit.

They decided to stop at Tours for lunch, allowing Millerkirk to consult his notes, which he had left at the hotel. Maybe they could sort out some of the theories.

"We can cross-reference what Haji and Stroutsel told you with some material I've gathered," Millerkirk said after giving the notes a brief perusal.

Tim actually began to feel hopeful now that his wild chase was being joined by someone with expertise, and gaining such a colleague made him feel more confident that he would actually be able to accomplish his goal. He was also more than a little moved by Millerkirk's desire to help. The man didn't seem the least bit annoyed at having his own research trip intruded upon, and even expressed genuine concern that Tim's vacation had been spoiled by something so jarring.

"I hope we can answer all of your questions and get you back to the island ASAP. Let's return to my notes. I want to pull something out. I don't want to mislead or get your hopes up too soon, but this whole business is ringing a bell. I told you about the 'supermanuscript'—this stuff of yours looks like it could fit in with some of the things I've been reading on that."

Tim sat at the sidewalk café having a café au lait and watched the late morning crowd stir across the plaza. Almost a week had passed since he and Laney and the girls had flown into Fort Myers and driven out to Sanibel Island. It seemed as if it had been months since he had seen or even talked to them.

The last few days had unhinged his easy pace, forcing him to explore unfamiliar regions of his own mind and soul, and he realized that the entire set of circumstances had probably changed his life forever. Gone was the regret he had felt for years, the restlessness and longing over lost dreams and opportunities, missing pieces of his destiny. As he sat in the heart of the Loire valley town of Tours, observing the lively pulse of the Saturday market scene, he discovered he was more singularly focused than he could remember himself ever being. A stranger in a strange place, instead of being exhausted and angry, he was enthusiastic, charged. He had become convinced that he actually belonged here on this pursuit, that it was his role, maybe even his destiny to play out this part of history. The quest had developed a power of its own, had surpassed anything he'd ever felt before, even in grad school. He himself had now become one with the search and its meaning.

Millerkirk broke into Tim's reverie when he sat down and put down two notebooks and a lightweight laptop computer on the table.

"Tim, I think we've got something—very solid." The theology and history professor grinned widely. "For the last five years I've been pulling together stuff on what I've called the 'supermanuscript of medieval history'—hinted at through the arcane, but never before proven. Until about two years ago I wasn't sure it even existed. I thought maybe I was reading too much into data or simply reading material wrong. Then I put together a data base and played with it several ways, and it all came together."

"What kind of supermanuscript?"

"I don't know. It's silly. I know it's out there, but I don't know what it is."

"Any theories?"

"I have a lot of those," he laughed. "At first I thought it was a translation of the Bible, or books of the Gospel hitherto unknown. I toyed with scrolls of Qumran, something like the 'Q' manuscripts, and a whole load of other possibilities. But after a while I gave up on the 'what' it might be and started looking at the 'who' that might be behind it. I figured If I could follow it back to the writer or writers, and their sect or tribe, then I might have a better shot at the 'what'— what it means."

"How did you get on to this? Stroutsel mentioned your 'post-it notes,' and 'billboards or post cards.' "

"Yes. Absolutely inappropriate, but very typically Jim Millerkirk. I used those terms once at a UN conference and only a couple of people got it."

"Well, I don't get it. I don't follow you."

"I'll give it a shot. In looking over a period of six hundred years, from roughly 600 to 1200 A.D., I've found evidence of and references to a message, an epistle of great importance. These traces come in a variety of places and ways, so I called them my post-it notes, billboards, post cards from the past. The abbeys in this area are ancient, and some of the manuscripts they've stored are even older. They've been handed down through religious orders, from royalty, as the spoils of war, some are from private collections, and estates. We continue to find old books, early printings, hand lettered volumes and older manuscripts."

"Stroutsel told me about the clay vessels at the château where the plate was apparently found. They were, what—about a thousand years old?"

"Yes, which is why I think your plate could be the key to some of the things I've been studying. Some of those documents or manuscripts may have the same origin, and I think I can prove it. Anyway, about these messages: in several abbey collections, as well as in the incredible collection at Mont Saint Michel and Avranches, there are recurring references to a letter or message from someone called simply 'W-E.' I've also found annotations and explanations by priors and archbishops about the epistle, and in some cases there are even whole letters about the explications themselves."

"It's almost as though it's developed a following or life of its own," Tim said, as much for his own clarification as a comment to Millerkirk.

"You're right. It seems that at times various monastic orders undertook a kind of coded communication: different abbey houses had different codes, if I can call them that. There are direct references, along with seemingly hidden messages, as though there was an attempt to cover up or hide something. Then I find that years later someone made references back to the earlier writings, written in the same type of monastic code."

"Are they always about the same thing?"

"Indeed, and that is why I am so obsessed with it. The central and recurring theme is this very important letter, this epistle. As Haji and Stroutsel told you, there have been legends and stories about a highly important item or artifact said to possess mystical or magical properties. Of course no one knows what the item is, just the stories about it. Well, the assumption has since been made, because it was found during the war, that this item could be your metal plate. That's probably why some governments are jumping through hoops now to figure out what it is your daughter found. You can understand the urgency, if the plate you have is also the 'magic' plate in all these old legends."

"What's the connection between the plate and the supermanuscript, the epistle of—what?"

"Of whom—W-E. The Epistle of W-E. Maybe it's just coincidental, maybe not. I'm the only person researching the epistle, but the stories about this plate are ancient. The sources are long since lost, but the stories and legends have come down in different ways, from tribes, monastic orders, sheiks or whatever; Christian, Jew, and Muslim.

"During that period of 600 to 1200, the plate was very important as a tradition, or at least something associated with it was. And here we get to the chase: I saw a very similar pattern in archives and abbeys in southern Britain. I changed a couple of index parameters on my data base, turned it on, and that's when I came up with an answer to the W-E mystery, or at least to the whom of the W-E is— William of Enright. Tim, I think William of Enright was the author of the W-E epistle. If we're lucky and if providence permits, I think we can put together the what; I think its in here," he said, tapping his computer and notebooks. He sat back and took a sip of coffee.

"So back again to my obsession—what's the plate all about?" Tim asked, trying to follow where the theologian was going. Millerkirk grinned again.

"I haven't got it all worked out yet, but I can't help thinking it's more than coincidental, that it's related. The main thing I can't figure is how close in time the Enright epistle and the plate are related. And if I knew what the plate meant, I think that would beam through and make sense, and I could figure it all out." Millerkirk stopped and studied Tim's reaction. "How about some lunch? It might help us think."

Tim looked around the plaza and the picturesque buildings bordering it and thought how it gave the impression of being a movie set. People sat at tables beneath colorful umbrellas, and merchants lined the square with carts and tables full of the local bounty of vegetables and fruits and flowers. As he and Millerkirk walked toward the L'Odéon Restaurant directly across the square from the train depot, they continued their discussion about the different theories.

"You know Haji and Stroutsel say the plate could be a kind of address plate. They both cite Mont Saint Michel."

"I've been through just about everything there and at Avranches, and I found references to the Enright letter, but that's all. I'm certain that you'd just be spinning your wheels going through Mont Saint Michel again. And although I'm sure the plate is part of the puzzle, I just don't know how."

Tim listened appreciatively to Millerkirk's conversation with the waiter. In a fluent, non-halting French he ordered for both of them starting with cream of watercress soup, Loire pike in buttercream sauce for Tim, and berry rooster in a red wine for himself. They split a paté salad and a bottle of Mont Louis vin blanc.

"It's said the best French in the country is spoken here," Millerkirk said, watching the waiter walk away. "Pressure was on. He probably thinks I'm nuts for having the rooster in red wine and ordering a bottle of white. Crazy Americans." He locked his hands behind his head, stretched his elbows and arms, and took a deep breath. "Tim, I'd like to take a mental break before I start with this computer. Tell me about yourself."

* * *

It was about an hour before sunrise on Sanibel. Dave couldn't sleep any longer. He lay there in the dark, running through the plan again and again, analyzing every move and every facet. It was as though he were watching a tape, stopping it, and blowing up details to large size, scanning them, then moving on. Timing would be critical. In seven hours he would strike. In seven hours he would have his daughter back and he would exact some just revenge. He was acutely aware that if his plan didn't work the situation could turn tragic. Earl had kept the police at bay, buying time, but Dave knew the clock was running out. When time was up, despite concerns to the contrary, the police would take over. He had only one chance, and he didn't want to consider what might happen if he failed.

Maybe they should have listened to Barb's impassioned plea; she was a mother who wanted only her child's safe return. But Valmer, Edward Earl and he each had their own agenda and each had, in his own way, a score to settle. Valmer wanted answers to why the old artifact prompted such international uproar, and why it had been such an enigma for so long. Edward Earl wanted Wasser, jailed and charged.

Dave wanted his daughter, but he wanted something else—a moment of warrior's justice with Wasser.

Barb had begged Dave to "just surrender the plate, get the girls and be done with it." She had urged him to bring in the Florida State Police, even the FBI. Earl had finally convinced her that even with a skilled police unit, Wasser had the upper hand. Now, staring at the ceiling in the dark Dave recalled Barb's anguished look as Earl laid the reality of the scenario before her.

"I've seen scores of kidnappings and abduction cases and I can predict how they'll play out," Earl had said. "Wasser will be on the plane, holding one last hostage, probably one of the little girls. That child will not be freed until the plate is in his possession and the plane is ready to move. Any sign of anything out of the ordinary at the hangar or near the plane, and he will be wheels up with the child and only the Lord knows what that could mean. Remember, he can see the exchange point from the plane. It's too damned close."

Barb listened, and realized with dismay that the former prosecutor, investigator, and intelligence man was probably right.

"Wasser knew what he was doing when he set up the exchange site," Earl explained. "It's perfect for him and absolutely impossible for police, even the FBI. There's no way to infiltrate that kind of open expanse. If the scenario went according to plan, Dave would get out of the van holding the plate over his head, Wasser's intermediary would take the plate, release the girls, tell Dave the other child would be freed once he and the plate were on board and the flight was cleared to leave. Once they were in the air, they would soon be in international air space and beyond arrest. It's a private plane so he can fly anywhere he wants. The Air Force is not going to shoot an American out of the air."

"Then have the police storm the beach house," she had urged.

"That would be a lost cause from the start, because there's no way to get down the drive without alerting the kidnappers and there was no approach possible from the beach without being seen.

"For one thing, Wasser is probably staying elsewhere, where he can't be recognized. Knocking down doors only happens in the movies. Try that in real life and someone, often the hostage, gets killed. We can't take that chance," Earl said. "In the second place, without some kind of information—a psychological profile, a record—on who is actually holding your friend and the kids, it's not wise to go in that way. As long as Wasser thinks he is getting the plate, the hostages are safe. Change that equation and you don't know what you'll get. Besides, I think your husband's idea is off the wall enough to work."

Now as Dave lay awake, with his plan spinning in his head, he could feel more intensely than ever his sense of mission and his desire for revenge.

Laney hadn't slept much. She was worried about Katie and wondering about Tim. She missed him, even more in these circumstances. Not being able to talk to him compounded her misery.

She rolled onto her side and studied the face of the sleeping child next to her. Even in her sleep Katie didn't seem quite right, like the tension and fear was still present in her dreams. Laney brushed a lock of hair from her daughter's forehead, and Katie stirred and snuggled closer. Laney thought about Tim. Was he back in the States yet? How had Dave or Valmer broken the news of the kidnapping, and how had he taken it? He would be frantic, she was sure, and blame himself. She felt the tears welling, and took a deep breath so she wouldn't cry. She couldn't lose control now; the sun would be up soon, and sometime during this day all of this would end.

Out in the greatroom Hertt sat nursing a tumbler of Markers Mark. It was the same glass he had filled hours before after his argument with Wasser, and he had only sipped at it. Most of the night he sat and thought about Katie, how much he hated Wasser, and the long list of mistakes he had made in his life. When Wasser had berated him for letting the redhead so close to the house, that was it. Hertt reckoned he'd get the plate, let the girls go, drive over to the hangar and give the plate to Wasser, then drive out of Wasser's life.

Father forgive me.... He hoped his family would forgive him. He was surely going to do whatever he could to make up for the past years, the hell and the pain he'd put them through. He thought he'd go spend some time with his Aunt Roy, and try to patch things up with his sister, get to know her and her kids again. Maybe it wasn't too late to start over. If he played his cards right, maybe he could meet a woman, get married and have a child, like the poor little kid inside the guestroom. He sighed and sipped his drink. Yeah, that would be great.

Stroutsel disclosed to Moshe and Anna what he had told Tim, the plate might be important, but it also might simply be old. Dr. Jim Millerkirk knew more about any possible significance, which was why he had sent Tim to him. The two Mossad field operatives were chagrined to learn they had been given the slip, though Stroutsel was able to direct them to the hotel in Tours where Millerkirk was registered. After they interviewed Stroutsel, Moshe notified Tel Aviv where they were moving. They knew they would have to act fast, because when they found Tim they would also find Tariq Abel.

Tim and Jim Millerkirk continued to hit it off well. They liked each other and conversation came easily. Millerkirk was a preacher at heart, with heavy academic pedigree. He was also an intellectual Christian with a strong belief in what he called disciple-ship.

"It's an adventure," he said, describing his 'walk with Christ.' "He is, as the scripture says, 'the way, the truth and the life,' and I know when I'm challenged, the Spirit is there. I can't imagine a greater adventure than putting our trust and faith in a master who calls us to serve."

Although the context was somewhat different, it sounded familiar to Tim—Haji and his serious devotion to Allah, Stroutsel and his 'Rock of Abraham' suffering, and now this. But Millerkirk didn't sound like he was proselytizing, nor like an evangelizing preacher in a tent crusade. Instead he spoke with an assured calm-ness and certainty, evidence of a deep and heartfelt conviction. Tim thought Jim Millerkirk was one of the most exceptional men he had met, even among the many powerful and wealthy men and women he had encountered during his own career. Millerkirk seemed to have an extra dimension, and as they sat finishing the meal, Tim concluded that that "extra" was the man's faith. Whatever it was about Millerkirk, it made Tim confident that he would actually be able to solve this ancient riddle, his arcanum, and perhaps soon.

The restaurant had emptied, except for the two Americans. They occupied a table by the window, and the manager didn't seem to mind that they lingered as they ordered deserts and more coffee and busied themselves with the computer and notebooks.

Jim Millerkirk told Tim how he identified with the supermanuscript's supposed author, William of Enright—what he wrote and how he wrote it, and how he must have lived. "What strikes me the most are his reflections on his seventh century world, as it came to him in pieces. I've taken to calling it a medieval memo."

"What do you know about him?"

"He was a fine storyteller. He would have been a great as what we call a pulpit preacher. He was a man of great intelligence, full of grace, and he devoted his life entirely to his faith."

Millerkirk's expression suddenly changed, becoming more serious, even urgent. His gaze quickly alternated between computer and notebook; he leafed through the notebook, tapped in some entries on the keyboard, stared and consulted the notebook while he gnawed on his knuckle.

"Excuse me, Tim—I just can't believe what I'm reading. One of our research associates booted several Latin documents into my program, and there were several which I hadn't had a chance to read yet, much less bothered to translate, because of the sequence. But they are genuine and they look like they fit with an earlier part of the Enright letters."

He scrolled through several pages on the computer screen, his eyes wide. "This is incredible! I can't imagine that this can be right—something must be wrong here. Whew!" He scooted his chair back from the table and started gathering up the notebooks. "I'm going back to the hotel and call Diane at the university and have her plug in a few pages, or at least get an accurate translation on some of these pages here," he muttered more to himself than to Tim.

Tim lifted his hands palms up and shrugged his shoulders, and Millerkirk responded with both hands in a kind of halt or stop gesture.

"I've got to stop. I must be reading or translating this wrong." He pushed the notebooks aside. "Back to William of Enright—I'll do this other stuff later. Are you bored by all this history?"

"Not at all. I'm anxious to hear it. Besides, you ought to let that computer cool down before it melts."

Millerkirk smiled. He leaned back in the chair and relaxed, stretching out his legs in front of him and crossing his ankles. "As a prelude, let me tell you I've been away from the pulpit for a while and I'm really into this, so if I start to preach, let me know," he chuckled.

"Hey, not to worry. A little old-fashioned religion would probably do me some good," Tim said. Millerkirk's whole demeanor was so engaging, Tim was sure that his brand of "preaching" would be as lively, interesting, and inoffensive as the man himself was.

"When you say old-fashioned, how old are you talking about? Remember, some of this goes back thirteen centuries. For everything we've learned, we have forgotten some things, attitudes buried under centuries of ignorance. Some of it is worth thinking about. For example, I come across lines like '...the sacred charge to cloak the acts in the mantle of secrecy to stay the hand of apocalypse from the cradle of faith.' Now, I used that one on my classes before. They go berserk trying to figure it out."

"Sounds a little like Jonathan Edwards, the 'Colonial firebrand,' huh?"

"And here's another one," Millerkirk said, looking through one of his notebooks. "This is one of the lines that I just translated. I don't know where it came from yet, but listen to this: 'The rotten heart of the labyrinth, a breach of all that is decent, an act of will, lay at the center of the maze, buried by a great act of courage and faith all those centuries ago. Still, the buried heart beats, caustic, corrosive, corrupt, and evil.' Wow. I'd love to know what that's all about. I hope Diane can translate. How would a congregation take that today?" Millerkirk smiled, obviously tickled by the arcane passage, but Tim could see it also troubled him.

He tried to ease Millerkirk back on track. "Before you slip back into burning your computer, I'd still like to hear about William of Enright."

In the ensuing history lesson, Millerkirk related the events of thirteen hundred years ago that impelled the evolution of civilization as it is known today.

"It began around 597 when the pagan Angles, Saxons and Jutes in the northern Britain were converted to Christianity by missionaries from Iona off the west coast of Scotland. Augustine led the effort to convert the pagans of the south with the help of Pope Gregory the Great. Gregory was from a wealthy family and trained for the legal profession, but turned to the church instead. He converted his vast estate and other homes into abbeys and monasteries. The power of the Roman empire had fallen by then, so kings of new countries as well as bishops and dukes welcomed the rising authority of the Church. He insisted on care and protection of the poor, settled disputes, gave advice on how to manage property and tolerated no political interference with the Church.

"Meanwhile, the Pope sent Augustine and his party of monks to establish a mission in Canterbury on land donated by King Ethelbert of Kent. Ethelbert's wife, a Frankish woman, was a Christian, and she convinced him to allow Augustine to begin work as the first Archbishop of Canterbury. It was during this time that King Edwin, one of the rulers up in Northumbria, was also being led on the path to Christianity by his wife, a princess from Kent. He had promised her if he were successful in a military campaign he would become a Christian. When Edwin won, he kept his word and called together a council to convince his pagan followers they should convert to Christianity.

"It had to be one of the most exciting moments in religious history," Millerkirk said, sipping from his coffee, "and the young William of Enright was there. He was the eldest child of the king's sister, in training to become a knight. His writing about the council meeting is powerful."

A rider on a motorcycle passed the L'Odéon Restaurant and slowed when he noticed Tim listening intently to the other man. The speaker paused only slightly to drink some coffee, and in doing so glanced at the motorcyclist. Tariq Abel passed by, confident that he was again close to his prey.

Tim was fascinated as Millerkirk continued with his historical narrative and the story of William of Enright's impression of King Edwin's council chamber.

"Christians from the Canterbury mission had spoken, and then an aged councilor rose to speak. He compared the life of man to a sparrow's flight through the hall. Man, the councilor said, is sitting at the table, by the fire eating, while outside is winter's chill and rain. On this point William's story corresponds almost verbatim with the account in *Bede's Ecclesiastical History*. It's a great story:

" 'The sparrow flies in at one door and tarries for one moment in the light and heat of the hearthfire and then, flying forth from the other vanishes into the wintry darkness whence it came. So tarries the life of man in our sight, but what is before and after it we know not. If this new teaching tells us aught certainly of these, let us follow it.' I memorized that years ago. Terrific analogy, isn't it?" Tim nodded agreement.

"Now, if you can, imagine what effect that would have on the king, much less young William. When the old man sat down, a pagan priest stood up. He said that although he had followed his gods with duty and devotion they had done nothing to favor him. The room was still. The priest then repudiated his gods and threw a spear against a pagan shrine in the council room, smashing it. King Edwin and his people became Christians that very night, and Edwin gave land for a church which became the York minster. Most importantly, young William of Enright asked Edwin to send him to Canterbury, and here our adventure really takes off." Millerkirk was a masterful storyteller and by now had Tim's rapt attention.

"The young William of Enright was a knight among priests, but he had an insatiable appetite for learning. He consumed manuscripts and books voraciously and would question the priests and the monks to the point where they would sometimes go out of their way to avoid his inquisitiveness. But he soon learned where they hid. There was no escaping his curiosity and desire to learn.

"He had been trained in the formal etiquette of the court and council, and his winning personality endeared him to the mission and its visitors. After a couple of years, he was given the task of organizing and administering what would today be called a library. The role expanded and William became the emissary who met with the travelers to and from Rome and elsewhere. Most importantly, he had direct contact with the growing number of pilgrims going to and returning from the Holy Land. He became the mission's principal contact with the outside world and brought its news into the mission."

"He was a kind of early chronicler, wasn't he?" Tim asked while pouring another cup of coffee.

"Indeed he was." Millerkirk explained how he had been able to locate and read most of William's writings, accounts of his conversations with travelers, stories they told of their journeys, and of the sights and experiences of Christians on the road to Jerusalem and through the Holy Land.

"The letters, really reports for the abbey prior, the bishop, and the civil leadership, are fascinating history, written with William's style of homiletic storytelling. His reputation as a great scholar spread as far as Rome and Jerusalem, and people sought him out for his knowledge and insight. That is probably how he became aware of the growth of a new religion 'Mohammedanism.' Some of his best writing is from late in his life, and it deals with the relationship of God and man as it practiced by different cultures. It's comparative religion, really, what we would now call cultural influence. He spoke with rabbis, and followers of what became Islam, and examined how they perceived Christianity. It's wonderful. He was a bridge builder."

"What an exceptional man. I didn't realize."

"You know, Tim, to read it now forces you to analyze your faith, to question the strength of your conviction. Do we really see ourselves as children of God? If one calls himself a Christian, what kind of devotion does he or she demonstrate? He wrote almost as though he was delivering a sermon, which back then was unheard of. I'm sure it unsettled some of the readers, but it was an early example of attacking issues of faith with the intellect. The beginning examination of Christianity in a pluralistic world, even as Christianity was only six hundred years old. I think the supermanuscript, the super letter, is from this time period. It's some great pronouncement, some piece of wisdom that profoundly changed things. I can find many references to it, but haven't actually located it. As I've read, and re-read some of references, I come to the conclusion the letter is hidden someplace, someway. I just haven't found it, or unlocked it yet."

Tim sat in the shade of an umbrella at the café outside the hotel while Millerkirk, enervated by the translation he had just read, had gone up to the hotel room to consult other resources and to call the university. Bright sunlight blazed down on the old French plaza. Tim's mind seemed to free-float with the clouds above the plaza. He was sure his mission was about to culminate with a definitive answer. Millerkirk would be the man who knew how to use the metal plate, how to decipher its ancient code. He would know which old door the key would fit.

Ruminating on the puzzle as he watched the market merchants close up their carts and head for home, Tim's intuition told him that the old metal plate was in fact the answer to the location of the "supermanuscript" of William of Enright. He'd had inklings earlier, but now after hearing more about William and his life, he was convinced. His pulse quickened—he was right about this, he was sure. He was also struck by the insanity of the strange sequence of events. Had fate not led him and Katie to find the plate, it would now be in the hands of Calamari Pasotti and Millerkirk's search for the supermanuscript would be perhaps doomed forever. A rich and greedy collector who cared nothing for the real and sacred value of an artifact would simply have had another prize for his collection, while the secret it held would be lost for eternity. The search for the insights and devotions of a good man from centuries ago would have been halted by the avarice of a lustful modern man. Fate? Divine intervention? The interruption of his dream vacation seemed part of a continuum in this long, historical drama. It had been and still was somewhat annoying, but it was a small price to pay for unlocking an old door, solving an ancient riddle and establishing an important piece of history.

Sorting through his stream of thought he continued to be puzzled by the intrigue that surrounded the plate. He didn't understand why Valmer had been so insistent that this mission be undertaken at once, and by him, or why Valmer had pressed him so hard to find the answers, or the warning about governments and national security. Why were the Iranian couple, or whoever they were, following him? Was misinformation fueling wider and wilder speculation, or was it simply when one government begins to whisper, all the others begin to eavesdrop?

Tim wondered if Valmer and his friends and their counterparts in Tel Aviv and Teheran knew more than they were telling him. He had a nagging suspicion that they more than suspected something and had sent him off like an explorer, looking into the wilderness, while experts with computers and links of knowledge waited safe and snug behind, ready to spring to action if he discovered something significant. Of course, he had come upon Millerkirk and his theory of the supermanuscript, but that was not on his mission agenda, and in fact, Valmer didn't know what he had learned yet.

Tim's mind raced back to Valmer, pictured him sitting in his office at the ominous start of this journey, prompting him in turn to visualize sunny Sanibel Island and his girls on the beach. He decided before any more time passed he would call Laney and the girls, just to hear their voices—finally. His anxiety over being out of touch still nagged at him, but he figured that soon he would be flying back to the island paradise. He looked at his watch: two thirty here; it would be nine thirty in the morning there. He'd wait until Millerkirk came back down and then he would go call them. He was anxious to ask Millerkirk about how the events of thirteen hundred years ago had been preserved, and where the metal plate had been before it was found in the Norman château some fifty years ago, but the need to talk to his family took precedence.

Tariq Abel sat at another sidewalk café across the plaza, behind the row of flower carts and their bright array of color, wearing what looked like a Walkman and headphones but was in fact a parabolic microphone. He waited for the other man, Tim's talkative friend, to return. Abel had been able to catch much of their dining room conversation and he wanted the rest.

Pasotti would pay him dearly for an ancient manuscript. He'd simply wait for these amateurs to find it, and then he would claim it. He sniffed and swallowed hard, the last line of cocaine he had taken in the lavatory still numbing the back of his throat.

Meanwhile Moshe and Anna took up a vantage point in a small parking lot on the third side of the square. Now there was work to do. They discovered that they had established a way of communicating without speaking, and were able to work as a unit. They could see the entire plaza from their point, and had been there long enough to watch Abel as he listened to Tim and Millerkirk. To their alarm they noted that Abel was hitting heavily on the cocaine, and they worried that the drug would make the already irrational terrorist even more volatile.

Tim felt more confident than he had since the trip had begun, and since the eerie first meeting with Valmer. He began to discount some of Valmer's warnings as those of a man who had residual traces of professional paranoia and operative's doubts coursing through his veins. The next twenty-four hours would surely bring some closure to this bizarre chapter of his life. Relaxing in the beauty of the quiet French afternoon, Tim was in an upbeat, almost joyful mood, until he saw Millerkirk walking toward him.

His face was ashen, his eyes glazed and distant, almost fearful. As he sat down he was obviously shaken, and he clasped and unclasped his hands, then clasped them again and rested his chin on them, shaking his head. He inhaled raggedly, as if drawing the strength to speak and closed his eyes.

"Jim, what is it?" Tim asked, alarmed.

"I...just a moment, Tim. Something—of a marvel. I was reading a manuscript which I had booted into the program before I left the university. It hadn't seemed important, based on where I found it, so I didn't get around to it until just now." He exhaled and shrugged his shoulders as though a chill ran down his spine. "I checked with the office and we both read it the same. It's only a partial, we don't have the complete document. It's from the Enright series, but I don't know its context. Is it something he wrote, or copied, or what? It's mystifying, and important."

"Why? How?"

Millerkirk leaned in toward Tim, looked to be sure no one sitting at other tables was within ear shot and spoke softly.

"This is part of an account which seems to state, really matter-of-factly, how…" he swallowed hard, "how Mohammed was in fact a believer in Zion and under the control of a radical and renegade Jewish sect."

"What? Mohammed a Jew?" Tim frowned.

"No, under control of a Jewish sect."

"How? I mean, that's just plain nuts!"

"What I mean is not that it actually happened, but that it was a rumor. Invented purposely, but very potent. Lots of people seemed to believe it, according to this account."

"A wild rumor?" Tim considered a minute. "Well, rumors have power and can change history. After all, near the end of the Third Reich all sorts of wild rumors circulated, that Hitler had a secret bomb that would annihilate the Allies any minute, and so forth, and because of that the war lasted longer than it needed to." He warmed to the subject. "In my own home town in the 1920s the Ku Klux Klan spread around that the Pope was going to take over America, that he had his own secret army stashed in the Vatican, and Catholics who wanted to run for President visited him there."

"And do you remember how powerful that kind of a rumor was back then?" Millerkirk asked him intently. "If I recall my American history correctly, the Klan took over the entire state of Indiana in the twenties just on the basis of such fabricated lies. They are intended to undermine the present order, and so they are very powerful. This ancient rumor was of that sort, I suspect. You've got to remember, the case we're talking about here was in the early seventh century, a dark time full of superstitions and fear. Very little learning. These discrediting rumors would have been spread with very clear goals."

"But what would the goals be of someone wanting to make people think Mohammed was a Jewish agent?"

Millerkirk let the waiter clear the coffee cups from the table before he continued. "Several. First, Mohammed's own powerful enemies in Arabia would be the very first to spread such a rumor. It was a critical juncture for Mohammedanism. It was the first generation of monotheism there, but two factions vied for power: which way to go, martial or spiritual? Peaceful or warlike? If believers were made to think Mohammed was nothing but a sham, the opposite, warlike faction wins." Tim nodded and crumpled his napkin on the table absently. This account was turning out to be more interesting than he had anticipated.

"Then," Millerkirk went on, "you've got to ask, who gets blamed if people believe Mohammed was an imposter, controlled by a Jewish sect? Obviously, the Jewish religion. The Jews were in Diaspora by then, already divided into sects and factions anyway; heap more blame on them, shatter their faith further. But the specific goal of a rumor like this was to hurt all faiths, even Christianity."

"But how would a smear about Mohammed harm Christianity, and who would want to bring about such a breakdown of faith as you describe?"

"Christians would be discredited because if you show one great religious leader as a fake, it casts doubt on all religions. Remember, Christianity is only about six hundred years old at this point, vulnerable, still sending out missions but already getting converts among the great and politically powerful. It's a time of superstition and cults all over Europe and the Middle East, easy to shake the faithful. If you can prove one holy man is a fake, then maybe all of them are. Make people think they've been duped. And unsettled people can add to the violence of an already uncertain world—seed a holy war, instigate turmoil, breakdown—make it more difficult for Christianity to survive. Rumors can be as potent as bombs with fuses, spreading with sparks to the blow-up and starting little fires all along the way."

"Well, maybe. I can see how such a rumor, spread along the trade lines of the world, would go like wildfire and undermine faith. But who would want to do that?"

"I don't know exactly. But there is a good deal more to this story through these early centuries. The purpose was to shake up the existing power structure, with the ultimate result being total destabilization. The big losers would be the kings, and the religious leaders who backed them. Chaos would reign as these evil forces used religious differences as a tool to usurp power for themselves."

"Jim, could this be the supermanuscript you've been looking for? You said you never had located it."

"Believe me, I've had that thought. If it contains an explication of the plot or the theory, then it becomes clear why it was hidden for thirteen centuries. Why it's been so cryptically mentioned, why it's so hard to get. A lot of people wouldn't want it to see the light of day forever."

They sat silently for a while. Tim did a few neck-rolls, trying to break the tension which had knotted his shoulders. Millerkirk entwined his fingers behind his head and tilted back to catch the last of the afternoon sun on his face.

Finally Millerkirk broke the silence. Another thing that puzzled him, he remarked, was the existence of more documents from the series which had contained the bombshell. These were with a group from about two hundred years after William's writings in the early seventh century.

"We just overlooked them until today. What threw us off is they date from around 800. What I think happened is they were re-translated, cleaned up and annotated later, so we simply overlooked them. They're from the ancient scholar Alcuin. Diane is putting them into the computer now. We should have those in a while."

"You've lost me," Tim said. "I remember Alcuin, but not well. He was before the period I was interested in when I was in school."

"Then I'll give you another quick history lesson. Alcuin dates back to the Germanic leader Charlemagne, around 760. I'm sure that you know he was a warrior without peer. After his armies conquered all of Gaul, crossed over the Pyrenees, and took Spain, his empire ran from the Danube to the Elbe rivers. He was an incredible man, exercised regularly, and believed in temperance in drink, very unusual for his time. And he loved learning.

"When he dined he listened to music or had someone read to him. He was a great practitioner of charity and assistance to the poor—in short, a good man. He was an ally of the Pope. Around 799 there was a riot in Rome and Pope Leo III actually ran to Charlemagne for protection. The story is that Charlemagne marched into Rome, took control, and on Christmas Day he knelt in prayer at Saint Peter's while Pope Leo crowned him Emperor of the Romans. Historians say he then thought of himself as a new Caesar. He created military districts, appointed courts to rule over them, created defenses to keep out the barbarians. He set up his central government in Aachen—Aix-la-Chappelle. He allowed the conquered people to live under their own laws, and ordered that all unwritten laws be put in writing. He encouraged the Church and even presided at Church councils. As an immense advocate of education, he set up church schools inviting scholars from all over to come to the school he set up in the palace.

"Here's where we get to the William of Enright connection. One of the scholars, in fact he became most famous in Charlemagne's court, was Alcuin, an English scholar, writer and churchman from the Episcopal school at York. Alcuin ran the palace school and even taught Charlemagne to read. He used Saint Augustine's *City of God* as a textbook.

"The *City of God*," Tim mused. "Stroutsel mentioned it as a possibility for the plate. He said Augustine's whole message was that God is present in all human affairs."

Millerkirk looked at him intently. "Yes, and that's the most important idea of all, isn't it? And—actually the one the lie—the rumor I'm talking about wanted to combat. Because paganism is easy to manipulate. But if there is one God and he is always present to help individuals or rulers—they can't be taken over.

"But back to Charlemagne. Together, Charlemagne and Alcuin set up schools for children and encouraged genuine education. Monastery and cathedral schools were improved, and Alcuin directed a reform movement in writing which led to the first modern script. He ordered monks to go through all of the abbey libraries and reading rooms and copy old manuscripts and classics and set up monastic libraries to preserve ancient manuscripts and documents.

"When he was still in England he did likewise. That is when he must have come across the William of Enright letters. He was so impressed he took them with him when he went to join Charlemagne. Now, this would have been some two hundred years after William wrote them. Alcuin spent several years translating and annotating the letters. I've read his translations and the originals. But this last group had no matching originals, so they were down our list of priorities. Because they were annotated by Alcuin I didn't catch the William of Enright signature. I didn't even think they were his, not until just a while ago. That's where this bombshell was found. I can't even imagine what the others may say."

This talk of history bored Abel, even though he knew old documents were worth money to men like Pasotti, which meant good business for him. He hoped these two would determine soon where they had to go to find what they were looking for—and what he wanted. He wanted to get out of Tours as soon as he could; he felt uneasy in small towns where he could be spotted. In the big cities like Paris, Berlin, Madrid, Dublin he could blend into the population and become invisible.

The talk of the Prophet's being an agent of Zion had struck him as being bizarre and ridiculous, but he was so buzzed on cocaine and obsessed with the thought of selling the documents and whatever else these two were chasing, the significance escaped him and barely even registered on the periphery of his mind. He had mentioned it to Pasotti when he called, but his account was so twisted that the astounding aspect of treachery, that the accusation about

Mohammed didn't register with the greedy collector either. Like a shark smelling blood, all that Pasotti knew or cared about was that he was close to obtaining a valuable artifact. Abel told him that when listed, the manuscript would be the envy of other collectors, and could command an astronomical price. Pasotti put up a front of being skeptical though, for fear that if he let on that such a rare manuscript could bring even more than Abel thought, the Iraqi would try to hold him up for more money. Or worse, sell it to another bidder. That stunning revelation was not lost on the two Israeli agents who continued to monitor Abel's calls.

Millerkirk prepared to drive up to Chartres, where he had planned to do some research in the old early thirteenth-century cathedral, and asked Tim to go along. It would give them a chance to brainstorm. Tim pulled the car out of the parking lot and waited for Millerkirk by the hotel. Perched on his motorcycle, Abel adjusted his helmet and watched, ready to follow. The Israelis stood by in a rented car, also ready to move.

"Did you know that Tours is where Joan of Arc bought her suit of armor?" Millerkirk asked as they drove away from the plaza as the afternoon sun cast direct shadows.

"You figure we should do likewise? There's a good chance that we're being followed."

"It might be appropriate. But I don't know what can protect us from the past."

Millerkirk described the newest translations of Alcuin's Latin manuscripts just received at the university as they drove. These writings dated from around 800 and provided more detail of William of Enright's incredible story written around 620. As he listened, Tim became frighteningly aware of the gravity and widespread impact of this historical research.

"Alcuin had discovered William's epistles on the founding of Islam, and the subsequent account of the plot to spread the cancerous lie," Millerkirk said. "Clearly, William had based the account on interviews and conversations with many of the travelers from the Holy Land. Mohammedanism was in its infancy when he wrote about it. Anyway, the travelers and pilgrims related stories of upheavals and intrigue, including the battles, the flight, the division in Medina, and the war to take Mecca. They described the growing legion of followers of this Arab monotheist, and impact the belief in Allah had in the Arab world. William chronicled the events as he heard them, and then he would evaluate and interpret what he thought they meant. The original documents are long lost now, but according to Alcuin's annotations, the Enright letters had been taken quite seriously and had been read by Church leaders in Rome and circulated to the principal members of several royal courts."

It had also been clear to Millerkirk and his staff that some of the Enright letters, particularly the theorized supermanuscript, were missing.

"I can tell from Alcuin's notes, like a preface to what William wrote, that there is a great deal more. I wish I knew where it was," Millerkirk said. "I found the tone and content of the old letters troubling, as well as the missing pieces of the puzzle."

"Could the plate be the answer? I mean, maybe it's the link or a clue to location of these letters?" Tim asked. Haji and Stroutsel had suggested the plate might be an "address" for something else. "The lines of the inscription about the 'warrior of light who guards the south' or the Latin passage about true light on sin? Could it fit?"

"I'd love to think it fits, Tim, but I'm not convinced there's a connection. I've read nothing of either William or Alcuin which makes any connection or even hints at something like the plate. I'm hitting a wall, a blank wall."

Tim's mood was sinking toward depression. Less than an hour before he had been near ecstasy thinking he was on the verge of solving his riddle and completing the mission. He had even entertained the thought of booking a flight back to the U.S. and to Sanibel that same afternoon. Now he felt as though he'd been tossed into a medieval dungeon with no way out, lost and forgotten. The charge he'd felt earlier from the thrill of the research was giving way to the dismay that he'd ever gotten himself involved in the first place. He was so tired—and he wanted to go home.

But part of him still trusted his earlier intuition. He honestly felt that they were heading in the right direction, that they would find the answer they sought. He prayed that this *would indeed be* the answer, and not just a wild goose chase for something else. He was then troubled by a feeling of guilt. Was he imposing his will on the Divine? Still, he wanted to be done with the pursuit.

Millerkirk highlighted certain points as he read. The story of the plot as chronicled by William of Enright had been circulated widely and the political implications were, of course, profound.

"You want to know who started this rumor plot. I don't really have enough to really say now, but it seems as though this story came to William from the Middle East through both Jewish and Muslim sources as well as from Christian pilgrims. It also appears as though some very influential people were intended to take it quite seriously and did so."

"I really have trouble understanding that," Tim responded.

"Don't underestimate the instability of that period of time. There were constant wars and battles for power involving kings, emperors, dukes, princes, bishops, archbishops, and even popes. The people themselves were virtually powerless, most of them ignorant and highly superstitious. At the same time, powerful economic interests were rising, controlling the trade routes for not only luxury goods but the absolute necessities. As a result, the religious structures and secular rulers came more into conflict. The secular powers began to realize just how potent the new monotheistic structures were. In many ways this plot was an assault on faith, but I think it really was about power, control."

"I remember Haji's telling me about the war against nonbelievers. The armed struggle it took to establish Mohammed as leader of both religion and state. You know there had to have been plots and intrigue."

"No doubt it was a bloody and violent period. There was

horrible opposition to Mohammed. He was trying to lead these people out of darkness, in his way, and through his 'revelations.' He had enemies everywhere, among his own people and certainly among Jews. And apparently among some Christians, or at least nominal Christians." Millerkirk tapped the sheaf of papers in his hand. "According to these there was a lot of stock put in the canard. William writes that the false story was pushed by one of the Germanic leaders, one of the heirs of Clovis."

"This is pretty deep water isn't it? Long way from a sunny beach on Sanibel," Millerkirk could see Tim was growing depressed.

"I'm sorry, Jim. Guess I'm feeling sorry for myself. This business you're into now is very deep and troubling. The plate seems peripheral."

"But it's still going to press on you, as long as the mystery remains unanswered. We've both got a load here, huh?"

"I really do appreciate your help," Tim said.

"At least we've got each other to kick it around with. William was for the most part on his own. Some of these pages reflect an awful torment, because he realizes that powerful secular forces are threatening religion. Listen to this. I'm translating from Latin, so I'll take some liberty: 'What a terrible thing I ponder. Troubled now I am to know how to act in legion with God and faith to protect and preserve this fragile trace of the sacred in an hour of man's darkness.' This is a sort of lament. He goes on: 'What is it the Lord would have me do?' Then he writes about how difficult it is know the best way to act, the best thing to do. Now here's another wonderful thought: 'This I know: once unleashed, such questions will not be dismissed. For what then should I pray?' Now this is just amazing to think about. Faced with this obscene and evil plot, he responds by asking how he should pray."

"Does he come up with an answer?" Tim asked calmly.

"It's like he's working through it. There are several pages. This would make a marvelous lesson for seminarians. What William gets to is the concept that he can ask for guidance, for help, for God's grace. But even before he asks, the answer pre-exists because God knows us better than we know ourselves. Now that, Mr. Calvin, is a whale of a theological concept."

"I can understand why you would be so impressed with William. It sounds like Saint Augustine—God is present and he helps. Simple but profound."

"He could have been a knight," Millerkirk said, "but instead ended up some kind of seventh century combination of Walter Cronkite, Joseph Campbell and Billy Graham, with a little Dean Acheson or George Schultz thrown in."

Day faded into early evening, and as they passed a road sign they saw that they were just a few kilometers from Chartres. Religion had always been a private matter for Tim, and he had never worn it obviously. Now he was surprised to find himself praying again. He had earlier issued a plea that the metal plate and the manuscript be tied together and the riddle solved so he could get on with his life. This time he found himself asking God to just give him the strength to see the ordeal through. His somewhat uncharacteristic mindset puzzled him, and he decided to explore the issue with his travelling companion.

"So Jim, why did you become a minister and theologian?"

"You ask now? That's good! Its a technique a professor might use," Millerkirk gave him a broad smile, as though he recognized why the communications expert was prompting this line of thought. "I went into this line of work because I wasn't good enough to play second base for the Phillies." Their chuckles broke the tension.

"Really, though, it's the adventure. I saw the needs of people and I liked the challenge of the intellectual. I think the mind of God puts order into the universe and reason into the minds of man. And I think we see the perfect person in Christ, and through that we see the heart of God. To me, it's the way we should live. Some things you just can't put into words, at least not completely. At the risk of sounding simplistic, I felt a calling."

"It's more of a commitment than most would make, or even be willing to make."

"Not necessarily. Hey, basically every human needs the same thing—love and faith. That's what the boss offers; love Him with all you've got, and He'll love you back. Have faith, no matter how tough it gets, *He's there*. Augustine's message, told anew in daily life. To me it's the simplest of concepts and the greatest of all adventures."

Tim mulled this over for a minute before he responded. "One thing I hope to take away from this experience is the same type of courage faith gives people. Haji, for example: he's devout and ready for a moral battleground, a spiritual warfare. Stroutsel is long suffering and full of pain, but still he clings to a sense of Godly justice. Compared to them, I feel like some kid who's been at a Bible school picnic."

"Don't be tough on yourself," Millerkirk said pensively. "As you mentioned Haji and Stroutsel I was thinking of how a Jew, a Muslim, and a Christian have worked together on this problem. We've worked together before on the UN commission of course; but I mean how in trying to figure out what's behind the plate, we've all come together into the puzzle. What a contrast everyone has provided with the different interpretations about these translations." Millerkirk squeezed his eyes shut in concentration before he continued.

"Here's what I think the plot might have been about. It looks like enemies of Mohammed may have cut a deal with the new secular and mercantile enemies of the Church leaders, both east and west, and possibly with a renegade Jewish sect or cult. None of these groups had any use for each other, and would've probably cheered each others' destruction. But this time they had a common cause, and they teamed up to spread this evil conjecture, with each faction circulating it among their own people and religion. I've been thinking about what William must have thought. He had to know the damage this could do, the foment and upheaval, and more war."

Millerkirk leaned his head back against the headrest and breathed deeply and exhaled, as though to expel tension. "But, to get back to your mysterious plate, east and west are looking for a warrior of light who guards the south while Christ is enthroned to the setting sun. It looks like we're all over the compass with that, Tim, and I'm not sure where to go from here."

"Well, at least we've gotten to Chartres. Do you want to go directly to the cathedral?" Tim asked, checking the road signs.

"Yes, please. Tim, this will be a real moment. We should be there in time for vespers and sunset. Trust me, this will be an evening you'll remember forever."

Moshe and Anna followed Tariq Abel on the evening road to Chartres. "I'm worried, Moshe," Anna said. "These two men are so gentle, so innocent, and I'm afraid that before morning this depraved man may to do harm to them."

Moshe nodded grimly. "I'm afraid you are right. He's motivated by the ancient evil. These men are innocents on a quest, leading with their hearts and love of mystery. They are unaware of how savage the world can be. The battle seems eternal."

Confession at Chartres

"What's the story on this place, Jim? You've seen it from both a theological and architectural standpoint," Tim asked as the car approached the ancient cathedral.

"Well, give me a moment to refer to this well-worn guide, which is better than my memory at this point," Millerkirk said, reaching into his bag and flipping to a dog-eared page. "Let's see, yes—here it is: Chartres, a charming village southwest of Paris, crowned by the magnificent cathedral first built in 1145. Burned fifty years later it was rebuilt between 1195 and 1220. Its twin spires are unique: one is Romanesque and the other is Gothic. The massive structure itself features some of the earliest examples of Gothic sculpture and architecture, with an emphasis on symmetry and clarity resulting in a stunning array of sculpture work on the jambs of the portals. For centuries, visitors have marveled at the beauty and intricate detail of the sculpture work which was ordered by Abbot Suger, who oversaw the quarter-century construction project.

"The west portal is particularly powerful with three massive doors lined with jamb statues of kings, queens, and Biblical prophets." Millerkirk gestured as he narrated, as though pointing out the different scenes. "Above the center door is a breathtaking sculpture of Christ on a throne as Judge and Ruler of the Universe. He is flanked by the symbols of the four evangelists, with the Apostles gathered below while the twenty-four Elders of the Apocalypse reside in the archivolts. Above the door to the right, in a smaller arch, you can see a richly-detailed sculptured depiction of the birth, the presentation in the Temple, and the Christ child on the Virgin's lap. The archivolts depict humans paying homage to divine wisdom. The left tympanum contains a scene of the Christ of Heaven and the Ascension. He is framed by the signs of the zodiac. These three arched frames contain some of the most exquisite sacred sculpture work in the world. Since the early thirteenth century the images of Christ and His heavenly entourage have stunned those who have beheld their beauty." He shut the guide book.

"Nicely done, Dr. Millerkirk. You could moonlight as a tour guide," Tim said as he pulled the car into a parking place and looked at the cathedral. The scene was stunning. "I know this is a major understatement," he said, "but this is incredible."

As they walked up to the cathedral they contemplated the grace of the building, apparent even from the distance of their parking spot. Millerkirk spoke of the "magic" of the windows of Chartres, the only one of the many Gothic cathedrals to have retained most of its original stained glass. Unlike stained glass of later centuries, these windows were often described as "translucent walls."

"It's one of the most amazing sights you'll ever see," he enthused. "The old glass does not so much allow light in as it changes it, a bit like a kaleidoscope. The windows act like a filter, and they actually change the sun rays and light. I've heard people describe it as God's poetry of light. It really is out of this world."

Tim checked the time. A little after 5:00 P.M. here, and midmorning on Sanibel. He decided that before it got much later, and before he even called Valmer, he would call Laney. But this time he would keep trying until he got through. It had been too long since he'd talked with her, heard her voice. The pain of separation cut keenly, and he couldn't shake the apprehension that had plagued him ever since the trip started and he hadn't been able to reach her on the phone. He gazed up at the magnificent stained-glass windows, so lovely out here, breathtaking when seen from inside, he was sure. He thought of how Laney would love this incredible old cathedral, especially the windows, and missed her even more acutely.

They headed for the main door of the cathedral, where Jim said he was going to the office and from there to the reading room for "a session with some manuscripts." As a member of the UN commission he had carte blanche as to where and when he could read.

"Look over there!" Millerkirk pointed to an artist who had set up a work station in the plaza in front of the cathedral. "I think that's Charles Warren, the American impressionist. I've seen his work and read about him. He must be painting here—that sure looks like him."

They approached the artist, a man not much older than Tim, who wore his white hair in a flattop and looked like an ex-Marine drill instructor. The canvas on his easel was being transformed into a rich painting of the cathedral rising above the village. Two other paintings were propped up next to an artist's box, and a pretty, dark-haired woman sat in a chair nearby, smiling at the interest passersby took in the work that sat drying in the evening sun. The painter stopped to examine some brush strokes and tilted his head close to the canvas again. He grabbed a rag to wipe the brush and noticed the two men admiring his work.

"Howdy," he said, his piercing eyes bright and full of life.

"Beautiful work," Tim offered, casting his eyes on the piece on the easel and those drying by the chair.

"Praise the Lord, thank you," the artist responded with a full and hearty smile on his face and in his voice. "My darling wife and I are just moved by the beauty of this place."

"You're Charles Warren, aren't you?" Millerkirk asked. "I saw some of your work at Mystic Seaport in Connecticut last summer. I remember your face and haircut from the picture."

"Yep. It's my 'Sergeant Carter' look," he said, grinning and running his hand over the close-cropped head.

"I'm Jim Millerkirk. This is Tim Calvin." They shook hands.

"This is Becky, my darling wife, and my manager too. I need a manager, don't I, sweetie?" Warren seemed to have a teasing, jolly personality.

Becky Warren smiled and squeezed her husband's hand. "Are you here as tourists?" she asked.

"We're here on research. I'm from the University of Edinburgh, and Tim is researching the history of an artifact."

"Have you seen the windows yet?" Warren asked, excitement in his voice. "They're unbelievable," he said, drawing out the last word when they indicated that they had not. "It's the light. Just like the Lord. Are you fellows Christians?"

At that, an engaging conversation ensued with the painter and his wife. From the Midwest, they were making their first trip to Europe and had found no shortage of scenes to paint. He was a burly, outgoing, colorful character with little inhibition, while she was quiet and reserved. They were so immediately likeable and their conversation so congenial, that they provided a much welcome diversion from the deep, tormenting mysteries.

They decided to watch the painting in progress for a while. Warren's work was rich with color and texture, a result of his applying some of the oil pigment with a palate knife and some with the fine-brush finesse of a creative master. The paintings had a tangible quality, almost inviting a touch; Tim could see why the man was such a success and why Millerkirk was so excited about meeting him. During the course of their conversation he found the man to be full of conviction, frequently giving credit to God for allowing him to express his artistic gift. Tim liked the guy even if he was usually uncomfortable with such evangelistic enthusiasm. Warren was fun to talk with, and before long they discovered a mutual interest in basketball.

Millerkirk excused himself to read and Tim mentioned his interest in seeing the windows, which prompted Warren to talk of "light—light in nature, light in his paintings, and the light of the Lord."

"It's in the Gospel of John: 'While you have the light, believe in the light that you may become sons of light'. Let your light shine, buddy." His robust voice had the same intensity as his painting.

"I've come to understand a great deal more about religion than ever, as a result of this trip. Thought about a lot," Tim said. "It has been, as they say, a growth experience."

"Well, you've got to remember this: being a Christian is not just being a part of a religion. It's a relationship, a one-on-one full-court press with the Lord." Warren's voice boomed as though he was giving a pep talk.

So the painter is also a preacher, Tim thought. Jim had suggested they get together for dinner with the Warrens, so Tim took his leave and said he would see them later. He wanted to spend some time studying the windows.

*   *   *

The plan was finalized but Dave still needed an advantage. He figured an element of surprise would get it for him. Wasser would be thinking only about the exchange, and wouldn't expect anything. Ideas and options rolled around in his mind, none of them acceptable, as he rummaged around the kitchen, getting ready to fix a pot of coffee. He opened the freezer to get the bag of coffee and his eyes fell on a piece of Jayne's frozen chocolate pie, wrapped in plastic. Cee had stuck it away a couple of weeks ago, saving it for one of those moments when she needed a "lift," as she put it. He took out the coffee and shut the freezer door.

He filled the basket, poured the water in the reservoir, and turned the coffeemaker on. As he put the bag back in the freezer he looked at the pie again. Its presence seemed almost like an accusation. He picked it up and looked at it for a long moment. That's it! He tossed the pie back in and slammed the freezer door shut. Grabbing up the phone he quickly punched in Jayne and Brian's number.

*   *   *

Valmer was restless, and found it impossible to sit still. Sleep the night before had been out of the question. It had been too long since his last contact with Tim. He knew that Tariq Abel had remained on the chase, though the ineffectual Iranians had given up the pursuit. His associates in Langley had relayed the status of the Mossad agents, which gave him some measure of consolation. If the untrained and inexperienced Tim Calvin got into trouble, then there might be some help nearby.

He was also uneasy about Dave's rescue plan. He was certain that with a little more time Edward Earl would be able to compel the wheels of justice to grind Wasser, but Dave was adamant about extracting a little "justice." Valmer was not convinced Dave's exotic plan would work, but there was no stopping him. Maybe he would succeed. At any rate, his wild idea seemed safer than any plan the police might construct.

* * *

Hertt had told Laney and the girls while they were eating breakfast that they would be free and back in their condo by dinner time. He was apologetic and assured them they would be "safe very soon." Katie was still in very poor shape, listless, limp, seemingly barely able to stand, and nonconversant. She seemed to brighten at the news that they would be home that night, but just barely perceptibly.

Elizabeth and Cee were encouraged and their behavior reflected it, though Cee unloaded a venomous assault on Hertt for his "criminal behavior and disruption of her normal routine." As punctuation she assured Hertt her daddy would get even. "I'm real sure he will, Freckles. I don't doubt it for nothing," Hertt replied, no longer wanting to scrap even with her. Cee, for her part, wasn't sure how to respond to that kind of capitulation.

Fortunately, for his own peace of mind, Wasser remained out of sight and earshot, and therefore wasn't witness to much of his henchman's apparent change of character. Confident that everything was under control, he remained on the phone, doing business and finalizing plans for his quick and perfect exit from the island.

* * *

"Testing—hello—one, two, three," Millerkirk said into the small voice-activated tape recorder he often used when reading old manuscripts. He had developed a system for his research, alternating between making notes, reading manuscripts aloud, and summarizing and capsulizing what he read by talking into his recorder. Often, when he played the tapes back, he was amused at some of his "aside comments" either to himself or to colleagues.

"I am in a stone-walled office, built in the twelfth century but now with some twentieth century appointments, such as a humidity-control device, indirect lighting, and personal computer terminal with an index to the ancient manuscripts, stored in special boxes. There is a separate file of the translation of some of the documents. I intend to scan them now."

He was astounded by what he read, and in his excitement could barely remain seated. He wanted to run and shout to Tim, but he was too transfixed by the events coming at him from the texts of the manuscripts before him.

"Here is a third link in the chain, a thirteenth-century connection," he dictated. "What had begun with William of Enright, discovered, read, updated and annotated by Alcuin, was polished and finished by a man named Howard the Tall. The seventh century observations, drawn through the ninth century, were handled again, and decisively, in the thirteenth century and with the benefit of hindsight and a study of history.

"Howard the Tall was a church advisor in the royal court of the king of England. Like Alcuin and William before him he was a scholar-historian and churchman. There had been another Howard in his lifetime and early training, so he was given the moniker 'the Tall' because of his towering height. He was a learned man, well read, and his passion for the dusty volumes of abbey libraries led him to the accumulated work of Alcuin, including his collection of the writings of William of Enright. Apparently, as Howard studied Alcuin's writings combined with William's work, he found something called the 'Epistle of Shame.' This is it—yes! I can't believe it! I feel like giving a war whoop, but that would be most inappropriate for a member of the august UN commission." He paused to clear his throat and try to retain his composure. "Let the record indicate that Jim Millerkirk is wild with excitement: This is the eureka moment! In this ancient volume before me is the missing 'supermanuscript.' Dear Lord, this is too much. Note: it is listed in the index as A109 dash 1225 dash X. I am taking photos and will ask for commission authority to validate. Gang, this could be the grand slam. Methinks the theory has been confirmed. I read on with exhilaration.

"Howard made it his mission to collect and gather the original texts of William, as well as Alcuin's analysis written two hundred years later. Howard then added his own touch. Today we would call it an update or analysis of accuracy. Howard sort of validated what both William and Alcuin had written.

"I can tell my blood pressure is up and my heart is racing. My hands are jittery and my palms are sweating. I don't want to leave out this excitement. As you listen to this tape played back you may notice my voice is up an octave or two—I may be singing soprano before this dictation is completed.

"But to continue: Howard put the final spin on the incredible and evil plot begun in the late six hundred twenties at a time when Mohammed's following had begun to grow in Arabia. William of Enright had picked up traces of the so-called revelation early and as he talked with more people returning from regions of the Holy Land, his base of information grew. Based on the notes he kept, listing who he had talked with and where they had been, and who they had talked to, he was able to separate the misinformation and political manipulations from the reality of the intrigue. Oh, Tim Calvin, you are going to love this—it's just like modern investigative reporting. William's astute observance of distant events, his knowledge of the changing world, and his personal contact with leading merchants, scholars, and people of the ruling class, gave him the information and power to stop, or at least partially stop, the traffic in the heinous 'revelation.' The point is that Howard directly tells us William *had* dealt with the plot to discredit Mohammed—and the new religion! We hadn't known that!

"So this seventh-century dirty trick has a smoking gun, William of Enright's Epistle of Shame, until now known as the theorized 'supermanuscript.' This bogus accusation about Mohammed, the so-called revelation, had been talked about in caravans, by pilgrims, in temples—wherever the provocateurs could spread it. It was in fact part of an evil conspiracy—I note William, Alcuin and Howard all used the term 'evil conspiracy'—to dislocate the power of the Pope and the Western Church, the Emperor of the East and the Byzantine Empire of the Orthodox Church, in addition to the primary target, the surging power of Mohammed. William and Alcuin both figured whatever Jewish power structure existed then would also take some hits. So that was it. In a nutshell, the whole scheme was an attempt to undermine leaders of the newly strong religious faith structure everywhere to increase secular power. Note to Tim Calvin: we actually nailed it back in Tours.

"In summary, William had been able to trace the corrupt path to the perpetrators, this group of world traders and anti-religious political intriguers. They engineered this insidious plot, confident that it would lead to their eventual acquisition of power when the ruling structure of the 'religionists' or Church-supported leaders tumbled. Secular pagan power-grabbers score one, monotheistic religionists zero.

"Wow. Dr. Jim Millerkirk, purveyor of the supermanuscript theory, is on the verge of being wildly giddy. My only companion at this moment of discovery is the dust dancing in the evening sunlight like a swirling galaxy. But hang on, because the plot thickens here. Note to staff: this is why we love history so much.

"Realizing the rumor about Mohammed as a monstrous threat against growing worship of one god, William had acted, says Howard.

244 | The Sanibel Arcanum

stoutly refuting the claims and unmasking the plot, William's Epistle of Shame was sent to Rome, Constantinople, Medina, Mecca, the Holy Land, and to royal courts of the west. He went up against a powerful cabal of fierce enemies, but his intellect and good faith were strong enough to stop the plotters.

"The widely read epistle had alerted both Church and secular leaders and those threatened by the conspiracy, giving them an opportunity to prepare, respond, and take preemptive action. Alcuin and Howard both note that William was modest about the details, but apparently quite a few royals and church leaders asked him for advice about specifics; after all, he had been a knight in training as a young man. Anyway, it seems like a few beheadings, stonings, and consignments to the dungeons took care of some of the plotters. Says here William got a deathbed confession from one member of a sect of Jewish ascetics, apparently one of the plotters. Oh, this is great—a deathbed confession in Venice from one of the plotters. Note: Millerkirk is not making this up—Howard says it is part of a William letter, but there is no evidence of the letter here. Note to check elsewhere, maybe on earlier disk of William."

Millerkirk stopped to check the tape in the recorder. He didn't want to run out in mid-sentence. Satisfied that he had plenty left, he continued.

"OK, despite that, traces of the story remained in the bloodline of history like a poison. That's what the first half of the Alcuin file is about; that two hundred years later trace elements of the diseased thought remained alive. In whispered tones in mosques and temples, in quiet talk in cloistered libraries and naves, amongst 'learned' leaders, rabbis and priests, and even among the worshipful, there was dialogue, gossip, rumor and conjecture about the 'real nature' of Mohammed and Islam. So we see the plotters had been stopped, but their tool of damage was still working and sneaking through time. Alcuin, finding the William letters, was able to apply the antitoxin of intellect. He followed William's own example and circulated his letter amongst the learned and powerful, warning priests and teachers to be vigilant for the foul story in whatever form it might reach them. And now, here is a copy of Alcuin's letter that clearly disproves the lie, including passages from William. Ah, but Howard writes— 'it had some potency, but still the evil strain remained.'

"Summary time, some bottom line judgment: The power of a thought, especially an impious or sacrilegious idea, can generate a vile influence even while largely dormant. So it was that in the world and time of Howard the Tall in the 1220s, the blasphemy remained. It remained as a curse to those who studied history, an evil oath to Christian and Islamic scholars who encountered ancient documents or tribal legend hinting that the founding of Islam was a conspiracy of such complexity and proportion that only God could know for sure. Howard's act, the final editing, annotation, and sealing of the manuscript for history, was the stake in the heart of the foul plot. Six hundred years after the launching of the terrible thing, it was stopped.

"Thank God for Howard. He wrote this passage with such clarity and power. As an aside, this is something either the UN commission or the Secretary General should circulate. Specific details for historical examination: The conspirators wanted to make the world think that Mohammed was an agent of the *B'nai Tzion*—the Sons of Zion—a Jewish sect with a reputation for strong political and economic alliances. The Sons of Zion were loyal to Talmudic law, and were renowned for their practices of ethics and reason. They were strong in number and respected by those with whom they dealt. Some of their followers were powerful merchants and well-connected with royal houses in both the east and the west, and others had business ties to Arabia. The plotters believed that by their linking Mohammed to the Sons of Zion, and spreading that his real mission was to deceive Arabia, they could undercut his growing power among his people, and destroy a powerful Jewish organization besides. So that's the specific context."

Millerkirk was soaked with perspiration. He had just read an epic of history which had been secreted, hidden, unread for centuries. The seven hundred and fifty-year-old manuscripts before him were the completion of a story that he had been able to get only in bits and pieces. Now it had a frame and structure. Howard's letter put everything in perspective. He pulled his handkerchief from his pocket and wiped his forehead and the palms of his hands. Popping a new tape into the recorder, he flipped it on and resumed dictating.

"Chartres tape number two. Dr. Jim Millerkirk reading from the Latin, original manuscript HO dash 1224 dash 1, in library at Chartres. Note to staff: this does not look like anything we have translation on. This is a Howard letter and it looks like some background; it reminds me of a history book in progress—Clovis had been converted to Christianity by his wife, a Burgundian princess. Clovis, his sister, and three thousand warriors were baptized on Christmas Day, 496. After the death of Clovis in 511 the Germanic invaders fell away from God. The empire was divided among his sons, provoking war.

The Goths, Visigoths, and Ostrogoths, strongest of the tribes, did bloody warfare for generations. Out of this cauldron of war and hatred one of the Gothic tribal leaders emerged more powerful and dominant. Acting in concert with a renegade off-shoot of the Rechabite sect called Brothers of the Guardian—*Havra Hashomer*—they contacted enemies of Mohammed.

"Hold on everyone—this is getting heavier. Old Howard really seems to have nailed this down. Bob Woodward, eat your heart out! The Brothers of the Guardian had been a cloistered and isolated sect who had taken Pharisaic law to the extreme. They had fallen out of favor and were embittered. By their teachings and practices they actually rejected some of the Torah, and tried to redefine Talmudic law. They became increasingly scorned by the Jewish population as a whole, were considered pariahs, in fact, and they began looking for revenge. Their lust for vengeance wasn't limited to the Jewish community, though, but was an ecumenical hatred. Interesting thought! By twentieth century standards they would have been considered a cult of hate.

"On the other hand, the Arab conspirators were members of wealthy and powerful tribal families who found old desert superstitions and polytheism useful tools for exercising power and control over a largely unenlightened populace. Howard notes some of these people apparently were interested in control of the caravan trade routes. But the swelling ranks of the Prophet and the religious fervor and zeal he was amassing threatened their hold on power. Mohammed also had armies and he was intent on taking Mecca as a holy city. Clearly this new faith threatened the old order. Military predominance would be their religion—if they could get rid of Mohammed.

"The Goths had problems with Christian leadership in Rome and Constantinople. Their murderous and barbaric ways had been decried by church leaders and many royal courts which owed allegiance to either Pope Gregory or the Emperors of the East following the pattern of Justinian.

"Howard nails it on this page: Gothic Christian, Jewish radical, and Arab merchant united in common evil purpose. They were— he's got a great name for it—'an unholy cabal'—forced together by their rejections in a world of superstition and decadent paganism, ready to listen to wild rumor. But particularly insidious were the Havra Hashomer, for by casting blame on and drawing attention to the Sons of Zion, not only would they discredit the one group that could keep them in check, but they would be able to continue with their evil deeds and plots undetected.

"Howard realized the monstrous lie was still around, but in the thirteenth century it had grown enormous horns: the militant Seljuk Turks, lineal descendants of the rival sect of Moslems, were threatening the world. The religion of Islam was being overpowered by radical preachers of holy war. The old lie, weakening the spiritual authenticity, fed into their power and they rode rampant, thus threatening the Christian world itself."

As Millerkirk read, his respect for Howard deepened. He was moved by the power of a faith that bridged six hundred years, kept alive by the light of truth and devotion of men who struggled against dark times and powerful enemies. But as riveting and powerful as what he had just read was, what he turned to next almost knocked him off his chair. Howard the Tall had retranslated the Epistle of

Shame, had the original letters and those of Alcuin copied, and added his notes on the line of descent since. He had compiled them into a "collection for the ages," to cast "true light on sin"—the sin of trying to destroy religious thought. So it said.

True light on sin. That was part of the Latin translation on Tim's metal plate. Howard had ordered metalsmiths to make seven plates, each like the one Tim's daughter found on the beach after it had been buried by Pasotti's turn coat courier.

"Note to Tim Calvin: this may be the closest thing to miracle I've seen. It looks like we have another grand slam. The plate *is* tied into all of this. Your hunch was right!

"OK—here's the story of the plate—this is too much: Howard had not been optimistic about the tide of events. There had been moments of epiphany, but there was a storm of violence on the wind as well. It was 1222 and there was a spirit of new thinking in England. King John had been forced into signing the Magna Carta in 1215. Legal reforms started under Henry the II were still in place. Cambridge University was thirteen years old and trying to rival the older Oxford founded some sixty years previously. There was a recognition of the importance of history and learning. The church was an important force in the society. But Howard had seen the ordeal of Thomas à Becket and realized the power of government and the power of the church could not always coincide. King Henry III had just recently taken the throne and it was unclear what course he planned to take, but it seemed as if secular materialism was rearing its ugly head again, as in the past.

"This is like a ringside seat to history. England and France were at odds with each other and there had been bloodshed. Christians in the Holy Land were being persecuted and slaughtered. The Seljuk Turks, a vile and destructive Asiatic band had captured Jerusalem and defiled the Church of the Holy Sepulcher. The early Crusades were not going well as Christian soldiers were being routed with high losses and heavy casualties. The Holy Land was falling away from Christian control and it seemed as though a terrible war at home and on the continent was approaching. Many hearts and minds were consumed with pessimism.

"Note to myself: these next couple of pages could be the source of a great piece on faith versus adversity. Random observation: His writings, and those of William and Alcuin, are examples of faith over greed, intellect over power, light over darkness. Howard writes he could not be confident of the immediate future, but he knew in his heart that this evil challenge to faith should not be forgotten, that in it was a lesson for the ages. He realized that regardless of what was about to happen immediately, future civilization needed to remember the exposure by William of the awful plan, the attempt to sabotage the worship of the one God in the world. But faith and goodness could survive even the most corrupt and insidious attack. This was one of the great victories over evil, and its story had to be saved.

"OK, here's more on the plate. Ah! The seven plates were carried by courier, knight, and missionary, chosen by Howard, to far ends of the known world as guideposts to where Howard had stored the manuscripts. Because of the uncertainty of the times Howard chose to hide the manuscripts in a place of safety and sanctuary. The inscriptions were written, Howard had said, so that only men of faith and good heart could decipher their meaning and find the hiding place of true light on sin.

"Query: Wonder what happened to the other six plates?

"This is odd. There are just two pages of the old manuscript left, an account of Howard's travel to Chartres in 1224 as an emissary of the King. The cathedral had just been completed, having been rebuilt starting in 1194. Howard was part of a royal party which was to meet with King Philip Augustus. It was hoped the dedication ceremony and the spirit it would evoke could ease the tension between France and England. Howard writes how he was moved by the beauty of the windows and the statuary work. It was during his extended visit he completed his work which recounted the story of William and Alcuin. His act of devotion at the new cathedral was to order the forging of the plates telling where he was sealing away, hiding for time and history, the full account of the Epistle of Shame."

Millerkirk was puzzled. He felt like he'd been driving down a smooth highway only to find a bridge out. There had to be more. He went to the computer, searched the index for more. He pored over the voluminous hand-written index books. He looked in the stacks, and on shelves and in cases for additional pages. He called the Archbishop's office. No, there was no more.

"Now this is incredible and a bit disconcerting. I know what the grand prize is. I know there is a supermanuscript, the Epistle of Shame. I have translations and records of its existence. But I don't know where it is. All we have is Tim Calvin's metal plate; and now we know what that is, but we must decipher its message. Providence is playing some kind of trick on us. We are putting together a puzzle but some of the pieces are missing. Where *is* the manuscript? The answer is still locked in the riddle of the Greek and Latin inscriptions."

Millerkirk pulled the notes out of his folder that had the translation from the plate.

> *Warrior of light who guards the South where Christ rules and judges enthroned to the setting sun. A second house on early spirit ground. Two sisters reach to heaven.*
>
> *For the love of God and all earthly issue. King of ages here resides true light on sin.*

Tim wandered through the cathedral. As vespers were being chanted he sat toward the back of the massive sanctuary, marveling at the high vaulted ceiling and the massive stone columns and pillars and the ornate woodwork. More than anything else he was captivated by the light. Devotional candles glowed along the side of the nave and on the altar, but it was the light coming through the stained glass windows which overpowered him. The evening sun diffused through the multicolored creations and poured down into the cathedral in a cascading symphony of color. The very air seemed thick with pastels and jewel-tones, swirling around him almost tangibly. He sat there, absorbing the color, losing himself in it. Vespers ended, and people came and went.

A group of musicians drifted in with violins, an oboe, a piano, and a French horn, preparing for an evening concert. Motionless, Tim watched them assemble. He felt as though his body had been immersed in color and only his eyes hung there in the space of light rays. They played Bach's "Jesu, Joy of Man's Desiring," the gentle tones riding on currents of color that changed as the sun set. Candles glowed softly and the quietly sweet music rang in tranquil resonance off the old stones.

Unbidden, and without pain, tears came to his eyes. He made no attempt to brush them away, and in his eyes the colors melded. The candle flames became spokes of light, rays emanating from a hot center and reaching into the diffused light from the windows. The music pierced deep into his heart, and with tears running down his cheeks, making large wet splashes on his shirt, he felt peace unlike any he had never known. He became overwhelmed with the love he felt for all who were dear to him, his beloved Laney, his children Elizabeth and Katie, his parents, and his friends. His mind drifted on a gentle, soft path through the people and places of his life, and he felt more than love. He was thankful for it all. He felt the presence of God, in a way so undeniable that he shuddered even in the depths of his mind. Haji defined faith as the deeply serious business of the work of Allah. For Stroutsel it was the rock, the basis for his existence after the horrors of the Holocaust and Normandy. And Millerkirk's faith was an exciting adventure. All of these men had experienced their faith in God as the foundation of their existence, present in all parts of life as Stroutsel had said, and now he had been given that gift here in the beauty of Chartres. God was reality, not so much an intellectual matter as it was an intuitive insight, a connection with source. It was an acceptance that all that is earthly is temporal and passing, as Bede had quoted the old counselor as saying. But beyond that passing material scene is a love so powerful, touched with grace, that life becomes an opportunity, its mission service, never beyond the light of God, he thought. Even though he had considered himself a "good" man, he had deluded himself. From this moment, when he experienced God as the reality of existence, he knew he would never think of good in the old way. Augustine had indeed been correct; God was present always, and that is what gave life meaning. He knelt there and listened, and opened his eyes to the wonderful color. He had been touched by heaven, the same one that had been a reality for William of Enright, Alcuin and Howard, and for Haji and Stroutsel for that matter. The plate and its divinely inspired message rejecting the lie which denied one God had reached across the centuries and brought him to this moment.

* * *

As Millerkirk left the reading room and walked into the side yard of the ancient cathedral he felt as if he were in another world, as if moving between centuries, his mind running between 600 and 1225. He was overwrought, now focusing his entire concentration on the code on the plate. Where was the original of the Epistle of Shame? What an incredible document that would be for theologians and historians. But what in the world did the message on the plate mean?

Charles Warren had changed location and was working on another small canvas that Millerkirk could not see, approaching as he was toward the back of the easel. Seeing the artist at work brought his attention to where he was, and Becky and Charles greeted him at the same time Tim approached from the front of the cathedral.

As Tim joined the group Millerkirk and the Warrens noticed his emotional state. "The cathedral got to you, didn't it?" Millerkirk asked softly.

"To say the least," Tim replied. "I feel wonderful...well, I'm not sure how to put it into words. I'll tell you about it later. How are you doing?"

"I feel like I'm lost in time. I've just been totally absorbed. We need to talk about that soon." Millerkirk moved around behind Warren to look at the work in progress. "What are you painting?"

"The twin spires. They're beautiful, like two saints, aren't they?" Warren asked. He deftly dabbed spots of pale golden paint on the image of the Gothic and Romanesque spires, showing the glow of the setting sun. His words stopped Millerkirk and Tim cold.

"What did you just say?" Tim demanded, his mind spinning.

"Like two saints," Warren repeated, puzzled by the question.

Tim's eyes raced from the canvas to the spires, his thoughts flying like sparks. The inscription on Howard's plate spoke of "two sisters reaching for heaven." Two saints, two sisters—could it be?

Millerkirk read his mind. "Tim, I think I know what you are thinking. I want you to take a look at something."

They excused themselves from the puzzled Warrens and headed around the cathedral.

"Let's look at the doors and those sculptures on the west entrance," Millerkirk said, referring to the exquisite scenes of Christ. Their pace went from a walk to a sprint.

Warren watched after them, and then looked at his wife and arched his eyebrows. "Man! Are they into something deep or what?"

* * *

Millerkirk and Tim had already seen the sculptured arches over the west doors of the cathedral, but now they studied them with a new intensity.

"There—the center piece is certainly Christ enthroned as ruler and judge of the universe," Millerkirk said.

"The spires have got to be the 'sisters reaching to heaven.' Millerkirk, it's falling into place."

"And this is the second cathedral built here. Remember, the first one was destroyed by fire."

"That would account for the 'second house now' passage. But what about the line 'early spirit ground'?" Tim asked. Millerkirk frowned, deep in thought. Then he snapped his fingers. "No prob-lem! It's the cathedral itself! Druids worshiped on this ground long before Christianity reached this part of France. The site had been a druid place of worship first, but now it's the 'second house on early spirit ground.' Old Howard would have known that; it's just part of the history of the place. He must have been so taken with this wondrous new cathedral that he hid the manuscripts here. They're here some place!"

"This is a mind buster!"

They stood at the south door looking up at the jamb statues on the south transept portals, their eyes moving over the marvelous carvings. Millerkirk saw it first and stopped abruptly. Tim turned to him questioningly.

"There it is." Millerkirk pointed toward a collection of four statues.

"What?" Tim looked where Millerkirk pointed. There in the cluster of four statues one stood out, a large stone warrior, a crusader.

"This has to be the final piece!" Millerkirk said.

"The soldier of light, who guards the south! Yes—yes!" Tim practically shouted.

"We've got to check this out," Millerkirk said as he dashed off toward the manse to find someone who could answer his questions.

"Ah, yes, you're talking about Saint Theodore," Father Marcel said, "a Christian soldier of the Crusades. He is indeed different from the other figures, standing at ease, a slight "S" curve in his body, very natural. The other figures are rigid. Did you notice his feet? They are on a flat platform and very lifelike. Those of the other statues you see are carved into the platform or are sloped and unnatural. Yes, Dr. Millerkirk, Theodore is quite different. His detail is more intricate, his face is more human. He is so much more lifelike than any of the other statues. It has baffled us for centuries. He stands alone."

Father Marcel had provided the final clue. "Yes," Millerkirk repeated softly, "Saint Theodore is different."

"Thank heavens for that," Tim punctuated.

* * *

They rested on the bench outside the main door and watched the sun drop below the horizon. The sky was full of small fluffy patches of clouds illuminated from the back by the mauve to orange afterglow of the sunset. Music drifted from inside the cathedral.

"So we've had the same goal after all." Millerkirk said.

"Traveling to the same place along an ancient road, Millerkirk. A place presided over and guarded by a stone Christian soldier." Tim stretched his legs. "To think just a week ago I was relaxing like this on the beach. It's amazing."

Millerkirk smiled and placed his hand on Tim's shoulder. "Well, they say the Lord moves in strange, mysterious ways. But that he'd move you all the way from Sanibel to the seventh century is more than an average miracle."

* * *

Dinner with the Warrens at the small restaurant turned out to be a celebration. Warren offered a blessing and then proceeded to order a bowl of garlic and another of sliced onion to accompany his dinner, which elicited a perplexed look from the waiter. Millerkirk recounted the tale of the old manuscripts. He was deeply grateful for the phenomenal success of deciphering the plate and the insight he gained. Warren and his wife Becky were amazed at the odd, tortuous story.

"I declare, prayers were answered." Warren said with gusto. "Tell you what—I'm going to do a painting of Saint Theodore for you. A way to remember all the years you worked on this. A way to commemorate the Epistle of Shame."

Tim was both serene and joyful. He could not fully account for his own personal experience in the cathedral except to say that he was "as moved by the love of God as he could ever remember." In this company he needed to say nothing more. Dinner ended and the Warrens took their leave. Tim went to call Laney and the girls. It would be one-thirty in the afternoon on Sanibel, he thought. Someone might be around the condo now. He would finally reach them, and then he would call Valmer to give him the good news.

* * *

Abel's head felt like fire. All the mumbo jumbo talk of Calvin's friend had come to him garbled, as if it were on slow speed. Abel was ready for action, ready to move on to another town, but first he needed to get the old manuscript for Pasotti. That was going to be really big money. His frequent calls to Pasotti had been like appetizers, whetting the rich man's desire. He told him it wouldn't be long before he had the priceless documents and said he would arrange for a transfer in Rome. But right now Abel was wired, a bundle of cocaine-fried nerves, fidgeting.

Moshe and Anna watched, aware that the risk of danger escalated with the darkening of the sky. They had continued to monitor Abel's calls.

"He is so loaded he will be unpredictable. Look how he's bouncing his legs, rocking his head back and forth. He can't sit still," Moshe said as he peered through his field glasses.

"He's like a caged animal, eager to pounce," Anna added.

"Yes. Well, I know how it feels to be caged," he said, sending her a thinly-veiled yearning look.

"And I know as field operatives we have no time for your caged feelings, so try to behave like a professional." She took the field glasses and looked at Abel. "Something tells me this evening could be dangerous, and possibly lethal."

Tim was elated as he waited for the transatlantic call to go through. If they could get the manuscript tonight, he figured he could catch the 9:00 A.M. flight out of DeGaulle which would put him into New York around eight. Then he'd get a connection to Fort Myers and be back on the island by late Sunday afternoon. He toyed with another option—sleep in and catch the later Concorde and still get to Dulles about the same time. Valmer could work it out. The thought of rejoining his family and resuming his vacation, combined with his experience in the cathedral, made him positively joyful.

The phone at the condo rang over and over with no answer. Again? Was everything all right there? Maybe something had happened to Laney's sister and they'd had to go to Fort Myers. He hoped not. He was so far away, and anything could happen.

He dialed Valmer's number, looking over the notes he had jotted about Millerkirk's explanation of the Epistle of Shame. There would probably be some international wrangling over ownership of the documents. He was sure seminarians, theologians, historians and maybe even politicians would be enormously interested.

It struck him for the first time that the mystery of the plate was solved. His quest was over. He would have no need for the manuscripts. Actually, Millerkirk could take possession of them as his UN commission resolved ownership issues. Surely no grave international crisis would erupt from the Epistle of Shame, not now at least. It could have provoked widespread chaos a thousand years ago, but now it seemed more the province of theologians and historians. On the other hand, making public a rumor that Mohammed had been a Jewish agent could provoke more nastiness in the Middle East, where ancient hatreds were a contemporary and ongoing crisis. And weren't the young man and woman, the Iranians, still around? Maybe he wasn't completely out of the woods yet. Valmer and his friends might have a take on that. He would leave such worry to the pros.

"Hello?" Valmer answered before the first ring was complete.

"Valmer, this is Tim. Great news—mission accomplished!"

"I'm glad someone has good news. There's a dearth of that here."

"We are in Chartres. We've broken the code. The Latin described this incredible old manuscript from the seventh century, and the Greek was the location. Millerkirk knows where it is. It's called the Epistle of Shame."

"You are quite sure this is accurate?"

Tim explained, starting with details of Millerkirk's early research. Valmer was familiar with the work of Alcuin, though William of Enright was new to him. Now and then Valmer intruded with a question, a challenge, which Tim was able answer to his satisfaction. As Tim explained Millerkirk's theory regarding the

Saint Theodore statue his mind flashed back to Valmer's liquor chest, the old knight's chest, and the old wooden desk where Valmer more than likely was sitting. Those two antiquities had seemed to foreshadow the odd course his life had taken in the past few days.

After giving Valmer the last details, Tim tried to describe his moving experience in the cathedral. He couldn't really find the words, though, and could only say that he had been moved to tears.

"Your news is indeed wonderful, Tim, and your experience in the cathedral seems to be the beneficial and satisfactory conclusion of a long trip. But I have bad news; actually, it's quite horrid, and...."

"What? What's happened?" Tim's heart pounded and his knees almost buckled. His suspicions had been right after all—something had happened.

"Now listen, Tim! Everyone is alive, but there is a problem. It's not an easy one, but we're doing what we can to correct it. Your wife and daughters and Cee Hockett are being held captive by a greedy lout named Ivan Wasser. Wasser means them no harm; he merely wants the plate and plans to exchange your family for it. David however, has taken matters into his hands. As we speak he is making final plans for a rescue. I have to tell you, though, it's not good here. Your wife was allowed to speak to David on the phone, and apparently your youngest is not well, and your wife is very worried about her health. I'm sorry to have to tell you like this. You must understand—I couldn't tell you until now."

Nothing Valmer could have said could have been more unexpected. Tim said nothing, thinking somehow if he did not acknowledge what he had heard it would not be real, that it would disappear. He could not be sure he had heard it correctly. His breath exhaled in a burst, as though his body caved in, his head felt like it was imploding. His mind felt like it had been blasted by a space laser, rattled, stunned, empty.

At last he tried to speak, but his mouth was so dry. "What...?" he croaked, a feeble crawl of a voice—it was all he could manage.

Valmer explained, in detail. Wasser's background, the monitored phone calls, Jayne's discovery, Barb and Dave's agony and Dave's anger, and finally Dave's plan of attack. He had kept the information from him "for his good and for the sake of the mission." He apologized for the "intrusion into his life, the manipulation of the affair, and the terrible consequence."

Tim felt distant, remote from the horrible news, listening as if to a news report involving strangers. Something in his brain clicked, making him feel analytical, calculating, dispassionate; there *was* nothing he could do. Another part was consumed by desperation and fear. The loves of his life were captives, pawns, and he was helpless. He wavered between paralysis and rage. He asked for more details. When Valmer described Dave's plan, Tim felt a fleeting moment of confidence, although it was severely challenged and undermined by the anguished worry and terrible dread.

Katie seriously ill? He shut his eyes and pictured his angel sleeping as he checked on her each night, her little face in peaceful slumber, surrounded by her stuffed "rabbie" and "huggy bear." He would kiss her cheek and whisper, "Daddy loves you, God Bless you." Some nights in her sleepy voice she would answer back "I love you too, Daddy, God Bless you."

This was what life was really about, and his greatest moments were when he checked on his sleeping children and secured the house for the night, knowing that his family was safe, sound, healthy, and well. But this time, when they had needed him most, he hadn't been on watch, he hadn't been able to protect them from this violent intrusion. The pain was hard to bear.

Valmer told Tim about Edward Earl and how he would accompany Dave on the rescue. "No guns will be used. They will rely solely on the element of surprise. Police will be on standby, and if necessary will try to intervene on the road between the beach house and airport, but we want to keep their involvement at a minimum because the probability of injury is much higher if police move in. Earl is an expert in these things, and knows the odds. Due to location and other factors, such as not knowing how many people are holding the girls, Dave's plan is probably our best hope. The kidnappers are not maniacs; they have no reason to want to harm your family. They just want the plate. There is nothing more I can say or do right now." Valmer told Tim they would be in radio contact and he would know as soon as the operation began.

"Meanwhile, you must concentrate on what you have to do. No amount of worry will help at this end, but it can distract you from your work." Valmer was silent for a moment, and Tim had the feeling he was still withholding something.

"What is it, Valmer? What else are you not telling me?"

"Well, I have another confession to make. That man whom you have seen, the Saddam Hussein look-alike, is Tariq Abel, a terrorist, a killer wanted by many nations. He is working for someone, probably Aoki Pasotti, but to be sure, he is out for himself. Tim, you must exercise great caution. Abel will try to take what you seek. Is there any way Abel can get to the document before you and Millerkirk?"

"No, nobody else knows anything about it or where it is," Tim said. "Millerkirk isn't entirely sure himself where we'll find it, or how to get to it."

"I can't emphasize enough—do not underestimate Abel. He hasn't survived for so long without being more capable and more ruthless than his adversaries and prey. And right now, Tim, that is you."

"Millerkirk has a plan of his own worked out." The distraction of the task at hand, and the creeping fear of Abel snapped Tim out of his depression, mobilizing his mind.

"I cannot be sure of Millerkirk's capability, so say no more," Valmer said. "I must resign myself to leaving the operational procedures to the two of you. Guard against being overheard and be extremely vigilant with your undertaking. Abel is a man with much experience."

Tim was exhausted. He resolved to call often for updates until he got home, and Valmer had promised to go to work immediately on return trip bookings. Now he needed to focus on what he had to do, but he wrestled with his emotions. Although it was a natural and probably inevitable thing to do he knew he should not worry about the girls, and Tim fought desperately to steel his nerves. He had to trust Dave to get his family out of harm's way: after all, his own daughter was also being held. Valmer was right, there was nothing he could do, it had to be handled on Sanibel. He remembered he had failed to tell Valmer about the Iranians who were also on his tail. He had not seen the young couple recently, but he could not be sure they were not lurking somewhere in the darkened town. He wondered why Valmer had not mentioned them; surely he must know of them. He needed a twenty-four-hour sleep.

Millerkirk was the picture of happiness as he sat in the café sipping coffee. He fairly beamed as he looked over a couple of sketches Warren had done of the jamb statute of Saint Theodore. Soon he could begin the formal retrieval process with the French government and make his report to the UN commission. Then he could return to the university with a treasure of the ages to study, and Tim could return to his family. He opened his mouth for a cheerful greeting when Tim approached the table, but as soon as he saw his face he knew something terrible had happened. Just hours before Tim had been so full of bliss, and now he looked as though he was caught in a painful trap.

* * *

Compassion came easily to Millerkirk. His experience as a pastor and his natural sense of grace and abiding faith helped him walk Tim through the agonies of the moment.

"You had your spirit and faith revived there in the cathedral. Now it's time to draw on that strength, put it to work. You can handle this."

Tim nodded miserably, then sighed. "You're right, and I'm trying. In the meantime, we have another problem to address. Let's walk for a while."

They paid their check and stepped outside the café. As they strolled up the street Millerkirk arched his eyebrows questioningly. "What's up?"

"We needed to be outside where no one could listen," Tim said. "When I was talking to Valmer, he told me an Iraqi terrorist has been following us. He's after the plate and whatever it leads to, so he can sell it to an art collector. According to Valmer the guy wouldn't have any qualms about whatever he had to do to get the treasure."

"We need to get it right away then, before he does—tonight," Millerkirk said quietly.

The jamb statues were larger than life-size, and Saint Theodore stood at the top of a carved column which itself crowned more stone. The carved-stone platform, mounted on the massive foundation, was rectangular shaped and resembled two sides of a miniature temple. The steps abutted the foundation stone and the carved and sculptured columns rose alongside, each on a similar base. Studying the Warren sketch, they noticed the ornate bottom work resembled more than a temple: the stacked levels looked like giant versions of a child's set of wooden blocks. Millerkirk pointed out the position of the spear in Saint Theodore's right hand. It was at a definite right angle and he had a hunch the shaft was a pointer.

Millerkirk had walked around the cathedral earlier, while Tim was on the phone, and tapped at and knocked around on the statuary on the south transept adjoining the Saint Theodore statue. By following a line from the spear's end down the column to the base block, the temple-like box shape, he found what he thought was space large and secure enough to hold the combined manuscripts. There in heavy stone, under the warrior of light who guards the south was the "true light on sin"—it had to be.

"How can you be so sure that's the place?" Tim pressed.

"I tried to think as Howard might have. When he came here, the cathedral was new, all of the statuary was breathtaking, astonishing to the thirteenth century mind. But out of all of it, the Saint Theodore is unique, so life-like, the features so vivid and real, it had to stand out. Perhaps he thought that others of the faith in the future might read the plate and solve the riddle and would notice how outstanding this statue is. Match that with what he had written, plus the Epistle of Shame, and the plate's message about the warrior of light, this has to be it, don't you agree?"

It made sense. It was somehow appropriate, Tim thought, that a Christian soldier had stood guard over the secret for almost eight hundred years. Had it not been for his child's serendipitous find, the stone warrior's secret might never had been known. Katie! It tore him apart to think of her in peril now. She just had to, she would make it. Focus—he needed to focus on what was going on here.

"It's important we do this without defacing the stonework. I'd planned to run this through the UN, but frankly, if we did that, with all the bureaucracy and the French government getting involved it might take years to happen. If someone is on our tail I'm afraid we've got to do this, for the safety of the document," Millerkirk continued. "I can claim some UN commission authority to cover us, but we've got to protect that stone work. The lights should go off in a few minutes. That'll leave only the front of the cathedral and the spires illuminated." He added that he had seen service lights over the rear entrance and lights on the walkway and garden. "I think they cast enough light for safety and security for the rest of the building, but it's not a lot. The area we're interested in is on the south transept, and will be in heavy shadows." They would be far enough away from the street lamp on the walk to give them cover.

"We sound like burglars, don't we?" Millerkirk chuckled.

"Yeah, but I don't want to end up in jail like one. What about the gendarmes? They're bound to think its suspicious, our tapping and digging around the base of a statue in the dark. How will we answer that? I don't know...." Tim shook his head. What a strange deal, a couple of guys like themselves plotting a nighttime raid on an ancient church.

"A good question, but not really a problem. Remember, this is Chartres, not New York City. Vandalism is unheard of—nothing happens here, so the police don't keep a tight guard on the cathedral. They'll be occupied in the restaurants and bistros, and we should have plenty of time to do what we have to do."

* * *

While they waited for time to get underway, Tim went to his hotel room to place a call to Valmer. "We're about set to go here. Any word there?" Tim asked.

"It's just before two. Wasser expects the exchange to happen at the airport in an hour. This old walkie-talkie isn't cooperating so I can't tell you what's happening. By David's plan something should be, but I have nothing to confirm it; we're in the dark. We have to trust David on this." Strain and anger wore on Valmer's voice. "Critical moments are passing on both sides of the Atlantic, and there's not much I can do about the outcome in either place. It's extremely frustrating," he said tensely.

As he and Millerkirk stealthily crept around the cathedral, Tim carefully looked around for signs of anyone lurking in the area, especially Tariq Abel. They had moved around the building and grounds and entered from the gate at the back, dashing from shadow to shadow cast by the building and trees, until they came to the south side. Because the hotel, cafés, and restaurants were in another part of town, this area was quiet. No cars moved on the nearby narrow streets and the higher ground of the cathedral gave them a good view of any nearby activity. The church itself was empty and quiet, and they were alone.

Abel could barely control his desire to laugh out loud at the childish and unprofessional behavior of the two Americans. What did they think they were doing, playing a game of hide and seek? Concealed in a dark alleyway, he had a clear line of vision to where

Tim and Millerkirk had stopped. He also had been to the cathedral to scan for a vantage point, and they could not have picked a better spot for him. They couldn't see him, but they were quite visible even to the naked eye, and certainly obtainable through his scope.

The only tools Tim and Millerkirk had were the ones from the trunk of the rental car. Both carried small flashlights. They agreed they were hardly prepared for this odd archeological dig, and certainly were ill-equipped to deal with potential hostility if the Iraqi were to show up. Still, what other course was there? Tim trained his light on the block base of the column, while Millerkirk set about tapping on the stone, as a person might tap on a wall listening for a stud or hollow space. He had wrapped the tire iron in his wind-breaker jacket so as not to chip the old stone. Millerkirk's flashlight was propped against an adjoining column and its beam climbed the statuary, illuminating the old knight in a bizarre, dramatic way.

While he held the light, Tim looked around and tried to take in the scene, to store it for playback at a time when he was at ease, not nervous and frightened by the task at hand nor wracked by worry about the well-being of his beloved gals.

"We're out our element—maybe out of our minds," Tim whispered.

Millerkirk nodded agreement as he continued to tap at the stone.

A gentle spring breeze blew through the chestnut tree, car-rying a bit of chill. The moon sidled along one of the spires, and the sky was pricked with stars which seemed to swim behind a few wispy grey night clouds. The air was rich with the scents of flowers and trees, and more prosaically, the distant aromas of sizzling butter and simmering sauces. The only sounds, aside from their own, were cars and a thin din of voices coming from blocks away.

Abel had been on the cellular phone again. Pasotti was not available but his assistant had been told the status of things, that Abel was "in control," and would soon "eliminate the obstacles."

Soon he would strike. Soon he would take possession. Soon. It had to be soon. He had them both in his scope. He took another snort of cocaine just to sharpen his senses. These idiots had to hurry. He didn't want to wait much longer.

"Listen to the difference," Millerkirk whispered as he tapped the base stone of Saint Theodore, then shuffled backwards on his knees to tap the column crowned by a monk holding a Bible. "Hear it?"

There was a distinct difference. The first tap was answered with a slight echo, a hollow sound. The other, in fact all the others, sounded like solid stone when tapped.

"But it's stone. How do we get in there—how can we get at it?" Millerkirk sat back on his heels and mumbled, more than spoke, as he faced the last piece of the puzzle.

"This may not work, but its worth a shot," Tim said. He took the tire iron and worked the thin flat end into the seam between the block base stone and back wall. He gritted his teeth and pulled, feeling as though the veins in his temples would explode. "If it's hollow, this is the only way in. The wall behind the statues is solid stone. It's got to be from out here."

Millerkirk squeezed his hands onto the jackhandle and together they pulled and grunted. They felt the slightest motion. Tim pulled the jack out to make sure it had not bent at the strain.

"If we can get this open, we'll let someone else close it. But I don't want to mess up the work. Hand me my jacket. I'm going to put it next to the stone so we don't scratch it." Millerkirk said.

After positioning the jacket against the stone and jackhandle, he lay on his back, directing his flashlight beam up at the seam between the top of the carved stone foundation box and the first inches of the cylindrical column supporting Saint Theodore.

"It's moving," Millerkirk said matter-of-factly.

They continued pulling, and after almost eight centuries the stone once again moved against stone. Air sealed away in 1224 blew into the twentieth century, while the breeze of the French night blew into a secret cube, and two trembling flashlight beams brought light onto a dark and ancient mystery.

They were transfixed by the power of the moment, at the private sanctuary of Howard's act of faith. A fine white powder, eight centuries of masonry dust, had settled in and coated a wide-mouthed clay vessel with a tight fitting top. A metal plate, not unlike the piece uncovered by Katie, lay also covered with stone dust. Millerkirk blew it clear and read.

"'For the love of God, true light. William of Enright, Alcuin, Howard the Tall of York.'"

There was nothing they could say. Their shadows flickered on the row of statues as they moved their flashlights over their find. Both men sat kneeling, gazing, and feeling a connection to something profound.

"I feel like we're explorers who have uncovered the past," Tim said after a long silence in the twilight and shadows. "We've found a bridge through time," he whispered softly.

"Tim, this is heaven-sent. I've got to get this to a lab and notify the Secretary General's office. Can you use your windbreaker to wrap the...."

Out of the corner of his eye Tim thought he saw a flash of light, a glint of something bright coming from across the churchyard and plaza from the dark recess between two buildings. There was nothing, just black.

Then a sickening metallic whine, a sound like a spitting shriek split the still night air, followed by a loud crack and sparks. Millerkirk saw flashes of light from the alley, and in the same moment he saw Tim pitch violently forward, his head jerking like the tip end of a snapping whip. The scene seemed to be in horrifying slow motion as Tim tumbled sideways, his arms flying up as his body fell, his eyes with a look more frightening than anything Millerkirk had ever seen.

Tim's back had been toward the alley when he heard the high pitched sound and crack. In the next instant he felt the back of his head burn, and the burn turned immediately to raging fire and then explosion. A screaming metallic monster filled his ears and deafened his brain and robbed him of balance. His vision blurred and his entire body was overcome with a violent nausea. His head roared and his eyes were like electronic circuits shutting down. His body seemed to be leaping in spasms beyond his control, he was hurtling into some black awful painful space.

The world around him raced in circles, and he spun into a dizzying chasm full of sickness and pain. With what seemed like superhuman effort, he put his hand to the back of his head and felt something wet, ragged, burning. It was like looking through a tunnel when he passed his hand in front of his eyes. The hand was red. He felt chilled to the bone, and numb. He heaved, and an explosive pain filled his head, the chills growing stronger.

"Tim! Tim!" He heard his name called with an urgency that frightened him. It was dark, and he fought his way out of the darkness. Collecting consciousness, he saw Jim Millerkirk's face. Millerkirk was cradling Tim's head, and he looked frightened. "Tim—stay with me!"

Tim opened his mouth to speak, but could only manage a gurgle and a slur. He wanted so badly to ask what was wrong. The fear and worry in Millerkirk's eyes confirmed that something was horribly wrong.

"You'll be all right, Tim. You've been hit, but you're going to be OK."

He could see in Millerkirk's eyes that it was bad. He could feel himself slipping away.

"Hang on, Tim. I'm right here—stay with me. Don't be afraid. Remember what we talked about—Saint Augustine, the plate—God is present in this too."

The pain faded to a dull roar which seemed to hover around him like a fog. He tried to focus on what Millerkirk was saying, but his mind wandered. Scenes, like vignettes of his life, swirled before his eyes. He saw Jesus with little children. Then everything played before him like a fast-forward tape. All that he had seen and done since his meeting with Juni in Chicago came back at him like a strobe camera. The countryside, faces, and Valmer's briefings flew by him. He felt like crying. He longed to hold his mother's hand and see her face. He wanted Laney there to wake him up from this bad dream. He wanted to hold Elizabeth and Katie and tell them he would always love them.

He was so cold, like ice. He looked up and Millerkirk was gone. He saw the spires of the cathedral and the moon. Would it end like this, away from his family? He had failed his girls. He was not there. He wanted to do something. He hurt. He could barely think. Pray—God, please save my girls. Forgive me. Peace. He remembered the light of the windows and music and how it had made him feel. But then, the pain and a distant rushing sound surrounded him and carried him away, like the tide at Sanibel. Sanibel. He was falling, falling, and everything around him seemed to be lifting away. The sound stopped and the world went black.

Across the plaza and churchyard in the alley, Moshe and Anna rushed Abel from behind. Moshe placed a garotte around his throat and Anna held a Beretta to his head. They could have killed him there; they wanted to. They had tried to move quickly, but hadn't been able to get to him before he fired three shots. They had watched him just dial a call from his cellular phone and hadn't expected him to shoot. Keeping her eye on Abel, Anna retrieved the phone and put it to her ear. A voice with an Italian accent yelled on the other end, halting abruptly when she said, "Good evening, Signor Pasotti."

Jim Millerkirk ran to the manse, crying for help.

Dave's Resolve and Jayne's Addiction

Just as Tim and Millerkirk had waited for darkness and deep shadows, Dave had waited for the tall sun of early afternoon before putting his plan into action. The first phase had already taken place. He had asked Jayne to prepare one of her special deserts, the deep, rich chocolate pie they called "Jayne's Addiction," one of the favorites of visitors to her restaurant. The tantalizing confection consisted of a blend of chocolate and nuts, with an Oreo cookie crust. But this one was loaded with an extra punch—Valium, Seconal, and an assortment of crushed sleeping pills which Brian and Jayne and the Hocketts had gleaned from their medicine chests and those of friends on the island.

At 10:00 A.M. on Sanibel, about the same time that Tim and Millerkirk were arriving at Chartres, Jayne walked up to the beachside entrance to the white beach house to make her delivery. Hertt saw her coming and scrambled Laney and the girls to the bedroom, and nervously smoothed his hair and straightened his shirt. The prospect of seeing Jayne and talking with her made him nervous. He met her as she started through the gate and stammered out a greeting.

"I was getting some desserts ready for the restaurant and I couldn't help remembering my best fan here," Jayne gushed. "I just had to bring you one of my special pies." She looked up at Hertt through her eyelashes.

"You…that is…I mean, you made this for me? I dunno what to say."

"Oh, don't say anything. I'm *really* happy to do it, after the nice things you said about my singing." She glanced coyly down, then back up at him. The blood pounded in his ears. "I brought it down now, though, because it really is best when it's fresh," she said. "But I'll have to warn you, it's for adults only. Your niece shouldn't eat any because it has liqueur in it, and I put a little extra in—just for you." She smiled her most dazzling smile and winked as she handed him the pie dish. "Careful, there," she said when Hertt fumbled and almost dropped the dish. "Don't let it stand too long now; you really should eat some with your lunch. Bye, now. See you later!"

Hertt managed to get his mouth working and promised that he would indeed eat some of the pie as soon as he got back inside. Jayne turned and sauntered back down the stairs, looking over her shoulder when she reached the gate to flash her dazzling smile and a wink one more time. She closed the gate behind her and blew a huge sigh. Phase one was done.

Hertt went back in the house and let Laney and the girls back out into the greatroom. Laney recognized the pie sitting on the counter.

"That looks good," she said. "Is the bakery making deliveries here?"

"Nah. It's a present, from the red-headed babe who sings down at the restaurant," Hertt preened.

"Well, isn't that cozy," Laney said sarcastically. But her heart pounded, and she fought to maintain her composure. She knew instinctively something was up and was heartened by the thought that some kind of a plan was in the works. Fighting the urge to share the news, she simply continued to encourage the girls that soon they would be released. The anticipation of a return to their own life seemed to give Katie a little strength. The morning passed with the girls whispering excitedly about their prospective release.

Around eleven thirty, while Laney and the girls were on the

pool deck, Hertt and Wasser devoured most of the pie, setting the stage for phase two of Dave's plan.

Dave had put the striking pin of the plan together in his mind, and then fleshed it out with the help of his friend, Dick Munch. One of the island businessmen, Munch was one of the "ol' boys" Dave shared breakfast with at the Quarterdeck. His special hobby was caring for and raising exotic animals on a beautiful, fairytale-like compound tucked away on his extensive acreage.

Dave had turned to Dick to develop the feasibility of his idea at its inception. He drove into Munch's compound and was greeted by the shrill squeal of an aviary full of yellow-nape parrots, birds of a striking combination of color, green with yellow around their faces and iridescent green and yellow eyes. They sported red epaulets on their wings, and light green fan-like tail feathers. The beautiful birds produced a piercing shriek that Dave thought sounded like the wild trilling of the Shiite women he had seen on CNN news reports.

As he and Dick walked through the aviary, a pair of Stanley blue cranes waltzed through, their large bulbous crowns looking like fanned cobra heads atop the long silver and blue grey necks and three-and-a-half-foot-tall bodies. Three other giant birds that drew Dave's attention included Abdom storks, huge swooping birds which had migrated from Europe to Africa and looked like small experimental aircraft as they breezed by; plush-capped turacos, a fierce species which eats rats; and blue-crowned motmots, with their stunning long, teardrop-shaped tail feathers. There were dozens of other birds. Zoos and private collectors purchased exotic creatures from Dick, or sent problems to him for study and rehabilitation. The two men stopped to look at the odd sight of several parrots that had defeathered themselves. They looked to Dave like survivors of a bomb explosion. Dave had been here before with Cee, and he was always amazed at the precise operation, as well as the exotic and beautiful creatures themselves.

But Dave had come on business that day. He and Dick stopped by the cage of ring-tailed lemurs and the adjoining cage of capuchin monkeys, often called organ-grinder monkeys, both frantic with activity. Dick was stunned when Dave first explained the special operation he wanted to conduct, but the more they walked and talked, the more convinced he was it could work. As soon as Dave left Dick had gone to work, building a number of "transfer cages" and picking out members of the invading "army."

Now it was time for the old drill instructor and warrior to enter the arena of combat, to rescue his beloved Cee and the Calvin girls, and to exact justice on the body and mind of Ivan Wasser.

Edward Earl planned to accompany Dave and Dick and their "troops," and would stay in contact with Valmer by using walkie-talkie units. When Dick's truck pulled into the Hockett driveway, Dave could see the large tarp-covered transfer cages on the back of the pickup bed. He pulled on a pair of coveralls, took a pair of bird handling gloves from Dick, and climbed up behind the cages on the bed of the truck, while Earl took up the vanguard with the van. Their faces were grim with tension, expectation, and uncertainty. Barb was worried, but tried to mask her fear; she trusted Dave, and knew that he was always successful at his undertakings, no matter how difficult. Dave's stomach rolled, and as the moment of execution drew near, he hoped that his plan was not too exotic or wild that it wouldn't work. His rage at the kidnappers had become his only focus. He leaned over the side of the truck and kissed Barb, and the two vehicles pulled down the road.

Just out of sight of the beach house, Earl stopped the van, and Dick pulled up behind him. Earl got out and carried a briefcase back to the cab of the truck. He opened the case and produced two silver gray Smith & Wesson nine millimeter semi-automatic pistols. "You should have these, just in case," he said. "Pray you won't need them, but having them is probably the best insurance."

Although wild, the plan was relatively simple. Dick would back the pickup down the lane of the beach house. Once in view of the house he would race toward the window to the left of the door.

If Jayne's description was accurate, the rigged opening on

the transfer cages would match the height of the window. From his position behind the cages on the pickup bed, Dave would yank the front of the tarp clear, grab a handle to slide the cage forward and thrust open the exit door. There was another lever which would either raise or lower the platform built on top of the pickup bed in case the cage and window heights didn't match. Dick had prepared well. The cages held an army of the feisty and irrepressible capuchin monkeys, a half dozen of the ferocious plush-capped turacos, and more than a dozen of the yellow-nape parrots led by Rosa, who had been trained to make an uncannily realistic impression of a police siren.

Katie lay on the lounge chair on the sunporch of the house and stared out the window at the pool. Even though she had finally drunk some juice, she was still weak. She sat transfixed by the sparkles of sun on the water. Elizabeth lay next to her, cuddling her; Liz's mood was brightened by the thought that her dad and Dave and Brian and Jayne were at this very moment moving toward freeing them. Cee watched TV and pouted because she had missed a craft class as well as her horseback riding lesson. She continued to glower at Hertt, even though he had begun to treat them quite decently, even kindly. He sat in a recliner chair in the great room; he looked as though he was sleeping. Usually he kept his eyes on them, particularly little Katie.

They had not seen a sign of the other man since he and Hertt had last met in the kitchen. Laney anxiously watched the beach and listened for any sound which could mean their rescue was on the way. The clock on the pool house showed it was a little after one thirty. Hertt had told her the exchange would take place at the airport at three. If something was going to happen here it would have to be soon. But it dawned on her that the plan might be to stop them en route to the airport. She was surprised that neither Hertt nor the angry man had begun to marshal them to move. Compounding her uneasiness was a feeling about Tim's well-being. There was nothing logical about it, but she was still anxious, and felt a fleeting prickle of fear. She quickly dismissed it as a by-product of having not seen or heard from him since the kidnapping, and as a case of nerves, natural enough in these circumstances.

Earl cleared the driveway and pulled onto the shoulder of the road just north of the entrance, almost hidden by sea grapes and Brazilian pepper. Dick pulled the truck in behind him, and positioned it to back in quickly down the small incline and around the twists. Dave hopped down from the cab and took up his position in the bed of the truck behind the cages and slipped the pistol into the pocket of his coveralls.

Earl tried to raise Valmer on the walkie-talkie. The unit seemed to be working, but he couldn't be sure because he got no response. Valmer might be on the phone. He knew Valmer had broken the news of the kidnapping to Tim, and Tim was of course dismayed. Earl was to check in soon because Tim would be calling for an update. Well, if the walkie-talkie wasn't working there was nothing to be done for it now. They had no choice but to continue. Earl would have to wait and call Valmer from the phone in the house as soon as the situation was under control.

Dick began backing the truck down the drive. As Earl pulled the van in behind the truck he could see that Dave looked grim, with an edge of fear in his eyes, a look that Earl had seen before on cops and field agents. He parked the van in a position that would enable him to round up the girls and drive them away quickly.

Laney heard the sound of a racing car or truck engine and spun toward the direction of the sound. Elizabeth bolted upright on the lounge chair, and Cee and Katie both looked questioningly at Laney. The racket brought Hertt bursting from his apparent torpor, and he started toward them, moving in what seemed to be slow motion. In the next instant a loud banging and crashing shook the house, causing Hertt to reach for the pistol in his shoulder holster. For an instant, Laney thought she must be dreaming. Hertt reached for the pistol as a loud siren-like noise pierced the air. He dropped the pistol and put his arms protectively over his face, his eyes wide with terror and confusion, as a swarm of shrieking, screeching green and yellow birds flew through the room, accompanied by a horde of hissing and screeching monkeys that bounded over chairs and couches and knocked over tables and lamps and climbed curtains and blinds. The animals chattered and screeched madly, while the shrieking birds swooped and darted .

Hertt ran and stumbled in an attempt to escape the uproar, and waved his arms in panic. In the instant it took to happen, Laney knew this was time to make a run for the beach. Elizabeth and Cee stood pale-faced and wide-eyed like frozen statues, their mouths agape. But Laney couldn't believe her eyes when she saw her listless Katie dissolve into gales of laughter as she watched the flying, tumbling, swarming, hissing onslaught.

Snapping herself out of her surprise and shock, Laney grabbed Katie and shouted at Elizabeth and Cee to follow as she darted for the stairs leading down the pool deck and to the beach. She felt a moment of panic when she looked back and saw another man, who she thought must be the other kidnapper, enter the greatroom. Then from outside she heard a voice.

"Mrs. Calvin—come this way, quickly! I'm a friend of Valmer—hurry!" He grabbed her arm and they hurried down the steps toward the waiting van, Cee and Elizabeth close behind. Elizabeth paused for a moment to look back at the chaotic scene inside the house. She wrinkled her nose in a look of utter revulsion, then bounded down the steps and ran to catch up with her mom and the others.

Dave followed behind the shrieking invaders as they flew and scrambled through the house. He was pumped and his heart hammered against his ribs as he stepped through the shattered frame and glass of the picture window. Hertt was in the corner of the adjoining room in a state of utter panic, ducking and waving at the birds as they flew at him. Dave saw him pulling at the revolver in his shoulder holster and reached for his own pistol, but just as Hertt pulled the weapon free he was hit by two or three turacos and dropped the gun. He ran toward the bar separating the greatroom and the kitchen, shielding his head with his arms, then he grabbed something off the counter and bolted through a side door. The sudden action caught Dave by surprise, and he started to take off after the fleeing man when he heard the voice from the ransom call—the voice of Ivan Wasser.

"What the hell is going on here, you idiot?" The sound came from the stairs from the loft overlooking the greatroom. Dave scooted into the hall behind the steps and watched Wasser come down the stairs. Stunned by the piercing sound and devastating ruckus of the monkeys and parrots, Wasser fired a pistol in the direction of some hissing monkeys.

Dave leapt forward, leading with his shoulder, and slammed into Wasser. Still under the effect of the Jayne's Addiction, Wasser was slow to turn and respond. He tried to spin to his right, bringing his hand and arm around to fire, but Dave crushed him in the midsection hard with his shoulder sending the gun flying from Wasser's hand and knocking the breath out of him. He crumbled and slammed hard into the bar. He tried to pull himself up with his elbow and was looking for his gun when Dave regained his balance and blasted him in the belly with a roundhouse of a right. Wasser doubled over in pain, and Dave gripped his chin and squeezed with a left hand made strong by all the clay he had ever wedged and worked. Wasser, dazed and out of breath, hung in Dave's vice-like grip.

"Look at me!" Dave snarled. "I'm the 'mudslinging stooge,' you little son-of-a-bitch!" Wasser returned his stare, the evil in his eyes apparent even behind the pain and surprise. Wasser spat and tried to scratch Dave's face and kick at his shins. The last bit of Dave's fuse burned out and the explosion went off. His grip on Wasser's jaw tightened and he could almost feel the bone begin to crack. Wasser screamed in pain, and in a lightning-quick move Dave let go of his jaw and grabbed him by the hair on the back of his head. He pulled Wasser's head back, tilting his chin up, and with all the power of his right shoulder and arm let fly a punch that connected solidly with jaw and cheek. He felt bone give way to the velocity of his anger and he dropped Wasser like a rag doll. He felt something brush by him—a couple of turacos diving for Wasser bloody face.

Dick Munch came into the room and pointed to the door. "Earl has the girls. They're OK!" he said. "You all right?"

Dave simply nodded. His heart was racing and he gasped for breath. He suddenly felt very tired, spent, like a used shell casing.

"You beat the hell out of that guy, ol' buddy. I didn't know you had it in you," Dick said as he surveyed Wasser rolling on the floor in pain and desperately trying to keep his face away from the turacos.

They stepped outside into the deceptive quiet. A small breeze blew through the Australian pines and the sky was a clear blue, while inside the elegant beach house parrots and monkeys ruled over a greedy lout bloodied by an angry father, picked over by mean birds, and soon to be charged with a major felony.

Dave caught his breath and walked up the drive to where Earl had driven the girls. He could see Cee's smiling freckled face through the front window. She opened the door and ran to him. He picked her up and hugged her and they held each other tightly.

"Celia—Cee, darlin'!" was all he could manage to say. Tears burned his eyes and his voice caught in his throat.

Earl passed them on the driveway. "I think I should go secure the crime scene and call the local law. By the way, the fellow who abducted them tore out of here in a rental Mustang. He blew right around the van. Mrs. Calvin and the girls say he turned out to be sort of a decent kind of guy. Took a real interest in the little one. But I'll call airport security in case he tries to take the plane."

As Earl walked toward the house Laney, Elizabeth, and Katie got out of the van and started toward Dave and Cee. Katie was chattering to Elizabeth about the monkeys and how funny they were. Her sparkle and liveliness were already returning, the nightmare of the ordeal seemingly erased by the circus comedy of a houseful of monkeys and birds. Elizabeth seemed almost overwhelmed with relief, and Laney greeted Dave with a broad smile, a big hug, and tears.

"Where's Tim? I thought he would be here—isn't he back yet?" Laney asked.

"He's still in France. He didn't even know about this until a couple of hours ago. But Valmer says it looks like he's about to wind up the trip and be back real soon," Dave looked at his watch as he spoke. "It's after nine over there. He's probably doing his thing right now."

Valmer's Clean-up

Between giving statements and answering questions Dave, Laney, Elizabeth, Katie, and Cee talked about the ordeal, what they had thought, how they worried or passed the time. Katie seemed to be snapping back; her energy was returning and she was hungry, causing her mother to marvel at the resilience of children. Laney fully intended to have a doctor check Katie over, to be sure she wasn't too dehydrated or malnourished, but the little girl's quick turnaround after their ordeal was gratifying.

Dick and one of his assistants got the birds and monkeys back into their travel cages, even though the captives had been delighted by the playful antics of the monkeys, the damage the small creatures had done to the sleek white beach house was extensive. Edward Earl presided over the crime scene and coordinated efforts between the Sanibel police and the state criminal investigator. Ivan Wasser had been placed under arrest and faced federal charges of kidnapping and telephone fraud. He had also been given first aid for a broken jaw and nose as well as facial lacerations, and had been carted off to Lee County Hospital in handcuffs.

Earl finished his business with the police and put in a call to Valmer. After he hung up he walked out to the pool deck where Dave and the girls had gathered and motioned for Dave. Laney watched with growing concern as the two men conferred quietly.

Dave suddenly stepped back as though he had been struck, and the color drained from his face. Earl put his hand on his shoulder, pulled him closer and whispered a few more words. Laney couldn't hear what he was saying, but the look on Dave's face when he walked over to where she and the girls sat caused Laney's concern to turn to alarm. He came over and stood next to her.

"Dave, what's wrong?"

"Come on, let's get you gals to the Hockett house. Barb wants to see her baby," Dave said with a forced cheerfulness that did nothing to dispel Laney's fear that something was horribly wrong.

"Dave, tell me. Is something wrong?" she demanded.

Dave looked at her with his back to the girls. "Not now," he whispered. "Once we get the girls to the house you and I should drive over to Valmer's." With a sinking heart she knew something had happened to Tim.

As soon as Moshe and Anna had seized Abel, they used his cellular phone to call Tel Aviv. They reported they had caught their "prize" and their control told them to proceed to the predetermined location while governments wrangled about jurisdiction and extradition.

Moshe reported that it would be difficult to learn more about the manuscript because Calvin had been shot. He was down and Millerkirk had gone for help.

Their assignment was to get Abel to a secure location. They were simply to leave the crime scene untouched, leave the weapon and phone in the alley, and to secure themselves and their prisoner. Legal offices would advise the French government and police agencies about the specifics of the shooting and the shooter.

Moshe wanted desperately to go to Calvin's aid, but the control stood firm. Tel Aviv would notify Langley about Calvin and the shooting. Moshe and Anna's priority was to get the terrorist to a secure location.

* * *

Valmer was exhausted. He had slept very little since the ordeal began. He worried about Tim. He worried about Dave's rescue plan. Now his walkie-talkie refused to operate and he was out of touch with both operations. When the phone rang he expected Earl or Tim, not an associate from Langley and certainly not the message he received. It was terse and preliminary, based on observations of an Israeli field team. Tim had been shot in the head. Tariq Abel was the shooter and he was in the custody of the Israelis.

Barb's beaming smile and tears of joy and the warm hugs and embraces temporarily distracted Laney. After a few moments of hugging and kissing, Cee excused herself to her room and then reappeared with her calendar.

"We have to find a way to make up for all of my missed classes. Why can't we go on Tuesday afternoon when Daddy goes to..." She was interrupted by the phone.

"Good afternoon—Hocketts," Dave answered.

"Who is this?" he said after a moment. "Hang on. Laney it's for you."

It was Hertt. He had called from the highway. He told her he had left the Mustang in the Publix parking lot off Summerlin and was on his way to a new life. He apologized for how he had been when he took them hostage. He said he had changed and wanted to know if he could talk to the little gal.

Katie took the phone. "Hello, who is this?" she asked in a small voice. "Yes, I feel fine." She listened for a while, nodding her head, then she laughed.

"The monkeys were funny," she said, and a moment later, "OK. God bless you too." She handed the phone back to Laney. There was a dial tone. Hertt was gone.

"What did he say, honey?"

"He said he was sorry. He said I helped him see things differently, and he said he wants to have a little girl and name her Katie. Mommy, do you think maybe he wasn't really a bad man after all?"

Laney was at a loss for words, and Elizabeth joined in.

"You know, Mom, after a while he did seem like maybe he wasn't so bad, even though he did scare us."

"What he did was wrong, with the hell he put us all through, and there's no other way about it," Barb snapped angrily.

"I don't know, Barb," Laney said. She picked Katie up and snuggled her in her lap. "You weren't there. It was strange, really; I got the feeling that in a way he was almost as much a victim as we were. I almost feel sorry for him."

"Well, you can feel sorry for him if you want to. I just hope the police get him and make him pay for what he did."

"I'd like to make him pay, too," Cee piped. "I'd like to slap him for calling me Freckles."

Brian and Jayne's arrival brought on another round of hugs and tears of happiness and joy. Cee and Jayne gave each other high fives for the success of their "secret rescue plan" with the mirror.

Laney was torn between the relief of being free and with friends and the nagging fear that something awful had happened to Tim. Neither she nor Dave wanted to let on to the others, but their pretense was wearing thin. She had to hear the truth.

It wasn't until they were well onto Periwinkle toward Tarpon Bay before she worked up the courage to ask Dave. Neither had said a word, as though the silence between them sealed a private pact.

"Tell me, Dave." It was a simple command. She knew it might be terrible.

"Tim's been hurt. He's been shot. In the head."

In the last three words Dave's voice broke and he clutched the steering wheel, gulping for breath and trying to regain his composure.

Laney felt all her strength drain out of her. Her stomach knotted and her heart twisted in her chest. She pictured Tim's smiling face, but couldn't cry for the numbness that gripped her.

She felt distant and removed from her body when they got to Valmer's. Jane met them on the porch. She circled her arm around Laney and led her into the house.

"Come with me, sweetheart," she murmured soothingly. Laney moved mechanically. Dave followed mournfully behind through the house and up the steps to Valmer's study. Laney sat on a padded wicker chair and Jane handed her a glass. She took a sip. It was strong.

"It's a gin and tonic. It'll help you relax, darling. Val and I have been through this before. We're here to help you."

Laney set the glass down on a table. The awful certainty began to hit her and she started to talk "People are shot and killed or terribly injured all the time. In some lines of work it's part of the risk of the job. But Tim's not in that kind of work. He is gentle and sensitive. He likes adventure but not this. He loves his daughters, he's just a good man who worked hard, who sacrificed to spend time with the girls." She broke off, unable to continue.

Dave's voice broke through the fog. "There's really nothing new. He was shot. The man who did it is a wanted terrorist. He is in custody. It happened outside the cathedral at Chartres." Dave was red eyed.

"Oh, God," Laney moaned. "Is he alive? Please tell me he's alive."

"I think...we think so," Dave lied, knowing only the sketchy information he'd gotten on the phone.

She felt a flash of hatred for the man who had shot her husband. She imagined Tim lying on a sidewalk bleeding and she flashed on the image of Bobby Kennedy lying mortally wounded. She began to cry, tears spilling down her face, as she thought about their life together, their tender moments. She'd give anything now to see him and touch him and tell him how much she loved him. Her mind rambled over the simple little things that made up the fabric of their marriage. His kiss as he drove off to work each day, reading to the girls, their romantic moments, and vacation times. How was she going to tell the girls, or his mother, or their friends? How was she going to live without him? Suddenly she felt as if an avalanche was tumbling on her and Tim was not there to help her. Wait—wait a minute, she thought, her mind was running too quickly. Maybe it's wrong. Maybe it's a terrible mistake.

Dave touched her on the shoulder. "Let's go up to see Valmer. He knows a little more."

As she walked into his study, she was struck by how tired and grave Valmer looked. The dapper and charming senior gentleman had become haggard and tormented. His computer screen occupied some of his attention. He was looking toward it and tapping an occasional key while he shouldered the phone and listened. He motioned for her to sit in a large leather chair.

He hung up and walked around the desk, and took a seat next to Laney.

"I am so deeply sorry. When I asked your husband to undertake this mission, I never expected..."

"You never expected? What *did* you expect?" The fog was swirling around her, and all she could see now was a mist of red. "My God, you had to know some kind of danger would be expected! Tim thought he was going off on a simple research mission, and you sent him right into a den of lions!"

"Mrs. Calvin, remember, he wanted to go..."

"He didn't know what he was getting into, and now this...I just want him back. I want him home! Damn you, damn you! I want my husband!" The last of her control dissolved and she collapsed in sobs.

"I know how difficult this is, believe me, and I am truly sorry. Jane and I will do anything to assist you. Please let me handle the details of getting him home." The phone rang. He got up and moved toward the desk and lifted the receiver. "Yes?"

As he talked Laney's mind raced away again. Getting him home. The words tore at her heart. She was usually a strong person, with a tough demeanor which some confused with insensitivity.

That was just her manner. But now the emotion was more than she could contain.

"An Israeli field team was in the area. In fact they've taken control of the man who shot your husband." Valmer placed the phone back on the cradle. "One of them remained behind and has reported that a man who was with Tim summoned help. He's alive and has been transported to a local hospital. We are making calls now."

Brian and Jayne had excused themselves from the restaurant to join Laney and Dave at Valmer's. Brian was tense and anxious and Jayne was fighting tears as they walked into Valmer's study.

"My French is rusty. I'm waiting for a call back from Langley. They have a greater capability to locate the hospital and the proper contacts. Would you mind taking Mrs. Calvin out to the porch? She can relax there, and I'll be out the moment I have news." As Dave escorted Laney out he looked back at Valmer. The strain was obviously wearing on him as badly as it was on the rest of them.

* * *

Millerkirk clung to his awkward perch on the narrow piece of shelving inside the ambulance, the vehicle swaying as it navigated the narrow streets of Chartres. His left hand clutched the clay container between his left arm and chest, and his right hand was on Tim's shoulder. Tim stirred and moaned, which the doctor said was a good sign.

Jim had run to the manse and brought two priests and their dinner guest, a retired French doctor, back to Tim's aid. Although there had been a great deal of blood, which worried Millerkirk, the doctor indicated that head wounds bled a lot and often looked worse than they were, which was the case with Tim.

Tariq Abel's bullets had struck the statues behind Tim and Millerkirk and had chipped off pieces of stone which had in turn become projectiles. Flying fragments of stone from Saint Theodore's column had struck Tim with enough force to knock him down. They had created some nasty gashes and lacerations, but did not appear, at least in the dim light from the streetlamp, to have penetrated the skull.

"A few stitches, a mild concussion, and a vile headache will probably be the worst of it. The doctors at the hospital will know more," the elderly physician offered in an impeccable English as Tim was loaded into an ambulance.

Tim came to in the ambulance and saw the medical technicians and Millerkirk looking down at him. He put his hand to his head and felt the bandages.

"I'm still alive? What happened?" he asked, wincing at the pain just speaking caused. His head hurt worse than he thought was humanly possible, but he felt almost euphoric at the mere prospect of even being able to pose such a question.

"First of all, you are indeed alive," Millerkirk said with a smile. "And what happened is you were a victim of Saint Theodore's getting shot."

"Excuse me?"

"Someone fired some shots, apparently at us, but missed and hit the stone instead. When the bullet ricocheted, a fragment of stone hit you in the head. It's just superficial, but we're on our way to the hospital just to be on the safe side. You're going to be fine."

"Laney and the girls will be glad for that, I imagine"

"I'm glad of it myself. You'll need a few stitches. That's about all. Close call, heh?"

"Who did it?"

"I don't have a clue. You suspected we were being followed, but right now it's anybody's guess. The police searched the alley. They found a rifle, a cellular phone, and a vial with what looked like cocaine in it."

"So after all the care we took to not damage the stonework, someone shot at it and chipped it up. How badly was it damaged?"

"Actually, the bullet hit the inner section we had just opened, so when it's closed up again there won't be any evidence of damage.

But don't worry about that right now. The important thing is to get you back on your feet and then get you home."

"I'm a mess," Tim said as he looked down at his bloodstained clothes. "I'm going to need some clean clothes."

Millerkirk smiled indulgently. "Let's get your head closed first."

Millerkirk translated at the admission desk and with the emergency room technicians. The emergency room doctor who worked on Tim spoke fluent English, had attended Johns Hopkins, and was a devoted Boston Celtics fan. He pronounced Tim fit to travel, remarking that "NBA players often took elbows which produced gashes almost as nasty," and complained about not being able to get crabs as good as those from the Chesapeake. He wrote a prescription for Tim's headache and told him the best treatment would be a "good meal and a lovely French woman to nurse him through his recovery." It was a thoroughly fitting conclusion to what had been the most unusual and bizarre few days in Tim's life. While Millerkirk went back to the hotel to get Tim's bag and to explain everything to the archbishop, who showed up at the cathedral after the incident, Tim asked for a phone.

*   *   *

Valmer had asked Laney to come back to his study, and invited the rest of the group along too. His associates in Langley had located the hospital where Tim was, but the night supervisor had refused to give information on any patient without authorization, which could not be obtained until morning. Meanwhile, Valmer had called an old friend in the State Department who in turn called the American embassy in Paris. Valmer explained to Laney that even as he spoke they were working through their consular affairs staff to get a status report on Tim. Laney could only nod mutely. She was exhausted, and all of her energy was going toward hanging on until news about Tim came through. As Valmer continued to detail the scenarios the phone rang.

"Yes?" His eyes went wide. "My God! I can't believe this."

The room was completely silent. Dave and Jayne each put an arm around Laney's shoulders, and she sat staring at Valmer, afraid to even breathe.

"Mrs. Calvin, I think you should take this call." Valmer handed the phone to her.

"Hel...hello?" her voice seemed to come from somewhere else. All eyes in the room were on her.

"Hi, kiddo, I miss you. Why don't you make reservations for tomorrow night at the Mad Hatter? How does that sound?"

"Tim Calvin, how dare you get yourself hurt like that," she scolded through her sobs. "Come home, honey. We need you."

Once she was satisfied that Tim's injury wasn't serious, Laney reassured him of their children's safety and well-being. He was relieved to hear that Katie didn't seem to have any lasting damage from their ordeal. The group was exultant and the drinks Jane offered on the porch in celebration were consumed with gusto. Hugging and back-patting and explanations of Tim's find circulated, and general good cheer and laughter were the order of the day, now that the worst was over.

After a while, Valmer excused himself to his study. "Please pardon my hasty retreat from this celebration, but I have some cleanup work to do."

Sunrise on the Horizon and Sunset at the Mad Hatter

Under the auspices of the UN commission, Millerkirk had taken possession of the manuscripts with the condition that they would be available for study by an international team of historians and theologians. It was his hope they could find a permanent home, perhaps, at the Ashmolean Museum on Beaumont Street, Oxford University's repository of antiquities. It seemed appropriate since William, Alcuin and Howard were English. But first he would recommend that the UN Secretary General sponsor some sort of world tour of the manuscripts. "In these troubled times it seemed a good lesson to teach; faith and good overcoming greed and evil," Millerkirk said. "With the tension of current world affairs, it might be instructive to examine how, long ago, powerful men of the world's three major faiths had turned their back on their own beliefs in an attempt to score political power." Millerkirk was sure that there was much that was positive and instructive which could come from his and Tim's discovery.

Tim woke with a powerful headache, but was excited at the prospect of getting back to his family on Sanibel and picking up with his vacation. He made a mental note that when he got back he would call his office and tell them he would be gone a few days longer than he'd originally planned.

The trip to DeGaulle went quickly and without incident, and it was a pleasure to have Millerkirk's company en route. He planned to be back in the States during the holidays and said he would make a visit to the Calvins part of his plans.

The Concorde flight was a blur, due in part to the medication. But the sunrise off the wing was spectacular. He left Paris at 11:00 A.M., 4:00 A.M. on Sanibel. He would arrive Dulles around eight, flying in with the sunrise. He was still groggy as he cleared customs, and moved somewhat slowly as he made his way to where private flights were handled. According to Valmer, Edward Earl had made arrangements for a Lear charter to fly him directly from Dulles to Fort Myers. En route he would be debriefed by officials from the State Department, the CIA, and the FBI, since his attacker was apparently an infamous terrorist. He realized now that the Saddam Hussein look-alike had been the one he should have been on guard for; ironically, the man was in fact a cousin of the Iraqi dictator. Tim had asked about the Iranian couple, the young man and woman, Valmer had surprised him by telling him that they were actually an Israeli field team who had captured the terrorist and quite probably saved his life in the process. The Israelis, among many others, had special plans for Tariq Abel. Tim felt somewhat foolish at misjudging the young couple, and his amateurish efforts at trying to lose them, but was glad to know his first impression of them had been right: they were indeed a decent and exceptional couple.

The pilot explained they were flying "eight miles high—only military aircraft fly in a higher corridor." Tim looked out the window and could see the terminator strip, the thin black line around the curve of the earth. For the first time he could see the planet's round spherical shape, looking very much like "spaceship earth," as Buckminster Fuller had once described it. This altitude provided a view very few ever saw, and he thought to himself that the trip had been like this view, something very few ever see. It had taken him to sights and experiences which had changed his life.

His sunbaked retreat, his kinship with the lizards and grains of sand had been shoved aside, but what had followed he would remember for the rest of his life. The nagging pain in his head was a small price to pay for the adventure, a minor toll for the incredible discovery and opportunity he'd had.

Tim actually found it pleasurable recounting his ordeal. As he'd gone through the debriefing he mused on what a great tale this would be for the girls. He was equally sure it would be just as entertaining as dinner or cocktail-party conversation, or something he could tell deep at night over drinks and cigars in his study. He reveled in what he had learned from the array of people his journey had exposed him to.

Now more or less finished with official work, he leaned back and looked out the window of the jet and enjoyed a moment of reverie, relaxing with his private contentments. From his lofty altitude he gazed out at the blue sphere below, marveling at how simple it looked from up there with its appearance of timelessness and purity.

He couldn't stop the misting of his eyes as he descended the steps from the Lear jet and into the Florida sunlight. There on the tarmac was the most wonderful sight he had ever seen. Laney and Elizabeth and Katie ran to him and covered him with kisses and hugs. Dave clapped him on the shoulder, and Katie and Elizabeth also clutched small American flags. Everyone of them gave up trying to fight their tears, and sniffles mingled with the joyful laughter of the reunion. For the first time since his fateful late night meeting with Valmer, now seeing his girls waving their flags, Tim Calvin realized that he had done something very unusual. It was small, mostly private, and quite arcane, but indeed quite special.

* * *

It was almost noon Sunday, by the convergence of international time zones only an hour later than when he had flown out of DeGaulle, even though he had been eight hours in transit. Edward Earl had dropped Dave and the girls off as he prepared to fly back to Washington. Tim scoured his memory to recall where he had parked the van in the long-term lot. They eventually found it and he cheerfully let Dave drive.

The large palm at the right of the toll booth seemed to wave a welcome home to him in the midday sun and breeze. Boaters were out in full force and the magic of the island began its traditional creep from his stomach up his spine.

"You're on vacation again, mister!" Laney squeezed his hand. "Aren't you glad you scheduled two weeks? You still have a week to go."

The scent and aroma of the restaurants' Sunday brunch offerings mingled with the fragrance of the blooms as they drove along Periwinkle. The cabbage and royal palms and waving Australian pine were a sweet treat for his eyes.

As they passed the community church, Tim watched the families, couples and senior citizens strolling out the door and into the sunshine toward their cars. He remembered what Millerkirk had said about "the Boss" who showed himself strong in the hearts of those who were loyal to Him. He wondered how it might be for those people leaving church, or for everyone, if there hadn't been loyal hearts down through the centuries. What if just that one generation had been duped? What if no one with faith and intellect had risen to fight the power and deceit? What if he himself had not been drawn into the ancient mystery, impelled by a quest for an answer for his own faith?

"Barb's got a little light lunch for us back at your condo," Dave announced. "We want to build a good base for tonight. Brian and Jayne have a couple of special items, a little French flair," he said with a wink and a grin. "The sunset should be spectacular. Like your better half said, you're on vacation, bud, and it's time to relax. We'll beach this afternoon, and you can take a little nap. Then tonight a wonderful meal and wine and we watch the sunset with our loved ones and have just a high old time. Sanibel magic, Mr. Calvin."

A nap would serve him well, in fact it was a mandate. An evening at the Mad Hatter would be an exquisite way to celebrate but it required the proper state of mind. The evening drive up to the pass was always an enchanting trip, mellow music choreographing the late evening shadows crawling across the island. How lucky he was—dear friends and an evening made merry with culinary bliss. The homecoming filled him with an overwhelming sense of well-being. Anticipating the sight of the sun as it sizzled into the water, igniting the heavens in a show of color before the stars began to prick the dark gulf sky, added to his satisfaction at being back. Brian and Jayne, masters of gracious hospitality, would provide hours of the finest dining he could imagine, and then they would join the Hock-etts and Calvins for port, coffee, and dessert and conversation that would stretch into the wee, small hours. Tonight he thought it might stretch until dawn.

What a change this is from what I've experienced, he thought. As they drove toward the island, he smiled as he pictured the long room of the Mad Hatter with its mirrored wall, the simple elegance of the fresh flowers, and soft pastels of artist C.W. Mundy. No doubt about it, the place was unique and a fitting end for the past week.

"Didn't you have the yellow fin with Thai noodles last year? You said it was awesome," Laney asked.

"Yeah, and now you've got me thinking about how tough the decisions will be tonight. I'm still in delicate condition and should not be thinking so hard, sweetheart," Tim said, grinning at his wife.

"Well, be ready for some major brain strain," Dave boomed. "Brian and Jayne have some great new tricks this season."

"I've learned the meaning of the word 'tricks' myself—bad and good—in this past week."

"We've definitely got a lot to talk about, bud," Dave laughed.

"We've got all day, and all night, and all week for that mat-ter. I am—I repeat loud and clear—I am going to become a grain of sand on the beach. I may get up a couple of times to do the stoop, but other than that, I'm staying put," Tim affirmed.

"Daddy can we still go nighttime crabbing too?" Katie asked with a smile.

About the Artist

Charles Warren "C.W." Mundy, a signature member of the Oil Painters of America, is an honored master artist. His work for the cover of *The Sanibel Arcanum* is an oil original which captures the exquisite color of a Sanibel sunset and introduces pieces of the intricate puzzle which is at the heart of the mystery.

Mundy's work is included in several important private collections. His reputation is gaining international acclaim. Among his corporate contracts are Gibson Guitar Company of Nashville, NBA Properties, United States Golf association, Mystic Maritime Graphics, Water's Edge Collection Red Farm Studio, Pawtucket, RI.

This leading American impressionist has received a Hoosier Salon Purchase Award, Hoosier Salon Merit Award for Outstanding Traditional Painting, Merit Award for Figure Work in Oil, Oil Painters of America National Exhibition, President's Award of Excellence, Modern Marine Masters Award, and the Hoosier Salon Merit Award for Outstanding Work in Any Medium, among others.

Mundy lives in Indianapolis, but he and his wife Becky are veteran and frequent travelers. Regardless of where in the world he may be, C.W. Mundy is usually painting.